ALLEGIANCE

THE NEW WORLD SERIES | BOOK THREE

Stephen Llewelyn

Published by Fossil Rock Publishing 2020

ISBNs:

978-1-8380235-9-1 hardcover
978-1-8380235-4-6 paperback
978-1-8380235-5-3 ebook

For Sally

Thank you for your unwavering
commitment to the cause.

The author also wishes to acknowledge:

Mum and Dad, thanks for your continued encouragement. Thanks to
Sally-Marie, Melanie and Fossil Rock for all the re-reads and for making
it all happen, along with Karl for the (audios) intro music. To my long-
suffering friends, including Les and Liz who have always been kind and
helpful in spreading the word. Thanks to Chris Barrie for his sublime
performance of the DINOSAUR audio book.
Special thanks to Adam and Gloria, who gave their names to new
characters within the series. Also to the experts who took time out of
their frantic schedules to answer my emails and questions about our
favourite subject. Cheers.
…And last but by no means least, to everyone who reads this book and
enjoyed its predecessors, a sincere thank you.
The crew of the USS *New World* will return soon in

THE NEW WORLD SERIES | BOOK FOUR | REROUTE.

No dinosaurs were harmed during the making of this book.

Preface

Dear readers, book three is here at last and I would like to relay my personal thanks to all of you for your enthusiasm and inspiration.

I re-imagined and substantially rewrote the book during this last summer. Normally, this would not be worthy of note, but 2020 has been such a difficult year for so many of us that I thought I would give a brief explanation as to why.

Originally, the main story was to take place against an underlying crisis besetting both sides. Reptiles, even today, often carry viruses communicable to humans – obviously, go back 100 million years and we would have little or no resistance to the ailments of the age.

The sudden onset of the pandemic in 2020 was shocking and disruptive to say the least. As my whole point in writing these stories is to provide people with entertainment and most importantly *escapism*, I decided to rethink.

Lockdown titles have been popping up all year and that is fine for anyone wishing to read more – however, I did not want to integrate the current real-world problems within this series.

As the seeds for the original story were planted in the last book, Revenge, I retained the theme in a minor way only, to avoid disruption in continuity. Otherwise, please be assured that this book is neither inspired by nor about the recent lockdowns.

In the spirit of the earlier books, I hope you will enjoy this tale about good people, bad people and, of course, *DINOSAURS!*

I raise my glass to you, and to a hopeful future for us all. Stay well.
Thank you,
Stephen

Chapter 1 | Zero

"Twelve ships approaching from a low prograde orbit, sir," reported the helmsman.

"Ready all weapons. Launch countermeasures," Captain Wolf Muller ordered clearly, from his command chair aboard the *Eisernes Kreuz*. He stood and moved to the tactical station. Looking over a young officer's shoulder, he viewed the approaching vessels for himself.

"Comms?" he called across the bridge. "Contact the *Sabre* and the *Heydrich*. Tell Captains Hartmann and Franke to ignore all hails and fire at will, as soon as they have a 'definite kill' targeting resolution. We're going to have to make a fight of it until our jump coordinates are confirmed."

"Yes, sir."

The incoming ships were orbital fighter craft. Relatively small and moving at colossal speeds, they made short work of their journey around the planet hanging in the sky before them.

"They're hailing, sir."

"Ignore them, Lieutenant." Muller turned back to the young woman at the weapons station. "Do we have firing resolutions yet?"

She frowned in study, checking her instruments. A moment later, she looked up to nod confirmation. "We do, sir."

"Fire," said Muller, with a practised calm.

Almost simultaneously, the *Sabre* and the *Heydrich* joined the attack. The fighters scattered immediately, but the intelligent warheads countered faster than thought. Ten of the little craft bloomed into split-second fireballs as the oxygen within their structures gave all to the explosive force of the ordnance directed against their hulls. In an instant they were simply gone, trace elements rejoining the eternal soup of the universe.

The two remaining ships took a wide, curving trajectory, increasing their speed to maximum. They were on the Dawn Fleet in a couple of heartbeats and launching rockets.

"Countermeasures engaged," reported tactical. All three capital ships began a computer targeted, withering fire towards the missiles launched against them. These small rockets eventually found their mark and three of the four missiles vanished in brilliant flashes. The fourth caught the *Sabre* top-centre of her port flank. It scored only a glancing blow, but the explosion violently shook the entire vessel.

A flurry of voices sounded out across Muller's bridge.

"Ten enemy vessels completely destroyed, Captain."

"Damage report coming in from the *Sabre*, Captain. She reports minor hull damage."

"We have new targeting resolutions, sir."

"A second wave of fighter craft on an approach vector towards our position, Captain. ETA three minutes."

Muller was about to order a second attack when the voice he had been waiting for cut through the general hubbub. "Sir, we have coordinates confirmed! Shall I give the command to jump, sir?"

Muller singled out the last officer to speak, and pointed directly at him. "Yes, give the order immediately!" he snapped.

"Good morning, ma'am, this is Lieutenant Colonel Davis Jonson, Chief of Staff's office. How can I help you?"

"This is Major General Lisa Green, Colonel. I need to speak with the chief right away."

"I'm sorry, ma'am, General Brassheim is indisposed at the moment. Can I make an appointment for a callbac—"

"Well get him re-disposed! This can't wait!"

Lieutenant Colonel Jonson wore a hunted expression. "He's a *five*-star general, ma'am, I—"

"Do you know who I am, Jonson?"

Jonson straightened to attention. "Of course, General, but you see, he's in the *shower*," he stated as quietly and apologetically as possible, under the circumstances.

"Son, I don't care if he's in his wife! This is an international emergency and I need to speak to the man in charge immediately!"

"Now, *Colonel*, do you wish to explain to General Brassheim how you decided to put this threat on hold rather than interrupt his shower?"

Jonson's eyebrows rose and his ears appeared to droop slightly as he gulped down his distress. "I'm fairly certain that I don't, ma'am. Please stand by."

General Green's monitor switched to a holding screen displaying a relaxing view of an aquarium while she tapped her fingers in agitation.

Three minutes later, a tall man, grey haired in his middle sixties, appeared in a shower robe. Still towelling his hair, he sat to take the call.

"Sir," Green addressed the chief of staff respectfully, "I'm sorry if this is a bad time, but it's urgent."

"Don't sweat it, Lisa. What have you?" replied General Brassheim, casually.

"Sir, a few minutes ago, we tracked three unidentified vessels in low orbit. We believe they took off from somewhere in mid-west Argentina. Despite their use of stealth tech, they were spotted by one of our satellites just before they left atmosphere. They ignored our hails, so a squadron of orbital fighters was scrambled to query them, sir. Our birds caught up to them easily, but when they too hailed the vessels, they were fired upon immediately – without provocation, sir."

Brassheim listened gravely. "Casualties?"

"We lost ten of the twelve craft, sir. None had time to eject – ten dead. Our two remaining craft report only a single indirect hit upon one of the enemy vessels."

Brassheim sighed angrily.

"It gets worse, sir."

"Go on."

"Immediately after the altercation, the three ships all jumped into a wormhole. A *single* wormhole, and right next to the Earth, sir."

Brassheim looked furious now. "Fools! They could have caused..." he tailed off. "What the hell could they have caused?"

"No one's really sure, sir. I *can* tell you they didn't give a crap though! They were going, and damn everyone left behind!" It was Green's turn to show anger now.

"Have you put Mars on alert?" asked Brassheim.

"Yes, sir. However, the ships do not appear to have arrived there. We don't have any clue where they went. They're just *gone*."

"OK, Lisa, is there anything we *do* know?"

Green nodded seriously. "The markings on the ships matched the black warship from the incident last November, sir – the one that also *disappeared*."

"Didn't that ship originate in the Middle East?"

"Yes, sir. These ships were smaller but we're clearly dealing with some sort of organised group force here. What's even more worrying is that their tech seems to be more advanced than ours – tell me how that's possible? Until today, we didn't even know three ships *could* jump into the same wormhole. It's remained theoretical – still on the drawing board."

"This is more than worrying, Lisa. We now have four warships armed with God knows what, all disappeared God knows where. There can be no doubt their intentions are hostile after the loss of our pilots and ships today.

"Have we heard anything back from Captain Bessel's mission yet?"

"No, sir. Nothing in two weeks now."

Brassheim gave her a hard look. "General Green, you may recall I was against sending another multi-trillion-dollar asset into the unknown. Despite this, and at your request, I talked the president into launching *Operation Arrow* and sending Bessel off on a rescue mission!"

The way I remember it, the president was happy for any excuse to remove the Newfoundland *from the public's view – after the 'Canadian problem'*, thought Green, privately. However, her reply was tactful, "I still believe that was the right call, sir. When the story leaked about the terrorist attack, which led to the disappearance of over a hundred people, we needed a response."

"Right, and less than two weeks after that warship launched from the Middle East, we fitted out one of the rescue Pods and brought teams in from all over the globe to make it happen."

"I know, sir,"

"I *know* you know, sir," he paraphrased sternly. "We were *not* ready. And now this!"

Brassheim slammed his fist down on the desk in front of him. "One of our ships is presumed destroyed! Then we find evidence that a wormhole *was* created and Douglas' ship simply vanished? Three months after that, possibly the most advanced warship on the planet is spotted leaving the Middle East and then *it* vanishes. We've totally lost touch with Bessel and the *Newfoundland* and now these three vessels destroy ten of our orbital fighters with horrendous loss of life! Did I miss anything? Oh, yes – and then *they* disappeared too!"

"Sir—"

"Lisa," Brassheim cut her off, "we have some very dangerous assets out there somewhere in the galaxy, and we don't even know where in the hell they are, damn it! And if the eggheads have it right, we don't even know *when* the hell they are!

"I want the team investigating the last ship in the Middle East recalled and I want a team sent in to Argentina to find out what in the Sam Hill is goin' on down there, too. Keep it under the radar, but get it done!"

"Yes, sir."

"We've had our best minds on this for almost six months now," he continued. "It's time they earned their salaries and told us where to direct our efforts."

"After it was concluded that the USS *New World* entered a wormhole through time, it changed the playing field for everyone, sir," Green answered, her colour also rising. "The high energy signature left in space, where the wormhole had formed, suggested there may have been an explosion. Douglas was no fool. Something happened to that ship. These unfriendlies appearing out of nowhere, and disappearing just as quickly, are making me think the whole thing may have been planned. Maybe Douglas' ship hasn't been destroyed, or lost in time – maybe it's been stolen!"

Brassheim sat back in his chair for a moment. "Now isn't that a comforting thought?"

"These ships *may* be in pursuit of our assets in the past, sir, but we've no way of knowing for sure," Green stated reasonably.

"That's as may be, General," replied Brassheim, leaning forward again, "but if someone's poking and prodding the timeline, we could all disappear at any minute.

"I've seen Douglas' file, he knows his trade, but if these hostiles are after him he won't stand a chance. The *New World* is a heavy-hauler, nothing more. God help those people if these criminals find them. This also begs the question, what do they want the *New World* for?"

"If my suspicions are correct, sir, it'll be the Pod they want. It's a manufacturing plant, fully stocked with equipment and material intended for Mars. They could theoretically build themselves a new..." she tailed off.

"*World?*" Brassheim enquired, raising an eyebrow irritably. "During the months after Douglas' disappearance, Bessel was sending queries to my office, one a week. Very politely asking when were we gonna go rescue the *New World*. Hell, I had him practically thrown out of my office at one point! He and Douglas go way back. I don't doubt he'll do everything in his power to find them, but another transporter carrying a Rescue Pod full of marines will still be no match for the ships the enemy is sending after them—" He held up a hand forestalling Green's correction. "*Possibly.*"

He leaned in close, filling the screen. "I want every resource thrown at this, Lisa. Tech, science staff – hell, archaeologists – whatever it takes! I meet with the president and the joint chiefs this afternoon and I'm gonna need some good news to offset all this. You have three hours. Is that clear, General Green?"

"Yes, sir." She offered a salute, but Brassheim was already gone.

"I'll just go online to the good news store and pick you something out," she muttered sardonically. "There goes my third star and lieutenant generalcy!"

Cretaceous Gondwana, 99.2 million years ago
Dr Dave Flannigan walked from his new field hospital out into the main Pod hangar. There were a few seats and a coffee table outside, where people could wait. He sat down exhaustedly, heavy lines etched into his face.

Major White broke off his conversation with the small team loading one of a pair of personnel carriers and strode to join him.

"How are they, Dave?" he asked, his expression full of concern.

With a weary nod of gratitude, Flannigan accepted a cup of coffee from one of the new nurses who had arrived with Captain Meritus. "Jim Miller and his daughter, Rose, are gonna be just fine – a few minor scratches and contusions, nothin' a good night's sleep and a few days' rest won't fix. Bluey has a concussion and some badly bruised ribs, but he should make a full recovery too."

After a pause in Flannigan's delivery, White felt obliged to ask, "Why do I get the feeling I've been given the good news and now I'm gonna get the bad?"

"Yeah," Flannigan admitted with a sigh. "Dr Norris was near death when they got her back here. I've removed the slug and any traces of clothing and dirt from the wound. We had to transfuse a couple o' litres of type 'O' into her veins, along with a broad spectrum antibiotic, and she lost some of her large intestine. She's held together with stitches and prayers, but despite being guarded, I am hopeful. It'll be a slow road but with a little luck and a lotta fight, she should make it."

"Will her state of mind be important?" asked White.

"Always," Flannigan replied adamantly.

"They took her son, Dave. What effect do you think that might have on her psyche?"

"What effect would that have on you, Major?"

White appeared thoughtful for a moment and then smiled. "I'd fight!"

Flannigan returned his smile tiredly. "That's what I'm betting Patricia will do, too."

"And Jill?" prompted the major.

Flannigan's anxiety deepened. "If anything, she's the one I'm most worried about, Major."

White's smile drained. "But I thought she just had a leg fracture? I know she got rolled around some, getting away from that dinosaur, but…"

"The Tyrannotitan – I heard." Flannigan was shaking his head. "Such cuddly names they give those things! Jill didn't pass out from stress and exhaustion. She's running a temperature and there's some evidence of early onset organ failure."

"*What?*" snapped White, jumping to his feet.

Flannigan raised his hands placatingly. "We don't know yet, Ford." He looked left and right before motioning the major to sit back down and then leaned forward, confidentially. "She's carrying some kind of viral infection. We've never seen anything exactly like it before. It's possible she was bitten by something out in the forest – we don't know. I'll need to check with the others she was with, over at the *New World* site and see how they're doing. I understand we have a couple of new crew over there?

People who have lived here for fifty years or more, maybe *they* can shed some light on this?"

"Kelly Marston is a palaeobotanist and a biologist, I'd try her first," agreed White.

"Yes, Major, I'm about to make the call. I just hope everyone else over there is OK."

On the one hand, he could not believe what he had done; on the other, the power to redress his situation was elating. Tim Norris stared at the smoking barrel of Heidi's nine millimetre pistol as if in a trance.

The smell of gun oil filled his nostrils, but before his senses fully returned to him, he was knocked down from behind. The detachment of guards who burst into the executive quarters, after hearing two loud and consecutive bangs, were all over him.

Heinrich Schultz struggled back to his feet from where he had landed, after leaping for cover behind an ornate antique sofa.

"Take the boy's weapon!" he bellowed.

Heidi leaned against a wall, propping herself up into a sitting position on the floor. She held her upper left arm tightly with her right hand. Blood welled between her fingers and ran down her side, pooling on the obscenely expensive carpet. Obviously in shock, she breathed heavily.

Tim was lifted roughly to his feet by a couple of guards, who dragged him to face Heinrich Schultz; the man who had ordered the deaths of Tim's parents, real and adopted, and who had brought them all to this point and this time.

The old man stood tall, straight and unyielding. He ignored his granddaughter and her condition, scrutinising Tim coldly.

"Take him to a holding cell," he barked at the guards. "He's not to be damaged!"

Two of the four guards carried out his orders instantly. To the remaining pair he snapped, "Take my granddaughter to the medical bay. When she is cleared for release by our doctors, she is to be transferred to a separate cell and must be guarded heavily and constantly!"

With that he turned his back on them all and stood looking west out of the window, his hands linked behind his back.

Despite her shock, Heidi looked scandalised. "*Großvater? Opa. Opa, bitte,*" she pleaded. She had not called Heinrich grandpa since she was a young girl, but it did not stir the old man. He continued to study the horizon, already planning his next move as the guards dragged her from the room.

Douglas sagged, like a man aged ten years in ten minutes. The comm call from Dr Flannigan and Major White had affected him badly. Flannigan had explained about Baines' illness and also told Marston where she could find the apparatus to test people, within his sickbay aboard the *New World*. He wanted her to make sure no one else was infected. White had filled in the rest.

Douglas volunteered to be Marston's first guinea pig and within minutes the test revealed that he too had the virus.

"Do you think Ah'm patient zero, Kelly? Could Ah have brought something aboard with me?" he asked, wretchedly.

"Let's not jump to any conclusions, Captain. I'll need to test everyone before we can even guess at what's happened."

Douglas slumped into a seat with his head in his hands. "Ah knew Ah shouldnae have let her go," he said.

Marston placed a hand on his shoulder. "Jill, you mean?"

He nodded without looking up.

"Captain Baines doesn't seem like the sort of woman to stay at home and do as she's told, James," she tried, sympathetically.

"If Ah'd tried harder, she'd have listened to me. Ah know she would."

Marston looked doubtful. "Perhaps, if you hadn't made her captain…" she tailed off when she caught his pained expression. "Sorry, James. That didn't come out the way I intended. What I mean is, she's a strong leader and she believed that she was doing the right thing."

Douglas sat back and sighed, running his fingers through his hair in agitation. "And how many paving slabs have we laid on the road to hell with that sentiment, Ah wonder?" he asked.

The skeleton crew began to visit sickbay as their duties allowed, and after several simple tests, a picture began to emerge.

"None of your people have tested positive yet, James," reported Marston. "I've still a few to see, but I suspect I may already have the answer."

"Go on," prompted Douglas.

"The only other people aboard who have any antibodies against this virus, so far, are Mor and myself," she answered, referring to Commander Morecombe Hetfield, the man with whom she had spent the last fifty years stranded in Cretaceous Gondwana. "And I think I know why."

Douglas' brows knitted in thought. "So have we picked something up from you guys?" he asked, perplexed.

Marston shook her head. "Not exactly. Some of the reptiles in this era seem to carry a virus that's transferable to us. This is not surprising – similar conditions occurred in our own time. Most of my crew came down with it at some point. Poor Vince, our palaeontologist, didn't survive it," she added, sadly. "You can imagine what a blow that was to our small collective, for so many reasons."

Douglas nodded. "Aye, we were incredibly lucky to have young Tim Norris on the passenger list..." Thoughts of the boy in their enemies' clutches resurfaced suddenly and he fell silent.

Marston gave him a measuring look. "That young man means a lot to you," she noted.

"Aye, they all do, Kelly. But you know how it is, no matter how hard you try to treat everyone under your command or care equally, there are always some who become closer than others.

"Ah never married or really wanted a family, but Tim... well, let's just say he's a young man any father would be proud of. And Ah don't know how Ah'm going to do it, but Ah tell ye, Ah'm getting him back!"

Marston smiled. "I believe you, James. However, for right now, I need to know how you're feeling?" she asked.

"How Ah'm feeling?" he replied, slightly taken aback. "A little glum, if Ah'm honest!"

"No," she chuckled, lightly. "I mean physically."

"Oh, Ah'm fine." He shrugged off her concerns.

"Hmm," she pondered.

Douglas frowned. "Hmm, what?"

"Let me see that snakebite wound on your arm." She helped herself before he could acknowledge, carefully unwrapping the dressing she herself had applied. "Healing beautifully – so, asymptomatic.

"You may be right, James. If this thing is kicking off again, you could be our patient zero."

Chapter 2 | Escape From Within

"She's still out," the man whispered through a ski mask.

His companion was in the process of dragging the second guard away from the door. "You'll have to carry her then!" he sibilated. "Come on, let's go!"

The first did as ordered and lifted the recumbent Dr Heidi Schultz over his shoulder in a fireman's lift.

Light levels aboard the *Eisernes Kreuz* were low, on a night-time setting. There were very few people abroad at this hour. The four guards, two outside the ship and a further pair in the medical bay with their prize, had been temporarily dealt with.

The men stepped outside gingerly, checking their escape route before committing entirely. Sounds of the forest filled the night with an otherworldly symphony of whoops, rattles and calls, syncopated with the occasional scream.

"I'm glad we're not heading out there again," whispered Heidi's bearer.

The other man nodded. His night goggles showed another couple of sentries walking away from them, just disappearing around the huge bulk of the *Sabre*. He gave them another moment and then, "*Move*," he hissed urgently.

Both men ran as quietly as they could across the compound to where three orbital attack craft were parked in a line. Although much smaller than the *Last Word*, each of the new capital ships carried one of these along with a tracked personnel carrier, a small, four-wheel-drive vehicle and six dirt bikes.

As they neared the small fighter craft, a hatch opened in the side of the first. The man carrying Heidi slid her off his shoulders and the two men carried her aboard bodily as the hatch closed behind them.

"Go!" they called through to the woman in the pilot's seat. She still had a sprained ankle from the Oxalaia attack they barely survived near the river, a couple of days previously, but as their only pilot she would have to do her best.

Bypassing all of the start-up safety protocols, she fired the vertical takeoff thrusters and the ship almost immediately began to rise in an explosion of heat, light and noise.

The night watch came running from all directions, but in their confusion failed to act before the ship was already a hundred metres into the air. By the time various comm calls had been answered, confirming the launch as unscheduled, the little craft was already beyond the range of their small arms fire. They had no choice but to let it go.

Dr Flannigan sat at a terminal in his office within the new infirmary. Despite the lateness of the hour, Dr Satnam Patel, Mother Sarah and Major White huddled around a comm screen in White's office. Flannigan's summons had fetched them from their beds so that he could deliver some very worrying news.

"Hey, guys," he said easily. "I'm real sorry about disturbing you so late. If it's any consolation, Sam Burton is down here in the hangar with me, setting up an extension to my new hospital!"

On screen, Sarah's features were still softened by sleep. *"No need to apologise, Doctor. What's happened? Are we expecting wounded?"*

"Nothing so simple, I'm afraid," replied Flannigan. "One of Captain Meritus' people roused me from my bunk down here about an hour ago. She was concerned about a few of our other patients who were showing temperatures."

White suddenly looked concerned. *"Could they have what Jill has?"*

Flannigan nodded. "I fear so, Major. After we treated her we moved her to a private room, but with the mess that poor Patricia Norris came

12

back in… well, it took a while for us to get around to her. Basically, what I'm saying is, she spent many hours on the ward and I screwed up. I'm sorry. Patricia was such an emergency we just…"

"*Hey, you're doin' great work down there, Doc,*" White stated seriously. "*You can only deal with one emergency at a time. So what do you suggest we do now?*"

"Sam Burton has a team emptying the cargo bay next door for us to set up a quarantine ward. We have no advanced cases yet, so we don't know how bad this is gonna get, but I thought you guys should know straight away. For one thing, all visits are cancelled, so please pass that along. I'll leave how much to tell everyone to you guys – but be advised, the word may already be out."

"*Understood,*" White acknowledged with a nod.

"I've spoken to Dr Kelly Marston on the *New World,*" resumed Flannigan. "Apparently James Douglas is also infected, but is so far asymptomatic.

"I suggested earlier, as you will recall, Major, that Jill may have been bitten by something out in the forest. Apparently, I was half right. It's actually James who was bitten by a giant snake-like creature." Seeing their looks of shock and concern he hastened to add, "Don't worry, he's fine, he's fine. I've got someone going through the palaeontological information we have, to find the culprit. This may shed a little light, but it's a terrific long shot. Even if we do find a match, palaeontology is fairly unlikely to help us with a biological problem like this."

"*The man we really need on that has been taken from us,*" Patel stated bitterly.

"Yeah," acknowledged Flannigan. "I would love to have Tim take a look at this right now. I'd love to have him here, full stop!"

"*Hear, hear,*" added Sarah, sadly.

Flannigan continued, leaning closer to the screen, "The one ray of hope we have is that, according to Dr Marston, the infection is only passed by direct contact, but even that is quite rare. Its main method of transmission is from bites, transfusions, bodily fluids, things like that."

"*Two questions, if I may, Dave,*" asked Sarah, holding up two fingers. "*Firstly, if this is correct we'll need to be on our guard, so how did cross contamination happen in your ward? And secondly, how did Jill contract this from James? I assume he didn't* bite *her?*"

"In answer to your first," replied Flannigan. "I'm not sure yet. Some of the less seriously injured on the ward are free to visit one another. Maybe the simple act of holding a friend's hand when they're hurting is enough to transmit the virus. Perspiration on a hand, followed by a subconscious wipe of the eye or mouth – it's easily done.

"Of course, there's always the chance that we may be dealing with another type of illness entirely from the one Marston and Hetfield have experienced."

He looked sullen for a moment and then grinned suddenly. "In answer to your second question – apparently, when James stepped aboard the *Newfoundland* for the first time, Jill was so excited to see him alive that she ran over – or hopped over – and kissed him. According to Marston it was no peck on the cheek, either! So that would explain that.

"I need blood samples from Marston, Hetfield and Douglas to begin harvesting antibodies so that, just maybe, we can begin to develop a treatment. Major, how doable would that be at this time?"

Flannigan saw White sit back in his seat, blowing out his cheeks. *"That's a big ask, Dave. Anyone we send out could be driving straight into an ambush. And if we fly, we risk unwanted attention, so..."*

"It's important, Major. And I need to begin work on it straight away. Not only for my patients, but also because I may be infected myself and need to work quickly, while I'm still able."

White nodded. *"OK, Dave. If that has the force of a medical order, I'll make it happen. I was considering asking Meritus to take an engineering team over to the* New World *to help speed up their repairs. Maybe he can kill two birds? I'll ask him to take his attack craft."*

"Won't that leave the Pod undefended, Major?" asked Patel, turning away from the screen and towards White.

"It will, Satnam, but I can't expect him to go out there unarmed. Schultz will want to make an extreme example of him, more than any of us, I'd wager. Anyhow, those ships are so fast he could be back here in seconds if we found ourselves in trouble."

"Us? In trouble? Surely not," Flannigan chipped in.

White snorted, *"And on that note, we'd better get to organising this ready for first light."*

There were no windows in Tim's cell, but as the lights intensified, he assumed the hour was now *civilised*. After being thrown into the small room with just a bed and a seatless loo, he had railed against his capture – banging on the walls until his arms and hands were a mess of bruises, but with the fading of adrenalin came the tears. He cried for his mother and father, whom he had never known. He cried for his dad, whom he had loved and he cried for his mum, whom he missed desperately. There were even a few left for himself and his hopeless predicament – trapped in the belly of his enemy's fortress with no help, no friends and no chance. He was alone.

Eventually, he had succumbed to a fitful sleep. Upon awakening, he enjoyed three or four seconds of confused bliss, before his situation resumed its relentless attack on his psyche, like a knife through the heart.

The force of his memories' assault took his breath away. He was utterly done for, had lost everyone he loved, would never again see anyone he cared for. Like a caged animal, he stared, dead-eyed at the wall.

The mind has many defence mechanisms, shutting down conscious thought being just one. However, the undercurrent, the thoughts beneath the thoughts, never sleep. Tim was blessed with a powerful mind. Young and inexperienced he may have been, but a strong mind will always fight – even when its owner is ready to give up. The thoughts beneath Tim's thoughts turned out regardless, ready for work. Strategies marched his neural pathways like an army on the move. At the moment, they could only mount a guerrilla defence, hiding from the overwhelming force of his conscious depression. Like any rebellion, it began small – hit and fade, hit and fade. After a few small victories, his under-thoughts became bolder, striking back at the despair harnessing their freedom. They sought to make just one significant breach and then…

Tim stood. "Right!" he snapped, roughly wiping dried and crusted tears from his eyes and face. "If my old life is over, I need a new job."

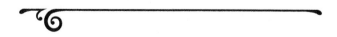

Woodsey seemed really down. Henry had never seen this side of him before. Rose had returned the previous evening, amid a storm of activity around the Pod. Henry did not yet know all that had transpired, but the prospect of seeing Rose again had completely taken over his thoughts. He still did not know how to reconcile feelings for his dream-girl with loyalty to his mother. Chelsea Burnstein had recently witnessed an alleged attack on the British politician, Alison Cocksedge, by Major Ford White. Rose had completely refused to believe it, despite Henry's mother's involvement. If he was honest, he had trouble believing such a thing of the major himself. However, his mother was unmoveable on what she had seen – or thought she had seen, he conceded.

Rose had taken a journey to the USS *New World* with her father to help the repair crews and get some space. Clearly she had now survived some kind of battle or crisis, and he could only hope that this, along with their recent geographical distance, may have closed some of the emotional distance between them – or at least sublimated it.

He turned back to his friend. "What's eating you, dude? Someone died?"

He instantly regretted his attempt at humour.

Woodsey gave him a look of sorrow which simply had no place on his face.

"What is it?" Henry tried again, with concern this time.

"You haven't heard?" the young New Zealander replied with a question of his own.

"Heard what, dude? You're worrying me."

"Tim's transport was attacked last night. His mum got shot. She might even be dead, I don't know. Captain Baines is in a bad way too."

"*Rose?*" Henry shouted her name, unconsciously grabbing his friend's shirt collar.

Woodsey held up his hands, gently breaking Henry's grasp. "She's OK, mate. And her old man. Bluey, the Aussie builder's a bit knocked around, but he's OK too."

Henry sagged with relief. "For one moment there, I thought I'd lost her." He breathed in and out deeply, dispelling his fears and then turned back to Woodsey. "Do you really think Dr Norris might be…?" He couldn't quite say the word.

Woodsey shrugged.

Henry suddenly felt his heart jump again as he noted one crucial omission from Woodsey's report. He was almost afraid to ask. "What about Tim?"

"Taken," said Woodsey, simply, a small crack in his voice betraying the emotion beneath.

Henry leaned heavily against a wall in the corridor where they had met, within the residential area of the Pod. He slid down to sit on the carpeted floor, staring into space. "Do you know any more?" he asked at last.

Woodsey slid down the opposite wall to face him. "Only that Schultz has him. You know, that crazy German doctor chick. Word is, she's taken him back to the enemy camp."

"But why would she want Tim?" Henry spoke the thought aloud. "He's just a kid, like us."

"Yeah, except he knows way more than we do, mate," Woodsey theorised, darkly. "If you were gonna set up shop in this crazy time, wouldn't you want a 'Tim' around to stop you from getting killed by eating the wrong leaves or trying to milk the wrong dinosaur?"

Henry frowned. "Dinosaurs don't have milk, do they?"

"Irrelevant, mate," Woodsey replied, sourly. "Although, I'd have the answer to that for you, if the skinny Pom was here. Ya see?"

They lapsed into silence.

After a long moment Henry spoke again. "I was gonna ask if you'd come with me – to meet Rose, I mean."

Woodsey raised an eyebrow. "After what she's been through, you want her to throw herself into your arms with *me* there?" he asked askance.

"Yeah. I mean no. I mean, I don't know! I just thought I could use the moral support if she… *you know?*"

Woodsey's other eyebrow shot up. Clearly he did not.

Henry looked embarrassed. "Come on, you know what I'm saying!"

"Look, mate, I don't have any more eyebrows left, so why don't you spit it out and save me a lot of time and effort reading something into this that isn't there?"

"In case she *rejects* me," Henry spelt out from the corner of his mouth.

Woodsey put his head in his hands theatrically. "Oh well, with everything else that's going on that really would be the end of the world, wouldn't it!"

"We can't get the parts we need over to you, Captain." Chief Engineer Hiro Nassaki sounded confounded and irate through the comm channel.

Douglas stared west across the lake from the aft of the *New World*, where the main engines were housed. He was high up within the ship, standing before one of the few rear facing observation ports.

Prior to the interruption, he had bleakly searched for any sign of the enemy, while dwelling upon a young boy in his care, held captive by that enemy. His mind was a playground where vengeance and worry took possession of the seesaw and bullied any other thoughts away.

He sighed deeply, pulling himself back from the darkness. "What's wrong, Hiro?"

"Sir, have you looked out of any starboard windows recently?" replied the chief.

Douglas frowned. "Give me a minute," he responded and made his way through the ship to see what Hiro was so concerned about.

He found a south facing porthole and looked out. "Oh," he vocalised his surprise. The problem was not difficult to spot.

When the *New World* crashed, she came in on a near flat trajectory, digging a trench about twenty metres deep into the earth. Inside the thirty metres of fuselage still showing above ground, Douglas was almost two thirds of the way up. It therefore came as a shock to see a huge face staring back at him, through the window.

Between the vast bulks of the *New World* and her sister ship, the *Newfoundland*, there was an obstruction – several, in fact. The two ships created an unnatural corridor down to the lake, funnelling any animals that wished to drink.

Douglas' head spun. The sight was almost too much to take in. He had seen the vast Argentinosaurus herd just after they had first landed in Cretaceous Patagonia. This animal was probably no bigger, but it was a hell of a lot closer.

Recovering from his initial shock, he stepped back towards the porthole, a boyish grin splitting his face for the first time in several days. He remembered Tim saying something about spotting a herd of sauropods in the area. He had not really paid it any mind. Many more pressing concerns had been grappling for his attention at the time. What had the boy called them? *Pata something?* he thought, then he had it. "Patagotitan," he said aloud, pleased with his recall.

The massive creature let out a huge bass moan, which Douglas felt vibrate through the hull. He placed his hands on the screen, laughing with wonder. There were a lot of them, more than could easily fit into the space. After drinking their fill, he hoped they would find a way out the other end of the bottleneck.

Ah can only imagine how many ways this might go wrong if they try reversing out! he pondered.

Still smiling, he said, "Hello, Mr Patagotitan." The smile gradually faded from his eyes as he once again recalled the young man who furnished him with the name.

His comm beeped, finally bringing these few blessed moments of release crashing back to Earth.

"Douglas," he answered.

"*You see the problem, sir?*" asked Hiro, sounding rattled.

"Aye," Douglas admitted. "We'd better not spook them. Ah'd not wish to see any harm come to such magnificent beasties, naturally. But also, Ah'd rather not find out how much damage they could do to ma ship. She's hurt enough already!"

"*Agreed. Any ideas, Captain?*"

"Er... wait them out?" Douglas tried hopefully.

"*Hmm...*"

"Singh here." They had hardly manned the bridge since many of the civilian helpers departed the day before. Instead, Singh had routed all messages to his personal comm, freeing him to assist Georgio Baccini. They worked tirelessly, stripping out damaged fuel lines around the thruster destroyed during their aerial battle, a few days ago.

Major White's voice came strongly through the comm link. "*Hey, Sandy. Just a heads-up. You're gonna have some company very shortly. Captain Meritus is bringing you some extra engineers to relieve you guys and let you get some rest. He will also bring back some blood samples to us, so that Dave Flannigan can work out what this new illness might be.*"

"That's great, sir. However, this is a bad time— Oh, no." Singh's words were cut off by the rumble of immensely powerful engines.

"*What's wrong, Lieutenant? We thought you'd be pleased?*"

"We would, but we have an animal incursion at the moment, between the ships. They're huge and blocking access from one vessel to the other. If Meritus' craft startles them, they might cause all kinds of damage. Sir, you *must* recall them! Or at least get them to set down at a distance."

"*I'm on it.*" The channel died for a few heartbeats. "*We've asked them to land away from you. Sorry, Lieutenant, but we decided not to give you too much advance warning in case our message was intercepted and the enemy decided to send a welcome party. Meritus' orbital attack craft is our only serious weapon. While it's outside the Pod, it's a target. The enemy's been quiet – we're not sure why – but we don't want to stir them into motion before we're ready.*"

"Understood, sir," replied Singh, over the thunderous stomping and braying of huge animals just outside their walls, dozens strong. "But I think we've got problems here!"

Tim's cell door slid open to reveal a couple of guards. Their expressions of arrogant disdain chimed eerily with uniforms resembling those worn by the *Schutzstaffel*, Hitler's own; the SS.

"You will come with us, *Herr* Schultz," one of them addressed him, curtly.

Tim stood and spoke bravely, "My name is Tim Norris!"

His heart gyrated in his chest as if trying to escape from within. By some weird science, the lurching of his stomach also seemed to vibrate his innards to water. He felt like a ghost from another time, 170 years in his personal past, but still many millions of years into the future.

The young man was so completely freaked out by his multilayered reality that he almost swooned. Sheer determination alone provided the mettle to face his nightmares.

He stepped out of the cell.

Hundreds of miles away, Heidi studied the stitching to her upper arm. *A neat job*, she thought.

Glancing up at her three rescuers, she nodded. "You did well to react before my *Großvater* fully secured me. He must have thought that even *I* could not escape while unconscious." She smiled wryly. "His philosophy of rule by fear has flaws, it seems. You showed me great loyalty last night."

"You're welcome, Doctor," one of the men replied.

Heidi observed them for a few moments more. She had a knot in her stomach; it felt like the tearing of a muscle group little used. She winced, but had to let it out. It was now or never. "Thank you," she said, hesitantly.

The man who had just spoken suddenly bore an expression of pure puppy joy. With his metaphorical tail beating the seat behind him, he basked in the glory of her recognition.

Schultz almost had to stop herself from following up with a 'Good boy'. Fortunately, her earlier gratuity of gratitude had left the well dry. *How can anyone stand being grateful?* she mused. *It feels like debt.*

She shuddered.

"Do you need a blanket, ma'am?" he offered hopefully.

"No," she answered coldly. She felt unclean, having ventured so close to the 'dark side'. However, her analytical mind recognised something new in the eyes of her followers; fear replaced by... *love?* She really could not tell for sure, having so little experience with sentimentality.

She shook her head irritably and stood.

"Right," she said, perhaps a little too forcefully. "I have been betrayed by my family. For this, they must die. I will then take control of this world and you..."

The three officers were hanging on her every word now.

"*You*... will be *rewarded*," she added. Seeing their reactions, she went for broke. "You will be *well* rewarded."

Heidi had never understood James Douglas, had always thought him a weak leader, in fact. She had only ever known the iron rule of the rod, but for the first time she began to catch a glimmer of something she had never taken seriously before – just a *slice* of the carrot.

Beck Mawar tossed and turned in her bed within the infirmary. She had been unconscious for more than a day. However, her vitals were strong and with the other crises overtaking him, Flannigan had barely managed to do more than periodically check her progress.

Sometimes, Beck's strongest links with the spirit world came during sleep, especially during the hypnagogic or hypnopompic states of falling asleep or waking. However, she was now trapped between worlds and could neither enter rapid eye movement sleep nor awaken fully. A harsh voice mithered her constantly; she could not make out any of the words which only increased the nightmarish qualities of her delirium. Occasionally, she would feel someone reaching for her, like an outstretched arm to a woman falling, but she could never quite grab it before being whirled away again. Like a rushing wind, she seemed to be travelling faster and faster between the planes of existence. At last, as if from nowhere, yet all around, came the voices. They gained in strength, working together to make her hear, to make her understand.

She awoke, suddenly and shockingly. Struggling for breath after her ordeal she began to cough, which drew the immediate attention of a nurse.

The woman raised Beck to a sitting position, plumping her pillows to provide back support.

"I must see Major White," Beck croaked hoarsely.

"I'm afraid that's not possible at this time," replied the nurse, and checking the name on the clipboard attached to the bed, added, "Rebecca."

"Call me Beck," she replied, automatically. "Please. I just need a minute of his time, no more."

The nurse nodded brusquely; there were no smiles from this hard matron. "I'll see if I can reach Dr Flannigan."

A few minutes later, Flannigan appeared by the side of Beck's bed looking exhausted. She instantly felt guilty. "Are you feelin' OK, Doc?" she enquired.

Despite the tiredness, his expression softened. "I'm pretty sure that was my line!" He winked.

She attempted a smile in return but fear and worry lines cut across her face, driving it away. "Doc, I must get a message to Major White. It's urgent!"

"Whoa, whoa! Slow down. You've been unconscious for many hours and we haven't been able to figure out why. Maybe you could answer a few question—"

"It's Dave, isn't it?" Beck interrupted him. She seemed to be looking disconcertingly over his shoulder instead of at him.

Flannigan nodded.

"Alright, alright! I'm telling him, give me chance!"

Flannigan's eyes widened in surprise. "Are you feeling quite yourself, miss?" he asked gently.

"What?" Beck answered, surprised. "Oh, sorry. I was just talking to… look, never mind. I have a message to give you and it's real important."

Flannigan frowned. "Very well," he allowed.

At last, she seemed to ignore whatever she thought was going on behind her doctor and stared levelly at him. "It's about the criminal, Del Bond."

"*Thanks, Dave.*"

"Major?"

"*That's the first thing to make me laugh in days!*"

"You're not buying it then?" Flannigan once more sat in front of the terminal in his office, adjoining the new infirmary. Beck Mawar had refused to calm herself until he promised to take her message to White personally. As the infirmary was in a state of lockdown, for all but emergencies, he commed White instead.

White was at his desk in his own office within the security department. "*She wants me to release the man who orchestrated the kidnapping of Captain Douglas and held Jill Baines hostage – is that pretty much the deal?*"

Flannigan looked down and scratched his head, mildly embarrassed. "You missed the bit about being told to do so by our dearly departed crewman," he added.

White gave him a look.

"I really liked Mario Baccini," Flannigan continued. "He was a good kid and I'm not sure about anyone using his name like this. It feels kinda disrespectful, you know?"

"*You're not buying this 'messages from beyond' charade either then, huh?*"

"Ford, how can I?" he replied candidly. "Beck seems a decent lady, and I really believe *she* believes. But this…? Surely it's crazy, right? Aaargh!"

"*What is it?*" asked White, concerned.

Flannigan stared. He was covered in hot coffee. The cup had been square on his desk and yet somehow travelled half a metre to empty itself all over him.

"*Dave?*" asked White again.

"Sorry," replied Flannigan at last, getting a hold over himself. "I just spilt my coffee. Major, maybe we should just re-interrogate Bond – see if any of her information pans out. What do you say?"

His cup righted itself on the desk.

"What the…!"

"*What's going on there, Dave?*" White was viewing Flannigan askance now.

"Oh, nothing, Major. I'm just a little tired and a little rattled. You know how it is."

White nodded. "*How are Jill and Patricia doin'?*" he asked gently.

"Patricia is still in a medical coma. I won't be bringing her round just yet – she's better off as she is.

"As for Jill, she's in a bad place, Ford. We're not able to do much more than hook her up to a saline drip and keep her cool when she burns and warm when she chills. I really need those blood samples."

"*I'll chase it up,*" replied White. "*I will speak with Bond again, just in case. Keep me apprised of any changes – White out.*"

"Get out!" snapped Heinrich Schultz peremptorily.

Captain Wolf Muller bowed and left wordlessly.

Tim was clearly catching the tail end of some kind of altercation as the guards hustled him into their master's presence. They bowed respectfully and stepped back to stand by the door, leaving Tim alone in the centre of the floor.

Schultz took a grand leather armchair facing him. He appeared almost enthroned as he steepled his fingers and stared penetratingly at the young man before him. After more than a minute he finally spoke, "You have been left alone to process your new position – your new identity.

"Believe me when I tell you, I have literally moved Heaven and Earth to bring you back to me. In a very real sense the future I am building is for you. As you see, I am now quite old."

Tim said nothing, but eyed Schultz guardedly. After arriving at his senses earlier that morning, he had indeed begun to process the Schultzes' revelation. Followed to its natural conclusion, he expected some form of recruitment speech next. However, Schultz seemed to be accentuating his importance towards something bigger still. Clearly, this old psychopath wanted more than Tim's knowledge of the Cretaceous. He wanted his grandson back – Timothy Schultz, Heidi's first cousin, back into the fold. The very thought nauseated him, but he was careful to remain expressionless.

He had not given up all hope that Patricia Norris, his adoptive mother, still lived. Certainly Captain Baines would have done anything to save her, as would the others. It was that which made them strong, made them great, made them unfathomable to a creature like the one seated before him now. He wrapped the thoughts of his mum around his heart like armour as he straightened and stared the old man down; an acute bearing of arrogance he had observed in the Schultzes. He felt sure it would play well with, quite literally, the grandfather of them all.

Tilting his head back slightly, he looked down his nose, speaking slowly and deliberately. "What, *exactly*, are you offering?"

Schultz nodded appreciatively, even favouring the young man with a wintry smile. "Good. You are learning, *Enkel*."

The dinosaurs remained almost stationary. Unable to reach the water's edge all at once, and with nothing else to do, they simply waited for the animals in front to move. Some of them chewed on the high branches of trees within reach at the edge of the lake.

The situation was far from ideal, but Hiro had work to do. So he spent a few moments noting the animals' behaviour.

Many smaller creatures travelled with the huge sauropods, presumably for mutual benefit. Before his capture, Tim had suggested they might be Notohypsilophodon Comodorensis. Similar, but a little more slender than Mayor Dougli Salvator, these quick, agile and highly alert little creatures served the giants well as sentinels. In return for this service, they received a bounty of broken-down plant matter, along with any scraps falling from the Patagotitans' mouths. In harder times, even the dung of their huge travelling companions would offer nutrition, yielding semi-processed vegetation and a plethora of insect life for protein.

Drawing inspiration from these smaller animals, darting around and between the giants' feet, his team began to move carefully through a colonnade of stanchion-like legs.

Carrying equipment and spare parts, they constantly alternated between holding their breath and holding their noses, whenever a free hand became available.

The stench was truly appalling, a situation worsened by the threat from above. Faeces fell around them like depth charges, dropped with abandon to flush them out.

Setting aside almost incomprehensible levels of unpleasantness, such a voluminous deluge might even kill a man by sheer blunt trauma.[1]

Despite this, their first foray was successful, emboldening Hiro to try for a second. Unfortunately, the arrival of Meritus' ship changed everything. The powerful engines spread panic among the herd, but the huge sauropods simply had nowhere to go.

"Go back!" Singh shouted into the comm. "Go *back!*"

Hiro and his team did not actually need telling twice. Suddenly, they were running like hell for the relative safety of the lift which had brought their equipment down from the Rescue Pod, nestled beneath the *Newfoundland*'s belly.

Hiro got there first. Turning, he reached for the last man in, dragging him from the path of a massive tail swipe as their steel enclosure shook with a deafening *clang!*

"Thank you," Hetfield acknowledged. "I'm too old for this crap!"

The open-mesh elevator doors were damaged and would only partially close, but at least the car was rising towards the ship. At seven metres above ground, their hopes were suddenly dashed when a huge body fell sideways, buckling the lift's mechanism and jamming them in place.

Dread gave Hiro's heart a squeeze. "Oh, no," he murmured.

His team were not the only ones in trouble. The herd's vast number of hangers-on squawked and ran in terror for their lives, their stable relationship degenerating into a domestic nightmare within the enclosed space. The relatively tiny Notohypsilophodons were no bigger than a Labrador, tails notwithstanding, and their situation was

---

[1]   It would also be the very devil for any commanding officer to make the death sound heroic whilst writing either their report or a letter to the deceased's family.

dire as they scrambled to find a safe path between the moving forest of monstrous limbs.

Hollow booms rang out across the lake time after time as vast bodies crashed into the hulls of both behemothic vessels. Some impacts were so violent that they forced the crews inside to hang on to something.

"Ma ship!" shouted Douglas to no one in particular. "Damn you, Meritus!"

"My ship!" moaned Singh, from a lower portal.

"Sekai!" shouted Hiro from across dino-highway.

The elevator, still hanging from the belly of the USS *Newfoundland*'s Rescue Pod, groaned alarmingly.

"Who's Sekai?" Hetfield shouted back.

"My ship," mouthed Hiro, through the tumult as body after huge body slammed her fuselage.

"Are you outta your goddamned mind!" screamed Hetfield. "Bring your head back over this side, son – we're in trouble here!"

As if to underline his words, the elevator lurched significantly to one side, swinging loose from one of its tracks.

The four men all looked at one another, hands reaching back automatically for walls that, although stationary relative to themselves, were now very obviously swaying. Hiro nodded to each of them in turn as he took a deep breath and with perfect simultaneity they screamed, "AAAARRRGGHH!"

The lift car fell.

"Henry, honey, I need to talk," said Chelsea Burnstein. *"I don't have a lot of time."*

Henry had stopped to answer his comm. After continuing a few steps, Woodsey realised he was suddenly talking to himself and halted to lean lazily against the corridor wall.

"What is it, Ma?" asked Henry. "I'm just on my way to see Rose."

"Can you come back to our apartment? Your father is away trying to drum up support for a separate civilian leadership – headed by himself, naturally."

"But, Ma, I haven't seen her since she got back and with everything that's happened with Tim's kidnap and his mum being shot and all—"

"*Oh my God! I didn't realise. Are Rose and her father...*"

"They're fine," Henry put her at ease. "But obviously, I'm real anxious to see her."

"*I understand, son, and I'm sorry, but it's real important and I need to see you alone. It can't wait.*"

Henry sighed deeply. "OK, Ma. I'm on my way."

Woodsey kicked off the wall with his foot to right himself and walked back to him. "Trouble at home?"

"Ah, who knows?" Henry answered dismissively. "I'd better go see what's happened."

"Do you mind if I carry on to meet Rose anyway?" asked Woodsey. "I really want to know everything that's gone on, but from the horse's mouth."

Henry nodded resignedly. "Yeah, sure. Please tell her I'll be along as soon as I can. This sounds important. Oh, and Woodsey?"

"Yeah?"

"Don't call her a horse. I'm in enough trouble as it is, without being branded as *your* associate."

Chelsea Burnstein turned the data-clip over and over in her hands. She knew that whatever she did next would have repercussions. Was she to trust a new friend, who seemed to have only the very best intentions for her and everyone like her, or did she stay within the known order of things – an order that had failed her all her life, but one within which her children must grow and live?

The doors to their apartment beeped and slid open to admit her only son.

As Henry entered, he could hear his sister, Clarrie, crying soulfully in her room.

"What's happened?" he asked urgently.

Chelsea waved him down. "It's OK, Henry. Your father called and told us about the Norrises. Obviously, he didn't bother to break it gently," she added harshly.

"I'd better go see her," Henry acknowledged, sadly.

"I tried, but she screamed at me that she just wanted to be left alone. Give her a little time, son. She'll need you then."

Henry looked unsure, but sat opposite his mother across the coffee table in their apartment's lounge. "So, what was so all fire important that it couldn't wait 'til after I'd seen Rose?" he asked, a little tetchily.

Chelsea frowned wretchedly. "I'm sorry, sweetie, but I just don't know what to do or who to talk to."

Henry leaned forward in his seat. "What is it?"

She showed him the data-clip. "This."

He held his hands out, palms up in bafflement. "And…?"

"It contains a message – a message that could not be transferred or transmitted, for fear of interception."

"OK," said Henry. "What's in the message?"

Chelsea shook her head. "It isn't for me. I'm meant to pass it on to…" She tailed off.

"Who, Ma?"

Chelsea took a deep, shuddering breath; she was clearly under enormous strain. "I'm to leave it for one of the enem—" she caught herself, "the *new* soldiers to pick up."

Henry was horrified. "One of Captain Meritus' people? Who?"

She looked afraid. "I don't know. I'm just meant to leave it in a janitor's cupboard in the recreation hall."

"Ma," began Henry, seriously, "who gave you this?"

Chelsea looked away, clearly not wishing to give up her confidence.

"Ma?" repeated Henry, more forcefully.

Still she looked away, stolidly tight-lipped.

"It's Cocksedge, isn't it?" he asked again. Suddenly, Rose's arguments all rang true. That politician was as dangerous as she was devious and now she had involved his mother in who knew what.

He stood and crossed to sit next to her. "Ma, you called me here to talk, so talk, will ya?" he added, sternly.

In answer, she merely opened her hand to reveal the data-clip once more. "Should we look at it?"

Henry took it from her and plugged it into his comm. He unfolded the screen to its full size and as the fold lines vanished into the liquid crystal, text began to appear.

They both read the information in growing concern and bewilderment. Was this an overture of peace or an act of vilest treason? It was couched in such language that reading it was like drinking in the knowledge through a crazy straw. Henry could only hope that if he sucked for long enough, he might just manage to get something out of it.

They looked at one another. Eventually, Chelsea posed the question that was on both of their minds, "What do you make of it?"

Henry thought some more, kneading the bridge of his nose as he tried to straighten the words out in his head. "I *think* she's saying that if *she* was in charge, we would have an unconditional peace – by *peace*, I assume she means surrender."

He re-read part of the document, "…would, were all things possible, obtain a multi-tiered peace package strategy through a process of… blah, blah, blah… obtainability through dynamism to arrive at an understanding… parties for the reconstructive redistribution of welfare pertaining to peoples remaining after the fact."

Henry blew out his cheeks loudly. "Ma, this is garbage, but I think it's a bid for power with the enemy's help, worded with so much double meaning that someone else could stand up and swear it was about peace and justice for all – or at least for any 'remaining peoples', and I hate to think what that might mean, if scrutinised!"

"What should I do?" asked Chelsea, tearfully. "She's my friend. No one has ever cared about my rights before, they were always too afraid of your father."

"Let's leave Dad out of this," replied Henry. "I know what he is, and he's got a lot to pay for, but he wouldn't sell us out to the Nazis."

"Do you really think that's what this is?" Chelsea was clearly tormented by indecision. "But I promised I'd pass on the message."

"OK," said Henry. "So why didn't you? I mean why, *exactly*, didn't you?"

She retreated from her son, rising to walk around as she sought an answer. Suddenly, she turned back to face him. "You know when your father sometimes gets that *look*? The one that says I'm going to get what I want and will crush anybody who stands in my way?"

Henry knew it all too well. He nodded.

"Well, it was kinda like that. She was talking of peace and a fairer, more equal new society for us all, but… I don't know. That Meritus guy was the enemy but in the way that an enemy soldier is 'the enemy'. Those people never actually got the chance to hurt any of us. Now, we have this new guy, this Schultz.

"Knowing all the things his evil granddaughter did to us here, I can't hardly imagine what he must be like."

"Added to the fact that Meritus would rather join *us* than live under his own boss," Henry chipped in.

Chelsea looked thoughtful once more. "I had started to believe in Alison Cocksedge. Still do, maybe. Everything she has said to me makes so much *sense*."

"Maybe that's because it's exactly what you want to hear, Ma?"

"Is that what you think?" Chelsea appeared more uncertain than ever.

"Perhaps. It's what Rose thought." He looked hangdog. "Before she went away we had a fight. She said that Major White would never do what he has been accused of by Ms Cocksedge, and that you were only seeing what you wanted to see – *believing* what you wanted to believe. I lost my temper and told her if she called you a liar then I would take your word before hers and… well, it got a little ugly."

"Did she call me a liar?"

"No," Henry admitted quietly. "She just thought that, with what you've been through, what we've all been through, you were too quick to believe badly of the major simply because he was a man."

He gave a look of abject sorrow. "*I'm* a man, Ma. So is Tim and Captain Douglas. Look what they've been through and what they've done for us. On the flipside, look at all Captain Baines has done for us, the risks she has taken with her own life to protect our people. Ms Cocksedge set out to ruin her! Surely we've seen enough good and evil on this trip already to know that no one has a monopoly, Ma." His eyes moistened in his passion and he wiped at them irritably.

"When are you meant to deliver this message?" he asked, finally.

Chelsea seemed lost in thought, or perhaps bad memories.

"Ma?" he prompted.

"This afternoon. By 2pm, latest."

"Right, I think we should give this to someone in charge. They may want you to drop it anyway, to see where it leads. You know that, right?"

She looked up, alarmed. "Do you think so?"

"Dunno. I'd wanna know who we're up against – potentially, at least."

Realising that she may soon have to face danger directly, she suddenly knelt before the sofa, looking up into her son's face, almost pleading. "Henry, I love the man you've become. You understand that, don't you?"

"I know, Ma, but Dad's just one guy. There's good and bad in all of us," he answered softly. "I'm going to make a call, OK?"

She nodded and let him go.

"And then I'm gonna check on Clarrie." Henry walked to the door controls mounted in the wall of their apartment and hit a red call button.

A tinny voice responded almost immediately, "*Security.*"

"Can I speak with Major White, please? It's an emergency."

Chapter 3 | Upside Down

"So, how do you like the new accommodation?" asked White, his customary lopsided smile mocking on this occasion.

"It's better," Bond admitted petulantly, "but hardly fitting for a man in my position."

"Your position being that of a man in jail?" White retorted. "I kinda think it's ideal."

"If you knew who I was, you would show more—"

"Save the garbage!" White cut off any further remonstration. "I'm going to ask you some questions and you're going to answer them – that's how this is gonna work."

"Or you'll torture me? As you did Lemelisk?" asked Bond.

"I didn't torture anybody." White nodded to himself. "So, we're dropping all pretence that he's Julian Bradford and admitting that one of your *colleagues* is actually the genetically altered arch-terrorist Sargo Lemelisk then, huh?"

"His past doings are nothing to do with me," Bond answered loftily. "He was a tool chosen by another. *I* am a strategist, engaged in essential work to save mankind."

White snorted. "You really buy your own rhetoric, don't you? Well, *Mr Strategist*, it's time to pull that Limey corncob from up your butt and start talking. I want to know exactly what *is* your strategy, Bond, and I wanna know now!"

Bond stared at the major in stony silence. Eventually, he replied indirectly, "You may not have tortured him yourself, Major, but you were part of it. So, let's not be coy."

"The torture, if you can call it that, was self-defence and not my idea, Bond. Let's just say I arrived too late to stop it. It would be a real shame if that were to happen again here, wouldn't it? Now, talk."

Bond said nothing.

White had no cards, so he decided to deploy the joker, face down, bluffing shamelessly. "I have reliable information that you have a mission within the enemy camp – a separate mission, one that may change the balance of power around here. Now, what d'ya say to that?"

Bond took an involuntary step back, his colour draining slightly. "What are you talking about?" he asked, but just a little too stiffly.

White was surprised by the reaction his accusation provoked and for the first time began to believe that the wild story, passed along from the medium by Flannigan, might just have a kernel of truth to it. He studied Bond for a long moment. Could this creature actually be instrumental in turning their situation around? He stepped closer to the bars of the cell. "Tell me what your purpose is, Derek."

Bond always insisted that everyone call him Del. He seemed to twitch even more than he usually did at the mention of his full name. After a moment's hesitation he stepped up to the bars, too, facing White. He nodded towards the solid wall between his cell and the one he used to share with Lemelisk, before provision was made to separate them.

"Take out the *rubbish*," he whispered, so softly that White could barely make out the words. "I hear him exercising, so I know the wall is not soundproof. Send the guard away and switch off your surveillance equipment. There must be no record of what I'm about to tell you." He grabbed White's arm through the bars. "None, Major. All our lives may depend on it."

White strolled through the corridors of the Pod's residential area as if shell-shocked. Just as he was wrapping up with Bond, one of his men had called him away to an alleged emergency. Unsure what he was walking into, he took a couple of guards with him. His head was spinning from Bond's revelation – could it possibly be true?

Without even realising it, he was suddenly standing before the door to the Burnsteins' quarters. After a few seconds, the doors opened to reveal Henry Burnstein Jr.

"Major, thank you for coming," the young man greeted, gesturing for the soldiers to enter.

White scanned the room quickly and, finding it empty but for the boy, his mother and younger sister, posted his men outside the doors.

"What's this about, Henry?" he asked, gently. "It's a bit of an awkward time—"

"Please have a seat, Major," Henry interrupted him. "I'm sorry, but this is real important."

White frowned. Nodding, he sat as invited and waited for the explanation.

The young girl was red-eyed from crying and her mother looked on the verge of tears herself. *Has Burnstein been up to his tricks again?* White thought darkly. He hated bullies. Cocksedge's accusation that he had beaten her had hurt him deeply. The very idea that anyone would believe such a thing of him cut him up inside. Now facing one of his principal accusers, Chelsea Burnstein, he really had no idea where this was going.

Henry dove straight in. "Major, Ma has been asked to drop a data-card carrying a secret message to a janitor's locker in the rec hall. The message is to be collected by one of Captain Meritus' soldiers and originated from Ms Cocksedge."

White sat back, stunned. Staring into the middle distance for a second, he stroked his chin thoughtfully. "Thank you for coming straight to the point. Have you seen this message?"

Henry nodded and pulled out his comm. Opening the screen once more, he turned it to the major.

White scanned it quickly. After he had read it, he leaned back slightly and placed a fist on his hip while raising an eyebrow.

Henry smiled sardonically. "Can you translate it, sir?"

White snorted. "It certainly goes round all the houses before it knocks on any doors! If I understand this doubletalk salad, and I have to reiterate the 'if', then after her defeat and disgrace a few days ago, Cocksedge is now practically asking for election funding from the Nazis!"

"That's what we thought, too. Ma was concerned about taking it straight to people who were enemies until just a few days ago, so we read it. I hope that's OK?" Henry suddenly looked very young and uncertain.

"You did good, kid," White replied unequivocally, then glancing at the boy's mother, added, "You both did."

"I have to ask you, Major," Chelsea spoke for the first time, still stroking her daughter's hair gently, "did you beat on Alison Cocksedge?"

White looked her squarely in the eye. "No, ma'am, I did not. Nor would I ever do such a thing."

"She had provoked you…" Chelsea pushed the point.

"Yes, she did," White accepted. "But that is neither here nor there. I am a soldier – I know there are times when one must fight, but I fight to defend what I believe in and the people under my protection. The abuse she accused me of is not in me."

Chelsea studied him for a long moment, years of fear and neglect racing through her mind like oncoming traffic across a roadmap of scars, blinding her. She had suffered so much to avoid being separated from her children, by a man who could buy anything, or anyone. She looked at her son, looked inside him to the man he had become and looked back to the soldier seated opposite. She knew she could never completely let go of the hurts of the past, but also knew that if she let them guide her future, she would never truly live. Her memories came to a complete and immediate stop. "I believe you," she said simply.

White's eyes glistened with emotion. He swallowed his embarrassment, clearing his throat. "Thank you," he replied seriously, never breaking eye contact. "I'm sorry, but I have to ask you to do something now – something potentially dangerous."

"You want me to plant the data-clip as requested," she stated. She had expected it.

"More than that, I want you to plant a camera in the locker, too. It will only be the size of a pinhead, with a fisheye lens. Will you do this for me, please?" White gave her a measuring look.

"Yes," she answered without hesitation. Taking Henry's hand she added, "I have to protect my children from these people. I'm still not a hundred percent convinced that Alison is wrong about suing for peace with the enemy, or that she's a bad person, but I feel that inviting them in here would be a mistake that we could not take back."

White considered before answering. "I think we're gonna have to agree to disagree about Ms Cocksedge's agenda," he stated diplomatically. "But I agree that allowing the Nazis aboard this Pod would be disastrous

– even lethal for anyone who doesn't match Schultz's ideal for the master race. Still, you're a brave woman, Mrs Burnst—"

"Chelsea," she cut him off.

He nodded and smiled his understanding. "You're a brave woman, Chelsea. Now, we have less than an hour and I need to make this happen." White got to his feet, at once the military man of action. "I will have Mary Hutchins bring the surveillance equipment to you here. No one will suspect her about janitorial duties. As she's *New World*, rather than Pod staff, there's less likelihood of any link to Cocksedge too. Very good. Thank you, we'll be in touch directly."

With that, he gave them all a respectful nod and left.

"Are you guys OK?" asked Meritus. He and five engineers from the Pod huddled around the broken doors to the crashed elevator car; only his pilot remained with their ship.

The car was badly distorted. Having swung before it fell, it had landed on a corner and crumpled. It would clearly never be useful again.

Three of the four passengers groaned; Hiro was the first to open his eyes. "YOU!" he spat, and without warning, launched himself at Meritus. "You shot down Sekai in the first place!"

Meritus stepped back, slightly shocked and more than a little bewildered as the engineers grabbed Hiro to calm him.

"Hey, we're all on the same side now, remember?" Meritus found his voice at last.

"All this is—" Hiro was grappled by several pairs of arms while he struggled like a leaping salmon to get at his erstwhile enemy. "Aarrgh!" he added in frustration.

"Lieutenant, calm down!" snapped Meritus, spotting Hiro's insignia. "We have work to do and injured to care for – get a grip on yourself, immediately!"

Hiro sagged slightly. Turning, he spotted Hetfield, clearly unconscious. "Commander Hetfield? Are you still with us?" he asked with concern. "Morecombe?"

The engineers released him to kneel and attend the old man. The other passengers either held or rubbed parts of themselves in obvious discomfort, but were at least starting to move. The crumpled steelwork had absorbed most of the shock from their landing.

"Morecombe?" Hiro tried again, taking the injured man's left hand and rubbing it.

Hetfield groaned and felt his brow with his right. It came away bloody. Wiping his eyes, he looked up balefully at the Japanese chief engineer. "Hiro, remind me to thank James for rescuing us from our retirement!"

The assembled officers and engineers chuckled with relief. Meritus took in the turd-strewn vista before him.

The Patagotitan sauropods that had caused all the damage were now wandering aimlessly in the lake's shallows, their fear and confusion already forgotten as they drank and generally milled about. It was a surreal spectacle. They behaved as though they suddenly found themselves standing in water, away from their lunch and could not quite remember how they got there. Conversely, the small Notohypsilophodons were still running around in distress, scattering ever further afield. Clearly they *did* remember how their neighbours had attempted to trample them all to death and forgiveness was yet to be forthcoming.

Meritus turned away from the animals and studied Hetfield, smiling at the old man's courage. He was clearly hurt but nonetheless cleaving to the healing power of sarcasm. It seemed to be working; he was now standing, with assistance.

Hetfield was eyeing Meritus in return, with suspicion, when a shadow fell across them all, causing the old man's eyes to widen in horror. He whispered, almost reverently, "Matilda!"

"Hi, Chelsea. Won't you come in?" Cocksedge gestured Mrs Burnstein inside, closing the doors on the guard stationed outside her quarters. "They're still keeping me locked away in here," she added scornfully as she guided her visitor towards the sofas. "I'll make us some coffee."

"I dropped off the data-clip as you requested," Chelsea stated nervously.

"Oh, that. I'd almost forgotten about it," replied Cocksedge airily. "Silly me. I thought you'd just dropped in to see a friend."

Chelsea forced a smile. "Of course, dear. But I thought you'd want to know."

"Thank you. And thank you for not deserting me."

Chelsea felt a stab of guilt.

"Did you read the message?"

"Was I meant to?" Chelsea answered obliquely, thinking as quickly as she could manage.

Cocksedge gave her a penetrating look. "Never mind. It was just my invitation for peace. I didn't bother to use any encryption. Someone could still have cracked it and I think that would only have looked suspicious, don't you? I have nothing to hide." She smiled her politician's smile. "Or should I say, *we* have nothing to hide. I'm very grateful that you agreed to be a part of this."

Cocksedge's insinuation that they would now go down together if caught was couched in the language of camaraderie, but Chelsea was not fooled. She breathed a secret sigh of relief, glad that she had shown the message to White.

"Everyone is treating me like some sort of traitor," Cocksedge continued, "and I'm only trying to work out a peace with the newcomers. I mean, really, isn't all this posturing and fighting pointless? We should be welcoming them, not attacking them. They might even be kind enough to take us home in their ships."

Yes, it's all so plausible, thought Chelsea. *I still believe it, even though I know it's not true. Oh, God. I just don't know what to think any more. I hope I've done the right thing.*

Cocksedge frowned. "Chelsea? Are you OK?"

She forced herself to brighten. "Yes, Alison. Forgive me, I'm just a little worried for my children with this whole situation. I pray we can avoid any fighting."

Cocksedge seemed content with this answer and began again, "Chelsea, I have another favour to ask of you – two in fact. I wouldn't ask if I was free to move about the Pod, you understand? Would you mind terribly, going back to the janitor's cupboard in the gym and collecting the newcomers' reply at 2pm tomorrow, please?"

Chelsea nodded. "Of course."

Confidence bolstered, Cocksedge continued, "The second favour is a little more difficult, I'm afraid. You know this Pod was built by your husband's corporation – several of his corporations in fact, I believe. He's a man with his finger in a lot of pies.

"Of course you do, what am I saying? Well, he will have certain override codes. Codes for the operation of the Pod, fairly minor stuff to allow the manufacturers to carry out any warranty work, things like that."

She paused as if deciding how to proceed. When Chelsea made no comment, she gave her a winning smile. "Chelsea, do you think you could tap into your husband's files and get those codes for me, please? They're sort of a 'back door' for the engineers."

Chelsea's eyebrows rose. "A back door? Is that really a thing? I thought that was just in sci-fi TV shows?"

Cocksedge gave a tinkling little giggle. "Yes, you'd think so, wouldn't you? But they really are 'a thing', I promise you," she insisted, lightly using the index and second finger on each hand to press the ever ready inverted comma bunnies back into service.

Chelsea's heart sank. *It's all true*, she thought. *Now I know. The only reason she befriended me in the first place was because of Hank's control codes over this Pod. I don't even know if he has such a thing, he's no tech. Although I wouldn't put it past him to have a way of taking control of someone else's bought and paid for equipment.*

Trying to hide the crushing emotional loss of being used by the first friend she had made in many years, she replied, "Alison, I wouldn't know how to find such things."

"Don't worry," Cocksedge smoothed over her concerns. "I can tell you where to look. As a Member of Parliament, I had access to all sorts of information about the joint venture – the Mars Mission. The contracts specifically stated that any override codes could only be used in times of emergency or product-wide malfunction. Well, I think this fits into the category of emergency, don't you? What with the military dictatorship to which we are enthralled declaring war on a superior force, and without cause?

"I can't tell you how much I appreciate your help and continued friendship, Chelsea. This is what I would like you to do…"

The tracked vehicles bounced along the forest trail heading east. Both were armoured and armed. The lead vehicle had an extended 'crew cab' allowing some fairly opulent and extremely comfortable seating to be fixed in the front compartment behind the driver.

Tim stared dispassionately at the back of the driver's head, an almost impossibly perfect specimen of blonde womanhood, dressed in similar fatigues to Schultz's personal guard. He believed she was Heinrich Schultz's private secretary, bodyguard and who knew what else.

They were on a mission to reconnoitre the *New World*'s crash site – not out to engage, merely to take stock. There seemed to be some confusion as to whose side Schultz's initial strike team were now on.

Heinrich had decided there was really only one person he could adequately trust, both to lead the mission, and to fully understand the situation.

"What is it that has your attention so completely, *Enkel?*" he asked from the opposite seat.

Tim turned back to the man who purported to be his grandfather.

"Perhaps it is Erika who interests you?" he continued, gesturing lasciviously towards the driver. "There are many Miss Schmidts among my entourage, although few are as skilled as *my* Erika." His use of the word 'my' very clearly stated his claim.

"Actually," replied Tim, "I was curious about that corpse over there."

Tim was gratified by the look of genuine surprise on the old man's face – he was clearly not used to being surprised by anything and Tim chalked this up as a very small victory. "Miss Schmidt, can you stop the vehicle please?" he asked.

"Sir?" Erika Schmidt asked Heinrich.

Tim swallowed. He really wanted to get out. Something had caught his eye certainly, but just maybe, if he was out, he could manufacture an escape. He could feel the bile rise in his throat with the word he must now utter, if he was to secure his chance. "Grandfather?" he prompted.

Schultz looked up abruptly, studying the young man. His penetrating stare burned into Tim like coherent light. Suddenly, he smiled. "Very well. Erika, pull over."

Tim passed the soldiers in the rear compartment and popped the rear hatch. A young officer ordered two of his men to lead an advance party, securing the area before the VIPs left the vehicle. After a few moments a guard of six men and women spread around the small clearing and were quickly joined by further troops from the other armoured carrier.

Tim stepped out and strode towards the half eaten carcass of a dinosaur. He was glad to be out in the open air but dismayed by the level of scrutiny he was under. He sighed and focused on his find.

He may have been out in the open air, but it could hardly be said to be *fresh* air. Squadrons of flies buzzed around the putrefying corpse.

It was fairly large, maybe seven or eight metres in length, he guessed. The complete animal would probably have weighed a ton or more. Although large portions of the tail were already scavenged away, most of the animal remained; its skeleton revealed to various degrees with little disarticulation. Most of the bones were still joined by the cartilage which had strung them together in life. The guts and chest had been almost completely devoured, the ribs left to enclose nothing but air.

Tim could clearly see the pubic boot; it was pronounced, large and highly suggestive, recognisable even. He glanced at the legs and particularly the feet. He shook his head; he had not really expected evidence there this early in the Cretaceous Period. He walked cautiously towards the semi-revealed skull of the creature, circled it and returned to the front of the mouth.

There was still flesh on the head. Tim expected this; skulls rarely made good eating and tended to be among the final scraps. He would have liked to see the nasals, to check for fusing, but did not have any tools to cut away the skin. He doubted any of the Nazis would lend him a large knife, so he simply tutted. It was a mystery.

Kneeling down, he looked up into the mouth of the skull. It was not lost on him that, had he done this a month or two ago, it would have been the last thing he ever did.

The teeth of the dead theropod were clearly and very obviously those of a predator. However, they were not like the Carcharodontosaurs he was already familiar with here, such as Mapusaurus or Giganotosaurus. Nor were they like the crocodilian teeth of the large Spinosaurs such as Irritator or Oxalaia, which also inhabited this continent. This animal was something different; the teeth were more rounded in section than the Carcharodontosaurs, and bore little resemblance to anything crocodilian. The clincher for Tim was the animal's front teeth.

He stood up quickly, taking a sharp intake of breath.

"What have you found?"

The voice from behind startled him and he took an involuntary backward step, almost tripping. Tim's engrossment aside, Schultz's approach had been absolutely silent.

"Well?" The old man raised an eyebrow, with unusual patience; he was not fond of repeating himself.

"It's a…" Tim could hardly catch his breath. "It's a Tyrannosaur!" he exclaimed loudly.

Schultz continued to stare.

"D-don't you understand what this means?" Tim stuttered, his words tripping over one another. "Hints. That's all we've ever found of *possible* Tyrannosaurs in South America. Hints! And this, this is a new species – I'm sure of it!"

"It doesn't look very new," Schultz retorted, wrinkling his nose at the semi-rotted cadaver.

"This is huge!"

"I wouldn't argue with that," replied Schultz, eyeing the giant remains drily.

Tim stepped back again and this time he fell on his backside.

A chorus of laughter from the guards encircled him.

Schultz gave them a look that froze them instantly into silence. "Get up!" he snapped coldly. Clearly he had no sense of humour at all where the family honour was concerned. "If this is a new animal – name it. I believe that is the tradition? Take some holos and get back into the vehicle quickly. We have wasted enough time."

Tim borrowed a comm unit from one of the soldiers to record the animal and its unique features. His had been taken from him upon capture.

"What's so special about this animal?" asked the guard.

"It's a Tyrannosaur, in a place where there were meant to be none," Tim explained. "It's less derived than the later Tyrannosauridae or Tyrannosaurinae, but it shares some features that will be carried through for the next thirty million years or more. It's like viewing a jigsaw with some of the pieces missing.

"See the foot? In later animals, those metatarsals will group so closely that the centre bone is almost crushed between the outer ones to help the animal carry its weight more efficiently. It's called the arctometatarsalian condition. This creature doesn't have it, but there are other distinctly Tyrannosaur features which—"

"Come!" snapped Schultz, already back at the troop carrier.

"*Schnell bewegen!*" the young officer shouted. Tim rushed a few last pictures and returned the comm to the soldier before he was rounded up in a flurry of movement and bundled back to their troop carrier.

Once they were underway again, he ventured, "That animal warrants further study."

"Perhaps," allowed Schultz. "I was impressed by your knowledge of these ancient reptiles and your enthusiasm. One day you may give whichever orders you desire, but that day is not this day."

Tim pondered this, Tyrannosaurs momentarily driven from his head. He was quite literally being offered the world, to take Heidi's place at Heinrich's side, with an army at his back. The thought was intoxicating, of course, but balanced by a cold awareness; his inner self was dying a little with every moment spent cooperating with Schultz's plans. Even though his was only a pretence, it was beginning to feel like Tim Norris had been locked in a room and beaten, so that Timothy Schultz could fly free.

He gave an involuntary shudder, when thoughts of his adoptive parents flooded his mind, massaging a little life back into the Tim beneath the Nazi veneer – and with those thoughts came inspiration.

"I will name that animal Patedosaurus Norrisi," he stated at last. In the privacy of his own mind he added, *To honour my mum and dad, Patricia and Edward Norris – two brilliant scientists and the best people I've ever known.*

"Matilda?" asked Meritus in confusion. Then he heard the snarl. He swallowed, turning very, very slowly to face the two-metre-long head of a female Tyrannotitan. With any hope that she had moved on to pastures new thoroughly dashed, his untrained eye saw something rather like a T rex – and that was pretty much all he needed to know right now. However, he had seen her before, skulking away through the trees when they rescued Captain Baines et al from their little excursion through the woods, after Heidi Schultz stole their transport. The huge scar running down Matilda's snout, cutting across the maxilla, made her instantly recognisable.

Four of the engineers Meritus had with him stumbled and skipped their way around to the rear of the crashed lift car, leaving him centre and forward, alone. Hiro's small team had already grabbed Hetfield and backed further into the car.

"Will she see me, if I stand still?" Meritus whispered out of the corner of his mouth, his eyes wide in terror.

"Shut up, you fool!" hissed Hetfield. "She's not stupid, even if you are!"

Meritus gulped as she sniffed him. Her jaws parted lazily, allowing saliva to drip to the ground in great oozing pearly globules. He tried not to breathe, but the slaughter stench nearly felled him; a reek so powerfully engulfing that it seemed to bond with his clothing and hair.

For the fifth engineer, still unsure which way to go, it all became too much and he suddenly screamed and bolted for the *New World*. This mistake made him suddenly interesting, drawing *everyone's* attention.

Matilda snorted, knocking Meritus from his feet as her head snapped round to follow the running man. She turned and roared after him.

The runner was flat out for his life. He was quicker off the mark than the giant predator, but that was when he made his second mistake. His odds were never great, but turning to look over his shoulder as he ran – like an extra from a Japanese monster movie – fatally slowed his progress, sealing his fate.

Matilda closed.

Hetfield closed his eyes, tight against the spectacle.

Meritus stumbled to his feet, breathless and gawping. It was heads or tails whether he was more shocked by what he had seen or by the fact that he was still alive.

The running man screamed when caught, but as the Tyrannotitan's devastating maw closed, bringing her teeth together like shears, he fell immediately silent. As the giant head flicked back to swallow, the man's head and torso vanished.

The legs were cut off at the thigh, sliding gracelessly from those jaws like hotdogs from the roll of a careless drunk, too liberal with the red sauce outside a club at three in the morning. Matilda sniffed at the severed limbs, and abiding by the three second rule, almost gently retrieved one of them from the ground.

As if struck by a sudden thought, she turned, almost hopefully, back towards the ruined elevator. Joy of joys, it seemed the burger van was still open to get another.

"Oh, crap!" shouted Meritus, backing up to the broken cage.

Matilda stalked towards them, the leg still swinging obscenely from her front teeth. Hinging at the knee, it appeared to kick out as she walked, the foot still booted.

Meritus saw an opportunity to distract the creature. He had no idea if this would work, how intelligent the creature was, or even if there would be any escape if it did work. He ran forward to meet Matilda halfway.

Rose opened the doors to the Millers' apartment only to be swept off her feet by Henry, who darted in to spin her round, squeezing the life out of her.

"Thank God you're OK." His voice was husky with emotion.

Rose extricated herself from his arms. "It took you long enough to get here," she replied harshly. "Have you any idea what we've been through?"

"Some," Henry admitted, cautiously. "Look, I'm sorry, honey. I was on my way over here earlier, when I got called away—"

"I know!" She cut him off. "Woodsey told me all about the mysterious message from '*Mum*'." The word was an accusation, after the way he had made his loyalties clear at their last meeting. She pushed Woodsey's description of Henry's state over the last few days, including the phrases 'lost puppy' and 'totally pathetic', from her mind. He needed to atone first.

He looked down sheepishly. "I'm sorry about all that. You were right, I was wrong, OK?" he asked, hopefully.

Rose crossed her arms giving him a sideways look.

Clearly more grovelling would be required. Henry sighed. "The reason I was called away was real important," he tried again.

"To your *mum*, maybe!"

"No, it's not like that, Rose – seriously. Something is going on. Look, I can't talk about it, but please trust me this was—"

"Really important – so you said. Tell me what was more important than checking whether I was still alive?"

"I knew you were alive, honey – and safe, I made sure of that." Henry tried to take her hand but she kept her arms resolutely folded.

"So," she began again, "what was more important than checking on me?"

Henry shook his head. "Nothing, my love. This wasn't more important – at least not t'me – it was just more *urgent*, you know?"

"It always is with your mother—"

"No!" he interrupted her this time. "This has nothing to do with Ma, at least not directly. It's just that she, and I, I guess, are involved." He leaned close to whisper. "I swore I wouldn't discuss this with anyone. All I will say is, it involves Major White and is real important to all of us."

Rose was intrigued, even forgetting to keep her arms crossed, but she was still unwilling to let him completely off the hook. "I'm not just *anyone*," she whispered.

Henry's frown of concern softened to his boyish smile. "You got that right."

Melt... *Damn*, she thought. A smile threatened to eclipse her scorn, so she grabbed a cushion from the sofa and beat him with it until they both fell, laughing, into the same armchair.

"What the hell! Are you *crazy?*" screamed Hetfield, his throbbing head complaining at the volume.

Meritus ignored the shout. Just before the halfway point where, unarmed, he intended to – there were no other words for it – face down a fifteen metre long, four metre tall, eight ton, carnivorous dinosaur, running flat out towards him, he spotted a pair of Notohypsilophodons.

The poor little animals had been crushed in the earlier mêlée. They spilled out of a huge, almost circular footprint, more than a metre in diameter; heads lolling horribly.

Meritus went to ground virtually on top of them. Crouched, ready to spring, he looked up at almost certain death.

Matilda lunged for him. Waiting until the very last split second, he jumped clear. Her jaws closed about one of the small Hypsilophodontids.

Backing off on all fours, Meritus scrabbled to get away, but to his everlasting relief the local queen seemed content with her lot. Everyone hates substitutions when ordering a meal, but once in a while, one gets a pleasant surprise.

The Tyrannotitan picked up both Notohypsilophodons in her mouth at once and stalked away victorious.

Meritus got to his feet and ran like hell. As he puffed breathlessly to a halt after his brush with death, Hiro stepped from the broken lift car and grabbed him by the arm, shaking his hand vigorously. "I'm sorry," he said.

Hetfield's lips twitched to a smile as he straightened to watch the giant predator leave with her consolation prizes. "Well, it's an ill wind that blows no one no good," he said.

Chapter 4 | Watchers

Two armoured transports crossed the river. Deviating from the now well-beaten track, they relied instead on game trails, many of which were strewn with debris from the recent hurricane. Fallen trees constantly slowed their progress and their twenty-mile journey was lengthened still further by several dead ends.

Smaller obstacles were pushed aside by the powerful tracked machines; others required some considerable effort to cut and tow out of the way.

Between the forests were great swathes of land that, but for scrub and brush, lay fairly open. These made for easier going and allowed them to make up time.

East of the mountains, the terrain was a weave of uniquely shaped, interconnected plains. The treeline marched irresistibly from the west and by claiming the most productive soils first, created a landscape of unevenly divided cells, each encircled by walls of encroaching forest. Still further east, the prairies were much larger and provided endless scope for greedy woodland expansion.

Nature's balance was struck by vast herds of herbivorous dinosaurs – most notably, some of the enormous sauropod clades, so common in Patagonia during the Mid-Cretaceous. Woodland clearance was their business and by keeping the forests in check, they opened up all manner of opportunity for plain-dwelling flora and fauna.

The forest answered these incursions with prodigious and tireless growth, and thus, this pendulum of destruction, countered by vigorous expansion, worked the region's eco system like a well-oiled clock.

The scenery was a joy, yet the hours passed awkwardly for Tim; a protracted hearing under the ferociously disapproving gaze of Hanging Judge Schultz. At least, that was how it felt – a trial made worse through lack of words.

As the miles passed under track and wheel, the roughness of the topography, coupled with the shaking of their transport, became mildly soporific for Tim.

Almost irresistibly, he drifted back to the smoggy, half-alive 22nd century of his memory. To say 'it was another world' was just bland language, a sin befitting the throw-away times in which he grew, perhaps. The two worlds could never be reconciled, in word or deed. One always sought the destruction of the other, but man's weapons of mass destruction were never quite equal to Mother Nature's tools of mass creation and rebirth – they were merely quicker, which was suggestive in itself.

Despite the dangers and the horrors he had endured, Tim felt in his bruised soul that this world was better. It had a future, for a start.

When he reduced the crisis they faced to comic book terms, the 'villains' in this piece wanted to provide humanity with a second chance in this beautiful, if not always idyllic, world. The 'heroes' wanted to return to a broken time and set everything back on its path towards ruin.

The practical sense in Schultz's aims chilled him. He could not help wondering, *Am I on the wrong side in this? Means and ends? Ends and means?*

He leaned his head back into the comfortable seat and closed his eyes. Without willing them forward, a parade of faces strolled before his eyelids: funny Sandy Singh, ingenious Hiro Nassaki, the ever dependable and honourable Satnam Patel and many, many others. The line of notables ended with his mum, Patricia Norris. It alarmed him that he already struggled to recall her features in any detail. The realisation was like a cup of freezing cold water down his back. *I am Tim Norris, Tim Norris!* he screamed in his head and then he had it. He knew what he had to do.

Opening his eyes, he saw a large lake through the thinning trees. The lead vehicle, in which he travelled, stopped abruptly, rocking slightly on its tracks.

Schultz nodded to his aide. The beautiful Erika Schmidt removed her safety harness. Completely in defiance of the cramped space, she somehow contrived to step gracefully into the rear compartment, barking orders as she went. The soldiers jumped from the rear hatch in rapid succession to secure the area up to the beach.

Schultz eyed Tim keenly; a calculating look Tim suspected was an attempt to divine his thoughts – his *real* thoughts and feelings. This was the closest he had been to his people since Heidi had captured him.

"Shall we take a walk?" the old man stated at last. The question mark merely denoted good manners, this was not a request.

Tim dutifully nodded and unbuckled his own safety harness. "After you, Grandfather."

"Hi, Jill. How are you feeling?" asked Flannigan, timing her pulse with his watch.

Baines looked pale and drawn but attempted a smile. "Like I'm missing out," she answered weakly. "What's going on out there, Dave?"

"Nothing for you to worry about at the moment, Captain. Captain Douglas has repairs in hand, over at the *New World* and Captain Meritus is bringing back some blood samples containing the antibodies I need. I'll soon have all this sorted out." He gave her a conspiratorial wink. "You'll be back in the game before you know it."

She frowned slightly. "What's he like?"

"Meritus?"

Baines nodded and Flannigan looked thoughtful for a moment. "Dunno, really. He was threatening to kill us all a few days ago and now..." He let the sentence hang. "Still, he saved you and the others. We're all grateful for that."

"But you don't trust him," Baines stated, reading her fellow officer's manner. Flannigan, usually so affable and easy-going, was clearly troubled by their new alliance.

"I really don't know, Jill," he repeated. "I wasn't going to mention this, but since we've been talking you seemed to have perked up a little."

Baines did indeed look a little stronger. Clearly being out of the loop was doing more harm than good. "Could you help me sit up for a while,

Dave, please? I'm as weak as a kitten." She smiled again, but some of the greyness was leaving her complexion to be replaced with pallor. It was an improvement.

"Of course," he answered, plumping up the pillows and helping her into a sitting position.

"Now, what weren't you going to tell me?" she asked a little more forcefully.

"There's been an attack. Over at the *New World* – a dinosaur attack." Seeing her expression change from intrigue to concern, he hastened to add, "None of *our* people were hurt – nothing serious anyway."

She relaxed, but only a little. "Go on."

"Sadly, one of Meritus' engineers was killed. The roar of the attack ship's engines caused something like a stampede—"

"Something *like* a stampede? What was the idiot thinking?" she interrupted.

"Calm yourself, Captain. I don't think it was like that. They arrived on site so quickly there was nothing they could do but land at a distance. Anyhow, the reason I brought this up was because Captain Meritus' actions on the ground were pretty heroic, apparently. Hiro hated the guy's guts for blowing up part of the *New World*, but now he's in the Meritus fan club, too."

Baines was astounded. "Hiro *forgave* him for blowing the ship up?"

"I *know*," agreed Flannigan, conspiratorially. "Clearly there's more to Meritus than meets the eye, but do I trust him…?"

"You don't know," Baines repeated his words back to him.

Tim walked to the lake's shore. They stayed within the treeline to avoid being spotted by anyone who happened to be looking in their direction from the *New World*. They would only be seen through powerful binoculars, but it was fair to assume that someone aboard would be keeping watch on the area.

For a crazy moment, Tim was tempted to dance along the beach waving his arms around. The odds were long that he would even be noticed, but it certainly *would* destroy his chances with Schultz. Reluctantly, he stayed where he was, squinting in the high sun towards the huge spaceship crashed at the opposite end of the lake, some five or six kilometres away. That was when his breath suddenly caught in his throat. *"What the hell?"* he externalised before he could stop himself.

Schultz, also staring at the vast bulk of the *New World*, registered the existence of *two* such vessels at the exact same moment.

Gawping in disbelief, Tim glanced at the old man and was rewarded with a similar look of bafflement in return.

"You know nothing of this?" demanded Schultz.

Tim shook his head, speechless.

Schultz nodded to his aide, who immediately handed him a pair of binoculars.

"The *Newfoundland*," Schultz read from the second ship's hull. "Well, well."

"May I?" asked Tim, holding out a hand hopefully.

Schultz gave him the binoculars and began to converse hurriedly with his aide. They spoke in German and Tim was unable to make out more than the odd word here and there.

"That's not possible," Tim gasped. He was scarcely able to believe his eyes.

Schultz looked at him sharply. "Explain."

Tim swallowed nervously, regretting his unguarded comment – did Schultz miss nothing? Memories flooded the young man's mind of all they had gleaned from their archaeological dig. It was only a few weeks since they made the discovery, but it seemed like a lifetime ago.

He very quickly ran through a list of pros and cons in his mind. Clearly he was going to have to explain *something* to his captors, to keep his position, perhaps even his life, but how much could he tell them? Eventually, he decided that any guesses or surmises made, based on events which played out twenty million years previously, could have little bearing on their current situation. The old man could see the second ship, so there really was nothing left to hide – he hoped.

Schultz and Schmidt listened in silence, fully attentive as he disclosed the few details he had. As Tim finished his monologue, Schmidt looked to her master for instruction. Seeing his faraway expression, she remained silent while he processed this glut of new and bizarre information.

Time, Tim thought. *This is all so weird. I'm on a beach with a Nazi dictator in the middle of the Cretaceous Period, explaining about fossilised bodies we excavated from a car crash that happened in the* early

Cretaceous – bodies of people looking for us, *and who were taking drinks with our captain little more than a month ago. It's lucky I left school when I did, because if I wrote an essay about 'what I did during the holidays' now, I'd be finishing it from a room with rubber wallpaper!*

While Schultz and Schmidt huddled, Tim drifted. As always, and even in the worst of times, he was noticing things. He listened to the chirruping of small animals hidden within the forest. A few heads popped up above bushes, to quickly vanish again.

"Notohypsilophodon," he commented absently to himself. "A small family group – hmm, interesting." He felt sure Notohypsilophodon was related to Mayor Dougli Salvator, an animal they discovered and named upon their arrival. Tim had only ever observed Hypsilophodontids as individuals or in very large groups; this was something new. "Such diversity," he wondered.

He moved a little farther away from Schultz and Erika. Despite the recent shock of discovering, effectively, two *New Worlds*, something else now had his attention.

The beach was covered with animal tracks. Many were vast, well over a metre across and clearly belonging to some variety of sauropod – perhaps the Patagotitans he had spotted in the area. He could see a large herd around the ships at the opposite end of the lake. Although he could not possibly divine their species, the fact that he could see them with the naked eye over such a distance was testament to their size.

His attention returned to the footprints. There were also some huge, three-clawed tracks among the sauropods. These too were almost a metre across.

Time... he thought again. Occasionally, tracks like these may be preserved in rocks for millions of years, astounding human observers. Would these be such? Survivors in stone, against impossible odds?

He had drifted so far into *Tim world* that some lesser details of his surroundings escaped his notice. The small family group of Notohypsilophodon, which had been keeping such wary vigil on his movements, suddenly disappeared in a flurry of activity and swishing foliage.

Barely aware, Tim studied the dried mud of the beach. Between and among the massive footprints of the super fauna were hundreds and hundreds of smaller tracks. Some were almost certainly Hypsilophodontids, but others were...

Abruptly, Tim came to his senses and looked around anxiously, the frantic disappearance of the family group finally sounding an alarm in his mind.

He strode hurriedly back to Schultz and, risking who knew what punishment, interrupted him.

The old man gave him another sharp look.[2]

"Sorry to break in," Tim apologised, "but we should be—"

A bloodcurdling scream cut him off.

"—careful," he finished in a hushed tone.

The instant their short-range comms came to life with reports, the forest came alive with raptors.

Their terrifying shrieks came from everywhere and nowhere as they leapt and jumped between the trees, attacking from all directions.

Taken completely by surprise, many soldiers were in the grip of several animals at once before they even realised they were under attack. The vicious little hunters gouged deep furrows through human flesh with their sickled claws, while jaws packed with razor sharp teeth clamped around limbs, tearing off chunks of skin and muscle. Blood was in the air from so many simultaneous wounds, surrounding the victims like red mist.

"Buitreraptors!" Tim cried.

His warning was lost to the rattle of automatic weapons fire.

"NO!" bellowed Schultz. "YOU FOOLS!" To his aide he barked, "Order our air support to these coordinates, now – before the enemy takes us!"

"Turkish delight!" muttered The Sarge to himself. Stationed at the aft observation portal aboard the *New World*, the sudden and unmistakeable sounds of battle took him by surprise. Grappling for his binoculars he immediately focused them, and his laser microphone, on the fracas taking place at the far end of the lake.

On maximum zoom, he could certainly make out soldiers, but he fancied the young man he had just witnessed diving for tree cover was the missing Tim Norris. "*Turkish delight!*" he repeated, grabbing his comm.

"Jackson to Douglas. Come in!"

---

[2]   A look Tim was beginning to think of as DEFCON 1. Schultz divided humanity into 'the enemy' and 'the ignored'; murder was *always* 'imminent or likely', he did not require five warm up stages. The next was where everyone died, and though certainly a condition, defence rarely had anything to do with it.

"This is Douglas, Sarge. Go ahead."

"Captain, I don't know if you can hear the weapons fire from the other end of the lake, but there's something big going on over there and I think I saw Tim Norris in the middle of it. Request we send Captain Meritus' ship to reconnoitre immediately, sir."

"What? Are ye sure?"

"No, sir."

"Good enough for me! MERITUS!"

The Sarge listened as Douglas bawled for their new ally's attention and passed along his request. Within seconds, Douglas was back. *"Sarge, Captain Meritus has relayed the order and his pilot will be taking off solo, any second now."*

Almost immediately after Douglas finished reporting back, The Sarge heard the attack ship's engines fire from farther along the beach. The roar of engines was partially drowned out by bellows of consternation from the sauropods, still milling around the treeline and shallows. The ship lifted and shot off towards the western end of the lake.

Within seconds, Meritus' man hovered above the scene. The green canopy below masked his view almost completely. Switching to the infrared band, a small battle suddenly unfolded before him. He wondered what on earth was going on, but was careful to record everything.

Several people were in trouble down there, being torn apart even, and he could not fail to recall that until a few days ago, they had been *his* people – he may even know some of them.

A chill shivered down his spine. This was all wrong for so many reasons. Their allegiance had become so confused. After a moment's introspection, he fell back on his decision to stick with Meritus. He knew where he stood with Meritus; with Schultz, who knew anything?

He relayed his findings back to his captain. "Two armoured vehicles, sir. Twenty-one people on the ground. Not sure how many still live. Less than half are moving."

"Destroy those vehicles," Meritus replied calmly, *"before they can be used against us."*

"Yes, sir," the pilot acknowledged.

"What the hell are you doing?" demanded Douglas. "Did ye no' hear? Tim might be out there."

"He *may*," replied Meritus, still annoyingly calm. "But those armoured and armed vehicles definitely *are*, Captain. We have to neutralise them to protect our own and deprive our enemy of their use. I don't need to tell you what would happen to these ships if they drove around the lake and opened up with those 50-cals, do I?"

Douglas opened his mouth to respond, but the distant explosion rendered it futile.

The Buitreraptors continued to tear into the soldiers with brutal efficiency. The pack was bigger than Tim had imagined; they were outnumbered at least three or four to one. Their human weapons were deadly, of course, but these animals were so fast that half the troops were brought down in the opening seconds. Even so, the dinosaurs were small and overwhelming firepower quickly began to turn the tide.

However, before anything could be decided, a deafening explosion shook the ground. One of the tracked vehicles was suddenly so much flame and shrapnel, its diesel tank and onboard ordnance fuelling a chain of secondary detonations.

Screams came from every quarter, human and animal alike. Tim was knocked to the ground by the force of the blast, his ears buzzing. Everything around him suddenly became a deadly slow-motion dream and he could no longer tell where he, or anyone else, was.

The ground shook again, but individual sounds seemed to merge. It was as though everything was simply too loud. Rolling onto his back, he gazed up at the sky between the branches. A fighter craft hovered. Somewhere in Tim's mind, a link was formed between it and the destroyed troop carrier, but he was yet to make a conscious connection. He could only stare.

For reasons he could not fathom, the craft suddenly turned and shot away to the north-east. The roar from the engines was thunderous, forcing Tim to cover his ears once more as he squeezed his eyes so tightly shut that tears ran down his cheeks.

The trembling of the ground increased as two further ships, drawn from distinctly similar lines, shot overhead.

As Tim wondered what was happening, strong arms lifted him from the earth and pulled him away.

Gleeson was glad to leave the discussion behind. It sounded more like an argument to him, anyway. Douglas had been furious about what he perceived as Meritus' 'cavalier attitude' regarding lives and Meritus had been scornful of Douglas' reticence to do 'what needed to be done'. Gleeson could see both sides but ultimately, the enemy had far too many dangerous toys for his liking. Therefore, seeing one of them go up in smoke was OK by him. He just hoped and prayed the lad had not been caught in the crossfire. He was about to find out.

"We're about three minutes away from the explosion site, sir," reported his designated driver, Corporal Jennifer 'Iron-Balls' O'Brien. "One of the attack craft has chased away Captain Meritus' ship and is… actually, I don't know where it is. They've gone beyond the range of our scanners, last seen on a north-easterly heading. Captain Meritus' guy is probably leading the enemy away from us and the Pod, sir. The second enemy vessel seems to have put down a couple of klicks further west." She turned to Gleeson for an instant. "They must have found a clearing there, sir."

He nodded. "OK. So any survivors will surely be making their way towards that second ship."

"Yes, sir. There is also a second ground vehicle – also making its way west."

"Yeah. Gotta be a rendezvous," he replied. "Head for that clearing—"

"What's this?" she blurted, before he could finish. "Sorry, sir. We've got incoming – from north-north-west."

"Meritus' fighter? Done a loop and returned?" he asked.

O'Brien shook her head. "No, sir. It must be another enemy vessel, but why it's coming in from the north is anyone's guess."

Gleeson placed a comradely hand on O'Brien's shoulder. "Pedal to the metal, Corp."

"I think we should try it." Major White was adamant, which surprised Mother Sarah, and Dr Patel.

"You really think he's on the level, Ford?" asked Sarah.

"It's impossible to say for sure, but if he is then this could be the magic pill we've been hoping for. If he's not... what can I say? He's no great threat to our security and of little or no intrinsic value as a hostage."

"I agree, to a point, Major," conceded Patel, carefully. "Bond seems to be rather unimportant to his friends and enemies alike. However, his *colleague* is a 'very different kettle of fish'. I believe that is the correct phrase?"

"Sargo Lemelisk," Sarah intoned heavily. "A known terrorist and murderer – possibly even the man who killed Chief Nassaki's brother, Aito. Can we really release him? Really?"

White sat back, sighing deeply. He was still struggling with the exact same question. "Trouble is, Sarah, they're a two-for-one deal. Bond's a... well, I don't know what you'd call him. He likes to think he's a tactician and a politician – maybe he is. He had us fooled for long enough, right? All that nonsense about being a philosopher and stirring up all the passengers? But the truth is there's no way he would make it to the enemy camp, on foot, alone. He just doesn't have the skills. All round, he's a less than credible insurgent. We all thought he was a joke! Schultz must have had a reason for sending him on the mission and maybe that was it – no one takes him seriously, and just maybe it will be that decision which settles all of this.

"We can't send him under guard or even with a bodyguard. If we did, Schultz wouldn't need to be a genius to figure out that something smelt—"

"Fishy," interjected Patel, with a half-smile.

"Indeed," agreed White. "That crazy psycho is the only person we *can* send with him, who would have any hope of being accepted by the other side."

"Assuming he does not simply dump Bond as soon as he is out of sight of the Pod," suggested Patel, playing devil's advocate.

No one could refute the possibility, so White said what they were all thinking. "Would that be such a loss?"

Sarah frowned. "You do realise you said that on the outside, Ford?"

White looked slightly abashed. "Sorry, Sarah, but it would mean two less mouths to feed and would remove a constant security threat in the heart of our operation. Neither of them might make it. And if they do, we only have Bond's promise that when the time comes, he'll do his best to make sure the Lemelisk threat is neutralised."

"We're talking about men's lives here," Sarah reproved.

"We're talking about evil men's lives, Sarah," stated Patel, unemotionally.

"Are we?" she asked, rounding on him. "How do we know that? If Bond is telling the truth, the biggest coward on this Earth may just possibly be the bravest man on this Earth!"

There was no answer to that either, so Patel slumped and brooded.

"Whether he's a hero or a liar, are we agreed about tonight? Well?" White prompted. "Are we agreed?"

Nothing…

"Come on, guys. Sometimes you have to make the *tough* calls."

"*Tonight*," stated Sarah and Patel together.

"What can *we* do about it?" asked Henry, exasperated. "There's a hundred armed personnel on this Pod, if they can't get him back—"

"So we just give up on him, then, eh? Sacrifice the Pom, is that it?" retorted Woodsey, angrily. "You gonna explain that to his mum when she wakes up?"

"Woodsey's right, Henry," Rose concurred quietly.

"I agree," Clarrie chimed in too. "Tim wouldn't leave *us* anywhere!"

"You stay outta this, little sis'," Henry laid down the law.

"The hell I will!" she snapped. "He's my…"

They all waited for her conclusion, but it never came. Instead, she hid her face in her hands, her shoulders rocking as she began to cry quietly.

Rose gave Henry a scathing look.

Henry pointed at himself. "*Me?*" he mouthed.

The four teens sat around their usual table in the bar. However, there was no bartender, no drinks for sale and pointedly, no Tim.

The room itself was simply available as a space, for people to sit and chat or think. Mostly, people sat in ones and twos, lost in private worries or whispered conversations. The life and light of the Mud Hole seemed to have winked out.

Realising everyone was against him, Henry tried again, "Alright, does anyone have any suggestions about *how* we might get Tim back?"

Rose answered excitedly, "Actually, I've been thinking about that."

"Oh, God. *This* should be good," Henry muttered under his breath. Then he caught her glare.

"Excuse me?" she prompted.

"Oh, good. I knew you would," he falsified enthusiastically, augmenting his sin with the supplementary, "Always thinking, that's my girl."

"*Really?*" asked Woodsey, in disbelief.

Rose took her comforting arm from around Clarrie and pointed at the New Zealander. "You don't want to mess with me today, sunshine!"

Woodsey's eyebrows shot up. "Charming."

"Yeah, yeah, alright, never mind all that," said Henry, impatiently. "Whenever we plan anything, it always just ends in a fight. Rose – what's your plan, honey? And you, just cut it out, will ya?" he added, also pointing at Woodsey.

"Yes, sir! I'll just sit here quietly awaiting your instructions then, sir!" he retorted. "Honestly, I've never known such treatment—"

"Then you've been lucky!" Rose cut him off. "Now stop chuntering. Does anyone want to hear my plan or not?"

"Of course we do, sweetie," replied Henry, chivalrously.

Woodsey put one hand on his head while placing the index finger of the other on his lips as he stared indolently at the ceiling.

"I suppose that's better," Rose commented sourly.

The strain of remaining silent almost immediately proved too much for the New Zealander and he burst out, "Honestly, you never listen to any of my ideas!"

"Do too," rejoindered Rose.

"You *so* don't! I mean, wasn't it Sigmund Freud, or maybe Cicero – one of those guys – who said, *I've* got time for *you*?"

Henry rolled his eyes. "Dude, that was Ronald McDonald. Look, we're getting side-tracked. What's *your* idea, then?"

"What idea?"

Henry sighed. "You said we never listen to your ideas, so what's your plan? Come on, we're listening."

"I haven't got one."

"But you said—"

"No, mate. I *said* you never listen to my ideas. I didn't say I had one."

Henry stared at him.

"*What?*" demanded Woodsey.

"Shut your mouth, will ya? I'm counting up to ten!"

"Well, that explains the pain on your face, mate. Would you like me to get you a crayon, so you can make notes?"

"Hey, I'm warnin' you—"

"*Boys!*" snapped Rose, slapping the table. "*I* have a plan, *OK?*"

"S'pose so."

"Sure."

"I'd like to hear it." Clarrie's small voice wavered with the shuddering of her breath as she resurfaced from her dark place.

Rose replaced her arm around the younger girl's shoulders and gave her a hug. "Right. We don't have much time, so listen carefully. If we're going to make this work, it will have to be tonight."

"Ah, now you see, I would, but I'm washing my hair— *Ow!*" Woodsey rubbed his brow where the corner of Rose's beer mat hit him.

Chapter 5 | Zeitgeist

The armoured troop carrier smashed through scrub and woodland, retracing its own tracks made earlier that morning. The mood within was already oppressive and the heavy green light, filtering through the forest canopy, seemed to darken it still further.

Of the twenty-one mostly fit young men and women who had arrived at the lakeside less than an hour ago, just nine still lived and many of them were wounded.

Tim was plagued by bouts of dizziness and nausea. His hearing returned but was dulled, overlaid by a constant whistling that filled his head. He hoped his ears had not suffered permanent damage.

The tiny reinforced windows in the rear of the vehicle, where he lay dumped by whoever had grabbed him from the beach, allowed very little light into the interior. Only the forest murk pervaded, the people around him mere ghosts in the gloom. Low light soothed his retinas, but his head banged to the double-time rhythm of his heart.

This condition became more acute as their transport crashed from the edge of the forest into brilliant sunshine. Tim was not the only one to groan and cover his eyes.

Stretching to relieve some of the stiffness in his muscles, he remembered his luxury seat behind the driver. It called to him.

Despite his craving for some measure of comfort, he was also eager to find out what was happening and stood awkwardly in the moving vehicle, almost falling as everything swam before his eyes. Covering his mouth, to stop himself from retching, he waited until he had control of himself before stumbling through to the forward compartment.

He found Schultz strapped into his own seat with Erika at the controls. The old man's immaculately tailored suit had a blood-soaked slash across the upper arm, while he wore a murderous expression across his face.

Tim fell into the seat opposite.

Schultz opened his mouth, but Erika spoke first, unintentionally cutting him off. Without taking her eyes from their path, she pointed out that their ship was waiting for them, 150 metres ahead.

Tim leaned forward in his side-seat, to better see ahead through the small front windows.

Out on the plain and freed from the restricting forest, Erika gunned the engine to close the distance rapidly.

I suppose this means safety – of a sort. Tim's thought had not even been fully realised when their armoured transport turned over. They were on their side before the occupants even registered the boom of the explosion.

Where there had only been ferns and scrub and solid ground, a pit was blasted, and their vehicle's right-hand track was blown completely off as it fell into the hole. With a dull thud, earth turned by the explosion was suddenly re-compacted under thirty tons of armour.

Tim was thrown back into his seat; the last thing he saw, their rescue ship, reduced to a ball of white light and flying debris. The resulting plume of fire and smoke climbed high into the sky.

Alarms rang from every quarter, competing with screams of pain and outrage. Tim was dimly aware of another ship landing between their transport and the fiercely burning remains of their erstwhile rescue vessel. Almost gratefully, he passed out.

"Everyone get back in. Come on, let's go, go, *go!*" shouted Commander Gleeson. Hurrying his foraging team back into their transport, he cut short their brief stop at the skirmish site with the Buitreraptors – the earth-shaking boom of yet another explosion to the west saw to that. Having found no survivors, they had already removed anything and everything useful from the bodies, mainly weapons and ordnance, and piled the fallen together. There were many raptors among the dead, the survivors long scattered in all directions away from the blistering inferno that claimed the enemy transport. Even so, Gleeson felt some scruple. As a former captain in the Australian Army, he did not like the idea of leaving fellow soldiers, even enemy soldiers, to the ravages of local wildlife.

Unfortunately, they had no time, and could only hope to stop and bury the bodies decently on the return journey – with any luck before they became despoiled. Standing to attention, he gave the fallen a solemn and respectful salute. That would have to do for now.

When another huge explosion tore across the countryside, he rushed the last man aboard their transport and jumped in after. "Floor it, Jen!" he barked at Corporal O'Brien as he threw himself into the cab's passenger seat.

The tracked vehicle lurched forward, chewing up the undergrowth as O'Brien found and followed the rough trail beaten by the enemy transports. They passed the still burning remains of the armoured personnel carrier Meritus' ship had taken out.

Bladdy 'ell, thought Gleeson, *nothing salvageable there!*

They had no idea what they were driving into or who was responsible for these latest detonations. All Gleeson knew was that he intended to follow the bangs and the smoke until he found someone to ask.

"That last boom," he queried O'Brien. "Any idea how far in front of us it was?"

"There's a high energy signature about two klicks west of here, sir. Reckon that's our boy!"

There was an excitement about O'Brien; Gleeson had seen it before whenever they went into action. *A natural soldier*, he considered appreciatively. *Me, I just like blowing stuff up.*

"Everybody ready in the back?" he bellowed. "We'll soon be in the middle of it, fellas – and we're going in hot!"

He wanted them to be completely prepared for whatever they encountered next. "I hate surprises," he confided to O'Brien.

"Yes, sir," she acknowledged respectfully.

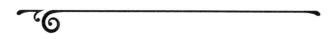

Tim was vaguely aware of his return to consciousness, though everything seemed out of focus. The world was in motion, he could tell that, but it felt like his life was all taking place in the next room – snatches of conversations overheard, among the scraping and bumping of furniture through a partition wall.

"Bring him!"

A harsh voice he may have recognised was barking orders and suddenly he was being lifted and dragged again, this time outside.

It would be nice to walk somewhere rather than being dragged all over the place, he thought imperspicuously.

Outside the crashed vehicle, the breeze revived him a little further into the real world – enough to be shocked by what he saw.

Heidi Schultz stood menacingly, holding an assault rifle before a backdrop of fiery destruction. Tim could quite believe it was a look she was born to.

The injured from the skirmish, and now the crash, stood in a forlorn group under the guns of Heidi's people – two men and a woman with a limp.

Heinrich Schultz stood apart and forward, his aide protectively by his side.

Tim was unsure whether the idea that shot through his mind like a bolt of lightning was a flash of inspiration or insanity, but before he even knew what he was doing he stepped forward.

His first step was uncharacteristically confident and the ones to follow gained ever more surety as he strode towards Heidi. Less than two metres before her, he stopped.

"Cousin," he greeted with a very small but deferential nod.

Heidi's eyes widened, just slightly, but he logged her surprise. "So, you have accepted this?" she asked.

"I've accepted that my old life is over. What else is there to do but look forward? And to that end—" He stepped to her right side, turning to face their grandfather. "Why would we need an old man? Especially one who is so willing to cast his own granddaughter aside, and after all you risked on his behalf." He looked sidelong to his left, gauging her reaction.

Heidi's surprise turned to uncertainty. The boy was behaving the way *she* would have in his position. It seemed natural to her, so why was she unsure about him? Her recent brush with the carrot, rather than merely the stick, had left her with deep questions. Nevertheless, if the boy was sincere, what an asset he would make.

Perhaps I should accept him at face value and work it all out later?
"I agree," she replied, with a small nod of her own, "*cousin.*"

"What! How *dare* you!" thundered Heinrich Schultz, taking a step forward. He stopped immediately when Heidi raised her weapon. Rage aside, he knew his granddaughter. After all, she was a blade fashioned by his own hand.

Erika Schmidt stepped in front of her master, but he shoved her roughly to the side. The normally catlike German beauty stumbled and fell, looking up at him in shock at first; shock which quickly turned to loathing.

Heidi saw it and laughed. "*Mein Großvater* – all the gratitude of a scorpion. And like any scorpion, his sting is ultimately aimed at his own back!"

She fired a quick burst into the ground in front of Heinrich. "Get back!" she snapped.

He did as ordered but with a look of purest murder in his eyes.

Heidi glanced at his aide, who had not bothered to get up from where she had fallen. "*Fräulein* Schmidt, would you care to join us to rebuild this world? As my cousin so eloquently stated, we do not need old men – only young and virile ones."

Tim frowned. "I don't think that was exactly what I said."

Heidi laughed again. Although humorous, it was a cruel sound. Tim managed to refrain from shuddering, but it required effort.

Who am I? he thought. *Who the hell am I?*

Erika sprang lightly to her feet, dusted herself down and glared at Heinrich.

He turned on her. "You will not dare betray me, child!" he spat, waspishly.

"*Ruhe!* Silence!" shouted Heidi. Then they all heard it, a high-powered diesel engine approaching through the forest from the east.

She took a few steps towards her grandfather. "I should shoot you down where you stand for your betrayal, old man." She glared at him, her workaday look of cold indifference now replaced by a mercurial hatred.

"However, our enemy approaches, and I think that you should end with a firing squad. Don't you, *Großvater*?

"Taking you back with me would be too risky. I could not guarantee the right outcome. I will allow the 'New Worlders' to do it for me. Of course, you could take your chances with the animals – I survived out here on my own, while working to *your* design," she added bitterly.

He stared furiously, but said nothing.

"Now I go to take control of the mission that was once *our* mission. *I* will usher in the new dawn and I *alone* will possess this world. *Auf Wiedersehen, mein Großvater.*"

She left him there, ordering her followers to cram the remaining soldiers into their attack ship.

Only Erika Schmidt remained with the old man as the ship lifted and set off west, towards the Schultz encampment.

As the swell of the massively powerful engines died away it was replaced by the moaning of a smaller power plant. The sound varied in pitch as the armoured personnel carrier scrambled over the rough terrain on a collision course with destiny.

Presently, it drew up close and half a dozen armed personnel burst from the rear hatch, taking up positions around the two left behind.

"Pete, see if that vehicle is salvageable," ordered Gleeson. "If it is, plot its location."

Pte Pete Davies saluted and climbed into the capsized vehicle to check its condition.

"Now, what do we have here? I'm Commander Gleeson. Give me your names and ranks. Then we'll have to decide what to do with you!"

The old man, already rigid, stood so straight-backed that he almost vibrated.

"Heinrich Schultz. *Dictator.*"

Gleeson's jaw dropped. When possibly the most beautiful woman he had ever seen introduced herself next, he barely registered her presence.

O'Brien leaned in close. "Still hate surprises, Commander?"

Major White knocked on the door, feeling a stab of regret and concern as he read 'Dr Patricia Norris' on the plaque.

"Come in," greeted a friendly male voice.

"Dr Fischer," said White as he entered. "Excuse the intrusion, but I have a few questions and very little time. May I?" he asked, grabbing a chair.

"Please," replied Dr Klaus Fischer, Patricia Norris' deputy and the man currently in charge of the Pod's microbiology department.

"Thanks," said White, seating himself. "I apologise for bursting in on you like this, Doctor, but it's real urgent."

"Of course, Major. Please call me Klaus."

"Ford," White responded in kind.

"Klaus, I need to speak with you about our new *friends.*"

"Ah," Fischer responded, knowingly. He had had a similar interview with Captain Baines – although, it had been Commander Baines at the time – a couple of weeks ago. "I suspect you wish to ask me about the German nationals among our guests – more specifically, about their attitude towards the new alliance?"

"You got it," agreed White. "Please don't think I'm pigeonholing anyone – I know a great many of them aren't German, but we are in unknown territory here and must use every asset at our disposal. I believe that at least one among them is working a double action for the enemy – at least we assume they're working for the enemy. Hard to imagine who else they would be passing information to, but who knows in this crazy world!

"I remember you standing by my side when Captain Douglas was taken hostage, ready to risk your life in a fight to stop the Nazis and their followers. The Germans who came with us as part of the original mission have been a hundred percent with us. So, as someone I trust, I just wondered if you or any of your colleagues have heard anything suspicious from the newcomers?"

"I thank you for your trust, Ford. So, you think they may let their guard down a little more around us?" asked Fischer.

"Maybe. Or perhaps one of you may have overheard something *they* thought was private?"

Fischer looked thoughtful. "I will ask my fellow Germans, of course, but I cannot think of anything out of the ordinary. It is my impression that they are loyal to Captain Meritus. Where he goes, they follow. Did you know he was Canadian, by the way?"

White sat back in surprise. "No, I did not."

"Yes, apparently he was a naval captain and commander of HMCS Victoria – a class of submarine originally bought from the British in the late 1990s and commissioned in 2000, however, the current class is Canadian built in partnership with the Japanese.

"His people largely keep to themselves, Ford, but they clearly hold Captain Meritus in some regard. It is said that he was against Canada withdrawing from the Mars Mission. Maybe he merely saw the Schultzes' plan as a way of saving a handful of his countrymen from the end of the world? Perhaps all of us here are guilty of that same sentiment to some degree?"

White nodded thoughtfully. "Hmm. When Canada pulled out, after the incident with the US government, it left a lot o' folks with egg on their faces, I remember that. But joining the Nazis? That's a hell of a course to take. He certainly hides the accent well."

"Indeed," agreed Fischer. With a wry smile he added, "I would imagine that a 'colonial' accent would not go over well in the Schultz camp!"

"No, I suppose not." White wondered what else might be hidden in plain view and the concern showed on his face. "We caught our insurgent on camera. Naturally, he or she was head to foot in black and wearing a mask. We suspect it was a man. I've got Rick Drummond, my ex-police security consultant, looking through footage from cameras around the Pod. He's hoping to match physique and mannerisms to one of Meritus' people – has the computer running scan-ware, taking everyone's proportions. Without a solid ID it's a hell of a long shot, but if he did manage to turn up any possible matches, it might at least give us a place to start.

"The guy may not even be among the German contingent. We're simply basing that particular hunch on Schultz's biases and prejudices. So here I am, just in case. Hell, Schultz himself isn't even German, just a puffed-up wannabe with a head full of twisted nostalgia for the Third Reich! Have the incoming Germans said anything about any possible plans from before they changed sides? Or anything more about Meritus, perhaps?"

"Not specifically, Ford. As I said, it seems he is well regarded by his people. Schultz, on the other hand, is viewed with fear and distrust, even by his own. Fear kept them in line – obviously, he's not a man to be crossed and none of them wished to be erased from history – but after arriving here and with everything seeming to blow up in their faces, they chose Meritus. They see him as their only chance to survive what comes next – whatever that may be. Might I suggest that many among *this* crew felt the same about Captain Douglas before we lost him. Hopefully, we will get him back soon."

"*I'll* sure as hell be glad when he's back here," White confided. "As well as fighting a war on two fronts, someone today asked me to make a decision about the rationing and distribution of toilet paper! *Toilet paper!*"

Fischer laughed lightly. "You think Captain Douglas will be keen to take such heady responsibilities back from your shoulders?"

"Either he or Jill Baines, when she gets back on her feet." A shadow crossed White's face, fleeting, but Fischer caught it.

"How is she?" he asked, gently.

"Dave Flannigan says she's a little better today, but it's gonna be a while before she can help us. Even when he gets this sickness licked – and I'm sure he will – she still has a busted leg to deal with."

"So perhaps Captain Meritus is the right help at the right time?" Fischer suggested.

"Maybe," White conceded.

"It seems," Fischer continued, "that many of the characteristics that make Meritus' people respect him are shared with our own Captain Douglas. Perhaps Meritus is Douglas in a... what is the phrase? A crazy mirror?"

White nodded sagely. "The same features, slightly distorted."

Fischer shrugged. "Perhaps."

The major stood, replacing his chair. "Thank you, Klaus. Knowing what our new ally's people think of him is at least something. Keep your ear to the ground, please."

Fischer stood too. "Certainly, Ford. And if you need me, you know where I am. Good luck."

White shook his hand. "Thanks," he said. As he reached the door, he turned back. "We may need everyone before this is through."

"I would have liked to strip more parts from the *Newfoundland*, Captain," said Hiro.

"Aye, but events have caught us up. You'd better be away to engineering. Good luck."

Douglas gave his chief engineer a shoulder squeeze, conferring his confidence to the younger man, before turning to Meritus. "Have you heard from your wee ship, Captain?"

"No, but when I ordered the pilot to lose his pursuit, I also told him to make his way back to the Pod under radio silence from here on in." Meritus shook his head, adamant. "We can't afford to lose that ship."

"True," agreed Douglas. He grinned. "So you'll be needing a lift, then?"

Meritus' lip twitched wryly. "If you'd be so kind, Captain. We seem to have gone full circle and now it's me who's the passenger on *your* ship."

"A *passenger?* Not quite how Ah remember it!" Douglas shot back. "What *is* your first name, anyway?"

"Tobias."

"Right, Tobias. To be just like old times, Ah'd have to show you one of ma wee rooms with bars."

Meritus bowed slightly. "I am at your mercy, Captain."

"James," stated Douglas. "It would be a lie to say Ah'm no' tempted, but Ah suspect you'll be more useful on ma bridge."

"Of course, Captain."

"Where Ah can keep an eye on ye!"

Meritus threw his head back and laughed; a deep, genuine laugh.

"Damn you, Meritus."

"James?"

"Ah didnae want to like you, but Ah'm beginning to. We'll be launching soon. This grand lady's been mighty hurt, largely thanks to you, Ah understand. So we'll have our hands full." He pointed a finger at Meritus. "Dinnae let me down."

"My allegiance is and has always been with the men and women under my command, James. I believe that our only chance of surviving the coming storm is to work together. It's my hope that we can."

Douglas nodded thoughtfully. "To the bridge, then."

The guard slipped away for a moment to use the toilet; the prisoners were not going anywhere, after all.

"*Pssst!*" hissed Bond.

Lemelisk frowned and approached the bars at the front of his cell. "Are you having a little crisis, Bond?"

"Very witty – *comrade.* Listen, we only have a moment. We need to get out of here!"

Lemelisk snorted. "Of course, why didn't I think of that?"

"No, shut up a minute! I regret not helping you make a fight of it when you tried to escape. I will not make the same mistake again. Now Heinrich Schultz is on this world, we need to be making names for ourselves if we want a large piece of the pie when all is divvied up. Here, we're just liabilities, easily discarded."

"I'm listening. What did you have in mind?"

"Not sure yet, just be ready. Any opportunity, take it. I'll be with you."

The flush of a w/c brought the hushed conversation to a close.

Gleeson's party travelled in absolute silence. They had not dared announce their prize over the airwaves. Gleeson believed it would be like painting a bullseye on their backs. Shock and brooding passed from one to another in an unending circle.

Eventually, O'Brien broke the most uncomfortable silence, "Commander, we're coming up on the *New World.*"

"Beaut'," was all the enthusiasm he could muster. "Better tell Captain Douglas we have prisoners and get him to air a couple of beds in the penthouse suite."

"Yes, sir."

Their tracked transport growled to a halt, dwarfed beside the 550-metre-long bulks of the *New World* and her sister ship, the *Newfoundland.*

The Sarge met them at the airlock, lowering a lightweight aluminium ladder for them to climb up into the ship.

Once everyone was inside, he asked, "No sign of young Tim, Commander?"

"Not by the time we got there," replied Gleeson, regretfully. "You were right though, Sarge. It was him on the beach. He's been taken away by Heidi Schultz," he added darkly.

A look of deep concern crossed The Sarge's face. "Oh, God," he muttered. Taking stock of the prisoners, he asked, "Who are *these* two, then?"

"Sarge, you might want to take a seat."

Gleeson told him.

"*Turkish delight!*"

Douglas was still chuckling as he and Meritus returned to the bridge.

"Well, that was awkward," said Meritus.

"For you, maybe. For me it felt like Christmas morning," retorted Douglas. He began to laugh again; he had hardly stopped since Gleeson's big disclosure. "The man himself! Locked up in *my* brig, with me, judge and jury – *in camera!*"

Meritus raised an eyebrow. "I'm not sure what's so funny, James," he commented, stonily.

Douglas stopped and turned to his fellow captain. "No? Then let me put it into plain words for you, Tobias. Ah want to take our people away from here. Far away. So that we can set up a new homestead, grow the food we need and live quietly while we build a wormhole drive capable of taking us home – with any luck without causing any major events which might disrupt the timeline. All these hopes are impossible with the enemy banging on our front door. Now we have *him*, we can throw a control yoke around our enemy and demand that they let us go without pursuit."

Meritus looked unconvinced. "Do you really think it will be so easy?"

Douglas sobered a little. "No," he admitted, honestly. "But you see, Tobias, we've had *no* cards to play all through this crisis. From the moment the first explosion sent us back to the Cretaceous, we've been fighting a rearguard action, never knowing where the next hammer will fall. This is *something* – a *big* something."

"I can see that, James, but have you reckoned for Heidi Schultz? She's every bit as insane as the old man, and as she split and left him there for us to find, it suggests a family fall-out. Wouldn't you agree?"

Douglas mulled that over. "Aye, that does seem likely. We'll need to interrogate him – both of them, in fact, the lassie too. We can squeeze that information out of them after we've returned to the Pod."

"There's also the two cards that Heidi is still holding," Meritus pressed his point.

"Two cards?"

"Indeed. Firstly, she has enough firepower aboard those ships to erase us from history – literally! And secondly, there's the little matter of the boy. Someone of importance to you, I understand."

Douglas' face fell.

"Captain?" asked Meritus.

Douglas did not speak for a long moment, his *bonhomie* completely shattered. "If Ah've to choose between Tim and everyone else, what can Ah do?" His answer was stoic and wretched.

There was no counsel he could give that would provide any sort of comfort, so Meritus changed tack. "I recommend keeping this little windfall to ourselves for now, James. We don't want Heidi to get any ideas about lighting this place up, do we? She needs the Pod, but I can tell you that the *New World* is on a 'would be nice to have' list – especially now she's damaged."

"And we all know who we have to thank for that!" Douglas snapped crossly.

Meritus' colour rose too. "Do you really want to go toe to toe with me about whose ship got damaged the worst?" he rejoindered, heatedly.

Douglas sagged a little. "Aye, alright, fair enough," he acquiesced.

Meritus brightened quickly, as was his nature, clapping a hand on Douglas' shoulder. "The repairs won't be finished 'til this evening, so we can't leave yet. Why don't we use these few hours to think it all over? Maybe there's some way we could get a message through to your boy, what do you say?"

"Well, it never reached me!" Henry whispered, hotly.

"Of *course* it did," Rose shushed him. "I sent the message to all of you."

The teenagers had split into two teams, taking turns to stake out one of the equipment stores off the Pod's main hangar. It was the turn of Rose and Henry, and they waited for everyone to go away after the day's shift. Henry's bright orange shirt was less than ideal for their purposes.

"I specifically said 'wear something dark'. Where *did* you get that thing, anyway?" she asked, disbelieving.

"Hey man, do you have any idea how much this thing cost?"

"Huh, you were mugged. Anyway, never mind that." She waved him into silence. Rose's idea was to acquire equipment over the next few days; equipment that would enable them to take their chances out in the wild. Her audacious plan involved making their way across country to the enemy camp and staking it out, in the hope of catching sight of Tim.

On the face of it, the plan seemed a little innocent and Henry harboured some rather serious, if secret, misgivings. Woodsey, on the other hand, had set his misgivings free, very publicly. After hearing the entire scheme, it had taken them a while to catch him.

Rose's strategy was not completely without merit, however. For one thing, she actually knew the way there – or at least where the tracks were that would take them there. Her terrifying adventure through the forests, pursued by a huge Tyrannotitan, had burned every detail of the area into her memory indelibly, including where the turning was located.

On the downside, they could not take any weapons with them; weapons would be missed. Otherwise, she banked on a two-day march, something she had never undertaken before in her life, and a week to watch the enemy from an as yet unknown 'safe location'. The rest of the plan they agreed to develop after taking stock of Tim's situation.

Woodsey thought the whole enterprise rather gung-ho[3].

They would need camping and survival gear, and rations. Rose had not been idle during her weeks in the Cretaceous. Her old life, as the 'pretty vacant' school mascot, captain of the cheerleading and netball teams, was over. Even before they landed on ancient Earth, she had worked hard to embrace their situation. Until recently, time had always seemed like a plentiful fuel one simply burned to drive one day towards the next, while waiting for something interesting to happen. Suddenly, she had so little. Every spare minute to herself was spent poring over Tim's palaeontological notes, attempting to take in as much as she could about the world around them; that or learning bush skills from some of Major White's fully trained soldiers and survivalists. She had made a few friends there. One of the female privates had taken Rose under her wing, augmenting the lessons with some basic combat skills.

Her father, Jim Miller, had made arrangements for her, using his connections as the Pod's manufacturing chief, so that she could learn from some of the best people they had. Jim wanted to give his daughter the best possible chance of surviving their new world, although the idea of her actually putting those skills into practice petrified him.

Rose felt a little guilty about putting his trust in her to work planning a raid on their stores, followed by a completely unendorsed 'jolly' through the land of the dinosaurs.

---

[3]   A description embellished with several, less printable phrases.

"Girls will be girls," she muttered.

"Huh?" asked Henry.

"*Shhh!*"

Henry was even less happy. Aside from Rose repeatedly telling him to shut up, his mother was to play messenger again tomorrow and he was very worried about her. He was well aware that Schultz's people did not mess around. Worse still, when he categorically forbade his sister from accompanying them on their search for Tim, she had exploded, threatening to tell the world of their plans – or at least the *New World*. He could only imagine how his father would react.

"Oh, *man*," he chuntered under his breath.

"Will you—"

"Shut up," he finished for her. "I got it the first time!"

"And *yet...!*" she hissed, glaring at him.

The business of the day was beginning to quiet throughout the hangar. Rose felt her heart rate increase. *Perfect,* she thought, excitedly.

2000hrs, *Factory Pod 4*, brig

"Stand back from the bars," barked the guard. "Shower time! You know the drill. We'll start with Mr Lemelisk – oops, sorry. Of course, I meant Mr *Bradford*, naturally."

Lemelisk glowered at him.

"Off you go," the man ushered Lemelisk from his cell towards the door. As they passed Bond's cell, the guard gave him the ghost of a nod.

An electric shock of adrenaline coursed through Bond's veins, setting his stomach lurching like a small boat in a heavy gale.

"Erm... Guard?" he asked, clumsily.

"What is it, Mr Bond?" the man asked, turning briefly to face him. "Assuming that's *your* real name."

With their single guard distracted, Lemelisk reacted instantly. A snap, hammer-fist atemi to the man's face stunned him, so that he did not even see the heel-first roundhouse kick which connected under his chin to launch him across the room. He was unconscious before even contacting the deck.

Lemelisk quickly stooped to take the man's stun rifle, knife and flak jacket. He would go through the pockets later.

"Let me out!" hissed Bond.

Lemelisk considered for a moment and then bent, taking the electronic key from the guard's belt to unlock the second cell's door.

"Thank you!" Bond sniped.

Lemelisk ignored him, pointing his new weapon at the prone man. He set the dial to kill.

"What the *hell* are you doing?" asked Bond in a frantic whisper.

"Leave no one behind who can come after you," replied Lemelisk, grimly.

"Don't be a fool!" snapped Bond, pushing the barrel down. "If they catch us they'll bang us back up in here, but if you've murdered one of them – unarmed and unconscious – they'll shoot to kill! Come *on*, Sargo. There's bound to be someone along to check on this fellow soon."

"Yes," replied Lemelisk, suspiciously. "And why *is* it that he was alone, do you think? They've always watched us in pairs until today – standard drill. And why did they decide I needed gym-time yesterday? They've never bothered before. And why did they leave *you* in your cell?"

"How the hell should I know – what am I, Google? Can we please *leave?*"

Clearly unconvinced, Lemelisk acquiesced to the general wisdom of that sentiment and made for the door. Hitting the opening stud, he checked the corridor, carefully.

No one...

This is too easy, he thought, but despite his misgivings nodded for Bond to follow him.

Heidi had made a big entrance back at the Schultz encampment. After landing, she had immediately ordered all personnel off the ships and out into the compound. Standing atop a small 4x4, she made a speech, and it was a surprising speech. Tim almost believed it. Her new followers certainly seemed to. This 'woman of the people' act was completely new, to her as well as everyone else, but she played it like an old hand. Tim always thought of her as a mere weapon, not realising just how brilliant and how truly dangerous she was.

Now they were alone in Heinrich's outrageously opulent field quarters aboard the *Eisernes Kreuz*. Tim was still mulling over the rousing words of this chameleon with whom his life seemed suddenly and inextricably entwined.

Two chameleons together, he thought wryly, *both of us pretending – playing polar opposite parts to our true selves. I wonder who will blink first?*

He watched her drag a brush through a tangle of blonde hair, transforming it to something of its former luxuriance.

Such a normal act. The thought popped into his mind, followed immediately by a stab of anxiety. *If I know she's a monster – acting the beneficent leader – then surely, she must know that I'm really... what am I? A scared teenager trying to stay alive in the monster's lair? Or am I a monster too – about to reveal my adult plumage to a completely unsuspecting world? I talked her into leaving that old man, that evil old man, to die out there – and it was so easy. Would she have left him anyway? I just don't know...*

Heidi replaced the hairbrush and turned to face him. "Now, cousin. What should I do with you?"

Here it comes, thought Tim, fearfully. *I hope it's quick!*

She scrutinised him. Heinrich Schultz had done the same, but Heidi's stare felt less penetrative. The old man appeared to see through him, but then maybe the full power of his stare had been a tool in itself? If people thought they had no secrets, maybe they were more likely to confess whatever they had left. However, this was not the old man, so perhaps he would be able to keep just one or two things from Heidi. Although definitely cut from the same cloth as her grandfather, there was no fast track to wisdom. One had to do the time. Tim began to hope.

"You impressed me today, Timothy."

His knees almost buckled with relief. He shifted his weight, changing his stance to hide the fact.

Act, act, act, his inner self spoke the mantra within his head. Mustering as much disdain as he dared, he replied, "How?"

She quirked a half-smile. "To step away from our *Großvater* and condemn him the way you did. You had no way of knowing how I would respond to such betrayal."

"*Betrayal...?*" he let the word hang for a moment. "The betrayal was all on his side as far as I could tell. More than anyone, you've been instrumental in bringing all of this about. That's how it appears to me, anyway.

"I owed him nothing, *he* owed *you* everything. Certainly more than a quick discard, once I arrived – and shot you," he added with a cold smile.

The light of anger kindled in her eyes.

Perhaps I am a Schultz, he thought. *Right, I've poked the hive – time to throw it into the neighbour's garden!*

"Am I right in thinking that his principal reason in dumping you was because I'm his grand*son*, rather than a mere granddaughter?"

She looked away, her anger redirected as Tim had hoped it would be. "I think that is probably true," she admitted.

"Well none of it matters any more, does it?" Tim pushed further. "*He*'s gone and *we* don't need him."

"And why should I trust you?" She stared intently at him once more.

His heart quaked in his chest. *Brazen, brazen, brazen, act, act, act!* "I may be Tim Schultz, but I'm also Tim Norris – you deserved better of him. And chucking you for being a girl is preposterous, pathetic even. You're far more brilliant and more dangerous than I could ever be." *Stroke, stroke, stroke.*

Heidi almost purred.

Clearly praise from family has been rare in this woman's life, thought Tim. He pressed on, "You will be familiar with the German word, *Zeitgeist*?"

"Of course," she replied, frowning slightly.

"Well, the spirit of this age is that we need only the young and the strong if we're to make this world our own. His money and power got us to a new, unspoilt Earth, but now... now he's just another mouth to feed. You were right to cast him aside – he's of no use to us here. You acted correctly... *Heidi*." He used her name uncomfortably.

When she did not reply, he continued, "Add this to the *zeitgeist* of any age and we have a winning combination, surely?"

"And what do you mean by the spirit of 'any' age, Timothy?"

"You already know the answer to that, cousin. You displayed it beautifully outside, during your rousing speech to the men." *Right,* he thought, *now for the double bluff – otherwise known as the truth. I just hope she doesn't see that this is exactly what I'm doing!* "The endemic spirit of ages is this – it matters not that you do the right thing, only that you *say* the right thing."

Chapter 6 | The (not so) Great Escape

Natalie Pearson threw the ball. Before it even reached the ground, Reiver snatched it from the air. Reiver, the zoologist's faithful but occasionally unruly border collie, usually expected to take his exercise in the gym hall. However, on this occasion, Major White had booted them out. He seemed to want to keep the area free for an 'unspecified purpose'.

Natalie was mildly annoyed, but then, things like that were to be expected. When the military become nervous – or more nervous than usual – freedoms are often curtailed.

She understood, really. They had their job to do. Unfortunately, the only other spaces large enough for Reiver to get up to speed were embarkation – if they were not wanted in the gym hall, they would certainly not be popular there – and the main hangar. How she would have loved to run her best friend out in the open air, where he belonged, but it was too dangerous for them. So, she decided on the hangar. Of course, this meant waiting for the place to clear after the day's activities.

Despite all the pressures and worries afflicting the human world, all her boy needed was his run and some mummy time to keep *him* calm.

This was time well spent for Natalie too, for it applied a balm to her troubled soul. It was also preventative. A bored border collie could be like a fight trapped in a jar; it paid to unscrew the lid every day to bleed off any excess enthusiasm. Otherwise, collateral damage could be at times adorable, often expensive.

Throw. Catch. Throw. Catch. They whiled away the evening.

Two distinctly separate parties watched the game from opposite sides of the hangar, each waiting impatiently for Natalie to leave. Both were out for nefarious purposes, although neither could be said to be fundamentally dishonourable.

Natalie eventually decided it was time to return to her quarters and for Reiver to take on water. After about half an hour, it would be time for a hearty meal too[4].

Rose and Henry watched in silence as the young woman and her faithful hound made for an exit leading to the Pod's residential area. With cameras all over, they donned masks, and were about to step out when Rose suddenly pulled Henry back down into their hiding place.

Across the cavernous hangar, two men, who must also have been waiting for Natalie to leave, suddenly sneaked out of another hatch. Rose was pretty sure that way led to security.

"Is that…?" She squinted in the lower light levels of the evening power cycle. "*No…*" she exhaled more than exclaimed.

"What?" Henry hissed, bewildered.

"That's Del Bond. I don't recognise the other guy, but I heard there were two men in the brig, both terrorists working for *them*."

Bond and Lemelisk ran to the main pedestrian hatch that led outside. The doors parted and they disappeared into the airlock.

Rose was about to stand up when she heard a dog bark and Natalie's voice echoing back down the corridor into the hangar, "Reiver, *no!* Come back here!"

Like a bolt of black and white lightning, Reiver shot from the hatch, head down, flat out. He made a beeline for the escaping terrorists, who were already outside and making a bid for the main gates.

"Come on!" shouted Rose, running after them.

"Wha'? *Hey!* Come back!" shouted Henry, charging after her.

---

[4]   To help prevent her beloved pet from developing 'bloat', Natalie never exercised Reiver thirty minutes either side of a meal. Bloat or Gastric Dilatation is a condition where the stomach fills with gas. Gastric Dilatation-Volvulus is where the gas-filled stomach then twists on itself. In both cases, if the distended stomach obstructs blood flow, this can cause shock and even kill. Unfortunately, control was often needed, as Reiver rarely listened to this particular health tip, even when she explained it really, really slowly…

Natalie popped out of the exit and slowed in surprise as she spotted the teenagers, also making for the main hatch. Quickly shrugging it off, she redoubled her efforts and ran after them, and her errant canine companion.

"That was too easy," Lemelisk spoke over his shoulder. "What's going on?"

"Run, you damned fool! Let's get out of—" Bond stopped, listening. "Oh, no. *Run!*"

He still had the stitches from his last encounter with Reiver and was not thrilled by the idea of re-acquaintance.

It was almost completely dark in the compound, but up on the wall walk a sentry was silhouetted against the skyline, standing near the gates. Lemelisk took aim and fired.

The soldier collapsed as a second voice from the darkness shouted, "Halt!"

Lemelisk fired blind, in the general direction of its source. The energy bolt from the stun-rifle threw just enough light to illuminate a second sentry as he dove for cover, hiding behind the mechanical digger permanently stationed there to open the gates.

Suddenly there were people – and a dog – running around and shouting in the darkness. In the chaos, Henry felt a sharp crack to his jaw and went down.

"Henry!" Rose screamed, but before she could do or say anything further, a powerful arm grabbed her around the waist, pulling her off her feet.

Felled by the rifle butt, Henry could only groan, temporarily knocked out of his wits.

Bond had managed to scramble up onto the digger to escape Reiver, who was jumping up the side of the machine and barking. "They know we're out now!" he cried.

"Shut up!" snapped Lemelisk.

As Natalie helped Henry to his feet, pulling him behind the digger for cover, another voice spoke, "Let the girl go."

Lemelisk snapped round to face the newcomer. There was little light to see by, so he pointed the short-stocked weapon at Rose, his other arm around her neck.

"Drop the weapon, soldier boy, or the girl gets it!"

The sentry, seeing no alternative, did as ordered.

Lemelisk called out, "Bond, use the digger to open the gates."

"What? I can't drive a digger! I'm a tactician, a strategist!"

"You're bloody useless is what *you* are!" Lemelisk pointed the rifle at the sentry. "You! What's your name?"

"Private Prentice," he answered, gruffly.

"OK, Prentice. Get up in that digger and open the gates or I drop this pretty little thing right here!"

"No!" shouted Henry.

Natalie tried to hold onto him and Reiver's collar as each struggled, tugging in different directions. All three went down.

"Move it, Private, or people start dying." Lemelisk risked a quick glance back at the Pod. He could hear shouting.

Private Prentice jumped lightly up into the cab and powered up the excavator's motors. Gradually, the drawbars were removed and, using the machine's arm, he nudged one of the gates open about a metre.

Lemelisk backed towards the gates, still holding on to Rose. Bond passed through the gap first.

"Let her g-go!" said Henry, his voice quaking with fear and rage.

"She comes with us," answered Lemelisk. "Let's call it insurance. Anyone follows us and she dies. Oh, and a word to the wise, pretty boy, don't think I won't do it!"

With that, Bond, Lemelisk and Rose vanished into the night.

Clouds hid the moon, diffusing the light into little more than an absence of total darkness. The *Newfoundland* was so big that, despite the tenebrosity of her time-wearied white paint, she was still visible from the starboard observation port. Hetfield and Marston looked out into the night, standing in darkness themselves, the better to see her.

"Goodbye, old girl," said Hetfield, at last. "Thank you for protecting us and giving us a home all these years."

Marston turned into his chest, crying softly.

"Hey now," Hetfield comforted her. "We've still got each other, Kelly, huh? Always."

"I know, honey, but all those memories, all our friends…"

"I know, I know. But they'll always be with us too, you know that. Remember how you explained it to Captain Baines? You and I haven't even been born yet – not really. So, in a hundred million years we'll see them all over again – our families and other friends, too. Then we'll end up back here and round and round we go. That's a comforting thought, isn't it? Even if we died right now, we'd still have all that and all our lives together to look forward to."

She smiled at him in the darkness. He felt rather than saw it. "I've loved you all these years and never more than right now," she said.

"I know, old girl. You never could kick the habit."

She chuckled, giving him a gentle thump on the chest and they stood in silence for a while, simply holding one another. After fifty years, they never *wanted* to kick the habit.

The gentle hand on Hetfield's shoulder made them both jump. "Sorry to interrupt, Mor, Kelly. It's time," said Douglas.

Henry pulled away from Natalie and ran through the gates after them.

"Henry! *Don't!*" she screamed after him. Trying so hard to restrain him caused her to lose her grip on Reiver too. The dog also bolted through the gates, following the bad man's scent.

Natalie found herself on the ground once more when a helping hand raised her to her feet.

"Are you OK, miss?"

"Is that you, Pte Prentice?"

"Aye. It's Adam, miss."

"What can we do?" Natalie asked, frantically.

"There are people on t' way. Tell them to send help. I'm going after the teenagers. I'll do what I can." The Yorkshireman squeezed her arm compassionately, stooping to retrieve his rifle before he too ran off into the darkness. She heard him call from the other side of the gates, "And get them to check on my mate up on t' walls, he's stunned!"

She was suddenly alone beside the excavator. A tear ran down her cheek. "Reiver, please come back."

From behind, she heard the approach of running feet. "Natalie?" A torch shone in her direction.

"Major White! Quickly, there's a man down up on the wall walk. They've—"

White never heard the rest of her words, the sudden roar from the sky so loud it almost stunned them. Despatching troops to retrieve the downed man from the wall, he dragged a struggling Natalie back towards the Pod as the *New World* hovered, just a few hundred metres overhead. Even the bruises he was suffering from Natalie's flailing limbs could not have dampened his spirit at that moment. The majesty of the ship that bore them here, and upon which all their hopes rested, was unmistakable.

She began to lower the vast cables which would allow the Pod to be raised and re-seated under her belly.

White realised that they all needed to get back inside immediately. He was about to hurry his men, more by touch than voice, when he realised that Natalie had stopped struggling and stiffened in his arms.

He turned to see what could have frightened her and all the joy of seeing the *New World* flying once more drained from his heart.

There were now two other ships in the night sky, invisible but for the flames from their thrusters and engines. Although smaller than the *New World*, they were still giants, and White knew, though he could not see, that they bristled with weaponry.

"Och, damn that woman! Will she no' leave us alone!" shouted Douglas, slamming his fist down on the arm of his captain's chair.

"Our launch must have attracted their attention," Lieutenant Singh pointed out bitterly. "What should we do, sir? Hiro has already begun the docking procedure."

Before answering, Douglas rubbed the stubble on his cheek, momentarily unsure what to do for the best. "If we break off, we could be putting ourselves in more danger still."

"I agree," said Meritus.

Singh looked unconvinced. "Sir?"

"Captain Douglas is right, Lieutenant. We should continue our docking manoeuvres. If we break off now, they will chase us down and if they can't get us to land and hand over the ship quietly, they may just blast us out of the sky."

"What's to stop them doing that anyway, sir?" asked Singh, eyeing the other vessels warily on the main view screen.

Douglas answered first, "Because, if they fire on us, we'll come down on the Pod. *Factory Pod 4* is the key to this whole affair. It's also their Achilles heel."

"And as long as we're willing to defend it with force," Meritus took up the baton, "they have to be careful, or their whole mission is finished."

"Aye," Douglas continued. "Back in our own time, the authorities will be wise to the fact that something is going on now. The Schultz mission will never get another chance to take a Pod and without one, they cannae build Nazi World! Their ships are formidable, but tiny when compared with the Mars fleet. Even if they could secure the resources to build their own, Ah very much doubt they'll want to travel home now. Pretty sure our governments will throw a hell of a welcome party if they do."

"So we've got them right where we want them, sir," replied Singh, uncertainly.

Douglas smiled. "Stand firm, Mr Singh."

A bang and a judder signified the first movements as the Pod began to rise from the sucking, clinging ground.

Captain Wolf Muller nodded for his communications officer to acknowledge the incoming call.

"Muller," he answered.

"This is Captain Hartmann, Captain. The *Sabre* and the *Heydrich* are in position. The *New World* has moved to dock with *Factory Pod 4*. Would Dr Schultz like us to prevent this?"

"Keep your station, Captain Hartmann. Tell Captain Franke to do the same. Prevent them from leaving *only*. Do not engage. Stand by." Muller walked across to communications. Quietly, he ordered the officer on station to summon Dr Schultz back to the bridge.

"Yes, sir."

Muller found it hard to believe she would leave at a time like this. This newfound cousin seemed to be distracting her. He did not approve. In fact, he was not at all sure about their recent change in leadership. Although the Schultz family were overlords and paymasters to the entire enterprise – and by extension, the world – taking orders from a slip of a girl made him nervous. Both were very obviously psychotic, but her grandfather at least had the benefit of experience. Muller blew out his cheeks, but his misgivings remained.

"Captain?"

He turned to find Heidi Schultz standing right behind him. *How* do *they do that?* he pondered, but greeted courteously, "Ma'am."

Heidi listened to his report and then ordered a channel opened to the *New World*.

Douglas put his head in his hands. "Oh, for the love of God. OK, answer it, Sandy."

Singh accepted the transmission, nodding to signify that the channel was open.

"This is Captain Douglas of the USS *New World*. What in the hell can Ah do for you, Schultz?"

"*Land that ship – immediately,* Kapitän."

"Ah'm afraid we have other plans, Heidi. We're leaving this place. And just in case you're planning on following us, we have your dear old grandfather as a prisoner. Ah'd hate it if something were to happen to the old fellow!"

Heidi whispered an order into the ear of a junior officer, who left the bridge on the run.

"*You* will *land,* Kapitän. *For I too have someone here that you will very much wish to see again alive, yes?*"

Douglas' face worked involuntarily as he chewed over her words in silent fury. While he deliberated how to respond, a huge *clang* rocked the ship.

"We're docked, sir," reported Singh, quietly.

For the first time since before the battle over the *Last Word*, the *New World* and *Factory Pod 4* were one. The idea of landing and capitulating to this creature, *again*, made Douglas' blood boil.

"If you have Mr Norris there, Ah'd like to speak with him," he stated at last.

"*You wish to have proof that he is still among the living. Very well, I have him here. Say hello, Timothy.*"

Fifty kilometres west, aboard the *Eisernes Kreuz*, Heidi nodded, and Tim stepped forward.

"Hello, Captain."

"Tim. Are ye OK? They've no' harmed ye?"

"I'm very well, at the *moment*, Captain. Thank you." He looked at Heidi, who nodded again, the beginnings of a cold smile on her lips. "I've actually discovered a completely new and unknown to science Tyrannosaur and named it Pat-ed-osaurus. I would also have you know that my real name is Timothy Schultz. I'm Heidi's first cousin by birth and am with my *real* family now. As for our grandfather, you can keep him. Heidi would have killed him anywa—"

His speech was cut off abruptly by Heidi's fist in his face. *"Fool!"* she snapped.

Tim spun and fell, hitting the deck with an angry red welt glowing hot beside the triumphant smile on his face.

On the bridge of the *New World* a shocked silence descended. Douglas looked to Meritus, who could only shrug – he had no idea if any of it was true.

"Do not make me shoot you down, Kapitän," Heidi continued.

"And lose *Factory Pod 4?*" replied Douglas. "Ah doubt you'll do that."

"So how do you plan to escape, Douglas? We can follow you anywhere you go. Shall we pursue you until you run out of fuel and drop out of the sky?"

Anger and indecision burned for supremacy within Douglas. Eventually, he conceded, "We'll land." With a sigh, he mimed cutting across his throat, to close the channel.

Singh obeyed and the *New World* set down once more.

Prentice could hardly believe the aerial display above him as the three capital ships faced off. On the other hand, the light cast by their engines was just enough to see by, so he made the most of it and sprinted after the escapees.

The running squaddie left the clearing behind quickly. Once inside the treeline, he followed the bulldozer road, cleared to reach the *New World*'s crash site some days ago. The trees reduced the wash of rocket noise significantly, so that clear sounds of an altercation could be heard from the trail ahead. A woman's scream chilled him. Now fully in the woods, it was pitch black, but he dared not light his torch for fear of becoming a target. He could still hear the dog barking and the concussive thuds of a stun-rifle. The girl screamed again, crying and shouting wordlessly, but at least she was alive.

The barking became a muffled snarl and a man screamed.

Prentice smiled to himself. *That sounds like one less for me to tackle*, he thought as he gained on them.

Spurred on by the girl's screams, he pushed himself harder. In the darkness, his boot snagged something on the ground, throwing him headlong. Getting back to his feet, he bent to see what had tripped him. To his horror, he found it was a body.

"Come *on*," he muttered, feeling for a pulse. "Only stunned, thank God. I'll have to come back for you though, lad. I'm sorry."

He listened. Ignoring the more distant roar of manoeuvring ships, he could tell that his quarry was moving farther up the road, away from him. More worryingly, he also began to pick out other sounds – closer sounds.

Prentice's focus switched fully to his immediate surroundings. Hailing from a modest background, he had joined the forces because it was one of the few ways one could receive decent food rations in the 22nd century. He had never wanted to be a hero. Nevertheless, as a trained soldier he had an instinct for when danger was closing, and it was closing now.

Silently, he pulled his rifle from around his shoulders. It was hard to be sure, but he believed the unconscious body to be that of the American boy. How could he get him out of here and fight off whatever was circling him?

"Aaargh!" he yelled, clutching at his leg as it collapsed beneath him.

Whatever had struck, had struck fast. His leg was bleeding copiously, his palm coming away soaked. What had it done to him?

His slick hand began to riffle through his jacket pockets for something he might use as a tourniquet, but almost immediately, he heard the creature stir again. His hand snapped automatically back to the rifle.

His thoughts whirled, *Damn! I'll bleed out before I get a grip on t' situation.*

Before that worry could fully take hold, he heard something else approaching from the north. Whatever it was came on swiftly, faster than a man could run. Prentice could tell by the sounds it made that it approached on four legs, and his concerns about blood loss suddenly seemed rather long-term.

From the trees at the side of the road, his initial attacker came on again, demanding his full attention. It was a two-legged theropod dinosaur of some kind; no more could be discerned in the darkness. All he could make out for certain was that it was crouched, preparing to spring.

He dove to his left, but as the creature leapt, the running intruder arrived to snatch it out of the air. Both animals went down together in a twisting snarl of teeth and claws.

Prentice was speechless for a second before managing to shout, "Flippin' eck! It's the bloody dog!" more in surprised acclamation of a life continued than to provide commentary for his companions.

Regaining his senses, he switched his torch on to reveal a circling pair of none more disparate carnivores. No imagery necessary, they were literally millions of years apart. The four-legged canine's sleek black and white fur shimmered as he moved through the torchlight, planted and compact. The bipedal dinosaur's red-feathered plumage rustled up on its neck and down its spine in warning, an altogether more willowy creature, yet by far the more dangerous of the two. Reiver's attack and distraction were as courageous as only a dog can be, but Prentice knew he had to even the odds or they would all die.

The light and human voice had no effect upon Natalie's beloved pet. He had grown up around human gadgetry and understood hundreds of English words – while pretending not to understand thousands more – but the dinosaur panicked. At about two and a half metres long, from its savage teeth to the tip of its feathered tail, it stood about as tall as a German Shepherd.

Prentice winced. The long sickle claws on the second toes of its otherwise birdlike feet made the gash in his leg throb reflexively. His torchlight clearly pained the eyes of this nocturnal hunter, and after a moment's open-mouthed posturing, claws spread wide, it attacked.

Fortunately, the torch was held alongside the barrel of Prentice's rifle. He fired.

The dinosaur fell out of the air and lay still.

Prentice kissed the barrel of his gun and then knelt to greet Reiver. "You good boy! You beautiful boy, you!" He hugged the collie tight for a moment, when a sudden weakness overtook him, forcing him to sit upon the earthen road. Going through his jacket pockets, he produced a strap and pulled it tight around his damaged thigh.

A groan came from the ground next to him. "You OK, lad?" he asked.

"Oh, man. What happened?" murmured Henry, blearily.

"You were stunned."

Henry sat up stiffly, blinking in the darkness. "Who're you?"

"Pte Prentice. Please call me Adam. Nice to meet you."

"You too, I'm Henry. Thanks for stopping by." He proffered a hand automatically when a sudden shock roused him to his senses. "Rose!"

"They're gone, lad. I'm sorry. I tripped over you in t' dark and then that *thing* attacked me, out of the woods. If it hadn't been for the dog..." Prentice tailed off.

"Hey, Reiver," Henry greeted their saviour. He was recovering rapidly from the effects of the weapon, allowing him to experience the full horror of Reiver's kiss of breath. The black and white face, demonstrating an unfeasibly long tongue, actually bore more than a passing resemblance to a Kiss *poster*, but in the inky blackness, the young American was as oblivious of any historic rock parallels as he was defenceless against the collie's affections.

Coughing and wiping his face, he asked, "Are you out here alone, Adam?"

"Aye, there was no one else. I asked for help to be sent but with those ships arriving, I doubt they'll be coming any time soon."

"That was brave," marked Henry, genuinely. "Thank you, again. Can you help me track Rose? Reiver can find Bond – he has his scent and seems to really dislike the guy."

A stirring on the road made them jerk round. Reiver snarled. The dinosaur was coming round already. Prentice could not help noting the stunning effect of the weapon was much briefer than it had been on the strapping young American beside him.

"Can you help me stand, Henry?"

"You're injured?"

"Aye, that thing mauled my leg before I even knew I was in trouble!"

Henry helped him to his feet. Reiver's snarl turned to a growl as the stunned dinosaur began making small vocalisations of its own. The sounds were subtle at first, a sort of *breathy* screech. It was as if the creature was stuck in a dream, its feet kicking as it ravaged imagined prey.

"I don't think so, son," said Prentice and shot it again. "A helpless target, Henry. Believe you me, they're the best kind! Let's go. We need to get back t' Pod."

Prentice could feel Henry shaking his head.

"No. I'm sorry, but I've got to go after Rose."

"She's your lass?"

"Yeah. I can't leave her with those murderers."

"I understand, lad, but there's nowt we can do about it. They're armed and almost certainly heading for the enemy camp. If you go out into that forest alone, you'll be killed, without doubt. And I can't come with ye – not with this gammy leg. Now, I smashed my comm when I fell, do you have yours?"

Henry felt his pockets. *"Damn,* must have lost it in the struggle."

"Aye, well, never mind. We need to find our way back and get help. What did you say t' dog was called?"

"He's called Reiver."

"Right, come on, Reiver. I swear, once he's got his leg fixed up, your uncle Adam's gonna find you the biggest bone you've ever seen in your life, lad!"

"There were several messages hidden in Tim's words, there," Douglas stated confidently. "One of which, Ah intend to disregard."

Safely back on the ground, all eyes on the bridge turned to him. When he lapsed into thought, Gleeson prompted, "Go on, Captain."

Douglas nodded. "Firstly, let's deal with the main message, that he is somehow related to those murderers. Could this be true?"

"I don't know, Captain," replied Singh. "Everyone was well vetted before the mission. As far as we know, he was orphaned young and adopted by Dr Patricia Norris and her late husband."

"Poor child," said Kelly Marston. "To lose everyone like that."

Douglas slapped a hand to his brow. "Oh, Ah'm a fool! Ah never got to tell him his mother's alive. *Damn!"*

"What were the hidden messages, then?" asked Gleeson, getting everyone back on topic.

Douglas sighed deeply. "The first was that he's still our Tim Norris."

"How d'you figure that, James?" asked Meritus. "If he is a Schultz, they'll have offered him the world – literally. He's just a kid, it wouldn't take much to turn his head, bring him into the fold."

"I can't believe that," said Singh.

"Really?" asked Meritus. "He's been offered power over a new society, a life of luxury, an army at his back, not to mention the pick of an extraordinary array of exquisite blondes!"

"No," Douglas interrupted them. "You dinnae know the lad. The very fact that he told us all that proves he hasnae been turned."

Meritus looked at him askance.

"Seriously," continued Douglas. "He took a great risk to say what he did. Ah just hope he doesnae pay the price for it."

"Am I missing something here?" asked Meritus.

"Actually, Captain, I'm kinda wondering how you arrived at that conclusion myself," queried Gleeson.

"Simple. Schultz wanted us to know she has a hostage. By playing the collaborator card, Tim is trying to get us to desert him and do whatever we have to, to protect ourselves."

Gleeson looked sceptical. "That's pretty thin, Captain."

"Not at all, Commander. You see, Ah know how that boy thinks. He's no Nazi sympathiser and to prove it he told us about the new dinosaur."

"OK, you've lost me, James," said Meritus.

"Very simply, Tobias, Tim is crazy about dinosaurs – has been all his life. He's telling us he hasnae *changed*. But it's much more than that. You see, Ah happen to know that Tim's adoptive father was called Ted Norris."

Hetfield spoke for the first time. "I'm really not seeing the through line here, either, James."

Douglas smiled. "Then Ah'll explain it to you, my friends. Did ye hear the way he pronounced the name he'd given his precious new Tyrannosaur? The deliberate pauses he made, Pat-ed-osaurus?"

"Patricia and Edward!" blurted Singh

"Hole in one!" agreed Douglas with a wink. "He's still Tim Norris and he's playing a very dangerous game, compacted with another dangerous game of plausible deniability, now. He also told us that Old Man Schultz is on Heidi's hit list and subsequently is no good as a hostage. Now for the message Ah intend to disregard – he wants us to abandon him and save ourselves."

Everyone fell silent as they processed his explanations.

"I still think that's putting a lot of trust in a young kid, James," stated Meritus, with a shake of his head.

Douglas turned to him directly. "We've been putting our trust in that laddie since Sandy worked out we were all trapped in the Cretaceous.

He's no' let us down so far. And that brings me on to my next point. Dr Patricia Norris' life is hanging by a thread just now. So not a word of this leaves this room.

"Flannigan says she'll need all of her willpower to make it back, and if Tim really is a Schultz, it might break her heart."

He looked to each of them in turn. "Not a word. That's an order, are we clear?"

Rose was roughly shaken awake in the deep blue of early dawn. Lemelisk had route-marched them through the night, to where the road turned off towards the Schultz encampment. After travelling a few hundred metres further west, he had decided it was safe to make camp for the night. For Rose, this meant being launched up into the low boughs of a tree with her hands tied around a branch with a set of zip-tie handcuffs, drawn from a pocket within Lemelisk's stolen security jacket.

He cut the tie, allowing her to rub life back into her arms. It took a few minutes to restore circulation before she could hang from the branch and drop.

"What are you going to do with me?" she asked, hiding her fear with forthrightness.

"I could think of a thing or two, my pretty." Lemelisk grinned lasciviously as he approached her.

Bond stepped into his path. "We have the better part of twenty-five miles to march through dinosaur-infested jungle. Mind on job, please, Mr Lemelisk."

Lemelisk grunted. Pointing a finger west along the vehicle-smashed trail, he said, "Fine. Let's move."

Rose gave him a look of pure hatred, which only made the man smile. Temporarily out of options, she began to walk with Bond following close behind. She could not feel gratitude towards him. What little she knew of the man suggested that his intervention was motivated purely by self-preservation. However, between him and the monster, Lemelisk, it made sense to try and befriend Bond, if possible.

As she pondered this, a chittering sound came from her left, among the trees. There was movement and a rustle of ferns on the forest floor, but whatever had caused the little commotion had already scampered out of sight. Tiny hairs stood up stiffly on her neck, her senses warning: beware.

The men had seen it too. They were scanning the foliage to their left when a similar disturbance struck up on the right. Lemelisk whipped the rifle from around his shoulders in one fluid movement and aimed into the trees.

For the first time since he had abducted her, Rose was actually glad he was there.

"Oh, this isn't good," muttered Bond.

"Be silent!" hissed Lemelisk.

Rose was half the age of Lemelisk, younger still than Bond, and so was the only one to hear the high-pitched chittering. Tilting her head, she froze, causing Bond to walk into her.

"Wha—" he began, but fell instantly silent as Rose spun to look past him, back along the trail. Frozen in place, she began to shake.

Turning slowly, the men followed her gaze.

Virtually no one aboard the *New World* or *Factory Pod 4* had been graced with even a wink of sleep, and thoroughly exhausted, Major White walked into the meeting he had been dreading the most.

"Tell me just what the *hell* was going on last night!" shouted Jim Miller. Incandescent with rage, he singled White out immediately.

"That's what I'd like to know!" seconded Burnstein.

White raised his hands in a placatory gesture. Burnstein spent half of his days in a rage, but the transformation in the normally so placid Jim Miller was far more shocking.

He shook with anger as he added, in a quiet, dangerous tone, "Ford, tell me what has happened to my daughter."

"I wanted to go after her!" shouted Henry Burnstein.

"You keep your mouth *shut!*" snapped his father.

"May I answer this, Major?" asked Pte Prentice.

White gestured for him to intercede, the short reprieve coming as a relief while he considered his position.

"Sir," Prentice spoke directly to Miller, his Yorkshire accent gruff with tiredness. "I was on duty on the wall last night, when my mate was shot. Luckily, it was only a stun blast and he's OK, but we were surprised because the attack came from within our own compound."

"Del Bond and Sargo Lemelisk had broken out from their cell while being taken for a shower," added White. "Please continue, Adam."

"Yes, sir. Lemelisk grabbed your daughter and threatened her life if I didn't throw down my weapon and open t' gates. Naturally, I did as instructed, for the lass' sake, but they took her. Young 'Enry 'ere ran after them in t' forest. It was a brave thing to do, sir. I couldn't afford to wait for backup, so I followed them all." He placed a comradely hand on Henry's shoulder.

"The lad was stunned and left for dead, sir. Unfortunately, in the dark I tripped over him and then we were attacked by a dinosaur. We were saved by Natalie's dog, bless him. I would have tracked them all night, sir, but it got my leg."

Miller noted the crutches leaning against the man's seat and his gaze softened slightly.

"I couldn't let the lad follow her on his own, sir. He'd have been killed."

Miller nodded. "Thank you for going after her, both of you," he glanced at Henry. "But what was she doing out there in the first place?"

"I have a confession," said Henry.

Miller, already on his feet, leaned on the table with his knuckles. "Go on."

Shame, fear and embarrassment fought for dominance on the young man's face. "We were staking out one of the storerooms in the hangar."

"You were doing *what?*" bellowed White and Burnstein simultaneously.

White jumped to his feet, pointing at the errant teenager. "Spill," he invited dangerously.

"Rose had a plan—"

"Rose?" asked Miller, angrily.

"Yes, sir, but I won't let her take the blame, sir. We were all in it together."

Miller could see the lad was trying to protect his daughter and so asked the next question more gently. "Who's 'we' and in *what* together?"

"The plan to rescue Tim—"

"Oh, for the love of God!" snapped Miller.

Henry jumped to his feet, angry himself now. "Well, none o' you guys were doin' anything!" he bawled. "He's our friend, so if no one else was going after him, we decided we would!"

Miller and White sat back down as a stunned silence descended.

White sighed. "That was brave, son, but stoopid. You should have told us what you were planning—"

"Right, so you could have stopped us, you mean?" Henry replied, still angry.

"You're damned right we'd have stopped you, you li'l idiot!" stormed Burnstein Snr.

"None of this matters now!" retorted Henry. "All that matters is getting them back and Rose most of all. She's out in the jungle with those murderers." He stood again. "I don't care what you do to me, I'm tellin' ya, I'm goin' after her. Alone, if I have to!"

"Alright, alright," White interjected, calmly. "Listen to me, son. You're not going anywhere – yet." He looked at Jim Miller. "And neither is anybody else, is that clear? We have enough missing persons to retrieve without a free-for-all, OK?"

"I promise nothing!" said Henry.

Miller eyed White cautiously, keeping his intentions to himself.

"Do you, any of you, really think that we would just leave Tim out there? Or Rose? But we have to act cohesively."

"When?" asked Miller.

"We have a stand-off with those warships outside," he answered. "We need to plan our next moves with cool heads, or we could lose a lot more yet.

"Hank, take Henry back to your quarters, please. I'm gonna post a guard on your door so that nobody does anything crazy, OK?"

Burnstein nodded and stood, placing a surprisingly gentle hand on Henry's shoulder. "Come on, son. We'll get her back."

Henry looked up at his father with shock and awe. "Dad? Are you OK?"

"Sure, let's get you home."

"And when do I get *my* child home?" Miller asked bitterly.

Burnstein gave him a penetrating stare. "Since we now have such a large military contingent aboard the Pod, I've been making soundings about the forming of a purely civilian government. After that Cocksedge chick stirred things up last week, the idea has taken form. Whether she stays locked up or not, I'm standing against her."

He took in the room.

"We clearly have to get these kids back. I'll do whatever I can, Jim."

Miller nodded, one father to another.

The Burnsteins left.

"Pte Prentice, get some rest. That's an order," said White, helping the injured man to his feet and handing him his crutches.

"Yes, sir. No argument from me, sir. But when you do go after them, please, count me in."

White smiled. "Count on it."

After the soldier had left, White turned to Miller. "Jim, I wanted you to stay because there's more you should know. It's about Bond and his 'not so great' escape."

Chapter 7 | Life, Death and Forgiveness

"Don't move," said Bond, breathless with fear.

"That won't help," Rose hissed.

"Ha, pygmies!" barked Lemelisk. "What're you afraid of, Bond?" He fired a stun blast at the foremost of the three Buitreraptors, felling the little creature instantly.

Even before its two compatriots leapt for him, their ruse had proved effective. Lemelisk was caught completely off guard when six of their packmates attacked from the brush cover to either side of the road. Striking snake-fast and with terrifying coordination, each exploited a separate window in the man's defences, shredding his clothes like paper to slash at the flesh beneath.

Lemelisk screamed as he went down under a deadly quilt of brightly feathered bodies.

"Cover your eyes and ears," Bond called out as he grabbed Rose, throwing them both to the side.

Rose reacted just in time as a fantastic flash-bang assaulted their senses. After a moment, she risked a quick look around.

Bond still covered her with his body, shaking his head dully as if stunned. She pushed him off, entertaining the idea of making a run for it. Two things stayed her hand. Firstly, she knew there would be many more of these creatures, and worse, out there, making her chances of getting back alone, slim. Secondly, and begrudgingly, she had to admit that Bond had probably just saved her life.

Reaching a decision, she helped him to his feet. He thanked her, still shaking his head to clear it.

"What was that?" she asked.

"A stun grenade. I filched it from our friend's pocket last night, just in case of emergencies."

"With the wildlife or with him?" Rose nodded towards Lemelisk's prone and bloodied form.

Bond gazed levelly at her. "Quite," he acceded. "I suppose we'd better drag him with us before the animals come round."

Rose gave a shudder as she stood over her abductor. "I say we leave him."

"I understand your feelings, young lady, but there is more at stake here than you know. I *have* to get back to Schultz's flagship. Regrettably, I don't think I can without his help. Arrogant fool he may be, but he's also a lethal killer. Just the sort we need to stand behind at the moment. Wouldn't you agree?"

"*We...?*"

He smiled enigmatically. "I'm sorry you were dragged into this, my dear. It was never my intention. I ask you not to work against me."

"Oh, *do* you indeed?" she scoffed.

"I do, and you should know that I'm here with the blessing of your ruling triumvirate."

"*What?*"

He held a finger to his lips, then bent to retrieve the stun rifle while grabbing one of Lemelisk's arms. "Help me, please. We must go before they awaken."

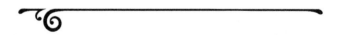

Jim Miller's face was red with fury. "You allowed those murderers to make a break for the enemy camp and take my daughter with them!"

"Jim, please, it wasn't like that—"

"No? Then just how the hell was it then, Ford? My daughter is out there with killers for company in a world full of flesh-eating monsters! What in God's name were you *thinking?*"

"It wasn't like that, *OK?* So don't take it out on me! You're her father, where the hell were you!"

Miller suddenly deflated as if he had been gut-punched and White immediately regretted his flash of anger. "Hey, Jim, look, I'm sorry. I didn't mean that. We're all worried and afraid and none of us have slept." He stepped around the table to place a hand of friendship on Miller's shoulder. "I'm real sorry, Jim."

Miller anxiously covered the lower half of his face with his hand, feeling the scrape of stubble as a tear rolled down his cheek. "But you're right. *Where* was I? What am I going to do, Ford? I've lost her. My little girl."

"Hey, now, she's a tough kid and incredibly determined. She'll make it and I won't rest until she's back, Jim. I swear it."

Miller sagged back into his seat. "I know. I just don't know how to proceed. She's my whole world, my whole life – everything."

White took the seat next to him. "I understand, my friend. We'll get her home, but unfortunately, the next move isn't ours. If we go off all half-cocked it will mean more lives. We have to show a little patience and a little faith – just for now."

As if on cue, Mother Sarah Fellows entered the meeting room, trailing Dr Satnam Patel. She moved quickly to comfort her friend. "Has anyone told Mrs Miller yet?"

White shook his head exhaustedly.

"Come on, Jim, let me take you home. We'll tell Lara together, OK?"

Miller nodded absently, allowing Sarah to usher him across the room. Upon reaching the door he turned. "Ford?"

"Yes, Jim?"

"I hope it was worth it. Letting Bond go, I mean."

White's usual upright military bearing seemed to have deserted him. A bone-weariness such as he had never known left him stooped, the weight of his cares forcing him to lean on the table for support as he answered, "I do too."

"You fool!" snapped Heidi. "If Douglas thinks you have defected, we lose some of our hold over him! And telling him that *unser Großvater* was of no use as a bargaining chip, closed another avenue we may have explored to further weaken his position."

She stood in the doorway to Tim's cell and eyed him sidelong. The livid red mark on his face was turning purple, working up through burgundy, the shape of her knuckles becoming clear in the flesh of his cheek.

"What sort of game are you playing, cousin?" she asked finally.

Tim sat on his bunk and gazed levelly back at her. "I thought I was helping," he said simply.

Heidi was not at all sure what to make of this cousin she had suddenly been landed with. He was clever, she knew that, very clever, but he was young too. Tim had had none of her training or upbringing. Maybe she expected too much of him? If Patricia Norris was dead, then his final link with the people of the *New World* was severed, surely? So why could she not bring herself to trust him?

She had always believed in the 'Schultz' way of doing things, through order, discipline and ultimately, fear. Yet, in recent days she had seen with her own eyes how the carrot often worked where the stick did not, seen even her *Großvater* become fallible.

I *would side with me*, she thought. *I have all the power. Anyone of sense would wish to wield such power. At very least they would wish to ally with or hide behind it, would they not? And yet I have seen a few kind words bind men to me and the rule of iron lead to betrayal. How does my cousin think? He's little more than a child, why can I not read him?*

Breaking into her thoughts, Tim asked, "Am I to be confined again, cousin?" He hated calling her that, hated that he was becoming more comfortable with it. This woman was deadly and probably insane. Even so, at this moment *he* was the insurgent, *he* was the betrayer waiting to strike, *he* was... like her after all?

"You may return to the bridge after you have cleaned yourself up and shaved. We have standards to uphold. You are a Schultz now, and that fluff on your chin must go."

Without warning she produced a cut-throat razor, flicking it open in one smooth movement. "Can you manage, or would you like me to help you?" she asked, wickedly.

Tim swallowed. "I can manage, thanks."

Treating him to a wolfish smile, she continued. "Apparently, someone escaped from the *New World* camp last night. As they hold, or *held*, two of our operatives prisoner, I have hopes.

"You will attend the bridge when your appearance has been remedied. I will take a transport and see who has escaped. If they are ours, they will almost certainly be making their way here."

"If that's the case, won't Captain Douglas work that out too?"

"Not necessarily, young one. He may believe they made for the *Sabre*, or the *Heydrich*, once they heard them pass. We know they have not done this, therefore they must intend to board the *Eisernes Kreuz*, and if so, I would know why. Even if Douglas does suspect this, we have two warships pinning down his position. It would be suicide to try and leave their camp."

"Heading out after them under the guns of those ships would be suicide," Douglas snarled.

Adding to their existing woes, everyone aboard the *New World* was confined to the ship to reduce the risk of spreading the contagion Douglas had contracted from a reptile bite. The ship and Pod were docked together as a single unit once again. However, communication with people just a few corridors away could only be executed via video link.

"We have to do something," retorted White.

"Ford, no. You're no' thinking straight. When was the last time you had any sleep?"

"I'm OK, Captain," White bridled slightly. "I can work through it."

"Actually, Major, perhaps you would benefit from just a little rest," Patel added, gently.

"Now would be the best time, Major," interjected Meritus from his seat next to Douglas in the *New World*'s meeting room. *"We're in a stalemate, no one can move."*

White slammed his fist down on the desk. "I've told you, I'm OK, damnit! Jim Miller's little girl is lost out there and by letting those criminals escape, we're at least partially responsible! Now, I don't need mollycoddling, I need a plan to get her back!"

"OK," said Douglas, *"let's get the full picture then, starting with Bond's escape. How did* both *of our prisoners manage to get, not only out of their cells, but off the ship entirely – kidnapping Jim's wee lassie along the way?"*

White and Patel glanced awkwardly at one another. Patel answered, "We cannot reveal that, Captain."

Douglas leaned in closer to the screen, an eyebrow rising with his ire. *"What's this now?"*

In the background, Meritus offered, *"They've let them go."*

"Captain, you're gonna have to trust us on this one. We can't discuss it here," said White. "All I can say is that holding Schultz aboard your ship, assuming it really is him, changes things. If we had known you had him... Well, let's just say we may have dropped the ball."

"Oh, surely not?"

White flared up again, not willing to be taunted. "Damnit, Douglas! I had no way of knowing you had him – that wasn't my fault!"

Douglas leaned back away from the screen, an amused look in his eyes. *"Ford, we here will get our heads together to plan our next move, but we need you rested. Away for yer bed now, son."*

White puffed out his cheeks in exasperation, rubbing his face to liven himself up. "Alright, you win! I'll reconvene with you shortly."

"Nighty night," Douglas and Meritus chorused with a wave.

White snorted. "I'll see you later."

After he had left Douglas asked, *"Satnam, Ah'm sure you have good reasons for keeping me in the dark here, but if we're to plan our next move, Ah really need the full scenario."*

"Actually, Captain, I have a vital task for you and believe it or not, ignorance of the reasons for what has transpired here, will better prepare you for it."

Despite his annoyance, Douglas was piqued. Leaning closer to the monitor once more, he prompted, *"Go on."*

"I need you to interview Heinrich Schultz. I suggest that, as someone who knows the man, Captain Meritus may be of help to you in this regard."

"OK. We can do that. So how does my ignorance mean bliss?"

Patel considered for a moment. "Captain, you know I have always held you in high regard, both as a leader and as a man."

Douglas felt a trap and viewed Patel askance while he waited for it to close.

"Schultz is a master strategist and a master of deception," continued Patel. "We now hold a piece of information so potentially devastating that we will not allow anyone with that knowledge to interview him. He's too clever."

"You think we might give something away?"

"Never deliberately, Captain. I'm sure you perceive how important this secret is?"

"Aye. Ah can accept that. If we have Schultz, though, wouldnae this lessen the danger?"

"We have *a* Schultz."

"Ah... Fine, it's probably time we should be about it then, eh?"

"Good luck, Captain," replied Patel simply, closing the connection. Finding himself all alone in a room grown suddenly silent and gloomy, he repeated, "Good luck."

Rose and Bond had dragged the unconscious Lemelisk no more than ten paces before they realised that moving him was going to be hard work.

Bond stopped, dropping Lemelisk's arm. "Wait. If we carry on like this, those little terrors are going to be awake and after us long before we can effect our getaway. Hang on." He pulled the rifle from around his shoulders, walked back a little way and proceeded to shoot every one of the little creatures again, to keep them down.

"Not very sporting," Rose commented upon his return.

"Fancy a rematch, do you?"

"Fair enough," she acquiesced.

Bond grabbed the unconscious man by the arm once more and dragged. "Come on."

"Do you think he might need a little attention?" asked Rose. "Some of those cuts were vicious."

"He'll just have to coagulate. I'm not hanging around here. Let's go."

After a couple of hundred metres, Lemelisk began to moan. As he roused, Rose felt both relief and dismay. Her ambivalence was equal parts fatigue – he was heavy to drag – and loathing, because he was such an odious presence to have around.

Helping the injured man back to his feet, Bond said, "Come on, Sargo. We need to move fast before those creatures wake up again. We'll do what we can for you once we've put some distance between us and them. You'll just have to tough it out."

Lemelisk said nothing; he simply tore a strip from his sleeve and, using his teeth, tied the scraps around the worst of his injuries. Fortunately, his legs had been unaffected. There was a gash in his side that would need attention but for now he simply applied pressure to it and strode away.

Bond looked at Rose and raised an eyebrow. "No need to thank us for getting you away from those *pygmies!*" he called after him.

Rose smirked. Lemelisk did not look round. "We go," he said.

The morning sun rose in the sky, heating the day. Under the forest canopy there was still coolness to be found, but this would gradually steam up to sticky discomfort as the hours marched on.

Making the most of the early conditions, the tired threesome walked through a world of mottled movement, where every breeze reset the background. Occasional direct rays from the sun blinded them, adding to the feeling of exposure and insecurity as they strode along the trail.

A low moan followed by grumbling, gurgling sounds came from the foliage to their left. They stopped dead in their tracks, senses heightened.

Rose stepped instinctively closer to Bond. Lemelisk turned to speak when a long neck parted the leaves, followed by a large barrel-shaped body. The animal was certainly some variety of sauropod dinosaur. Rose had read about many such creatures among Tim's notes. She was not sure of the species but gave a sigh of relief, nonetheless.

Bond felt the tension leave her. "Are these safe… *safesauruses?*" he asked quietly.

She nodded. Lemelisk was immediately obscured as three more large creatures stepped out from the forest to surround him, filling the trackway. All broadly the same size, Rose wondered if they formed a crèche; hatchlings born and grown up together that stayed in a group for safety. The sauropods were around five metres in length and plodded about on four stout legs, their long necks reaching for food from the trees while their long tails swished erratically, sending messages incomprehensible to their human observers.

The rumbling and moaning continued as they spoke to one another. At 1.6 metres tall, Rose was fairly slight, but standing on tiptoe, she could just see over the animals' shoulders. Each neck raked up steeply, giving the false impression that the front legs were longer than the back. At a glance, they appeared more giraffe-like than some of the other sauropods Rose had seen out on the plains.

She giggled nervously as she reached out a hand to pat the massively muscular shoulder of the nearest animal. The long neck curved back in a graceful arch, bringing the head down to look at her. Rose gazed into an innocent, almost bovine countenance. As she placed a hand on the animal's cheek, its large, babyish eyes blinked twice.

"Aww, how cute was *that?*"

The nostrils, high on the creature's head, sniffed at her. Rose tugged a fern from the side of the road and offered it carefully. If she remembered correctly, these dinosaurs used their peg-like teeth to strip leaves rather than chew, so she held on tight.

The sauropod sniffed the fern, obviously cautious of this new delivery system, and then took a bite. To Rose's absolute joy, it stripped the leaves easily, leaving her the stem.

"You're *beautiful,*" she breathed, tears welling in her eyes.

Even Bond plucked up the courage to pat the creature's long neck, smiling uncertainly.

"We're not visiting the zoo! Come on!" hissed Lemelisk. The 'pygmy' experience had clearly taught him caution, even around animals that were not obviously aggressive.

His ill-tempered comment was wasted as all four sauropods snapped their heads to stare back along the road, ending the moment completely. In a heartbeat, their whole demeanour changed. They bellowed and stamped, swishing their tails dangerously.

Bond pulled Rose away, a nervous reaction which further fed the creatures' agitation. They may have been at the lower end of the scale in terms of dinosaur intelligence, but they were in perfect tune with their surroundings.

Before he could move away from the group, Lemelisk was shouldered aside to hit the ground hard. He cried out in surprise, cursing profusely.

The sea change in their situation became immediately apparent when they all heard the roar. This was no pygmy.

Rose came to her senses immediately and grabbed Bond, dragging him into the trees and around the stamping sauropods.

"What is it?" he asked.

"Don't know, *don't want to,*" her voice rose in nervous singsong. "*Run!*"

Lemelisk also managed to get clear, and having narrowly avoided a trampling, was away on his toes, without troubling to look back.

"Why did we bring him with us, again?" Rose asked breathlessly.

James Douglas, fifty-year-old captain of the USS *New World*, felt like he was on trial. Never before had he encountered such a penetrating stare or felt so uncomfortable in an interview – and he was the interview*er*.

Schultz sat like a statue behind the bars of his cell. The only movement from the man had been when Meritus strolled in – Schultz's right eye had closed ever so slightly. For Douglas, the gesture brought to mind the sort of squint a cat gives, when it imagines crushing its owner for some slight or breach of protocol – such as purchasing the wrong brand of biscuits.

Meritus appeared nonchalant. He was good, but Douglas did not believe it for a second. He must have been unspeakably uncomfortable under the veneer.

When questioning someone, Douglas always believed in letting the tension build, rather than ploughing straight in. It was a technique which had served in the past. However, the prickly awkward silence only seemed to force Schultz ever further into his comfort zone. If it was an act, it was a damned good one.

The combined force of the two captains' dumb austerity was failing, crumbling even.

Damn the man! thought Douglas. He gave up. "OK, Schultz, we have some questions for you."

An hour later, Douglas and Meritus sat in the *New World*'s mess with Chief Hiro Nassaki and Lieutenant Sandip Singh.

"What manner of creature *is* he?" asked Douglas. The interview had so far achieved nothing. Schultz had refused to speak or even acknowledge them with more than a glare. "His stare burns like coherent light! Doesnae the man even blink? Ah cannae believe he never even asked the whereabouts or condition of the young lassie we captured with him."

"Maybe I could try, Captain?" suggested Hiro.

Meritus was already shaking his head. "That would not be a good idea."

"Oh?"

"Ah think Captain Meritus is suggesting that Schultz is a wee bit, erm… *prejudiced*," replied Douglas, apologetically. "If he willnae speak to us then…"

Hiro nodded understanding. "I thought so, Captain. That's why I dug this back out."

He dropped a small and distinctly homemade looking device on the table, almost knocking Singh's drink over. Singh glanced at the object, surreptitiously leaning away from his friend and colleague.

"Is that a taser?" asked Meritus with interest.

"It used to be," replied Hiro. A shadow crossed his face. "It packs a little more punch now. I souped it up for the interview with Sargo Lemelisk."

"Lemelisk was involved in the death of Hiro's brother three years ago," Douglas explained for Meritus' benefit.

Hiro wore a look of regret. "I was not permitted to finish questioning him about that. Perhaps there will be another time."

"Are you OK, Hiro?" asked Singh.

"I am. Why?"

"I just wondered if you were turning a little bit, you know, what's the word… *psychotic?*"

Douglas put his head in his hands. "That's what Ah love about you, Sandy. You always know just what to say."

Singh pointed to himself as if to say, 'Me…? What did *I* do?'

Meritus leaned forward, frowning. "Hiro, what was your brother's name?"

"Aito."

"Aito Nassaki," muttered Meritus, lost in thought.

Hiro stood abruptly. "You know what happened to my brother?"

Douglas raised a hand gently, gesturing Hiro to sit, but the engineer ignored him, eyes only for Meritus.

"Not exactly," drawled the Canadian. It was rare for his accent to show, he was clearly deep in thought. "A Japanese man named Aito… Something about that has snagged a memory, but I can't quite put it together. I'm sorry, Hiro. Let me think on it some. I'll tell you everything as I remember it. I promise."

Hiro sat down, his expression an odd mixture of hope and hurt. An idea struck him and he straightened. "I know someone who'll know about it!"

"Schultz," supplied Singh. "Of course."

"Thank you *again*, Sandy," snapped Douglas. "No, that's not the way. What we need is some way of applying pressure to the man."

"Exactly," said Hiro, taking the taser back from the table. "Torture!"

Douglas slapped a palm down on the table. "Now look here, Hiro, Ah understand your need to find out about your brother, but we have more immediate concerns right now. There are two warships out there!"

Meritus put a hand on Douglas' arm. "Actually, Captain, we don't really have a better idea at the moment."

"*Yes!*" said Singh.

"No, damnit! We are not the Gestapo!" shouted Douglas.

Meritus turned to him, always so reasonable. "Then what do you suggest, James? Asking nicely isn't working."

"Exactly!" said Hiro.

"*Yes!*" repeated Singh.

"*No!*" Douglas glowered at them. "Will you two just cut it out or do Ah have to split you up? We're no' torturing a man in ma custody – and that's final."

"Captain Baines would," muttered Singh.

Douglas leaned forward across the table. "How's that again? Ah cannae be sure Ah heard ye correctly?"

Singh looked abashed. "Did I say that on the outside?"

"Hole in one, Lieutenant."

"Sorry, sir. You're my favourite, Captain. I've always said so, haven't I, lads?"

Douglas snorted. "So now we've got that cleared up, we only have Schultz and the warships to deal with, eh?"

"Deal!" exclaimed Hiro, standing once more.

Everyone else sat back.

"Care to elaborate, Chief?" asked Douglas.

Hiro sat again. "Make a *deal*, sir. There must be something he needs. Almost everything, for a man in his position, I would imagine, sir."

Meritus snapped his fingers, pointing at Hiro whilst looking at Douglas. "Now that isn't bad! Assuming we can offer him something we can all stomach or tolerate, at least."

Douglas considered for a moment. "Ah have to admit, Ah've spent more time than Ah ever thought Ah would pondering revenge these last few weeks. Ah wonder what that must feel like for a man like Schultz...?"

"Perhaps you should ask Miss Schmidt, Captain?" suggested Singh. "She must know the old man as well as anyone, if she was his aide?"

"I can't run any more," complained Bond with the last of his breath.

"Neither can I," Rose confessed. "We've been jogging for over an hour – I'm *dead!*"

Lemelisk stopped and bent to place his hands on his knees while he panted. "You soon will be! Can't you hear all that behind us? That's the sound of violence heading this way."

"You would know," sniped Rose.

"And you should listen, pretty girl!" he snapped in return.

They had not yet caught sight of their pursuer, a situation for which they were extremely grateful. After they ran away from the small group of sauropods, the sounds of animals fighting had followed, haunting them. The herbivores were mostly peaceful giants, but they were strong, even at such a tender age. Whatever the predator was, judging from the sounds of battle, it had not had things all its own way. Rose could only assume that the interloper had been forcibly ejected from the restaurant. Unfortunately, the very next scent it came across had been their own.

Lemelisk had led them in and out of the trees, across streams, up small escarpments; anywhere with half a chance of losing their pursuit. They had shaken it several times, but always it rediscovered their scent.

"Can we make a stand?" asked Rose.

"Not with this," Bond replied, tapping the stock of their only stun-rifle.

Rose frowned. "I thought those new Heath-Riflesons were really powerful?"

"Maybe, but this one isn't—"

Before Bond could finish, Lemelisk interrupted him. "Yes, and why *is* that? We grabbed a rifle which looked like an augmented weapon, but which seems to have been powered down so that it can't seriously hurt anyone. Can you explain that, Derek?"

"Damn you! Don't call me by that name!"

"Answer the question then, *Derek!*"

Bond turned the rifle on his persecutor. "I'm warning you..."

"Boys… *boys!* Stop it and grow up! If it doesn't work properly, it doesn't work properly. So what *can* we do?"

Both men continued to mutter under their breath.

"*Oi!* Focus!" snapped Rose.

"Do you have another flash bomb?" asked Bond, grudgingly.

"Just one left – after the one you stole from my pocket."

"Now look here, if I hadn't taken that—"

"*Enough*, you two!" Rose sighed, like a schoolteacher breaking up quarrelling children. "Well, I suggest we try it. We're exhausted and starving. At least we'll get to see what's after us and maybe even choose our ground, yeah?"

Another roar, much closer this time, demanded their attention.

"We could climb a tree," suggested Bond.

Lemelisk was already shaking his head before he had finished speaking. "We don't actually know how big this thing is. We could just be trapping ourselves, like bread on the shelf."

"Well, what do *you* suggest then?" Bond retorted crossly.

Before they could start bickering again, Rose jumped in, "We should hide where the trees are thickest."

"And what if the creature is small enough to dodge between them?" asked Bond.

"*Well…* well, then the stun rifle may help us," replied Rose, thinking quickly as she went.

"Very well. I suggest we draw this nice, civilised English chat we're having to a close," snarled Lemelisk. "If we don't move immediately, there'll be more than cucumber sandwiches on the menu!"

Bond and Rose dashed left of the road, Lemelisk to the right. They pushed several metres into the bush until it became difficult to move, even for them.

Bond quivered slightly while Rose calmly wiped some extremely large and horribly poisonous-looking insects from his arms and shoulders. It was hard not to be impressed as she gently brushed leaves aside to give them a view of the road.

They waited for the creature to approach – it was an alarmingly short wait. They had barely hidden themselves in time.

The dinosaur stalked cautiously, stopping to sniff the air every few steps.

"What is it?" whispered Bond.

Rose instantly grabbed his arm. Shaking her head, she used her other hand to place a finger over her lips.

The dinosaur was a theropod. This was perhaps unsurprising as all strictly carnivorous dinosaurs from the Cretaceous were. However, it was another creature they had not seen before. A little taller than a man, it was in human terms monstrous, of course, but was no giant by the standards of the time.

Its head was deep but short, with large, bony ridges above the eyes. The jawline curved upwards and sported a particularly savage dental arrangement.

That's a hell of a smile, Bond thought, but kept it to himself.

The animal's deep brown skin and scales were flashed with red and orange stripes all along its body. With such obviously powerful hind legs, it looked incredibly dangerous, especially at their proximity.

Rose sighed as she took in its proportions; no wonder running away had failed them. She guessed that from nose to tail it must have measured about eight metres.

Tim had left her a plethora of information about this time and place, thoughtfully removing all else, unless it related directly. Digesting a mountain of data, spanning more than 180 million years and covering the entire world, would have been her very own Sisyphean task otherwise. She would never have known what she actually needed to know.

However, despite Tim's trimming of the information, it was difficult to think and recall. Right here, right now, she was afraid, but a name *was* forming in her mind – and it was a tongue-twister. Rose whispered almost silently into Bond's ear, "Ekrixinatosaurus, of the Abelisauridae family."

Among its most notable features were the tiny, vestigial arms. Comparatively, and literally, far smaller and less dextrous than the famously mocked appendages of Tyrannosaurus Rex[5], they simply hung from its sides, seemingly useless.

"Fire in the hole!" shouted Lemelisk.

They all covered their ears, their eyes tight shut.[6]

---

[5]   Despite being roughly the same length as those of a man, the arms, or forelimbs, of *Tyrannosaurus rex* are believed to have been powerful enough to lift upwards of 200kg each. It is still uncertain how *Tyrannosaurus rex* used its forelimbs or for what.

[6]   They naturally covered their ears with their hands, which was once again very unsporting of them.

The Ekrixinatosaurus turned towards the voice and snarled menacingly. The small grenade bumped off the end of its nose, making it blink.

It bent to sniff the unexpected gift...

"It hasn't gone off," Lemelisk muttered to himself, taking a step forward. *BANG!*

Dr Dave Flannigan was regretting having the new buzzer installed in his office. Someone was ringing it like a novelty doorbell and driving him crazy.

"Alright! Enough already!"

He looked to see who required his attention so urgently and sighed. Adjusting his mask, he grabbed his white coat and made his way across the isolation ward.

"OK, Jill, what is it this time?"

"Bored. Want to leave now."

Flannigan snorted. "OK, Captain, we'll go through it again, shall we? Yes, you're obviously feeling better – God knows, *I* know you're feeling better – but you're *not* better, ya see? You did notice that that was exactly the same line I spun you half an hour ago, right? And half an hour before that?"

"I can't just lie around here, Dave," stated Baines, plaintively. "We're in the middle of a crisis."

"Yes, we are, Jill, but as luck would have it, we seem to be awash with captains at the moment, to deal with it all!"

"Oh, right, and let the boys have all the fun! You shouldn't have told me what was happening!"

Flannigan chuckled. "You nagged me, remember? Now, I give the orders in here, Captain. And my orders are that you will stay here, being good, until I tell you otherwise. For a time there, we nearly lost you."

Baines drummed her fingers moodily. "Dave, you may not have noticed, but Captains Douglas and Meritus are both in lockdown."

"So are you!"

She pouted. "When I'm back in charge, I'm having you replaced."

Flannigan threw his head back and laughed heartily. "Until then, is there anything *else* I can do for you, Captain?"

"Actually, I've been thinking. I need to get a message to James. It might help him with Schultz."

"That I can do for you."

"Why are we always dragging this idiot?" Rose griped as she ran in an awkward, crabbing motion, holding onto Lemelisk's right arm.

"I thought he'd be useful," replied Bond.

"I can't imagine how," puffed Rose. "We hardly need a draught excluder!"

"Just save your breath and keep *running!*"

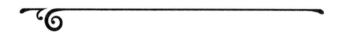

Captain Emilia Franke, commander of the *Heydrich*, strode boldly into the shadow cast by the *Sabre*'s huge wing. "Why did you want to meet out here, Aurick?"

Captain Aurick Hartmann stepped around one of his ship's landing struts to greet her. "You know how it is, Emilia, eyes and ears. What our paymasters lack in ingenious bugging devices they more than make up for with spies."

Franke's expression was professionally neutral. "Very well, I'm here. What do you wish to say?"

"Emilia, it seems to me that our orders to sit here and simply keep the *New World* pinned down lack imagination. I might possibly even suggest that our new *leader* is showing a certain lack of *leadership.*"

"*You* might, Aurick."

Hartmann studied her, considering his next words carefully. "Our whole mission rests upon our taking that Pod away from the enemy. If young Miss Schultz is perhaps out of ideas then—"

"*Doctor* Schultz, Aurick. There has been far too much dissent on this mission already. If we're to cleanse this world and rebuild the Aryan race, then we should begin by mastering ourselves."

A flash of annoyance crossed Hartmann's face. "Quite. Which brings me neatly on to my next point. Our *actual* leader is just over there, probably snugly within their brig."

"What are you saying? Get to the point, man."

"I'm *saying* the next move could be ours to make, if we want him back. I'm sure *Doctor* Schultz does not. So you see the problem? Which side of the fence are you on, Emilia?"

For the first time, Franke appeared uncertain. Eventually, she asked, "What do you suggest?"

Hartmann nodded slightly, pleased to have placed her on the back foot. "I suggest that we contact the enemy and arrange a meeting with Meritus. That alone might drive a wedge between their *fools' alliance*."

"Meritus betrayed us, Aurick. What do you hope to achieve with him?"

"Did he? Or did he merely betray Schultz?"

"You think we should make a private deal with Meritus? You're hedging close to treachery, Captain. The old man might even call that treason."

Hartmann held up placatory hands. "All I'm saying is, our leaders are down, or confused. We hold the bulk of the power on this world and, perhaps, it's down to us to put *Operation Dawn* back on track."

Franke considered. "I have no problems with offering a meeting to Meritus, Aurick. But be advised, I built my entire life's reputation upon effective leadership and loyalty to the cause. I'll be watching carefully and if the talks come to nothing, I want to go for maximum damage to the enemy's morale."

"Very well. What do you have in mind?" asked Hartmann, cagily.

"Simply this," began Franke. "We're all bluffing at the moment. *They're* bluffing that they'll fight, even though it would be suicidal – hoping that we won't risk damaging the Pod. *We're* bluffing that we'll shoot them down if they move – which we would only ever entertain as a last resort because it would effectively destroy our mission.

"We *did* have a hostage in the boy Norris, although now it seems we're to embrace him as part of the new leadership. However, one thing we still know for certain is that we have an asset free within Meritus' ranks – an asset capable of getting messages to us. I suggest we use that asset to sow general discord. Also, and most importantly, should they call our bluff, I believe that now is the time to trot out our ace in the hole. We know how emotional these 'do-good' types are. With their engineering team potentially conflicted and in disarray, it will hamstring any efforts they make to leave, should they try."

Hartmann smiled wryly. "Are you suggesting we spend our 'ace in the hole', as you put it, in a hostage exchange? Him for Schultz?"

Franke shook her head. "No. Douglas would never make a deal like that – it would undermine his whole position. I've studied him. He's a most curious mix of soft and strong, but he's no fool."

Hartmann stroked his chin thoughtfully. "Maybe Douglas wouldn't make such a deal, but what might a younger man, less experienced, more emotionally volatile do, if we dangled the right carrot and tipped our hand?"

Franke smiled coldly. "Why don't we see what happens?"

"Hello, Captain. May I say, I'm very pleased to see you well and back with us."

"*Thank you, Dr Fischer,*" replied Douglas. "*It's good to see you too. Ah'm only sorry it has to be over a video link.*"

"A small matter when compared to our other discomforts at the moment, Captain. Please call me Klaus."

"*Aye, thank you. And you're right about that. One of those* discomforts *is the reason Ah'm calling. Ah'm sorry, this is awkward, Klaus – even more awkward for not being in person.*"

"What is it?"

"*You may be able to help me – help us, Ah should say. Captain Baines has made a suggestion. She's something of a fan of yours, so Ah hope this'll no' cause offence.*"

"I understand, James. I'm sure Jill only has all of our best interests at heart. However, *mein* heart sinks, because I think I've guessed what you are about to say."

"*Ye ken?*"

"I believe so. Does your request involve a masquerade, trading on my family heritage, by any chance?"

Douglas squirmed slightly on the small comm screen. Unconsciously, he tugged at his ear. "*Aye, something like that. Ah'm sorry, Klaus.*" He chuckled lightly to relieve the tension. "*You people are all so damned clever, you're always ahead of me.*"

Fischer smiled sadly. "It's OK, James. I know how serious things are. After all *you* have been through, please make no apology merely for asking me to suffer a little indignity."

"Would that it were only that, my friend," replied Douglas, regretfully. *"There's also the not so little matter of the virus, which may still be present aboard ma ship. We've vented and circulated the atmosphere but if it's still in us, well..."*

"Even so, it's the very least I can do, James. Now, tell me, what do you need?"

"Come on, Hank." Mother Sarah was losing patience. "If MI6 know you have the codes, you must have the codes. All we're asking for is a little co-operation here."

Burnstein frowned in annoyance. "Why the hell were some Limey secret agency watching me?"

Patel answered. "Probably because you are or were one of the richest men in the world and neck-deep in Mars Mission politics, not to mention the logics train.

"Please, Mr Burnstein. If it is known by a middle tier British politician, it will be well known by the enemy that you hold backdoor codes for the critical systems aboard this Pod. By helping us now, you may actually be protecting yourself from their machinations. If *they* come for you, they will be unlikely to use phrases like 'please help us'."

Burnstein sighed angrily. "This is a goddamned conspiracy!"

"Yes," stated Sarah and Patel together.

"Hank, listen to them," Chelsea Burnstein pleaded. "The enemy's agents have already approached Alison Cocksedge, who approached me to get these codes from you."

"What?" Burnstein exploded.

"Hank, wise up, will ya?" snapped Sarah. "You may not have your fortune in the here and now, but you still wanna be a player, don't you?"

Burnstein eyed her cautiously. "What are you sayin'?"

"I'm sayin' that this is your big chance to help."

"Help the military *in secret*," he responded shrewdly. "There's no kudos with the public in that. But of course, if this thing all goes south and everything comes out, then I'll be the guy who sold the Pod access codes to the Nazis! How exactly does this help me become a player?"

Sarah buried her head in her hands. "Will you just stop thinking of yourself for one darned minute!"

"That's easy for you to say. It wouldn't be you taking the fall for treason!"

"Mr Burnstein," tried Patel. "No one is saying that this is not a risky business, but if the enemy do succeed in taking this Pod from us, you, as a Caucasian male will surely be among the more fortunate—"

"Are you outta your goddamned mind? My family escaped to the US of A in the 1930s – they were Jews!"

Patel winced slightly.

Sarah took up the baton, "Hank, there are risks – we know. Your forebears were clearly brave, now it's your turn. Be the hero!"

"Goddamnit!" swore Burnstein. "So what do you want, huh? You want me to sell the codes to the Krauts?"

Patel winced again.

Sarah fired up, jumping to her feet. "Henry Burnstein Snr! Dr Klaus Fischer and his wife, Dagmar, are willing to risk their lives to help us get away from here! So, as a member of the ruling triumvirate, I am *ordering* you to man-up and do the right thing for once in your darned life!"

"Please, honey," Chelsea tried once more.

Burnstein sat back down, giving her a direct look. "So, they tried to get to me through you, huh?"

She nodded.

Burnstein sighed, looking away from his wife, while taking her hand. "OK, I'm in."

"Not a chance, laddie!" snapped Douglas. "Would you allow this, if you were in my position?"

Meritus shrugged. "Honestly, I don't know. You'll still have doubts about me – I understand that, considering the newness of our relationship. But on the flipside, James, if we don't reach out, we'll be locked in this stalemate forever – or worse, we'll force them to try and take us."

Douglas visibly seethed. He was feeling the strain at the moment and the invitation from the enemy for talks, specifically with his new ally, made him very nervous. "Will ye stop being so damned wise and reasonable!"

Meritus grinned at the backhanded flattery.

"It's no' that Ah distrust you, Tobias," Douglas continued more calmly. "It's just that Ah have to consider all the lives on this ship. And another thing, what the hell do they want with ma chief engineer?"

"That I *don't* know. I do appreciate your position, James, but this might be an opportunity. Schultz is out of the picture. His crazy granddaughter has taken over the show but is nowhere to be seen. I don't know… it's just a feeling, but maybe we can use their absence to build a bridge? It worked between us, didn't it?"

Douglas gave him a penetrating stare.

"But you're not a hundred percent sure you can trust me," Meritus added with understanding.

"Ah want to, laddie. Can you believe that, at least?"

"I do, James. And I totally understand, but how do you want me to answer? It's your call."

"Maybe," agreed Douglas, "but there's also Miss Schmidt to consider."

Meritus frowned. "What happened there?"

"Oh, she wouldnae talk. Trained by the man himself Ah don't doubt. The only time she spoke at all was when Ah mentioned that now we had Schultz, she might as well play ball."

"What did she say?"

"Only that she had known Heinrich Schultz since she was eight years old, and she had never known him to be anywhere he didnae want to be." He sighed. "We clearly need intel. Set up your meeting, Tobias."

The attack ship left the *Sabre*'s bay, rising slowly into the air. The pilot oriented the little craft towards the south, gently leaving the landed warships behind as it crossed the river. Huge Cretaceous crocodiles on the banks forewent their sunbathing, plunging back into its quick-moving waters to escape the noise.

Within moments, the fighter alighted softly within the *New World*'s palisaded enclosure.

Captain Meritus and Hiro Nassaki stood on the recently turned earth, just outside the Pod's pedestrian hatch. With them was Major White, looking a little more refreshed, Corporal Thomas and a small detachment of decidedly '*New World* only' troops.

Once the ship's engines had powered down, the security personnel ringed the three officers as the whole group approached the newcomers with caution.

In answer, a second squad of six soldiers, all in battledress, disembarked from the enemy craft to take up positions around it. One of their NCOs said something they did not quite catch and two officers strode from the boarding hatch to stand roughly ten metres in front of their ship.

As the groups closed, Hartmann nodded in greeting. "Meritus."

"Hartmann, Franke," returned Meritus.

Franke stared at him coolly, offering no acknowledgement.

Meritus gestured to his companions. "This is Major Ford White, US Army and this, as I'm sure you already know, is Lieutenant Hiro Nassaki, the *New World*'s chief engineer."

"Gentlemen," said Hartmann, congenially. "I am Captain Aurick Hartmann, commander of the *Sabre* and this is Captain Emilia Franke, commander of the *Heydrich*."

"Captain, Captain," answered White, politely.

Hiro merely stared balefully at the pair.

"Now, I'm afraid, Major," began Hartmann, "that I must ask to speak with Captain Meritus alone."

"No can do," replied White. "I'm sorry, Captain. I have my orders."

Hartmann scratched his neck unconsciously while he considered. "Very well, gentlemen. As you can see, I have stood my men off some little way. Will you not at least do the same? What we have to say is not for all ears."

White nodded for Thomas to retire a few metres. "OK, Captains, we're here. What did you wish to discuss?"

"Peace terms, Major, naturally."

"You're willing to surrender then?" asked White.

Hartmann threw his head back, laughing. "Hardly, Major. But I would be willing to accept yours, should you wish to tender it?"

White gave his customary lopsided grin. "Sorry, I never surrender on a Friday, it upsets the whole weekend."

"*Enough!*" snapped Franke, speaking for the first time. "We are not here to listen to your ridiculous attempts at humour."

Hartmann sighed. "I'm afraid my impatient colleague has a point, gentlemen. The situation as we see it is like this: you have our *ex*-leader, we have some of your personnel."

White wondered at '*some* of your personnel' but did not interrupt.

"You have *Factory Pod 4* – for now – but we have the military might. Stalemate. Did I miss anything?"

"Only what you were about to offer," quipped Meritus.

Hartmann laughed again. "Ah, Tobias, but I have missed you. You would be welcome back into the family, you know."

"I rather doubt that, Aurick." Meritus winked at White. "The old man and his crazy granddaughter would rather burn me at the stake than take me back into the fold."

"Maybe, my friend," retorted Hartmann, "but *they* are not here."

"I can't see how we can make any kind of a deal with *you*," said Hiro, finding his voice at last.

Anger flashed across the face of Captain Franke and she gave him a piercing look. She opened her mouth to respond, but Hartmann put a hand lightly to her arm, forestalling any retort. "And why do you believe this to be so, Lieutenant Nassaki?" he asked.

"Let's just say the Nazis were never big on the idea of the family of humanity," Hiro replied scornfully.

White eyed him with caution. Knowing the engineer as he did, he dreaded what he might say next. Hiro was not the man he would have chosen for this embassy, but Hartmann had been insistent. *I wonder why?* he thought.

Hartmann nodded, as if in agreement. "I understand, young man. You think that we're monsters, out to kill all who do not comply with our 'ideals of the master race'."

Hiro crossed his arms. "Pretty much. I also think you're all—" he switched to Japanese.

White thought it was probably for the best, but Hartmann surprised everyone, Hiro most of all, by replying – also in Japanese.

"You look agog, my young friend. You see, I learned a little of your tongue from one of my crewmen, also an engineer. He lives a very full life within our new civilisation. Perhaps, if you will not listen to me, you may be persuaded by him?"

He turned and nodded to the sergeant who had spoken earlier. She saluted and ran into the ship. Within moments, she returned with another.

By his movements, it appeared to be a man, but head down, his face was obscured by the peak of a cap.

He stood beside Hartmann, who gestured for the newcomer to introduce himself. Removing his cap, he lifted a smiling face towards Hiro.

The chief's knees buckled instantly.

White moved to catch him before he collapsed. "Hiro, what is it?" he asked, urgently.

The chief managed to lift his head, staring dumbly, but when the stranger spoke, White almost dropped him in shock.

"Hello, brother," the man greeted warmly. "It's been a while."

"Ah," Meritus confessed, absently, "now I remember."

Chapter 8 | Trial By Water

The forest light dimmed as afternoon wore on. Terrifying shadows replaced the terrifying movements of mottled sunlight through the underbrush.

Lemelisk had revived once more but appeared very much the worse for wear. His violent ordeal with the raptors had weakened him. Subsequent blood loss and the further effects of two stun grenade blasts added significantly to his troubles. Indirectly, this added to the group's troubles too. They may have been ravenously hungry, but the scent and occasional drop of blood from Lemelisk's wounds left plenty of breadcrumbs for their nemesis to follow.

This deadly game of hide and seek had pressed them hard all through the day. Rose gave Lemelisk a wary appraisal. *We need something to eat or he's not going to make it,* she reasoned, unable to help the next thought which followed, albeit naturally, on its heels. *If he collapses, that thing will catch him and just maybe lose interest in us.*

She reproved herself silently, mindful that 'good people' really should not think such things. Also, in this new life, she recognised those kinds of self-serving notions as part of her past – a place she did not intend to revisit.

This thought brought forth a weary sigh. Being *better* was hard sometimes. Wiping sweat from her brow, she caught a whiff from her own armpit and wrinkled her nose. What *would* month-ago-Rose have made of her – that she was some sort of disgusting swamp creature, probably. She chuckled softly.

Bond noticed. He also noticed that, even in her tattered and filthy condition, she was a lovely looking girl. Perhaps nature's earthiness even polished this gem, in a way that all the make-up and 'product' in the world of man never could. His thoughts returned to Lemelisk and his threatening attitude towards the girl as he too considered the question of whether they could afford to lose him.

"Why do you laugh, Rose?" he asked at last.

"Just thinking what a fright I must look. It would have mortified me a few weeks ago – doesn't seem so important now—" She broke off suddenly and darted into the brush. "Hey, Del. Look!"

Bond stepped after her, following her gaze. They were at the edge of a long, narrow plain that sloped gently downwards to the west. Set within the low-lying valley, a river wended its way in from the north, widening to a bow as it turned due east. It was a beautiful scene, but Rose's attention was focused just in front of them.

At the edge of the treeline, benefitting from the extra sunlight, were what appeared to be fruit-bearing plants.

Bond's eyes widened greedily. "Could we eat those?" he asked.

Rose shrugged. "I know we're starving, but I think we should be careful. I read in Tim's notes that flowering plants and those bearing fruit appeared about twenty-five million years before this time. We've seen plenty of flowering plants, with it being spring and all, but this is the first time I've seen anything resembling fruit."

"Can we expect normal seasons in this time?" asked Bond.

"The Cretaceous is strongly seasoned, according to what I've read. We'll see, I suppose." Rose pointed at what they very much hoped would be their first meal in nearly a day. "Also, according to Tim's notes, I believe these are actually what's known as *false-fruit*, but these fleshy and prettily coloured seed cases may still be edible by certain animals."

Bond raised an eyebrow. "Would that include us?"

Rose held out her hands, palms up – it was anyone's guess – so Bond turned to Lemelisk, bringing up their rear. "Sargo, how would you like a bite to eat?"

"Yes, I do need food. Have you found some?"

Bond winked at Rose. "We certainly have. Here, try one of these…"

Lemelisk took the highly modified pinecones, which looked like purple, red and green berries, and popped one in his mouth.

"Wait!" Rose called out, scowling at Bond. "We don't know if they're edible."

Lemelisk chewed and spat out the red berry disgustedly. "I would say the red ones are not. Yuck, that was bitter!"

Unwilling to accept defeat, he tried a green one. He chewed again. His faced screwed up in horror as he spat that one out too.

Bond cracked a smile. "Good, was it?"

"A bit tart," Lemelisk wheezed, skewering him with a glare. "Feel free to have a go!"

"Certainly, I'll just see how you get on with the purple ones first – you're doing so well."

Lemelisk scowled, muttering in what sounded like Russian. He sniffed the last berry, showing more caution this time. He took small a bite from it. It was about the size of a grape and as he bit, juice ran over his lip. He chewed this one gingerly. After a moment, his expression cleared and he placed the remainder of the cone into his mouth, chewing thoughtfully.

"Well?" asked Bond, impatiently.

"Give me chance. I'm tasting it," replied Lemelisk tetchily.

Bond raised his eyes to the heavens. "For the love of God, Sargo, we're not after a gastronomic review! Are the damned things edible or not?"

"Well, I haven't gone into anaphylactic shock yet, so I *assume* they're OK!" snarled Lemelisk.

"Look, it was a simple questio—"

A roar from the forest behind silenced them both.

"Shut up, you two!" hissed Rose. "He's found us again. Quick, grab some purple *whatever-they-ares* and let's get out of here!"

They set off at a quick jog down towards the river, skirting the forest's edge to benefit from the limited security the trees offered. A crashing behind them made them turn. It was indeed the Ekrixinatosaurus that had tracked them most of the day. Not standing around to wonder at the creature's tenacity, the trio immediately dove back among the foliage.

They were still about half a mile from the river. Returning to the forest impeded their progress significantly, but there was simply no way they would have survived a running race to the shore. If they made it, such a large body of moving water would scatter their scent completely and finally shake the bloodhound on their tail – unless the animal saw them crossing.

Doggedly they moved between the trees, smashing noisily through the brush. Every now and then they stopped, listening for signs of pursuit. On one of these occasions they heard the dinosaur crash back into the forest; clearly it had found the point where they dove for cover.

"I'm naming him 'Custard'," Rose announced quietly.

Bond stared as if she were mad. "*Custard?*" he whispered.

Rose nodded shakily. "Then I won't be so afraid of him."

Bond's eyes softened and he smiled, encouragingly. "Custard it is, then. At least I can pronounce it! Come on, we should try another hop."

In their bid to escape, they had found themselves turned around many times throughout the course of the day, with only the position of the sun to guide them. After being forced to leave the trail behind, losing their way to the enemy encampment became a constant concern, but one naturally driven back by the more pressing fear of the reaper at their heels. Being chased through the forest by a one-and-a-half-ton predator will drive out most things, but their geographical worries were suddenly assuaged.

Out on the plain, running more or less parallel to the treeline, were several vehicle tracks. As the trio dashed between the trunks, ducking low branches, the tracks came into view here and there, given away by flattened ferns. All of them led down towards the river.

Things are looking up, Rose dared to hope. Another roar came from behind, this one much closer. *Hmm...*

The river was close now. "Can you swim?" Rose asked.

Bond, right behind her, replied, "What? Erm... I *think* so."

"Great."

They suddenly emerged into dazzling late afternoon sun, just fifty metres from the river's northern shore, as it turned east. The heavy flow from the recent storms had mostly drained from the hills now, and where it widened, the river was stony and shallow. Lemelisk was nowhere to be seen.

They looked at one another. Bond shrugged. "I haven't heard any screams," he said.

A few nail-biting seconds later, Lemelisk burst from the trees shouting, "RUN, *RUN!*"

They ran, splashing haphazardly into the shallows. To their surprise, the shallows remained shallow way out into the middle of the flow. Turning to check for Custard, Rose could see no sign of him, but she could see where all the vehicle tracks joined to descend the bank into the river.

They had found a ford.

Varying between shin and thigh deep, the freezing cold water passed unhurriedly over the treacherous, stony bed. It slowed them tremendously, while the overall shallowness deprived them of any way to hide.

They lurched and slipped, beginning to lose hope. "Oh, *this* was a great idea!" snapped Bond, acerbically.

"No, wait!" cried Lemelisk, stopping midstream. "Look! He's not following. Ha! He's afraid of the water!"

"Is he?" asked Rose. "Or is he afraid of what's in the water?"

"Oh, why did you have to say that?" asked Bond, shaking his head despairingly.

Custard was indeed behaving strangely. He had them, surely, but seemed content to stalk along the bank, stopping periodically to sniff the air.

"I don't think he's afraid of water," said Rose, quietly voicing her darkest thoughts. "I think he's sensing danger."

"*I* think we should go," supplemented Bond. "If Custard's scared, I don't want to embarrass myself this far from a toilet."

Rose nodded, not taking her eyes from the Ekrixinatosaurus. "Agreed."

Lemelisk seemed rooted to the spot.

"What is it?" Bond called across.

The stricken man slowly raised his arm to point upstream to where the waters turned north, narrowing and deepening significantly.

Rose turned slowly and then she saw it. Terror tore the breath from her lungs as she breathed the name, "*Oxalaia.*"

Bond was shaking. "W-what the hell is *that?* Sh-shall we call him 'Rhubarb'?" he quavered, as a vast sail rose out of the water. The creature swam strongly, using the sideways motion of its tail like a crocodile.

The Ekrixinatosaurus, lately known as Custard, sensed he was about to be deprived of a kill, and bellowed his frustration. Oxalaia was a beast of a different scale altogether. Possibly the biggest carnivorous dinosaur species in Cretaceous Patagonia, it was unmoved by the diminutive intruder, snapping terrier-like from the bank.

Rose was shaking so badly now, that her teeth were chattering. Impotent tears ran down her cheeks. "C-Commander G-Gleeson told me about these, when he c-came to blow up the enemy b-battleship."

Bond took a step forwards and placed a gentle arm about her shoulders. "I'm sorry," he said simply. A moment later, her words penetrated his own fear and he asked, "*These?*"

Rose had no chance to reply. A huge, dry-throated roar split the air from behind them and they jerked around, hanging on to one another instinctively.

Bond nodded stoically. "At last, final and indisputable proof that it doesn't matter how bad things get, they can *always* get worse."

Now behind Rose and Bond, Custard backed further up the bank, away from the river, the arch nemesis suddenly no more than a sparrow at a cockfight. Oxalaia rose from the water to stand obscenely tall in the shallows to their right, while on the opposite bank there now stood a magnificent adult bull Mapusaurus – fifteen metres nose to tail, and more than seven tons of killing machine in his prime. This was by far the largest Mapusaur they had seen yet, and the fact that he blocked the humans' last pathetic hope of flight was not lost on them.

After their shocking meeting, Hiro and Meritus had once again locked themselves away aboard the *New World*, staying as far from everyone as possible during their walk through the Pod.

They made straight for the bridge to bring Douglas up to speed. Douglas, Singh and Georgio tried to prop up their chief engineer emotionally, all stating the obvious, that it was a miracle to find Aito alive, let alone here.

It sounded empty, even to them. The best Douglas could do was order Hiro to get some rest.

Naturally, everyone was overjoyed that Hiro's long-presumed-dead brother had been magically restored to them, but there was a dark undercurrent: Where had he been? What had he been doing? Why had he allowed his family to grieve so?

As Douglas understood it, Hiro's father had practically died of a broken heart after his loss. The situation was a mess, and not knowing where all the pieces would land made him nervous. Were that not enough, he now had to force another Christian into the arena, to face the lion.

"We're very grateful to you for this, Klaus," he said. "Ah'd shake you by the hand, but you know how it is."

Dr Klaus Fischer acknowledged Douglas' comment with a smile. "I'll do my best, Captain. I suppose I should get to work."

Douglas nodded. "Sarge, take Dr Fischer down to the brig, please."

"Yes, sir. Follow me, please, sir."

Douglas escorted the two men from his bridge and stood a while in the corridor as he watched them go, concern etching deep lines into his face. "Ah don't like bringing anyone aboard with the risk of this virus about. And that's without what we're asking of the man."

"I understand, James," said Meritus, appearing at his shoulder, "but what choice did we have? Our interrogation was a washout. We couldn't even get anything out of the girl."

"Hmm," agreed Douglas. "But the fact that we're bringing Fischer's wife aboard tomorrow, too, makes things even worse. It's brave of them to work with us like this. We can't even offer them any protection because it has to look like they were aboard all along. Ah fear for them."

Fischer walked into the brig cautiously, looking around as if shocked by where he was. Fortunately, little acting skill was required. The idea of sentencing himself to spend the night in a cell next to a mass murderer, on what was effectively a plague ship, was all the motivation he needed.

Schultz eyed him curiously.

"You'll stay here until we can find a better place for you," The Sarge stated roughly, all courtesy gone. "Get in."

As soon as Fischer crossed the threshold, the cell door slammed and locked behind him. A shiver ran down his spine. He may have agreed to this, but now he was here, he could hardly believe it was happening. He steeled himself and turned to face the prisoner in the next cell.

They stared at one another and Fischer knew immediately that he was out of his depth. Evil emanated from the man in waves. *This must be what it felt like to stand next to Himmler or Hitler himself,* he thought. His flesh crawled. Schultz was not just a killer, he was the money behind some of the world's worst terrorist organisations and without doubt, the architect of some of their worst atrocities too, whether *they* realised it or not. Fischer was a clever man, a doctor of microbiology. No fools made it onto the Mars Mission science team. It was a 'merit only' ticket, selected from the 22nd century's finest. Yet the man next to him was *the* leading exponent of organised crime, and all that went along with it, in a world of nearly fifty billion souls.

Fischer cleared his throat. "You're Heinrich Schultz?" He spoke in German. "It's a pity we had to meet under such *unfortunate* circumstances."

"And you are…?" the old man replied.

"My name is Dr Klaus Fischer."

Schultz was tall and still straight-backed, despite his years. Nevertheless, he tilted his head back slightly, the better to look down even further as he menaced his new companion. His eyes were of the starkest light grey and the coldest Fischer had ever seen. When he spoke again, there was an air of disapproval in his voice that made the microbiologist quake.

"*Yes*, I've heard of you. You were one of the last-minute replacements on the mission, I believe. One of the people whose appointment impinged upon my plans to take over this ship.

"And now you are here to spy on me, of course. Why else would they put a German national in here? If you are hoping to win me over with charming conversation about the Fatherland, Doctor, or that I will talk in my sleep, you will be sadly disabused."

Fischer quailed again at the force of the man's malignant stare. Forcing himself to stand firm, he replied, "Were I informed of your plans, things may have been different, perhaps."

Schultz's eyes narrowed. "What's this?"

"You've heard my name, *Herr* Schultz, but do you know who I *am?*"

After a long pause, Fischer thought he would have to press the point home, but Schultz surprised him by suddenly asking, "Why don't you tell me?"

"Nice knowing you!" shouted Lemelisk, wading for the deeper water downstream, and away from the three giants penning them in.

"Wish I could say the same!" Bond retorted. "*Damn* the man!" He tried to manoeuvre Rose behind him, but there was really nothing he could do. "Any preference on a direction?" he asked. He could feel Rose shaking with terror – they were almost certainly about to die, horribly.

She turned to him. "You're really not such a b-bad guy," she said through chattering teeth.

He smiled and was about to return the compliment when her expression changed. "What is it?"

"Just an idea," she said. "It's believed that large predators would attempt to avoid direct confrontation with one another where possible."

"OK. And?" asked Bond, hopefully.

"Well, *this* may just be the safest place to stand – temporarily, at least. Let them worry about each other. Running might just draw attention to us."

He looked at the massive creatures that bayed for their blood. "Oh. I was hoping for a little more than that," he admitted, disappointedly.

Oxalaia approached them, but as Rose had hoped, the giant's attention was fully on the Mapusaurus stepping into the river. The two males squared up to one another, jaws open wide, posturing like a couple of WWF superstars pouting for the cameras.

Bond took Rose's hand and backed them away, slowly slipping into deeper water. The Ekrixinatosaurus watched them keenly, keeping pace from the safety of the opposite bank.

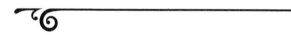

Hiro had not honestly expected to rest and when he lay down his mind was instantly overwhelmed by confusion and pain, but against all expectation he soon drifted into a dreamless sleep; his body simply shutting down for a few hours while his subconscious carried out repairs.

He was so deep under, that it took several beats on his door and rings of the chime to rouse him. Stepping carefully across the floor, avoiding the myriad half-finished electrical projects strewn about – he had been caught out like that whilst in a quasi-wakeful state before – he made his way to the door.

The last time Georgio Baccini had called on him like this, he had dashed in, charged with excitement after speaking with the spirit of his dead brother. This time, Georgio looked about how Hiro felt.

He invited his friend in with a nod. Now it was he who had spoken with a brother believed dead. If this was irony, it certainly left him overwrought.

Both men sat heavily at the billet's small dining table. "How are you?" asked Georgio.

Hiro was not sure how to answer that. How *was* he? Elbows on the table, he put his head in his hands, rubbing his face and eyes to revive himself. Eventually, he managed, "Overjoyed, betrayed, confused, ashamed…"

"Oh?" Georgio cocked a wry eyebrow. "Well, it's good that you're covering all the bases."

Hiro snorted gently. "I don't know what to make of it. I'm not sure I even truly believe it. Is it possible this is all some sort of trick?"

Georgio nodded thoughtfully. After a moment's consideration, he announced, "My mind's clay – we need coffee!"

Hiro nodded. "Make it a strong one, please."

Presently, Georgio returned with two steaming mugs.

"Did you make it strong?" asked Hiro.

"I'd say test it by seeing if your spoon stands up on its own, but I think it's already dissolved."

"Perfect." Hiro chuckled, taking a pull at his coffee. He winced, closing one eye altogether. The coffee was *strong*.

After a few coughs, he tried again, adjusting to the chemical shock. Georgio had not touched his own drink yet, but merely stared into it. Hiro suddenly realised how hard this was on the young Italian. Georgio would surely give anything to have his brother returned to him, but it was impossible. Hiro had been granted the greatest gift he could have imagined and all he could be sure of was that he didn't know how he felt about it. He was suddenly ashamed, not for his brother's sake this time, but for his own.

"How are *you*, Georgie?" he asked.

His subordinate looked up in surprise. "*Me?*"

Hiro nodded. "The elephant in the room might not be trumpeting, but we still know he's here, right? I would give anything to have Mario back too, my friend. And now I have my own brother here and I don't know how to relate to the situation – or him. I'm sorry, Georgie. I appreciate how ungrateful this must seem."

The Italian reached across the table to squeeze his friend's arm. "You've got nothing to apologise for, Hiro. Under the circumstances, I can't deny feeling Mario's loss even deeper than usual, but that's a separate issue. I'm *so* happy for you. Aito's back and you've a second chance!"

Hiro smiled, a warm smile this time. "Thanks, Georgie. You're a real friend. I know deep down that this is a miracle, but I'm in shock. He's back, but *is* he back? Is he really a Nazi sympathiser or just a clever survivor? Will I ever be able to trust him or truly bring him home? Relate to him, even?"

"We can't know any of that for sure just yet, Hiro. So don't waste energy on it. Even if your worst suspicions about Aito are confirmed, he's alive. *Alive!* That means there's hope. It means that change can happen, the future is no longer written."

"That's a loaded term to use around here!"

Georgio grinned. "Well, if the future *is* going to get messed up, I suggest we mess it up for the better!"

Hiro frowned slightly. "What do you mean?"

Georgio leaned forward conspiratorially. "You're Japanese, I'm Italian, but if the Schultzes had any delusions about resurrecting the Axis powers, I say we crash that party, drink their booze and steal their stereo! I might even pee in their pool!"

He raised his mug.

Hiro grinned and clinked. "Agreed."

"*Cheers!*" they said together.

"Let me get this right. My great, great, great, great, great, great, great, *great*-grandfather, I am sure you *will* have heard of, *Herr* Schultz."

Schultz scrutinised Fischer closely. "Go on, Doctor."

"His name was Eugen Fischer, professor of medicine, anthropology, and eugenics, *and*, as you will certainly be aware, a prominent member of the Nazi party. You will have a certain familiarity with his seminal work on eugenics, yes? Hitler himself referenced my ancestor's ideas and research before publishing the Nuremberg Laws of 1935.

"*Herr* Schultz, not wishing to slight your achievements or your lineage, I think that even *you* will not be disdainful of *my* family's credentials from those critical years, almost two centuries ago for us."

Schultz stared at Fischer, not his usual, surgical stare, dissecting the man's thoughts. This was a wide-eyed stare of wonder, but the moment passed quickly, his eyes narrowing once more with suspicion. "Fine words, *Herr* Doctor, but what proof do you offer to substantiate them?"

Fischer shrugged. "I offer none. My conduct alone surely provides you with proof that you can trust me."

"Explain."

"I manufactured a situation where I would be arrested and placed in a cell next to you. My own wife carried out the intellectual theft which led me here. It was also she who disabled the cameras and listening devices within this brig. I have some important information for you, so it was vital we were left alone for a while. She will be arrested soon, for her part. I will be exonerated and leave her to languish here, for now. She, and I, make this sacrifice for you."

"Why?" asked Schultz, shrewdly. "You never offered assistance to my granddaughter when she could have made use of it."

"She never made us part of her plans – we knew nothing of her mission or your overall strategy for repopulating this ancient world with humans from *preferred* stock." That last comment cost Fischer. He hated the principles upon which the Nuremberg Laws were founded, but had sworn to do his best here.

"We have little time, *Herr* Schultz. I have something for you and I'm hoping you have something for me…"

Bond and Rose swam with the strengthening current as the river deepened and narrowed downstream, eventually fighting their way to the southern bank. Rose grabbed a handful of reeds and reached out for her companion as he floated by. As it turned out, Bond could swim, just not particularly well.

Clawing their way through the reeds, they gained the bank beyond. The cover was useful. They could see and clearly hear the aggressive posturing still taking place a hundred metres upstream, but there was no sign of Lemelisk. More worryingly, Custard seemed to have vanished too.

The clearing around the ford offered little cover between them and the trackway west that disappeared into the forest.

"What do you think?" panted Bond. "Make a run for it and hope those monsters don't see us?"

Rose considered. "It's a gamble." She was so glad she had studied the material Tim had left her. Even so, palaeontology was a far cry from zoology in the real world. "We're just a mouthful to such apex predators. I don't know if they'll be particularly interested in us while they're focused on each other. On the other hand, whoever loses this 'wee-weeing contest' may take a snap at us just to offset their embarrassment!"

"You're not filling me with confidence, young lady."

Rose frowned apologetically. "No. Me neither. Well, we can't stay here all day. Shall we?"

Bond offered his hand and she shook it. "Let's give it a go," he said.

They crawled through the reeds that climbed the bank, stopping dead when a giant snake reared to tower above them. Swaying, its jaws parted wide in threat.

This creature was nothing like a python. Rose realised that straight away as the threat of imminent death once more sharpened her observational awareness to a scalpel's edge. Her mind raced as she noticed the vestigial remains of forelimbs and teeth that, to the untrained eye, looked more 'dinosaur' than 'snake'. Her mind was working so fast now that, having made all these observations, Rose found she even had a few nanoseconds left over – she filled them with screaming.

From the shallows of the ford upstream, Rose's cries were answered by a huge, throaty double-roar from the challengers as they stopped circling and lunged for one another.

The Oxalaia had possessed this spot for some time and for good reason. Everyone crossed the river at this point, and many slipped or got into trouble while doing so. The wily old spinosaurid merely had to wait and lunge, in true crocodilian style, whenever food perambulated by. His vast size was usually enough to send any competition fleeing for safer feeding grounds, but the Mapusaurus was less easily impressed. He was at least equal in overall proportions to the Oxalaia, but his head and jaws, the business end of any predator, were actually somewhat larger.

They clashed. The thud of muscle, bone and ivory, driven by tons of mass on either side, met with a meaty thump and clack which could be felt all the way over in the reeds.

The snake certainly felt it. Poised well above the terrified man and girl, ready to strike, the sounds of ferocity from the nearby giants seemed to alarm the creature, for it dipped violently. The terrifying motion caused it to slip past Rose, barely missing her. As the massive body writhed from side to side, it swept Bond's legs from under him. He cried out, sure he was done for, but with a swish of heavy reeds, the monster was gone.

Almost hyperventilating, Bond let out a wordless roar of panic mixed with relief, mixed with more panic. "Can we p-p-p-please go now?"

Rose helped him to his feet. "I think I've had a wee," she admitted, miserably.

Finding his wits, Bond grabbed her hand. "Let's get the hell out of here!"

They ran.

Mapusaurus had the lower jaw of Oxalaia in his own jaws. The shark-teeth of the carcharodontosaur gouged angry furrows in the spinosaurid's flesh while it bellowed in rage and pain. Oxalaia's power was in the mandibles, but nevertheless, he repeatedly dropped his top jaw like a deadweight. The maxilla, armed with crooked crocodilian teeth, acted like a saw as both animals struggled and thrashed for advantage. Litres of blood streamed into the river as the protagonists bled from horrific wounds to their faces and mouths. The scent of blood in the water would usually have drawn every aquatic predator for a mile in either direction, but none dared get caught up in this titanic struggle.

The dinosaurs broke apart suddenly, the Mapusaurus' head bobbing as he sought new weaknesses.

Oxalaia stood with jaws yawning wide in threat, blood dripping from his teeth, chest heaving.

A group of tiny pterosaurs saw an opportunity and swooped in to clean the gore from his large crocodilian teeth and gums. They shared a symbiotic arrangement that benefited both species, but their timing was lousy. After a few moments' recovery, Oxalaia's head lifted to roar at the sky, snapping at his diminutive dentists in agitation. Some of them vanished into the gaping maw, while others learned the importance of scheduling.

This distraction created just the opening the mighty Mapusaurus had been waiting for. He snapped instinctually. Coming from below, the massive jaws snapped around the spinosaurid's neck, terrible serrated teeth slicing flesh like a monstrous bear trap. His lunge was so forceful that he slipped on the wet stones.

Sensing a last chance, Oxalaia twisted his head and whole body at the same instant, in a desperate attempt to shake the Mapusaurus' grip.

Already off balance, Mapusaurus struggled in a sideways, crabbing dance to regain a footing. Fortunately, this motion delivered him into water deep enough to support his vast weight, preventing his ribcage from being smashed by the rocks below. He went down with a deafening slap, displacing tons of water in an instant as he disappeared into a whirlpool of white water and voluminous air bubbles.

In moments, the beast resurfaced, roaring in fury. Were these human combatants, the anger would be ascribed to the embarrassment of being thrown from the ring. However, the mighty Mapusaurus knew only that any sudden disadvantage could mean death – his blush, merely the blood of injury.

Oxalaia was equally possessed of a hunter's cunning and instantly recognised a fresh opportunity; this time to bring the fight into *his* domain. Diving into the deeper water, he lunged towards an adversary fashioned by nature for terrestrial living. For Oxalaia, with his crocodilian lifestyle, it was the perfect killing ground. It was certainly no place for any land animal caught out of its habitat.

Mapusaurus knew this; animals such as he did not live to reach such an age and size by being stupid. With a hugely powerful flick of the tail and massive, taloned claws scrabbling for purchase on the rocky bed, he gave all to drive himself back towards the shallows. With the river flowing strongly around his knees, a depth still well over a man's head, he was back on a secure footing and roaring defiance once more.

Similarly, Oxalaia, also a veteran survivor, knew when advantage was lost. He submerged deeper, to swim out of the Mapusaurus' reach.

Both animals were hurt, but neither critically so, and they both wanted this prime spot as their personal larder. Nature rarely endorses gifting and sharing, and almost never between predatory species, so Oxalaia resurfaced to face his enemy once more.

He stood near the northern shore of the ford, with Mapusaurus near the south, and with the gameboard reset, the dinosaurs roared their threats at one another. Claws grasping, teeth gnashing, their demonstrative gestures escalated as negotiations continued via the sign language of violence – appearances had to be maintained, recovery time purchased.

During the ruckus and confusion, the fleeing humans gained the treeline and rushed down the track. It was a thoroughfare created several days ago by heavy vehicles smashing through the forest, but it was hardly a road. The going was rough, and their waterlogged clothes made them clumsy. Bond tripped over a root, striking his head hard against a trunk as he went down.

Rose bent to help, realising with dismay that he had knocked himself unconscious. She dragged him into the relative cover of the trees, but before she could do anything further, she was snatched away from behind.

She screamed and her scream was rewarded with unpleasant laughter.

"Who is it?" she cried out.

Lemelisk spun her round to face him, holding tightly on to her arm. "There's nothing like a good blood sport to get the heart pumping again, is there?" he asked with a maniacal glint in his eye.

"Er... you look better," she noted cautiously. "Quick, help me with Bond."

He barked another laugh. "We don't need him, he's past it. We're young and it's good to be alive, pretty girl."

Rose did not like where this was going at all. Managing to jerk-twist her arm out of his grasp, she turned and ran, hearing his laughter follow.

Bond groaned but did not move.

Lemelisk left him where he lay to sprint after his quarry. He really had never felt more alive and decided that this enthusiasm should be taken out on someone.

Rose ran for all she was worth, but she was exhausted, starving and terrified, her wet clothes weighing her down.

Lemelisk was fired by endorphins and driven by the basest and most primitive urges. He quickly closed, taking her to the ground in a rugby tackle. Turning the girl over, he stood, bringing her back to her feet, securing both wrists this time. He leered horribly. "Why fight it, my pretty?"

Rose looked around him, hoping to see Bond, but they had turned a corner in the trail and there was no sign of him. In desperation, she raised her knee hard into the attacker's groin.

Lemelisk was a highly trained fighter and he saw the attack in her eyes before she even moved. He dropped his right hand to block before she could connect. He laughed again. "Now, now, don't bruise the goods, pretty girl, eh? Let's see what else you've got for me." He grabbed for her again, tearing her shirt.

Rose was frantic, the terror of the last few minutes threatening to overwhelm her completely. She would rather have fallen to the dinosaurs, in their honest predation to stay alive, than become a victim of this monster. In one last-ditch effort, she pulled away from him with everything she had left. She broke his grip, but as she moved backwards, she lost her footing and fell flat on her back.

He laughed raucously. "Better! That's the idea—"

Rose never found out what foul innuendo was to come next because the words stopped when he noticed her staring, not at him, but over his shoulder.

An even more primitive instinct overtook him instantly. The base code of all life – survival. He spun round, light-footed as any fighter, but within a fraction of a second, he knew the fight was over and he had lost.

His scream took on a mid-range, breathy quality as his head disappeared into the wide-open maw of Ekrixinatosaurus. The teeth met with a clack and the dinosaur, victorious at last, snapped its head back, swallowing Lemelisk's still living head whole.

His very dead body fell backwards[7], to land between Rose's legs. Blood sprayed from his severed neck, covering her from face down to crotch in gore.

She screamed.

Custard grinned toothily at her as it took a step forward, pinning Lemelisk's torso to the ground with one large, three-toed and taloned foot. Rose screamed again and the creature looked down, fixing her clearly with its binocular stare while tilting its head in puzzlement. Rose's terror spiked as the head ducked quickly, grabbing one of Lemelisk's legs. The dinosaur tore the limb from the body as easily as if it were a drumstick on a buffet tray and began to chew enthusiastically. The noise of cracking bones, along with the stench of raw meat and bowel, made Rose heave.

She was so terrified now, that her mind had completely closed down. Her body was on full autopilot as she scrambled backwards awkwardly on hands and buttocks, kicking with her feet. After crawling a few metres, she somehow got up off the floor and ran. The petrified young woman only made another five or six metres before she was grabbed for a third time and pulled into the trees.

Her piercing scream ended abruptly as Bond slapped his hand across her mouth.

Her eyes were so full of terror that it took long moments before she realised who it was and what was happening. Eventually, she nodded that she was back with him and tried to control her ragged breathing.

She was covered in blood and worse; it was all over her face, it was in her hair, even in her eyes and ears. Bond had not the heart to ask if she was OK.

---

[7]   Ahem, headlong.

They could still hear the sloppy, crunchy evidence of Custard's culinary excitement, but listening carefully, they could also make out another sound, just on the edge of hearing.

Even the sounds of battle from the river seemed to have stilled and Bond fancied he heard the thumping of very heavy bipedal footsteps running away. What was happening? Then two *crack-booms* rolled out across the valley, one straight after the other.

"Oh, for the love of God, what now?" he whispered.

Ekrixinatosaurus grabbed what was left of Lemelisk and sloped off into the forest to enjoy the rest of his meal in peace. This place was just too damned noisy.

The rumbling sound resolved into a low moan, constantly rising and falling in pitch. At last, the penny dropped, and Bond realised what he was hearing.

Dragging Rose after him, he stepped out into the middle of the track as an armoured vehicle rounded the corner at some speed. The noise and smell of the powerful diesel engine was like food and drink to the survivors. At that moment, neither cared whose side had found them, only that they had been found.

The vehicle's brakes squeaked noisily as it rocked to a halt in front of them – probably a condition brought on by the river crossing. A hatch opened in its roof and another blonde woman climbed out to sit on the small turret which housed two fifty-calibre machine guns.

"Heidi, thank God!" Bond exclaimed in relief.

She stared down at them, a wry smile twisting her lip as she took in their condition.

"Bond. So it was you. I thought as much." She frowned. "Is that Miss Miller with you? Hiding underneath all that, oh dear, is that blood? When we heard two people had escaped from the *New World*, we did not expect Dr Miller's daughter to be one of them. Well done, Derek. She may provide us with useful leverage."

Bond twitched at the use of his given name but was in no mood to correct his saviour right now.

Heidi continued, "I expected to find you with Sargo Lemelisk. He is not with you?"

Bond shrugged. "In a way, he is."

"What is your meaning?" she asked peremptorily.

He pointed down at the bloody stain and tattered scraps left behind after the dinosaur's retreat. "Here he is. He's had something of a bad day, I'm afraid – and rather too much custard," he whispered for Rose's benefit.

"Hmm...?" queried Heidi, leaning forward to look over the front of the vehicle. "Oh, I see. How careless of him." She accepted Bond's explanation without question. "Well, this promises to be a remarkably interesting debriefing. I assume you will not refuse a ride back to camp?"

"What is it you have that you think I might want?" asked Heinrich Schultz. He eyed Fischer warily, clearly distrustful of the man, not to mention this sudden change in his fortunes.

"Oh, I don't think you *might* want this information, *mein Herr*. I *know* you will. You see, my dear wife has procured the backdoor security codes for *Factory Pod 4* from Henry Burnstein Snr. Some of his largest enterprises played a major part in its construction, with many of the other components provided by the Nassaki Corporation – as you will no doubt be aware.

"As all the codes were changed a few weeks prior to the *New World*'s launch from Canaveral, along with many of the personnel, I assume that any accesses you acquired previously, via your extensive network, are now useless?"

Schultz stared impassively, neither confirming nor denying this.

Fischer continued, "Dagmar, that's my wife, made it look like *I* had stolen them, to throw suspicion onto me. That ensured my arrest so that we could have this conversation. She left just enough clues for the *New World* staff to deduce that I had been set up as a, what is the phrase the Americans use, a patsy? Anyway, they will find the clues before long."

"And what do you require in trade for these precious gems you offer, Doctor?" asked Schultz.

Fischer studied him for a moment. "You have been betrayed. You can no longer trust *any* of your own people out there. Obviously, you know that, and it occurred to me that a man such as yourself would plan for exactly such a scenario and have contingencies in place for it."

Schultz remained motionless, again, giving nothing away.

"There are dozens of your people aboard *Factory Pod 4* already, under the command of Captain Meritus." Fischer stopped talking when Schultz twitched slightly. The movement was virtually unnoticeable, but he had been looking for it. *Good,* he thought, *we have a nerve at last!*

"They are traitors – of no use to me," stated Schultz, airily.

"That may not be strictly true," replied Fischer. "They follow Meritus, certainly, but only out of fear. Fear of you.

"After they lost your battleship, the *Last Word,* was it? After they lost it, they feared reprisal. Now, what would happen if they thought they could earn your forgiveness, perhaps even your gratitude?" Fischer knew he was throwing candles to light up a storm here. He doubted Schultz even knew what gratitude meant on anything more than an intellectual level. He just hoped his argument sounded plausible.

"What I'm saying is, your future plans rest with this Pod, with its equipment and its seed stocks, and most importantly, with its people – at least the people you deem worthy, after your coup. Everything your cause – and I hope by extension, my cause – requires is already here."

Schultz still said nothing, so Fischer threw down his last card. "Douglas wants to take this ship away from here. He wants to make a deal with Captains Hartmann and Franke, possibly give them some of the seeds we have, and make a new start on the other side of the planet.

"From what I've heard, Hartmann is ready to make such a deal, but Franke is a fanatic. She is more likely to blow us, the *New World* and the Pod, all to hell! So you see the problem."

"And you think that with security access to this Pod I could somehow effect this coup of yours, from inside this cell?" asked Schultz.

"If you really are destined to be the new *Führer,* then, yes, I believe you will find a way. If you are not, then we will either be killed by your crews outside or by the stupidity of this one. Their leaders seem as liberal with their incompetence and division as they are in their alleged beliefs!

"Either way, when Douglas launches…"

"We'll find out," Schultz completed, then fell silent for several minutes as he considered.

Fischer sat on his bunk, afraid to say anything more for fear of over-egging the pudding. He prayed he had judged it *just* right.

"Very well, Doctor," Schultz announced suddenly. "Give me the codes and I will give you something to assure our launch."

Fischer stood and walked to the bars between them. Screaming inside his head, he strove with all his might to keep his expression neutral as he reached his hand through the bars.

Schultz took it and shook it once. His touch was papery dry; it was like being caressed by an old library, in which every publication was obscene.

Fischer forced himself not to recoil. Instead, he used the jerkiness of his movements to click his heels and nod in salute. It felt disgusting, but seemed to pass muster.

Henry waited outside the door. Eventually it opened, revealing his younger sister in her nightie. Clarissa's eyes were puffy. They were always puffy these days. Ever since Tim had been taken and Patricia Norris shot, she seemed to spend most of her waking hours crying and her sleep battling nightmares.

"Hey, Clarrie. Can I come in?" he asked.

She nodded and padded barefoot back to her bed to sit down. He closed the door behind him and pulled the only seat in the room over to face her.

"How are you?" he asked gently.

She gave him a look of such sadness that it broke his heart. Failing to find an answer, she instead asked, "How are you?"

"Yeah," he agreed with chagrin. "Stoopid question, right?"

Clarrie shrugged. "Thanks for asking, anyway."

Henry nodded, a little distractedly. "There's something I need to tell you, but I need you to keep it secret, yeah?"

Suddenly intrigued, she moved to sit on the edge of the bed, closer to her brother. "What is it?" she whispered.

"Clarrie, I'm leaving."

Her eyes widened in horror and fear. "No!" she mouthed, but no sound left her lips.

"Look, it's gonna be alright." Henry moved to sit beside her on the bed, putting his arm around her shoulders. "I'm going after Rose, Tim too, if I can."

"I'm coming with you," she replied immediately.

"No, Clarrie."

"Yes! I don't care what happens or what our father thinks, I'm coming. I want to be with you and I need to find Timmy, Henry. Don't you understand?"

"I do, Clarrie, really I do. That's the point. I'm going to go see Jim Miller, Rose's dad. I know he'll be thinking along the same lines. I want to steal some gear and a couple o' dirt bikes and go find them."

She grabbed his shirt desperately. "You can't go without me!"

"I can't go *with* you – you have to understand. Hey, I totally get it, OK? I know how desperately you wanna do something to help Tim. I wanna help him too, sis, but I'll be able to move faster and easier if I'm not worried about you."

"That's not fair, Henry."

"No it isn't, Clarrie. I know that and I'm real sorry, but you want me to bring 'em both back, right?"

"Of course, but I *need* to go with you, Henry."

He took a deep breath; he knew this was going to be hard. "This is gonna be real tough on both of us. Do I wish you were coming with me? Sure I do, but it's gonna be dangerous, Clarrie, and taking you along would make it even tougher for me. I know you don't wanna hear that and that you hate me for saying it, but you must know it's true."

She looked down, her face crumpling as she began to sob. "I don't hate you, I love you. And I love Timmy. I should be there. I just wanna help."

"I know. I love you too, but the most important thing is getting those two back. I know you've got the heart of a lion, li'l sis, but you really would slow me down. Our best chance is for you to stay here and take care o' Ma. I doubt she'll be ready to understand my choice. Look, please don't think I wouldn't change this if I could."

"You really think you'll have more chance without me?"

"I'm sorry, but yeah." Henry felt terrible saying it, but it was true.

She nodded slowly. "I hate being young. If the only thing I can do to help is stay here, then OK."

He smiled at her. "You may be young, Clarrie, but that was a real mature decision. We both want what's best for the people we care about and I need this to succeed. If you were out there too, it would tear me in half. Knowing you're safe here will give me strength and courage – and I think I'm gonna need both." He studied her seriously for a moment but then softened. "Besides, if you go, who's gonna take care of Woodsey? He'll be pathetic on his own."

Tears streamed down Clarrie's face, but she giggled and squeezed her brother tightly.

"They want to meet with you again?" asked Douglas. It was getting late and he looked tired. They all did.

"Yeah, but just me this time. Before you answer, let me say that I understand your concerns. I just think this might be an opportunity. I've begun to care a lot about our alliance and about the people aboard this ship, James.

"I expected my life under the Schultz regime to be cold and harsh, but it *was* going to be *life*, or at least, survival – which made it better than the alternative. I didn't think I would actually get the chance to live again and be around people I care about. I suppose what I'm saying is, I want us to get out of this mess, together. I want this to work."

Douglas studied him closely. Eventually, he nodded.

Meritus stood just outside the palisade gates with Major White. "Are you armed?" asked White.

"I have my sidearm, Ford. It'll be OK, I don't expect any trouble."

It was almost dark. Meritus could not clearly see White's features, but was close enough to sense the major's misgivings from his very aura.

"*Right*," said White.

Meritus grinned. "Back in a few."

"Good luck."

This time Captains Hartmann and Franke had insisted that the meeting take place outside the compound and with only the three of them present. Douglas and Singh had both insisted that, at best, this was a trap to take Meritus away from them. Meritus was not so sure; he knew Hartmann fairly well and believed him to be an honourable soldier. He would never have put his life in Franke's hands alone, but always the rough with the smooth – that was life. Certainly, one could never know for sure, so he set his comm to record, just in case.

The solid black of their attack ship was still discernible against the general and deepening greys of the plain at night. As he neared his destination, a voice called out to him.

"That you, Tobias?" The voice was Hartmann's.

"Guilty," Meritus replied, jovially.

"Yes, you are. Lucky for me," said Franke.

The muzzle flash of a firearm blinded Meritus, the sudden unexpected bang making his ears ring. One of the two officers in front of him fell to the ground.

Jim Miller dragged his feet exhaustedly across the carpet of their apartment to answer the door. As it opened, his face lit up with surprise. "Hello, Henry. What can I do for you?"

Henry was not really in the mood for pleasantries; his conversation with Clarrie had upset him, so he cut straight to the chase. "Are you going after her, Jim?"

Miller blinked. Opened his mouth, closed it. Finally, he asked, "What have you heard?"

"Nothing," replied Henry. "I just know."

Suddenly stern, Miller took a breath to speak, but then appeared to change his mind. "You'd better come in, son," he invited.

"Dagmar? What are you doing here?" asked Fischer, playing his most concerned and perplexed.

The Sarge answered for her. "It appears we owe you an apology, Doctor. We found the culprit, the one who really broke into Mr Burnstein's secret files in the end, didn't we, Mrs Fischer?"

"*Dagmar?*" asked Fischer again, in shock this time.

Mrs Fischer rolled her eyes. "Do change the record, Klaus!"

"This has to be a mistake! Sergeant Jackson, I demand that you release my wife this instant!"

"Sorry, no can do. Please come with me, sir. She'll not be harmed – Captain Douglas would not allow it, even for this scum," he added, pointing at Schultz. He leaned forward threateningly. "Although, accidents *can* happen to people in custody, if they don't do as ordered."

Schultz twisted his lip sardonically.

Fischer gave him a secret look and left with The Sarge.

"What the hell is going on?" shouted Meritus, his ears still buzzing.

"Murderer!" snapped Franke.

"Say, wha— eh?" answered Meritus.

Sounds of running feet could be heard from behind him, along with Major White's voice at full roar, "What's happening? *Meritus?*"

"You'll pay for this," screamed Franke as she pulled Hartmann's body back towards their ship.

"What?" asked Meritus again, completely at sea.

White arrived on the run with at least a dozen troops as the engines fired up on the small enemy craft. "Quick, get back inside. Let's move it, people. *Go!*"

"What the...? I don't know what just happened," Meritus protested as they jogged back to the safety of the compound.

"C'mon," White replied, "we'll sort it out inside."

Meritus was fast-tracked back to the relative isolation of the *New World* once more. "An opportunity!" bellowed Douglas. "That's what you said to me! What the hell was that?"

"I don't know," repeated Meritus for the nth time. "I walked out there, someone shot someone, I ran back! Will everyone please stop shouting!" he shouted into the sudden silence. "Erm, thanks," he added quietly.

Taking his comm from a pocket, he set it on one of the bridge consoles and hit playback.

Everyone listened in silence as Meritus and Hartmann greeted one another, then they heard a bang as someone shot someone, followed by the sounds of everyone running back.

"Well, that clears everything up," Douglas noted, witheringly. He was exhausted and in a foul mood.

"At least you know it wasn't me," retorted Meritus, plaintively.

"Aye, but what was the point?"

"We've been blindsided," offered The Sarge. "Whatever the reasoning was behind that shooting, it was planned."

"Aye," Douglas agreed again. "But would anybody care to hazard a guess at why?"

"To set up Captain Meritus?" suggested Singh.

"I would have thought I was in foul enough odour with those guys already," he answered.

"Maybe, but what if that was an execution – with benefits," added Singh.

"*Benefits?*" asked Meritus.

"Sandy's right," Douglas chipped in. "Franke wanted Hartmann out of the way and decided to get a two-for-one deal by implicating Captain Meritus while she was about it?"

"I believe it makes sense, sir," agreed Singh.

"Damned right it does," said Douglas. "OK, pinning it on Tobias here could be seen as a sagacious move, fair enough. So, what we really need to know is why did she need rid of the man in the first place?"

"Captain, forgive the interruption," said The Sarge, turning away from one of the bridge's view ports. "Obviously, this is a critical situation, but we also need to debrief Dr Fischer, sir. If they're up to something over there, his information might be even more vital."

Douglas nodded. "You're right. Did he get the goods?"

Sergeant Jackson smiled fleetingly. "He did, sir, and please trust me when I say that what he found out could be crucial to us at this time."

"Very well, Sarge. Wheel him in."

Before anyone had chance to move, the comm binged. Douglas swore.

"*New World* bridge – Lieutenant Singh speaking."

The main view screen lit up to reveal a woman in black military fatigues. "*I am Captain Emelia Franke,*" she stated crisply.

Douglas stood and walked to the centre of his bridge. "James Douglas," he responded curtly.

She scrutinised him briefly. "*Your reputation precedes you, Captain. I've looked forward to this meeting.*"

Douglas nodded slightly, not in any way taken in by her flattery. "How can Ah help you, Captain Franke?"

"*You have two things that I want, Captain,*" she replied. "*Firstly, that traitor who hovers at your shoulder. Captain Meritus committed a murder this evening. Captain Hartmann was a dear friend of mine and I have promised his crew justice.*"

"A dear friend," sputtered Meritus. "You shot him!"

"Please," Douglas said quietly to calm him. He turned back to Franke. "So Captain Hartmann is dead, then."

She nodded. "*And that murderer—*"

"Are ye planning on dancing around this all night, Captain? We all know what happened. Now, can we move on? What's the second thing Ah have that ye'd like?"

Franke's eyes flashed dangerously. "*I demand that you release Heinrich Schultz.*"

Douglas nodded to himself. "OK, Ah think it's fair to say that that was nay surprise. What are your terms, Captain?"

Franke stepped closer, to fill the screen. "*Send Heinrich and that murderer out.*"

"Or?" prompted Douglas.

"*Or we come in,*" she snapped.

"Ah'll need time to clear this—"

"*Captain!*" said Meritus and Singh together.

"Silence on the bridge!" Douglas thundered.

Franke sneered. "*You call this discipline, Captain? I suppose you need to get permission, from your civilian masters? The priest and the Indian,*" she added with distaste.

Douglas' jaw clenched with anger, but his voice remained level. "You're well informed of our processes, Captain. Give me one hour and you'll have my answer."

Franke nodded. "*One hour, Captain.*"

The screen had barely returned to standby mode when everyone spoke at once.

"Silence!" barked Douglas once more. He turned to Meritus. "Yes, Ah believe you. No Ah dinnae think you murdered that man, nor am Ah about to turn you over to her." He moved to stand in front of them all. "That woman is as mad as Schultz himself. The last thing we need is them getting together again. Sarge, bring in Dr Fischer."

"You wanna go now?" asked White in disbelief. "You pick your times, Jim!"

"I'm sorry, Ford," replied Miller, "but we both know this ship could move out at any time, if Douglas is successful in his plans. I just can't take that risk. I'm not leaving her."

Standing in the Pod's main hangar, White rubbed his hands down his face in exasperation. "OK, but you're not going alone."

Miller was shaking his head. "I appreciate the offer, Ford, but they need you – all these people need you, right here."

"Tell me about it," replied White, the frustration in his voice obvious. "I'd come if I could, Jim. You know that, right?"

Miller smiled sadly and nodded. "I know. Besides, I have help. Henry is coming with me."

"What? Burnstein's boy? Are you nuts? He's just a kid."

"I'm eighteen and I'm going with him," said Henry, surprising White from behind.

White blustered but gave up. He had enough on his plate already. "Jim, what I actually meant by not going alone was, I have a couple of volunteers who've asked to go with you."

"Really?" asked Miller, brightening. "And who *are* these crazy people?"

"Corporal Jennifer O'Brien and Private Adam Prentice – they're both damned good soldiers, Jim. If anyone can get you through this crazy caper and get you home again, they can. Prentice's leg's all stitched up and he's requested he be allowed to finish what he started.

"Dewi Jones offered to go too, but with the Sarge locked away on the *New World*, I need him here." He leaned in close. "Although I trust the man himself, I can't be a hundred percent sure of some of Meritus' people. And we still haven't found Cocksedge's go-between, either. Besides, I don't think even Jones' strength could help you with your task. You'll need stealth."

"Thank you, Ford, but are they sure? This could be a one-way trip."

White gave him his customary lopsided grin. "With everything that's going on right now, that could be said for any of us, my friend. What makes *you* so special?"

Miller smiled and pulled White into a back-slapping embrace. "Thank you," he acknowledged simply.

"You got it," White replied.

They were interrupted by shouting. "Henry, just what do you think you're doing?"

Henry had expected big trouble should his father discover their plans, but it was Chelsea Burnstein who was screaming the place down as she ran towards them. Hank Burnstein ran after her, trying to slow her down. Two surprises for the price of one.

Steeling himself for the worst, Henry heard his name being shouted again, this time from the opposite direction. "Ah great!" he muttered, hanging his head as Woodsey ran towards them, too.

"You can't go without me, mate!"

"He's not going at all!" bawled Chelsea. "Jim Miller! I'm surprised at you!"

A very loud argument ensued. For once, Hank Burnstein just found a small shipping crate off to the side and sat in silence, pinching the bridge of his nose.

"You can't come, dude," said Henry.

"Why not?" asked Woodsey, his colour rising.

"Two reasons. One, I need you to look after Clarrie. You'll be the only people our age left and if we don't make it…"

"You want me to *marry* your sister?"

"No! Will you just… ah, hell – never mind. The second reason is, you're all your dad has left. You gotta stay, for him, man."

"OK, but only as long as I don't have to marry your sister. She looks too much like you, dude. I just couldn't, I mean, not even in the dark…"

Henry took a breath to snap out an angry retort, but without ever intending to, released it as laughter instead. "You idiot! Come here!" He pulled his friend into a back-breaking bear hug.

Then he turned to his mother and all amusement left him. "I have to go, Ma."

Tears streamed down her face as she pulled him close. "I love you so much."

"You too, Ma."

His father pulled her away, gently for once, and held out his hand. "I'm proud of you, son. Do what you gotta to bring your girl home, but take care of yourself."

Henry took his father's hand. "I will, Pa. Take care of Ma and Clarrie, *please?*"

Burnstein smiled grimly. "We're all we have now, right?"

Henry returned his smile. "See ya around, Dad."

They kitted up quickly, dressing themselves and loading the four dirt bikes White assigned to them.

"Good luck, Jim," said Mother Sarah.

"Thank you," he replied. With no idea how she had got to hear about all this, he nevertheless pulled her into a hug, gratefully. "Please look after Lara. She's furious with me for leaving her alone."

Sarah bit back her annoyance with Lara Miller and simply nodded. "Of course I will, Jim. God go with you, all of you, always."

Just as they were about to leave, Burnstein grabbed Miller by the arm. He stood a hand's breadth taller than the Englishman as he stared down into his eyes. "Miller, that's my only son you got there," he said, meaningfully.

"Burnstein, when I get out there, I will have just two priorities. One will be my little girl, and the other will be your boy. Whatever happens, even if it means my life, that won't change."

Burnstein nodded and offered his hand. "Thank you, Jim. Godspeed."

Chapter 9 | Eleven O'Clock Rock

Douglas gave a nod of respect. "Thank you, Klaus. You've done better than Ah could have hoped, and your timing could not have been more fortuitous."

"You're welcome, James, but there's more." Fischer sat at one of the bridge science stations, his seat turned around to face the room. He leaned forward intently. "We have another spy on board the Pod."

Meritus and Singh looked surprised, but Douglas and The Sarge merely shared a meaningful glance. "We're aware of that, Doctor, but what else can you tell us? Ah think Ah have an inkling about what you're going to say. So, please speak freely."

Fischer was encouraged, but then looked uncomfortable. "The spy is among Captain Meritus' people." Looking towards Meritus apologetically, he added, "I'm sorry, Tobias."

Meritus appeared almost immediately thoughtful, but not shocked or even surprised. After a moment he said, "I hope you will believe me, James, when I tell you this has nothing to do with me?"

Douglas watched his new ally closely. "Actually, Ah do," he replied, and was surprised to find that he genuinely did. "But Ah also suspect that, despite the suddenness of this news, you've already a shortlist in your head."

Meritus shifted in his seat uncomfortably.

Douglas continued, "Ah understand, Captain. There's nothing worse than finding a betrayer within your own trusted crew. Believe me, Ah've

157

been there and have a wardrobe full of t-shirts to prove it! But Ah have to press you."

Meritus nodded. "I hate admitting to doubts, but if forced, I would begin with Lieutenant Richard Weber."

The Sarge raised an eyebrow and nodded to Douglas.

"Tell him, Sarge."

The Sarge gave Meritus a direct look. "Lieutenant Weber is already a person of interest for Major White's NASASEC consultant, Rick Drummond. Drummond used to be a detective, so he has a nose for these things. Moreover, Weber is one of three close matches for the physical parameters recorded by our hidden cameras at a pick-up and drop-off point within—"

"The Pod's gymnasium?" asked Fischer.

"That's correct, Doctor," The Sarge confirmed.

"Does everyone know about this but me?" asked Meritus, a little irritably.

Douglas clamped a hand on his fellow captain's shoulder. "Sorry, Tobias, but please understand. We didnae know who to trust."

Meritus sighed deeply. "I get it, but am I always going to be an outsider? I gave up any chance of going back when I joined you guys."

"Ah know, laddie," said Douglas, gently. "But once again, Ah ask you to be patient. Whatever Ah think of you personally must always come second to any decisions Ah make as captain. *You* know that. We're holding so many lives in our hands here."

"OK," said Meritus, straightening. "So, how do we prove whether or not it's Weber?"

Before Douglas could answer, The Sarge said, "We don't. We keep the suspects in our back pocket until we need them. Needless to say, Drummond has people watching them – discreetly, of course." He switched back to Douglas. "But at the moment, sir, might I suggest we have more pressing concerns? Captain Franke will be back to us in less than thirty minutes."

Major White watched morosely as the ten-ton excavator drove in through the Pod's vehicular airlock, throwing clumps of mud all over the place. *We*

really should hose those things down before they come back in here, he thought, vaguely irritated.

The machine was retrieved from gate duty at about the same time every evening, so hopefully the enemy, encamped in their ships across the river, would not perceive this as suspicious.

White stepped back into the main hangar, and as the massive doors clanged together behind him, they also closed a metaphor. The boom filled the cavernous space as he sent a silent prayer after Jim Miller's small but courageous team.

He had sent them out into the night, each draped in a hastily manufactured heat-reflective cycle poncho, to keep them from the prying infrared gaze of the enemy vessels, but with precious little else.

Taking a deep breath, he focused on his next task. The fate of Miller's team was now out of his hands and he had to move on.

The emergency hospital, hurriedly set up to treat Meritus' injured after the destruction of the *Last Word*, lay across the bay. Unfortunately, a number of his own people were also in there now, courtesy of Heidi Schultz.

As he approached the entrance to the temporary infirmary, he looked around warily, taking note of everyone's positions within the hangar.

Once content that he was out of earshot of anyone else, he pressed the call button on the door's intercom.

The screen lit up almost immediately to reveal a matronly figurehead wearing a no-nonsense expression. "Yes?" she snapped peremptorily.

White frowned slightly. "I need to speak with Dr Flannigan, *please*."

The woman looked down her nose. "Dr Flannigan is in his office, you can comm or message him directly."

"No, thank you. I would—"

The screen switched off.

"Why you—!" Bristling with annoyance, White pressed the call button again, holding it down gratuitously.

"Yes?" came the curt response once more.

"I don't wanna send a *message*, nurse. I wanna speak to the guy!"

"He will answer his comm, *in* his office, Major."

Black screen, again.

"Damnit!" bawled White, drawing attention from others in the hangar. This time he pressed the call button repeatedly to a rowdy rhythm that would have been more at home in a football stadium than a hospital waiting room.

"Yes?"

White tripped over his words in his attempts to control his language. "Nurse!"

"Matron."

"*What?*"

"My position is matron, *Captain.*"

White leaned back from the little screen. "It's Majo— Oh, I see. Very good, *Matron.* Now will you ask Dave Flannigan to attend me here, *please?*"

"The doctor gave strict instructions that he was not to be disturbed."

Black screen.

"Aaargh!" White bellowed.

"Are you OK, sir?" asked a helpful voice from behind him.

"Yes, *damnit!*" White took a breath, controlling himself. "I mean, yes, Crewman. Just a little trouble passing on a message, but I'm fine, thank you. Please resume your duties."

The crewman saluted and scuttled off, leaving White to turn back to the comm with a vengeance. For a moment he considered shooting it off the wall, but quickly came to his senses. "Right," he said, smiling sweetly instead. "Try again."

He pressed the call button.

"Yes?"

White's patient smile slipped a little, but he did his best to keep his voice even. "Matron. Thank you for answering so quickly. I am about to give you a direct order, do you understand?"

The matron squinted at him, her mouth contorting like she had found a surprise vinegar centre in the middle of a Belgian truffle. "I understand."

"Sir. You understand, *sir.*" White suddenly found his most charming smile.

"I understand…"

White mouthed the word, helpfully willing her on.

"*Sir,*" she managed at last – she must have swallowed the vinegar.

"Very good, Matron," replied White, as if speaking to a child, then his manner changed completely as he bawled like an NCO, "Now tell *Lieutenant* Flannigan that *Major* White expects him to attend this station immediately! Is that *clear?*"

Matron's mouth pinched, almost to a singularity, as she nodded brusquely and disappeared.

White paced impatiently.

Presently the small screen lit up once more, this time revealing the rather tired countenance of Dave Flannigan. "Hey, Ford. Everything OK?"

White visibly smoothed his feathers and, seeing just how exhausted Flannigan looked, felt a pang of guilt too. "Yeah, I'm sorry to pull you away, Dave, but this is real important and not something I could put in writing, if you know what I mean?"

Flannigan seemed to revitalise immediately. "Of course, Major. What are your orders?"

White leaned in close and spoke quietly. "Secure your patients – we're going for a ride."

Flannigan's eyes widened. "Yes, sir."

"Oh, and Dave?" asked White before breaking off. "What's the deal with that matron?"

Flannigan's serious face split into a broad grin. "Do we really have the time to get into that, sir?"

"*Tim!*" Rose shrieked as she tore from her guard's grasp to run and jump into his arms. Tim went through a whole gamut of shock, disbelief, joy and horror as she launched herself at him. He wanted so badly to hold his friend to him and never let go, but knew he could not. Worse, what he would have to do next was going to hurt like hell – him most of all. What was she doing here?

Holding her from him, straight-armed, he snapped, "Back off! This is a fresh uniform!"

Heidi laughed.

Rose turned to look at her, slow to understand the situation. After a moment, she did indeed notice Tim's fresh uniform. Before that moment, it had been a collection of mere garments – hand-me-downs to cover her friend's modesty, in effect – but now she realised with a creeping horror that they represented something more. She could only whisper, "What have they done to you?" before rounding on Heidi, shouting, "What have you done to him? Answer me!"

Heidi laughed again. "I did not realise how spirited this one can be." She tilted Rose's chin to inspect her features. "Hmm, very beautiful –

under all that filth. Blonde, blue eyes – I approve, cousin. Along with your intelligence, she will make good breeding stock."

It quickly became a competition to see which of the teens was more shocked by her suggestion. Tim regained his composure first. "I will make my own decisions in that regard, cousin."

"Cousin?" Rose repeated dumbly, stepping away from him as the awfulness of this unthinkable truth settled upon her. She shook her head, disbelieving. "*Tim?*"

Inside, Tim felt another nail drive into the coffin around his buried heart. There was nothing he could do or say to help her through. He could only pray that at some level, deep down, she would know that he was still him – and every bit as trapped as she was.

Bond took Rose by the arm. "Well, if the boy doesn't want her...?" He left the question hanging.

Rose snapped around, appalled.

Heidi stared at him in surprise and then snorted derisively. "Help yourself. I have no need of her. But know this, Bond, you will be completely responsible for her and you will both be watched." She smiled nastily. "Who knows what those fools may have done to you while you were their prisoner. I would rather not waste stock like her, but if she steps out of line, I *will* extinguish the problem – immediately."

He eyed her coolly. "May we at least get cleaned up before we see the old man? I'm sure your grandfather will not appreciate us soiling his audience chamber in these tattered clothes?"

The temperature in the room seemed to drop. Bond felt it. He had no idea what had just changed but was nevertheless instantly on his guard.

"*Mein Großvater* is gone," Heidi stated curtly.

Bond's eyebrows shot up. "*Gone?*"

"We no longer need old men," Tim supplied, pointedly.

Rose stared at her former friend as if he were an unknown species.

Bond glared at him. "Might I ask *where* Heinrich Schultz has gone?" he tried again.

"He betrayed me, so I allowed him to be captured by Douglas' rabble," Heidi declared. "Knowing how conflicted and undisciplined they are, he may already have been killed by now. Or maybe he's running the place. Who knows? We will move on them soon enough."

Bond visibly sagged. "I came here, by the skin of my teeth and now he's over *there?*"

She raised an exquisitely shaped eyebrow. "Oh, do not worry, Derek. You now answer to me."

"Don't call me by that name," snarled Bond.

Tim frowned questioningly. "And why shouldn't we do that, Bond? What is it about Dere—"

"That's none of your business, Mr Norris!" Bond cut him off.

"That's Mr *Schultz*," Tim snapped.

Bond stared at him in wild disbelief, but Heidi merely nodded, affirming the young man's statement.

"*No!*" cried Rose, collapsing to her knees.

Bond snapped her back to her feet angrily and handed her to one of the female guards. "Have her cleaned up and brought to my quarters." He turned to Heidi. "I assume you will allocate me a private suite, in accordance with my position?"

"Your position, *Derek*, is whatever I say it is. Take the girl away."

Bond caught the guard by the arm as she turned to leave. "And find her a new set of clothes to wear – something nice!"

Heidi's lip curled in an unpleasant approximation of a smile as she addressed the guard again. "Very well. Assign *Herr* Bond a suite and get the girl scrubbed and into a pretty dress."

The comm rang insistently, demanding attention. "This is it," cried Singh. "Party time!" He answered the call, moving the signal to the main viewer once more.

"Captain Franke, welcome back," said Douglas. He nodded to The Sarge, seated on the periphery of the main comm camera's field of view.

Jackson bent to his station for a few seconds before sitting back, his composure suddenly relaxed as he returned his attention to the screen – a man looking forward to a show.

Franke looked stern as ever, but paid little heed to the soldier with his arm in a sling. "*Your answer, Captain Douglas,*" she demanded. "*As Captain Meritus is no longer on your bridge, may I assume that you have reached the sensible decision? The only decision.*"

Douglas frowned, collecting his thoughts for one last moment. "You made two demands, Captain. To answer your second first, our esteemed guest, Mr Schultz, has made it quite clear to me that he wishes to stay here."

Franke hissed. *"Don't play foolish games with me, Douglas. I can and will destroy you if—"*

Douglas held up his hand. "Please, Captain, allow me to finish. We asked Mr Schultz, but he was unequivocal that he can no longer trust anyone on your side. Apparently, you have something of a track record for betrayal, murder and changing sides, that sort of thing.

"Naturally, we argued that you had *your heart set* on having him back, but what can Ah say? He knows you far better than we do." He nodded to Singh to begin the *New World*'s engine start sequence.

"I warned you, Captain. If this—" Franke began.

"Please, Captain, if you'll forgive me?" Douglas interrupted again. "You also asked us to hand Captain Meritus over to your custody."

Franke glared at him. *"And?"*

"Well, Ah put the situation to him, and he replied…" he scratched his ear subconsciously while he feigned remembrance, "now what was the phrase he used? Oh, yes, that was it. He said, bite me!"

The huge thruster rockets beneath the *New World* fired, tearing the still night air with flame and distorted sound that ripped across the landscape for miles in every direction.

The wildlife, once more grown accepting of the sleeping giants nestled in their midst, exploded from the forest's roof in terror. At 2300 hours precisely, the USS *New World* left Patagonia and even Gondwana, forever.

On the bridge of the *Heydrich*, Franke appeared almost demented with rage as she shouted, "Launch! Launch!"

"Captain," said the lieutenant at the pilot's station, tremulously.

"Yes?" snapped Franke.

"We've lost power, ma'am."

"What? Impossible!" As the words left Franke's lips, all illumination on the bridge went dark, to be replaced by emergency lighting. "Lieutenant! What the hell is going on?"

"I don't know, ma'am. We've lost main power."

Incandescent, Franke bellowed at the comms officer, "Open a channel to the *Sabre*, now!"

"Yes, ma'am. We've got audio only."

The channel opened and Franke heard a voice respond, *"This is the* Sabre."

"Who is that? Never mind! Is the *Sabre* ready to launch?"

"Yes, Captain. The New World *is taking off—"*

"I know that, you imbecile! I need you to shoot that ship down!"

"Shoot it down, ma'am? But what about the Pod—"

"Don't question my orders," thundered Franke. "Launch immediately and shoot down the *New World*!"

"Yes, Captain. At once!"

Nothing happened.

"*Sabre...?*" asked Franke, dangerously. "You do not appear to be lifting off."

"Stand by, Captain. We seem to have lost main power..."

Franke swallowed, completely at a loss. What the hell was happening? Reaching a decision, she snapped her fingers at the comm officer once more. "Get me the *Eisernes Kreuz*, immediately!"

"Yes, ma'am."

"This is Captain Wolf Muller of the Eisernes Kreuz. *How can we help you,* Heydrich?"

"Wolf, this is Emilia. The *New World* is taking off and both the *Heydrich* and the *Sabre* have been disabled."

"What? How?" asked Muller in disbelief. *"They have no weapons—"*

Franke cut across him, "We don't know how, and it doesn't matter! You must launch immediately, or we'll lose them – all of our equipment is down bar the comm—"

Aboard the *Eisernes Kreuz*, Heidi listened closely to the irate conversation between her captains and suddenly exploded. "You idiot, Franke! You stupid fool!"

"What?" came Franke's baffled response. *"Who is this? How dare you!"*

"Be silent!" snapped Heidi. *"Mein Großvater has activated the kill switch code! And you, Dummkopf, have now transmitted it to us!"*

The lights aboard the *Eisernes Kreuz* winked out.

"I will have you executed for this, Franke!"

"What kill switch code? What are you talking about?"

165

"I'd like to know that too, Doctor?" asked Muller, suddenly looking mutinous.

"*Mein Großvater* had all of his ships and vehicles installed with a kill switch programmed directly into the firmware. Should any of his people turn against him he could shut them down with a simple alphanumeric code passed through a comm signal."

"But why would *Herr* Schultz want the code to be passed from ship to ship?" asked Muller, incredulous.

"*Because,*" explained Heidi, as though speaking to a moron, "if *he* was aboard one of these ships, *he* would know he had sent it and refuse any incoming messages. By the same token if he was *not* aboard any of his vehicles during a rebellion, he could guarantee that none of them could be used against him – at least, not within his window of escape! Why? Because the first thing any of his unimaginative officers would do upon losing power to their vessels, would be to call the others! *Imbeciles!*"

"*And you didn't see fit to tell us this?*" Franke bawled through the comm.

Heidi was momentarily at a loss. "I never thought he would give up the codes to *anyone*," she said, almost to herself.

"*Well, look where your damned paranoia has left us now!*" shrieked Franke. "*I was making a deal to get him back – he was almost within my grasp! And now you have—*"

"You were doing *what?*" shouted Heidi, matching Franke's tone. "I gave you orders to stop that ship, orders which you have spectacularly failed to carry out! I did not give you permission to make any private deals to supplant my authority!"

Clearly, Franke's rage had led her to say too much and the comm went still.

Heidi gestured to the comm officer with a cut across her own throat.

"Channel closed, Doctor."

Heidi stepped within inches of Muller. "Get this ship operational with despatch, Captain, before we lose everything. And, Captain, if *I* lose everything, *everyone* loses everything. Do we understand one another?"

Muller swallowed. "Indeed we do, Doctor." He turned away to issue orders for repair and engineering teams to begin dissecting ship's systems.

"Comms officer," barked Heidi. "Call the *Sabre*, I wish to speak with Captain Hartmann."

Within moments a channel opened between the ships. "*This is the* Sabre, *how can we assist you,* Eisernes Kreuz?"

"This is Dr Heidi Schultz. I wish to speak with Captain Hartmann immediately."

A slight pause followed, causing her to frown. "Well?"

"Ma'am, Captain Hartmann is dead."

Heidi's eyes widened in shock. "Dead? How?"

Another uncomfortable silence…

Heidi knew well when people were afraid to speak. Eventually, the officer aboard the *Sabre* continued, "We're not really sure, ma'am."

"Explain! Your captain is dead and you don't know how? The truth, immediately, or it will go badly for you!"

She almost heard the officer gulp. "We've been told by Captain Franke that he was murdered, ma'am. Shot dead by Captain Meritus during a secret meeting…" He tailed off and Heidi could sense the reticence to say more.

"What are you not telling me?" she asked, dangerously. "The truth, now."

"Captain Hartmann was shot, ma'am. The only people present were Captains Meritus and… Franke, Doctor. That is literally all we know, ma'am."

The slight pause before disclosing Franke's involvement made Heidi immediately suspicious, as it was clearly meant to. The officer was probably quite genuine in that he had no solid facts, but he obviously harboured doubts about the death of his captain. Wisely and without proof, he had said all he could. She approved of this. This officer might be useful in the future, perhaps even a replacement for Hartmann. "Very well. We will be joining you as soon as possible. *Eisernes Kreuz* out."

She stepped up to the bridge's front view port and stared out into the night, balling her fists; someone was going to pay for all this.

"We have a direction, Captain, but does anyone have a destination in mind?" asked Singh.

"Good question," replied Douglas, but then a look of sadness crossed his face. "Once again, Ah wish we could tap the well of knowledge that was Tim Norris."

"He's still alive, sir," said Singh, offering encouragement.

"Aye," Douglas smiled. "True. Does anyone have any ideas?"

"As a matter of fact, I do, sir."

"OK, Sandy. Let's have it."

"Do you remember some weeks ago, although it seems like years, when we were sat around the table in the next room discussing where to land?"

"Aye. Are you suggesting we go home?" asked Douglas. "Well, for me at least."

Singh nodded. "Blighty, exactly. I seem to remember Tim making some crack about the animals being 'cuddlier' there."

Douglas was not convinced. "Hmm, but if Ah remember correctly, did he no' add something about there being some 'real horrors' there, too?"

"So where do you want me to fly us, Captain?"

"Very well, Sandy, take us to where Britain will be 99.2 million years from now."

Singh grinned. "Aye, aye, Captain. I'll keep her below Mach five, so that we don't overshoot your little island, sir – following a bearing of north-north-east."

Douglas was about to object to this slight on the stature of Great Britain when the rest of Singh's statement caught up with him. "Really?" he asked. "North-*north*-east? From Patagonia? Don't you mean north-east-by-north?"

"No, sir." The ship was flying by instruments now, allowing him to spin his seat to face Douglas. "I'd show you on the map, but I'd have to draw you one first."

"Are ye saying somebody moved ma house while Ah was away?"

Singh smiled. "More that it hasn't arrived yet, Captain. Fortunately, Tim uploaded several mid-Cretaceous geological maps to our computer's library. They're the only guidance we have. We really wouldn't have had a clue otherwise. They're not what I'd call accurate, at least, not by our usual standards, but you know, with a hundred million years of continental drift…"

"It's the best we've got," Douglas finished for him. "Do these maps give any indication of what the terrain will be like when we get there? Or the environment, for that matter?"

Singh nodded his understanding; they really were 'off the map'. Trying to cheer his captain, he said, "As far as I can tell, Britain in this period was largely made up of a string of tropical islands and vast lagoons."

Douglas was nonplussed. "Ah'll no' be seeing any heather then?"

168

Singh chuckled. "You don't think that sounds like paradise then, sir?"

Douglas looked at him askance. "Islands and lagoons, you say? Have you any idea what kind of things live in the water in these times? And Ah thought the dinosaurs were bad enough. No, wait, we'll have them too – Ah cannae wait!"

"At least Europe will be free from jackbooted Nazis for millions of years, sir," tried Singh.

"*Maybe*," replied Douglas sourly. "That will rather depend on how successfully we manage to hide a ship the size of a small hill! Hitler may have failed to get boots on the ground in my country, but he didnae have spaceships with equipment that could spot mouse droppings from the moon, did he?"

Singh frowned. "You're right, sir. I'd better start scanning. I mean for a hiding place, not… you know, mouse poo."

"Aye. And we've less than two hours to come up with something." Douglas walked to the forward viewports and stood with his hands clasped behind his back. Anxiety gnawed at him. Anxiety about what was to come and for their people left behind. *God help them*, he thought. *God help all of us.*

Chapter 10 | Proof and Pudding

Miller pulled over, allowing the other bikes to catch up with him. "I think we should camp here for tonight."

"But we've only travelled a few miles," Henry pointed out.

"True, but now we're away from watching eyes," explained Miller, "I think it would be pointless to go further. In the dark we may miss any signs of Rose or her captors. As for the third enemy vessel, well, since Captain Douglas put the lights out on those other two, I suspect they'll soon come to *us*, don't you?"

They had all heard the *New World* leave; it would have been impossible not to, amid the night-time still. Her roar grew quieter and quieter, until she broke the sound barrier. The boom carried over the darkened land with the finality of a door slamming shut.

Alone then... No one said it, no one dared. Rather, they busied themselves with setting up the simplest of camps, all preferring to share in the pretence of 'see ya later'.

Henry took Miller aside. "Jim, what's your plan for tomorrow? Do we follow Rose's trail? Or wait here, like you say, hoping she made it to the enemy ship and that they'll come to us?"

Miller was about to answer but changed his mind at the last second. "What do *you* suggest, son?" he asked gently.

Henry thought for a moment. "They were on foot. They may have made it all the way, maybe not. I think it's still possible we could catch up

171

to them. Even if we can't, we've a pretty good trail to follow and we have speed. If we guess wrong, we can always double back. We could split up, I guess, but that just sounds like a stoopid line from a movie."

Miller grinned, clamping him on the shoulder. "That's what I was thinking too. We get a few hours shut-eye, then we follow Rose."

Bond felt like a new man after a shower and a hot meal. Now alone in his cabin with a stunning young lady – clothed in a long, blue satin dress which matched her eyes perfectly – he could barely reconcile this vision with the bedraggled, matted creature, soaked in gore, with whom he had arrived.

Rose glared at him.

"That's better, isn't it, my dear? I must say, you are very beautiful, Rose."

"Pervert!"

Bond's eyebrows shot up in surprise. "Excuse me?"

She continued to glare so he suggested, "Let's play a little game before bedtime, shall we? Help us relax, hmm?"

"Only if you want to be wearing them around your neck!"

Again, Bond looked surprised. "Wear what around my— oh." He chuckled as her threat of violence became clear.

He sat at their quarters' glass-topped dining table which doubled as a workstation. "Please," he said, inviting her to sit opposite.

She sat with reticence, having little choice.

The tabletop lit up to reveal a computer terminal. Two smaller screens lifted up from the surface, one either side.

Rose frowned. "What's this, *Battleships*?" she asked sarcastically.

Bond smiled indulgently. "What a nice idea, but no, I think we've all had enough battleships in our lives recently, don't you?"

"Don't tell me, let me guess," replied Rose. "Strip poker."

Bond looked genuinely shocked. "No, I rather thought we may have a little Scrabble."

"Strip *Scrabble*?"

Bond appeared haughty now. "Will you stop talking about stripping! Honestly, and I thought you were such a nice young lady."

"And I thought, just maybe, you weren't such a bad man after all!" Rose retorted harshly. "HA!"

Bond frowned at her but began typing into his uplifted console anyway. "I've picked up a few tricks about computer games over the years. Have you heard of poking?"

Rose bridled, jumping to her feet. "You dirty old man! I'll have you know, I've been training with some of the female soldiers back on the *New World*. They showed me techniques that will stop a man like you from even thinking about anything like that for a very long time!"

Bond, once again, merely looked surprised. "I don't know what you're talking about," he replied calmly. "A poke is a cheat – you know, extra men or unlimited ammo, that type of thing? I'm setting up the game, that's all." He looked around the room suspiciously. He had not seen any signs of surveillance, but he knew they were there, so he added clearly, "I like to win the games I play, as much as the next man."

Sure enough, a Scrabble board lit up on the tabletop and Rose sat back down cautiously.

"Right," announced Bond, brightly, "I'll go first, shall I?" Without waiting for an answer, he typed his first word, which appeared on the board automatically. Once complete, the board spun to favour Rose.

The word read 'WATCHED'.

"Seven letters on your first go?" asked Rose in disbelief.

Bond sighed with annoyance. "The magic of pokes," he explained caustically. The look he gave her was clearly meant to be significant. "Oh," he brightened once more, "and that's a double letter on the 'H' making it a score of twenty. Your turn."

Again, the look. Rose thought she could see where this was going, but dared not begin to hope, let alone trust; not yet. She glanced down at her letters. Not much to go with, but in order to keep the game going, she placed the only word she could see, 'ENDS' – reusing the 'D' from the end of 'WATCHED'.

Bond's brows knitted, not sure what to make of that. He placed 'FRI' in front of Rose's letters to create the word 'FRIENDS'. "Drat! Just missed the double word score. Still, I get a double letter off the 'E' so that makes twelve."

"That was my double letter score," Rose pointed out. "You can't reuse it!"

"Yes, yes, you can," Bond blustered, brushing her point aside. "*Trust* me."

He winked.

Rose gave him her cross face as she pondered, *Is that him trying to send me the message that I can trust him or is he just a stinking cheat?*

"My last word was 'FRIENDS'. Now, how do you answer?" he prompted.

Rose frowned, but raising an eyebrow, she added an 'A' beneath the 'H' in 'WATCHED' – HA.

Bond was clearly nonplussed as he replied, "That's very poor word use, young lady!" He placed an 'E' and an 'S' above the 'C' in 'WATCHED', spelling 'ESC'.

"What's that supposed to mean?" asked Rose, truculently.

"It's an abbreviation, like on your computer keyboard," he explained.

Rose looked scandalised. "You can't use abbreviations! That's against the rules!"

"Read the rules to Scrabble, have you?" asked Bond indolently. "I mean, actually *read* them?"

"Er... well, I—"

"Didn't think so," he cut her off. "Once again, you'll just have to trust me. Now, my word is 'ESC' – what's your answer?"

Scratching her head unconsciously, Rose typed 'HEN'. When the letters appeared on the game board, they fell below the 'W' in 'WATCHED' to create the word 'WHEN'. *Watched, friends, escape, when*, she thought. *I wonder how he'll respond to that.*

Bond's initial cheat, allowing him to begin the game with letters of his choosing, was no longer able to help him. He frowned in thought for a moment before placing the letters 'SU' before the 'N' in 'WHEN'.

Rose looked him in the eye, trying to read the meaning there. *'SUN'? Does he mean sunup? Sunday? Or could he perhaps mean* soon *but doesn't have the letters? Damn, this is frustrating!* She cleared her throat and asked, "How much time am I allowed to find a word within these made-up rules of yours? My letters are hopeless."

"Take as long as you like," replied Bond, smoothly. "I'm sure we'll be here for at least a day or two."

Ah, thought Rose. *Probably soon, then – not sunup.* She yawned and stretched.

Bond nodded. "Yes, I think I've had all the relaxation I can stand for one day, too. Time for bed. You may take the top bunk."

"That's very chivalrous," Rose admitted, grudgingly.

"On the contrary, my dear girl. If you fall out, it will hurt you far less than it would hurt me. In fact, if you do fall out, it won't hurt *me* at all." He smiled cheerfully. "Goodnight."

As the *New World* crossed theoretical time zones, ship time was barely into the small hours when the sun began to rise in the east.

"Shall I reset the ship's chrono, Captain?" asked Singh.

"Eh?" asked Douglas, startled out of a dark reverie. "Oh, aye. Good thinking, Sandy. We'll all feel a bit jet-lagged, but best we get used to it."

"Yes, sir."

Douglas returned to his pondering. Patagonia had been a horrifying place at first, still was perhaps, but weirdly, it had also begun to feel like a home of sorts. Straight from one unknown to another, they would all have to adjust again, to a completely different location, climate – everything. Douglas had another problem too.

How the hell do Ah hide over half a kilometre of gleaming white spaceship?

Singh broke into his thoughts for a second time. "Captain…" he said ominously, "we're about to fly over Britain."

Douglas stepped towards his pilot carefully, standing behind Singh's station as they looked out of the forward viewports together.

The sky was a bright, perfect blue. The sea beneath them was deep azure, working up through aquamarine as it neared land. From their bird's-eye view, this 'tiering' of the sandy bed was obvious. Singh slowed the *New World* to a crawl as they took their first long look at their new home. The shallows twinkled palest turquoise as they kissed beaches almost white under the bright morning sun.

"I've been reading anything I can find about Britain a hundred million years ago, Captain. Our information's not exhaustive, but during the Cretaceous – more or less about now – the sea levels began to rise. Britain itself is a geologist's bonanza. Basically, three continents slammed together – Laurentia formed what would one day become Scotland. Avalonia created most of England—"

"Never heard o' the place," Douglas interrupted with a wink.

Singh grinned, continuing, "And lastly, Armorica, which includes much of what will be Brittany and Normandy, is believed to have also crashed in from the south."

"Another Norman invasion, eh?"

"Indeed, Captain. This one was a little before William I, however. The collision of the main plates began about 300 million years ago – that's 400 million years before you or I were born."

Douglas whistled. "So, even though the collision occurred that far back, we'll still no' recognise the place yet, Ah suppose?"

"No such luck, sir. This is nothing like the Britain we left behind. As hypothesised earlier, we should expect a landscape of lagoonal environments around a chain of islands. Where we find larger landmasses, like the one we're passing now, we'll probably see terrain criss-crossed with many rivers and lakes."

Douglas gazed balefully out of the viewport. "Well, that's certainly no' Lands End."

At a glance, their aerial view did indeed reveal Singh's prophesied tropical paradise. Moving slowly inland, they crossed a patchwork of sandbanks separating myriad tidal pools. Where the beautifully clear water receded, the sand was already dazzling in the burgeoning sunshine. A huge estuary joined the ocean a few miles to the north. From the air, the churning accumulation of mineral-rich silts over the vast delta was clear; everything nutritious to everything else. Douglas had never seen a place so *alive*. It was as if the forces of evolution were laying out their secrets one by one for him, in a series of cut-away images.

Singh continued, "The rising sea levels will lead to large-scale chalk deposition, particularly in the south of England, apparently…"

The pilot read from his notes and Douglas did his best to pay attention, but the vista below took his breath away. It was all so glorious.

Further north, the land began to rise towards a mountain range. There was no basis in fact for his guess, other than rough dead-reckoning and fancy, but he wondered whether they just might be the ancestors of North Wales' Cambrian range – a much brawnier great uncle, perhaps?

Whether these behemoths were indeed destined to become Snowdonia or not, in kinder days far ahead, the simple act of pinning a familiar name on this alien landscape calmed him a little. Everywhere he looked there was life, life, life… but then a specific movement caught his eye.

Singh increased altitude to a safe 3000 metres. As they approached the mountains, he sent footage from cameras mounted in the nose of the ship to their main viewscreen. The *New World* passed over an inland lake and on its shores was a reminder that this new paradise also had a serpent – many, in fact.

Below, they witnessed a tussle between a giant crocodile and a dinosaur. With an involuntary shudder, Douglas recalled a terrifying game of hide and seek on the night of his escape from the *Last Word* – one where he had been forced to scramble under the only shelter available, his own shuttle, while pinned down by the vast, sail-backed Oxalaia. This creature looked a little lighter than Oxalaia but was certainly built along similar lines and appeared no less bad-tempered.

The cause of the fracas was the corpse of a giant fish, washed up on the beach. The lake did not seem big enough to provide a home for such creatures, but due to the fluvial nature of their environment, almost every body of water was joined with every other; a vast hydro-highway connecting all life in this part of the world.

"That's our rude awakening, right there," Douglas noted, sourly.

The influx of Captain Meritus' personnel had put living space at a premium aboard the Pod. All the guest quarters were filled with people sharing. As most were military, this was nothing new to them. However, Lieutenant Weber, sharing a room with Sergeant Hans Baier, and four other men, was finding his lack of privacy irritating.

Forced to retreat into the toilet, he sat perusing aerial shots of planet Earth taken from the *Last Word*'s flyover, before their ill-fated ship had landed in Patagonia, east of the *New World* – never to fly again.

The word was out all across the ship that they were heading for a location that would one day become the British Isles. Although at the moment, they were a very different set of isles and many hundreds of miles west of where Britain would exist in the 22nd century.

Along their flight path was a much smaller island chain. Africa, although joined, had not fully coalesced into a single landmass by the mid-Cretaceous. A vast body of land, thousands of miles long and shaped something like a moose's antler, extended from the north-western shore out into, and almost bisecting, the expanding Atlantic. The tiny islands Weber studied were mere specks on the seascape, perhaps a hundred miles westwards of the Mauritanian and Western Saharan coasts – as they would become known in future millennia – out in the North Atlantic. The islands were roughly midway between the encampment the *New World* left behind in Patagonia and their destination.

Cretaceous continental Africa, being further south than in the time of man, placed these small islands almost precisely on the equator.

In a time yet to be gifted with satellite navigation, these islands looked ideal – easy to spot, easy to search and centrally located. *Perfect*, he thought. *Now all I need is leverage.*

His initial plans, as part of the task force assigned to deprive the *New World* of her Pod, had gone spectacularly awry. However, despite a change in venue, most of the pieces remained on the board still to play for.

I'll wait and see where they finally put down. Doubtless, they'll try and hide this ship somehow. So I'll need all the facts before I make my move.

"Captain, some of these mountains look like extinct volcanoes. Hang on – let me put this on-screen."

Douglas stood from his command chair to approach Singh once more. The large display came to life, showing footage from the *New World*'s cameras, this time revealing a plan view of what looked like a near circular lake, bounded by craggy peaks.

"You're not suggesting we put down in the lake?" asked Douglas.

"No, sir. I don't think she'd stand it."

"Corrosion?"

"Pressure, sir. Her hull's not as intact as she once was. If we went down…"

"Hmm," agreed Douglas. "OK, Sandy, what's your plan?"

Engaging the autopilot to keep the ship steady, Singh left the pilot's seat and walked around his console to stand before the screen. He pointed to the southern shore of the lake. "Although it's difficult to see from this angle, Captain, there's a very large cave here."

"Big enough for us?" asked Douglas, hardly daring to believe.

"Not quite, sir. At 550 metres the *New World* is just too big to go all the way in. She will, however, *partially* fit in."

"OK," said Douglas, slowly. "How does that help us?"

Singh turned to face him. "I'll need Hiro's help on this and certainly Dr Sam Burton's and Dr Patel's help, too, now that he's filling in for Jim Miller. I think I've a way for us to hide.

"You know we've several small, remotely operated vehicles? They were designed to help us find the mineral reserves we required on Mars—" he raised a wry eyebrow, "in another life. Well, these ROVs could be cloaked using basic lens technology – they're so small it would be fairly easy and wouldn't drain our resources too badly."

Douglas nodded. "OK, Ah'm with you so far. What do you suggest we do with these tiny, invisible flying robots?"

"We build much larger lenses that they can carry – carry and deploy as part of a larger system, whenever we're threatened. If we mount a sensor station at the top of one of these mountains, we can scan for any approaching ships—"

"Maybe," interrupted Douglas, "but the enemy warships are all stealthed up. We cannae see them with our instruments. Can we?"

Singh grinned. "I think I may have a way around that too, Captain."

Douglas slapped a meaty hand on Singh's shoulder. "Good man. Tell me."

"Yes, sir. I wanted to have options ready for you before we landed, so I've already been swapping messages and ideas with Hiro, during our journey. I suggest we instruct Hiro to begin straight away, sir, and bring Drs Burton and Patel up to speed as soon as we've landed the ship."

Douglas nodded again. "Aye, that makes good sense, Lieutenant. Tell him to proceed. You can fill in the details for me later. We cannae run forever and we're sitting ducks at the moment. Even in the air, they have a massive advantage over us. Nor do we know how long it will take them to regain control of their ships, either. They may already be on our tail."

Returning to his station, Singh replied, "Yes, sir. Coming about."

Wolf Muller, Captain of the *Eisernes Kreuz*, sighed. Unable to put it off any longer, he sent a message to Dr Heidi Schultz, requesting her presence on the bridge.

It was the middle of the night and his entire crew were exhausted after wresting control of their ship back from the clutches of Heinrich Schultz's kill switch codes. Despite this, Heidi appeared crisp and fresh as she strode onto the bridge.

Damn her! thought Muller. *She's going to want to leave immediately.*

"Are we ready to leave, Captain?" she asked without preamble.

Muller sighed – again. "The *Kreuz* may be ready, but her crew aren't, Doctor."

"Meaning?" she demanded.

"Meaning, they're worn out. I recommend just a couple of hours—"

"We leave *now*, Captain. *I* cannot afford to lose the *New World*'s trail while *you* take a nap!"

Muller nodded wearily. "Very well, Doctor." He turned back to his exhausted crew and barked, "Ready the ship for take-off! Bring all assets back on board! We leave in ten minutes!"

After an unenthusiastic round of acknowledgements, the crew blearily went about their business.

Schultz frowned with annoyance. "Discipline is becoming lax aboard this ship, Captain. Maybe the *Eisernes Kreuz* needs a new leader – someone who will motivate the men."

Muller was too tired to bridle at her insinuation and threat. "They're not machines, Heidi. They're giving you everything they've got. If you're planning on taking over my job, I suggest you try and understand that. It will probably save you a mutiny down the line."

"Are you threatening me, Wolf?"

"No, just straightforward advice, but I can't force you to take it."

Heidi's first impulse was to punish this man for his insolence, but she bit it back, instead saying, "Have her ready in ten minutes, Captain." She walked towards the exit and paused a moment. Turning, she addressed the crew loudly, "Well done, everyone. Thank you."

They stared at her in genuine astonishment, but Heidi merely spun on her heel and left the bridge.

Tim Norris sat alone in his quarters. What was it to him if they fixed their ship or not? If successful, they would only pursue his friends again.

I really need to find a way to neutralise this vessel, he mused. *I wonder if I could get my hands on the codes that were used to disable her?*

Dangerous thoughts, he knew, but he was all too aware that he should be *doing* something, anything, to help his friends escape the Nazis. He had high hopes that Captain Douglas would have understood his message, rubbishing Heinrich Schultz as a hostage, but surely he could do more.

An idea struck him. Perhaps he was looking at this the wrong way. Rather than attempting some kind of action against his... what were they? *Family? Captors?* He was no longer sure. Maybe he should instead focus his efforts on coercion.

As he counted his assets, he arrived at a conclusion that left him disgusted with himself. Gravely, he considered what he was becoming.

To him, it seemed that Heidi Schultz was a genius, certainly, and a psychopath, but perhaps that was not strictly true – or at least not the whole truth.

Tim never thought of himself as a genius, but if they truly were from the same stock, then he had at least some of the Schultz intelligence. However, where he deviated from their model was in his upbringing.

The Norrises were poor, but they had a great line in credit as far as love and stability were concerned. 22nd century Britain may have been a grotesquely unpleasant, built-up monstrosity *outside*, but inside, their home had always been a place of love, friendship and teaching. His brilliant and, more importantly, *kind* adoptive parents may not have been able to afford many of the things he wanted, but had nevertheless furnished him with everything he *needed.*

Heidi had known none of the perks a loving family can provide. Her models had been cruel, her regime, harsh. So, was she really a psychopath or just *galactically* repressed? Moreover, if correct, could Tim really use this against her? Could he *bring himself* to use this against her? Was he actually beginning to pity this beautiful, gifted, billionairess supervillain whom no one had ever loved?

He sighed, feeling yet another nail driven home into the coffin around his buried heart, but what choice did he have?

Despite his rationale, he knew this was going to cost him dearly. He would teach Heidi about family, about trust, about belonging and then he would find the worst possible time to take it all away.

Hovering just three metres above the lake's surface, the *New World*'s landing thrusters turned purest mountain water to froth. Singh kept her steady, while the ship's sensors checked and mapped out the cave he hoped would become their new home for a while.

The readings came back, plotting a full picture of the cave's interior on the viewscreen. In particular it flagged any obstacles or protruding rocks which might pose a threat to the vessel's superstructure. Once complete, Singh smoothly spun the *New World* through 180 degrees to begin some of the most delicate flying he had ever undertaken – backing more than half a kilometre of spaceship into a cave.

After a few minutes' careful sleight of hand at the controls, he had the ship in as far as she would go. The lake ran into the cave for a little under 200 metres – roughly a third of the ship's length. Although huge, at more than three kilometres long, the cavern began to close down around the half-kilometre point, making further ingress impossible.

They were, of course, incredibly lucky to find a cave even of this size, but unlucky in that seventy metres of the *New World*'s prow still remained outside – glowing most conspicuously in the sunshine.

Douglas studied the sensor readings. The vast space inside the mountain was almost cone shaped. "Can we deduce how this cave was formed?" he asked.

"Some kind of volcanic event would be my guess, Captain," replied Singh. "It is odd, though. The floor beneath us slopes up slightly – only by a few degrees, barely noticeable – but that suggests that a huge explosion, followed by a vast lava flow, must have descended from higher still.

"It's a strange arrangement. I believe the next mountain along was formed mainly by volcanism, rather than tectonic movement, and actually burst *through* the mountain we're hiding under – which is earlier, geologically. It must have arrived with one hell of a bang!

"According to Tim's notes, the mass extinction at the end of the Triassic Period has never satisfactorily been explained. The event at the end of the Permian Period, fifty million years earlier still, seems to have been more studied, perhaps because it was far, far worse. Life on Earth almost ended with that one. It's a miracle we're here at all. Hmm... interesting."

"Oh?"

"Well, I'm just musing, Captain, but perhaps these clues of extreme volcanism, all around us here, are completely buried from our sight by our own century."

"Erm... it's not likely to happen again any time soon, is it?" Douglas asked cautiously.

"No, sir. I think we can put the 'no' into 'volcano'. It's long extinct. As far as I can tell from our surface scans, these rocks seem to date from roughly the Carboniferous-Permian divide. That's about 300 million years before our own time in the 22nd century, Captain, just after most of the world's coal seams were laid down. This particular volcanic event, as I said, occurred maybe a hundred million years later at the end of the Triassic Period.

"When you lay out all the mass extinctions end to end on a geological chart, it shows just how fragile life truly is. And so, I can only conclude that..."

"Yes?"

Singh favoured Douglas with a boyish grin. "It's a funny old world, isn't it?"

Douglas smiled. "Such long periods of time. And Ah thought *we* were a long way back in the past. You're a font of knowledge, Sandy. Ah'm very impressed."

"Oh, I'd like to take credit, sir, but in truth I've only just now looked into it. *Weeell*... you know how our fortunes have been sliding in recent weeks – be just my luck to set us down *inside* our very own Vesuvius!"

"Don't even joke," agreed Douglas. "Good work, Sandy. Now, how do we hide our rather prominent white nose before it catches too much sun?"

"If we can manufacture a series of lenses to partially cover our protruding prow, we can then use the ROVs to manoeuvre in sync with any passing ships, keeping line of sight, to make sure that any flyovers see only what we want them to. The light will be passed from lens to lens and effectively bend around us, you see?"

"Aye, that's good, Sandy, assuming we can make and deploy all this in the time we have. However, we also have the problem of not being able to see their ships. You said earlier you had a plan to solve that?"

"Indeed, Captain. While you were in captivity aboard the *Last Word*, I studied every piece of sensor data we collated from their initial flyover." Singh shrugged. "There wasn't much, but *then* the enemy's second fleet flew over the Pod. They didn't seem interested in concealment. Indeed, as previously, I rather think they wanted to frighten our people. Fortunately, the Pod sensors scanned them automatically, looking for an ident – the way it would have with any ships passing over it on Mars, had it ever arrived there. Interestingly, these scans revealed another piece of the puzzle. All of the enemy vessels must share similar engine design – presumably scaled up for the battleship, *Last Word* – and these engines all give off a high frequency sound wave, invisible to most of our passive sensors, but caught by one of the Pod's parabolic microphones. If we set up four high-powered microphones with overlapping fields at a station atop one of the highest mountains in this range, we should be able to see – or hear, I should say – any ships coming towards us. The rub is, if they're travelling supersonic, they'll arrive before we have any warning."

Douglas scratched yesterday's stubble. "If they're looking for us, they'll probably slow down over land. Do we have any microphones powerful enough for this duty?"

"Sort of."

"Sort of?"

"Yes, sir. We have some very powerful seismic sensors which will do this job for us, but we'll have to do a bit of tinkering. They're calibrated to read the tiniest of structure-borne sounds. We'll have to modify them for use through air – which naturally doesn't transmit sound as well as a solid medium."

"This sounds like a lot of work, Sandy, and we don't have much time."

"Yes, Captain. I know you ordered the majority of our personnel to take a rest cycle during the journey. They've had a few hours now so I suggest we get them all back out of bed straight away, sir."

Rose jerked awake. The ship was taking off. What on earth was happening? She jumped down from her bunk and shook the still-snoring Bond harshly.

"Wha?" he asked blearily.

"Wake up," she snapped. "We're taking off!"

This seemed to rouse him and he moved to a sitting position, legs over the side of his bunk, to rub his face and neck. Semi-revived, he stood and walked a little stiffly to the window. The ground was very definitely moving away from them.

"Kind of them to warn us about strapping in before take-off," he noted witheringly.

"What should we do?" Rose's concern was evident in her voice.

Bond turned to her. "We get dressed, I think."

She ditched the dress and reached for the rather more practical military fatigues she had also been given. The shock of the ship's sudden take-off had her distracted, but she soon regained her senses and began to consider other things, such as modesty and privacy. "Well? Turn around then!" she barked.

Bond, startled out of his own reverie, complied immediately. "Of course, my dear." He gazed resolutely out of the window; he *was* a gentleman after all.

Unfortunately, it was dark outside and before he even realised the ramifications of this, he caught Rose's reflection. Snapping his eyes tightly shut for decency's sake, he asked, "Are you finished yet?"

Bond the gentleman fervently wished he could 'unsee' what he had just glimpsed, whereas Bond the inner man proceeded to torment him with a looped replay behind his eyelids.

"OK, I'm decent," stated Rose. "Thank you for not looking."

"You're welcome," he acknowledged, weakly. Bond wore his boxer shorts and a t-shirt to bed. So, still playing the part of an English bloke, he simply pulled on a pair of trousers, stepped into his boots and within mere seconds was ready to go.

As they left their quarters together, they bumped into Tim, still under guard, on his way to the bridge. Rose recoiled in disgust from a boy who had hitherto been one of the best friends she had ever made.

Tim tried to disguise his pain. "Where are you two going?" he asked, sternly.

Bond gave him a sour glare. "I don't answer to you, boy," he replied. "But if you must know, we're going to the bridge."

"Fine," Tim retorted. "So am I! She had better come with us too." He grabbed Rose's hand tightly and dragged her after him. Rose struggled, forcing him to stop and face her.

"You will come with me," he said slowly and forcefully, but all the while squeezing and releasing her hand.

Rose looked for the hidden meaning in his eyes.

Tim raised a wry eyebrow and said, "Well?"

More hidden messages, thought Rose. *First Bond and now Tim. I don't know who to believe or trust.* A tear welled at the corner of her eye.

Tim wiped it gently away. However, his words were harsh. "No weakness here. You understand?"

He looked deeply into her eyes. It was a fleeting second, but long enough for Rose to fancy that she had at last reconnected with Tim again, rather than the Nazi collaborator he portrayed.

She pulled her hand from his grasp roughly. "I can walk by myself, *thank you!*" She strode away haughtily, following Bond to the bridge.

Tim watched her go for a few heartbeats, wondering, did they have an understanding?

The comm rang with an incessant quality, eventually making any pretence of hypnopompic hallucination impossible. The noise, it seemed, was irritatingly and depressingly real.

Damn!

Groaning, Major White reached out to grab the source of his annoyance. Controlling the urge to throw it at the wall, he answered the call gruffly, "White."

"*Ford? Douglas. Sorry to wake you, but we have little time.*"

"Of course, Captain. How can I help?"

"*Rouse the whole Pod. Get 'em all up! We need some equipment, and we need it now.*"

White came to his senses quickly. "No problem, James. Send me a list and I'll have it taken from stores directly."

"*Aye, that's the problem, Ford. We havenae built it yet.*"

"Oh." White rubbed his eyes. "I'll put the Pod on a yellow alert status, then. That should get their attention!"

"Good man – Douglas out."

White opened a comm link to the duty officer within his security headquarters.

"Security."

"This is White. That you, Jonesy?"

"Yes, sir. How can I help you?"

"Sound a yellow alert, Corporal. We need the whole Pod awake and at their stations. Captain Douglas has work for us."

"Right away, sir."

"I'll be with you directly, Corp – White out."

White splashed a little water on his face to revive himself and, racing through his ablutions, quickly dressed and ran from his quarters.

On his way to security, he could feel the whole Pod coming alive around him as people were shocked awake by the yellow alert.

Turning a corner, he bumped into one of Meritus' men. Lieutenant Weber was fully armed and dressed for battle.

"Why are you armed, Lieutenant?" asked White, calmly.

For the briefest moment Weber looked unsure of his answer. "Yellow alert, sir. I, erm…"

White frowned, but then clamped a hand on the young officer's shoulder. "Richard, isn't it? This is not a military vessel, Richard. Yellow alert status is more likely to signify some kind of technical failure or environmental issue."

Seeing a chance for salvation, Weber affected chagrin. "Sorry, sir. My training in these situations was always so clear."

White nodded and smiled. "I understand, son. Better to be too ready than not ready at all. Please check your weapons back in at security, you won't need them. Not this time. Come, I'm heading that way myself."

Weber fell in silently beside him. Despite relief at his narrow escape, he was furious about his opportunity being so suddenly thwarted; almost the entire ship had been asleep, and now they could not be more alert.

White strode into security, as always, exuding confidence for his troops' benefit, but found Corporal Jones alone. "Jonesy," he greeted. "Check Lieutenant Weber's weapons back in, would you?"

Jones stood behind his desk to salute the major. "Morning, sir," he returned the greeting as his expression turned to puzzlement. He eyed Weber suspiciously. "I have no record of Lieutenant Weber booking *out* any weapons, Major."

White looked enquiringly at Weber.

"I kept them – in the quarters I share with my men," he answered haltingly.

"You mean you *smuggled* them in there," stated White, accusingly. "We ordered all weapons to be checked in when we allowed you aboard with wounded. Those were *your* captain's orders. I stood next to Captain Meritus when he gave them. Check your weapon immediately, Lieutenant."

Weber struggled with indecision for a moment and then pulled the assault rifle from around his shoulders. Making it ready to fire, he covered White and Jones. "Get back! Get back or I will terminate you both right here."

"What the hell?" shouted White.

Weber nodded to Jones. "Corporal, get some binders and tie the major's hands."

Jones looked to White for instruction.

"Never mind him! I am giving the orders now!" snapped Weber.

White nodded. "It's OK, Dewi." He held out his hands, wrists together for Jones to tie.

"Behind your back, Major," Weber spat, disparagingly.

White turned angrily for Jones to bind him.

"And you, Jones," continued Weber, "step into that cell, and Corporal, leave your keys and comm on the desk, here."

Jones did as ordered.

"OK, Major, walk."

"Where?"

"The infirmary – *now!*" Weber shoved White back out into the corridor. They had not travelled more than ten metres before running men and women approached them, skidding to a halt.

"Stand back! All of you!" Weber called out.

With a sinking feeling, White recognised all his security people as those recently off duty – none of them were armed. None were part of the skeleton force he had left to guard the sleeping crew. *So much for centralising our weapons cache*, he thought angrily. *Damnit!*

With a nod from him, White's people stood back, allowing them to pass.

Weber knew that White's people would make straight for security, Jones, and *many* guns. "Pick up the pace," he ordered, prodding White in the back with his rifle.

Sam Burton and Satnam Patel looked over the specifications forwarded from Hiro's terminal aboard the *New World*. Ship and Pod were still sealed from one another to prevent potential spread of the reptile virus, so they would help the chief remotely.

Burton massaged tiredness from his eyes when his office comm sounded. "Burton."

"Doctor, it's Corporal Jones, isn't it."

"What is it, Corp?" drawled the New Zealander.

"We have a hostage situation in the main hangar, sir. Major White has been taken prisoner by Lieutenant Weber. He's forced his way into the infirmary."

Burton and Patel blinked at one another. "Report this to Captain Douglas immediately, Corporal," said Patel.

"Already done, sir. Captain Meritus is attempting to make contact with the man, to see if he can be talked down."

"What do you need from us, Corp?" asked Burton.

"At this time there's nothing we can do but wait for his demands. I have the area sealed off, but thought it best to inform you, as head of ops, sir. The situation down here could quickly become unstable."

"Understood, Corporal. Please keep us informed of any developments."

"Yes, sir. Jones out."

Burton and Patel sat back heavily.

"I knew we should never have trusted those guys," said Burton.

"And yet, Captain Meritus has proved himself to be a stalwart ally," argued Patel.

"I'll give you that, Satnam, but his people are a mixed bag of survivalists, soldiers and fanatics. We just don't know which way they're gonna bounce. That's why we took all their weapons – or so we thought. Wonder what else is waiting to snap us in the backsides?"

Patel's brow furrowed with concern. "Come, Sam. Let us proceed with alacrity."

Burton nodded and stood. "To manufacturing, then."

White found himself on the floor of the isolation unit within Flannigan's new infirmary – Weber stood behind him, weapon up.

Matron stepped cautiously to the side, avoiding both men. At first, she had stubbornly refused entry. It was not until Weber threatened to start shooting people, beginning with White, that she had acquiesced, albeit indignantly.

This was the place reserved for patients worst affected, at least at first, by the virus. Two of them were barely conscious. The third propped herself up on one elbow from the recumbency of her sickbed. Mind still awhirl with phrases and situations from the trilogy of books at her bedside, Baines gave the young, black-uniformed man a quick look up and down. "Aren't you a little short for a storm-trooper?"

"Where is the doctor?" demanded Weber, ignoring her question as he locked the hatch behind them.

"He is attending the main ward," reported Matron. "What is the meaning of this, Lieutenant?"

"They have our master in custody, Nurse Runde. We must free him and return to our people," answered Weber, proudly.

"*Matron* Runde!" she snapped.

Weber's eyes narrowed. "I hope I can count on your support, Runde?" he asked sternly.

"Captain Meritus ordered us to work with—" Matron sighed theatrically, "*these* people. To the best of my knowledge, that order has not been rescinded."

Weber attempted a smile. "It's Gloria, isn't it?"

"My name is *Matron* Runde!"

Weber soured. "Very well, Matron. I put it to you that Meritus is a traitor. We are here to take this Pod and build a new, Aryan society – to claim this world for the master race and the new *Führer*. It was our oath before we left the polluted future behind to embark on our great work – have you forgotten?"

Matron Runde did not answer at once. Eventually she asked, "So, what do you propose?"

"Captain, our systems are coming back online," reported the young officer at the helm, triumphantly. "The *Heydrich* is ready for action!"

"Do we have weapons?" snapped Franke.

"Yes, ma'am," answered tactical.

"Sensors online, ma'am," called another officer. "We have incoming. It's the *Eisernes Kreuz*, Captain. She's hailing us."

Franke nodded for the comms officer to answer.

The cold voice of Dr Heidi Schultz spoke through the comm. *"Franke, once we have landed, you will board my ship immediately and alone. You are to be questioned."*

"Questioned about what?" replied Franke, equally frosty.

"Our entire fleet was disabled because of your actions. There are also questions regarding the suspicious death of Captain Hartmann. How do you respond?"

"My loyalties have never wavered, Doctor. I will obey my standing orders and continue to serve the ideals of this mission."

Schultz nodded, satisfied, as the connection was severed.

"Tactical?" demanded Franke.

"Yes, Captain?"

"Train missiles upon the *Eisernes Kreuz*."

The tactical offer got to his feet in alarm. *"Captain?"*

Franke unholstered her sidearm. "You question my orders, Lieutenant Devon?"

He swallowed. "No, Captain." He sat.

"Now, damn you!" bellowed Franke.

The *Sabre* and the *Heydrich* lay parallel to one another across the river from the abandoned earthworks and palisade created by the *New World*'s crew. Franke watched the night sky as the *Eisernes Kreuz* came about to land behind them, doubtless to create the basis for a three-sided enclosure.

"We have a resolution," the tactical officer reported, tremulously.

Franke had the light of insanity in her eyes as she screamed, "Lieutenant Devon, *fire!*"

"Excuse me?" asked Douglas in astonishment. "You dinnae wish to go?"

"Correct," asserted Heinrich Schultz, coolly.

"Firstly," continued Douglas, recovering quickly from his surprise, "Ah dinnae recall giving ye a choice, man! Secondly, *why* would ye prefer to stay here?"

Morecombe Hetfield placed Schultz's breakfast tray on the small shelf under the serving hatch built into the cell door.

"Why are *you* here, old man?" asked Schultz.

Hetfield's face lit up with amusement. "You're calling me old man, *old man?*"

Schultz's eyes narrowed; they seemed almost fashioned by nature to do so. "I mean, you are too old to be a part of this expedition."

Hetfield smiled, holding in his secrets. "Well, that'll give you something to puzzle over during your trip downstairs. Unless Captain Douglas decides to let you stay, in which case you will of course be *most* welcome."

He sneezed over Schultz's breakfast. "I *do* apologise. What with this virus about and all, can't be too careful. Still, we haven't the rations to waste, so I'll just leave it here in case you decide to eat it. Shame, I understand that eggs are your favourite, too. Isn't that right?" Hetfield winked. "Maybe you'll get better luck at lunchtime, assuming you're not in the front line of a hostage situation by then, of course. *Auf Wiedersehen.*"

Hetfield nodded respectfully to Douglas and left.

"You allow a prisoner in your custody to be treated so, Captain?" asked Schultz.

"All Ah saw was a man bringing you your breakfast. Eat it or leave it – Ah dinnae care."

"I see you have removed Mrs Fischer from the cells, Captain?" Schultz tried another tack.

"She's still helping us with our enquiries. She was only bundled in here to make sure she couldnae get up to any more tricks while we prepared a more suitable place to hold her. As with young Miss Schmidt, we don't want you plotting together now, do we?"

Douglas could almost feel his lie being unravelled by the powerful mind before him. *Schultz's stare really is a force of nature, or perhaps* un*nature,* he thought. *Maybe that's a neologism, but it works for me.*

He refocused to the problem in hand. Lieutenant Weber's demand had been simple and predictable; the hostages in exchange for Schultz and a ship.

"Well?" Douglas tried again. "Why do you wish to stay and remain captive among your sworn enemies?"

"My sworn enemies, Captain?"

"Ah'll have your answer, Schultz, no' another question. Why?"

Schultz smiled, pitiless, reptilian – ironic, given that his meddling had placed them all in a world ruled by such creatures. Perhaps he *did* belong here. However, when he spoke, his voice was at once rich and fluent.

"How quickly we have become used to these clear skies and oil painting views, Captain – a world of bounty and beauty. How quickly we forget the world of concrete and recycled plastic we left behind, with its deadly weather and where the very air we breathed had to be filtered, lest it poisoned us. A world built on weak policies of compromise and proliferation, under-provision and overcrowding. Recall that world, Captain, recall it well – a dying, no, an almost dead world. Fix it in your mind. All I have done has been to heal our planet and provide a future for the human race, free from the hell that *we* created. Was it not Martin Luther who said, 'they threaten us with death; they would do better to threaten us with life'?"

Douglas glowered. "Your arguments all sound so credible, wise even. Until you get to the part where you're happy to kill anyone who doesn't fit into this new social landscape you wish to create and literally delete everyone else from time itself!"

"Ah, but Captain, you refer to the people from our history – the small, the great and the terrible. They will not be *deleted*. They will be, to trade upon your own metaphor, *saved*. They'll live on within our history and within us."

"They'll no longer be people," interjected Douglas. "Indeed, will never have been people. Just characters trapped within the characters on a page, little more than fiction. Not real."

Schultz scrutinised him for a moment before answering. "They're already dead, Captain. We cannot hurt them, but if their memory survives—"

"But if they never *were*, we may as well liken the incredible bravery, effort and sacrifice of The Few, who flew in the Battle of Britain, with the heroism of Frodo Baggins! Or compare Mon Mothma with JFK! It's preposterous and it's wrong, can ye no' see that? And what about the fifty billion souls alive right now, back in *our* time…?"

"*Are* they alive, Captain? None of them will be born for millions of years and one false move here could, without malice aforethought, remove them from the future altogether. Perhaps you should concern yourself more with what *is*, rather than what was or may be – or not."

Douglas held no deep religious beliefs, but he could not help feeling that what he was experiencing would have once been described as the temptation of the devil – so plausible, so wise, so *reasonable.* An evil there for all to see, yet few saw. He resisted the urge to shudder, reminding himself that he conversed with a mass murderer of such complex and far-reaching criminality, that even the man himself could have no way of knowing how many lives he had ruined – or ended.

"You speak well, Schultz. Not the frantic babble of a madman Ah'd expected. However, if you had control of this ship, you would kill everyone aboard who did not fit into your model of a master race. How can you justify that and remain credible?"

"Captain," answered Schultz, reasonably, "the human race has but one natural state – war. I simply aim to reduce the likelihood of our future continuing in the way of our past – even though our future is technically *in* our past." He smiled, this time almost charming.

Douglas was beginning to realise just how dangerous a man Schultz was. A monster who could change his form at will. "You may not have noticed," he answered slowly, "because you seem to have missed the beginning, but your new world has begun exactly like the old one – with violence."

"Of course, Captain." Again, so reasonable. "This is because we here are not all *one*. My aim is to remedy that. Then, there will be no more need of war."

Douglas barked a laugh. "Are ye kidding? How many times has white man gone against white man, black man against black man or any other permutation you care to name? It doesn't matter what ye are, it's what ye do that counts. There are people aboard this ship with whom Ah've no physical relationship apart from being the same species, and yet Ah tell ye, they're family! If they required my life, they could have it. Ah'm not talking foolish martyrdom, Schultz, because ye see, Ah know they'd do the same for me. *That* is the family of man. *That* is the true link we all share. Once you strip the trimmings away: eye colour, skin colour, hair colour, height and build. We're all the same inside. Just the three branches of mankind."

"Three, Captain?" asked Schultz, a glint of interest and amusement in his eye.

"Aye, three. The good, the bad and the indifferent. Ah know which Ah am and Ah know which you are, and that's good enough for me!" He strode towards the brig's exit.

"Captain," Schultz called him back.

Douglas turned.

"You haven't given me your decision. Will you send me away with this boy, or keep me here?"

"The answer will be obvious to you, Heinrich."

"It will?"

"Oh aye. Ye'll know as soon as nothing at all happens, or when you suddenly and without warning find yourself hauled out of here by armed men. Enjoy your breakfast!"

Schultz's fists tightened around the bars of his cell, the muscles in his jaw bunching. He spoke to a closing door, "Very well, Captain. Have it your way."

Descending on thrusters, the *Eisernes Kreuz* was twenty metres from the ground when her tactical officer called across the bridge. "Captain Muller! The *Heydrich* is powering weap—"

The remainder of the report became lost and unnecessary as multiple explosions shook the entire ship.

Alarms went off all over the bridge. Anyone standing was thrown to the deck.

"Taking off and now landing without securing everyone in seats! Have you guys even *heard* of health and safety!" bellowed Rose with righteous indignation.

Tim took her hand, shouting over the din of klaxons and screams. "This isn't landing – IT'S CRASHING!"

Despite the terror of their situation, Tim saw an opportunity – should they survive. He reached out to Heidi. "Cousin, don't die alone!"

They were all strewn across the deck, but Heidi's face betrayed no fear, only anger. Tim's words took away that anger, replacing it with shock and something which may have been wonder. After a moment's hesitation – for moments were all they had left – she took the proffered hand, even returning his squeeze.

In the seconds before death, the mind makes all kinds of spiritual, intellectual and instinctual connections. The teenaged male within Tim's soul could not help noting that if he had to go, then in the scheme of things, dying with an outrageously stunning blonde in each hand was not in fact the worst way.

The *Eisernes Kreuz* listed horribly. Explosions tore through her fuel system, after the *Heydrich* targeted her engines.

Two of the four thrusters began to stutter and lose power, leaving the vertically opposite fore-starboard and aft-port thrusters fighting to hold the vast weight of the ship in the air. Automated stabilisation programs kicked in to save her, but as the damaged thrusters fired and cut out sporadically, even the computer could not compensate and she went down, nose first, listing to port.

The rending of the collision broke the *Eisernes Kreuz*'s back, leading to secondary explosions all along her hull. Fire suppression ran at maximum to protect any surviving systems. The rest of her fuselage slammed into the ground with a boom of seismic proportions.

The *Heydrich*'s engines had fired up in time with their first volley. Franke's ship was already off the ground and in motion as the *Eisernes Kreuz* came down, but in her insanity Franke had not given thought to *where* the *Eisernes Kreuz* might come down.

Landing nose first and twisting to port brought her aft end down towards the *Heydrich*'s engines. The pilot, fully aware of their predicament, had no choice but to fire the main engines to create space between them. He was almost successful, but the violence of the burst from the *Heydrich*'s engines caused the wing of the *Eisernes Kreuz* to explode. Huge shards of metal and composite material cut through the *Heydrich*'s main rocket engines, bringing fire with them. The resulting explosion shot the *Heydrich* forward, allowing the main body of the *Eisernes Kreuz* to miss her.

Aboard the now captainless *Sabre*, a young officer watched the spectacle with both awe and excitement. Whatever the outcome, the chaos fired his blood. He opened a channel to the *Heydrich*, "Captain Franke, this is the *Sabre*. Did your weapons malfunction? May we assist you?"

The *Heydrich* was somehow still airborne, despite the damage to her engines from exploding shrapnel.

"This is Captain Franke to all survivors. The usurper's power has been broken. We will shortly retrieve our leader from the enemy and complete our mission. Remember your oaths—"

The young bridge officer aboard the *Sabre* began to laugh as he ran across to the tactical station. "Train our weapons upon the *Heydrich*." In the background they could all hear further explosions from the *Eisernes Kreuz*.

"Are you sure, Lieutenant?" asked the tactical officer.

"Our future lies with the new regime, trust me. We have the only undamaged large warship on this planet now. We have the power. If Dr Schultz survives this *she* will have to rely on *us*. The old man is gone and probably finished. Train our weapons." He turned to the comms officer. "Switch off that sanctimonious old crow's address, would you? I think we've all heard enough."

Aboard the *Heydrich*, the tactical officer screamed, "Captain! The *Sabre* is targeting us!"

"What's this?" bellowed Franke, disgusted by the duplicity of this move whilst utterly skipping over its irony.

"We cannot take another hit, Captain. We're barely airborne as it is!"

"Helm, take us out of here," Franke commanded. "Flank speed!"

The *Sabre* let them go. Manoeuvring to a safe distance from the wreckage, her senior officer refocused the crew towards search and rescue. Under a red sky, the *Sabre*'s teams worked bravely into the small hours to help the survivors.

The *Eisernes Kreuz* burned...

Chapter 11 | Phoenix

A massive explosion shook the tree in which Jim Miller slept. Needless to say, he woke with a shock, but before he could cry out, a hand was slapped across his mouth. He hoped it belonged to Private Prentice.

It was still dark, and from the way he felt, he guessed he had not been asleep long. Utterly exhausted, both physically and emotionally, he had not so much as stirred when the enemy ship joined its counterparts, just a few kilometres away. Fortunately, his arboreal companion had been more aware.

The explosion, however, had woken every creature for miles. Even through the trees, he could see that the sky was lit by the red-orange glow of a vast conflagration.

"What the hell—" he began, when Prentice covered his mouth urgently once more and Miller suddenly realised why.

The light, thrown by who knew what manner of destruction, cast many shadows in the forest while dispelling others. Among them was one really *big* shadow. Now fully aware, Miller wondered how he had not noticed it at once. It had a depressingly familiar shape, this shadow.

Oh... my... God... he thought slowly. Gently removing Prentice's hand from his mouth, he gave the soldier a nod, showing that he now understood their situation.

After Douglas returned to the Pod with the *New World*, the stories had flown around in a frenzy, with every little adventure adding to the whole. Miller had been particularly interested in the stories of the old couple, Hetfield and Marston, and their fifty years living in the Cretaceous. Combining their stories with his own, he fancied he could now place a moniker upon this shadow standing before him, head several metres in the air.

Matilda. His mind conjured the name as he silently cursed his luck. *Why does she keep coming after* me? he thought plaintively.

The recent explosions had shaken the ground, so it was fair to assume that Corporal Jennifer O'Brien and young Henry Burnstein would also have been rudely awakened. Otherwise, they had no way to communicate the threat which stood in the middle of the track between them. Miller hoped that their colleagues' very silence meant they were aware, rather than in some way incapacitated.

A shudder of fear ran through him, this time not for himself but for the young man he had sworn to protect. He liked Henry and cared for him, despite the relative brevity of the young man's relationship with his daughter. All their lives were accelerated now. Where every minute was filled to bursting, the quickening of emotions was only to be expected.

In the stillness following the explosions, he second-guessed himself. Should he have stayed with Henry? What could he have done to protect the lad that a highly trained soldier like O'Brien could not?

The veteran Tyrannotitan heaved a huge sigh, bringing him back to his own, very real, very close problems.

Focus! Miller chided himself.

Apart from the occasional deep breath, the giant was otherwise eerily silent and unmoving. Her breathing was slowing markedly, the recent turmoil already forgotten.

She faced west. Miller guessed she had picked up their scent, probably before the explosions, and followed. Their bikes were buried under ferns and twigs. Enough to bamboozle the casual human observer, but against the advanced olfactory senses of an apex predator, he knew their ruse was pitiful.

It was dark in the forest, of course, but thanks to the fires, no longer pitch black. Both men sat rigid, nestled within the fork between two large branches. A miserable bed for the night – but not any more, it seemed.

To human eyes, their friends were invisible in the blackness, but Miller was not taken in. He remembered nestling in rather more comfort back aboard the Pod, lounging across one of their sofas as he listened to

Rose recite from Tim Norris' *Cretaceous Living* notes. Something about a theory that many theropod dinosaurs would have had excellent eyesight, perhaps equal to or even surpassing that of an eagle. Some may even have had extraordinary night vision. Thinking of the descendent dinosaurian birdlife from his own era, this was quite easy to believe.

Memories of Rose and their life before cut to his heart. It was almost with perversity that while his memories misted over the comforts of hearth and home, another part of his brain was creating a list: *Superb sense of smell, incredible eyesight, probably good hearing, oh and while I'm at it, fifty feet long and capable of carrying all four of us off in its jaws at once! Damn!*

The whole idea of a motionless target being invisible to certain dinosaurs, including but not limited to the mighty Tyrannosaurus rex, had been rendered preposterous over a century ago. However, for Miller and his party, it was literally all they had, bar fighting their way out of this – and he could only shiver at *that* prospect. So they stayed put.

Fortunately, O'Brien and Henry, assuming they were unharmed, appeared to have the same plan, or at least the same lack of one.

Still, the giant dinosaur remained perfectly motionless. Thanks to Hetfield, Miller now knew that it was a female, although that knowledge in no way made him feel any better about his situation.

What's she waiting for? He was dying to ask the question aloud, although he doubted the others knew any more than he.

The huge head swayed, very slightly.

Miller clenched. *This is it!*

The slight movement recurred, but to the opposite side, followed by a small dipping motion ending with the nose rising again, the jaws parting slowly.

These were truly unique creatures, their ways almost unfathomable to their mammalian observers, but then the predator released another deep sigh, putting Miller in mind of a sleeping dog. *Now there's a dangerous postulation. Could she actually be asleep? Immediately, so soon after all this ruckus?*

In a way it made sense. To the uncomplicated mind, all that mattered was now. A few minutes ago may as well have been last year – forgotten, irrelevant. She had found a scent, but she was tired, so she slept. To senses perfectly attuned for hunting, the scent would be there for hours – there was no rush. Could it be that simple?

The attack that followed was not what Miller expected. The assault was entirely directed towards his nostrils and he gagged, doubting any of them had ever smelt anything so rancid.

This time he clapped his own hand over his mouth and nose, struggling to hold his breath. One whimper could break the spell and get them all killed.

Can these animals sleep standing up? Is that possible, too?

He knew that horses and elephants did, even cows *could* sleep while standing, although they rarely did so. Perhaps more importantly, some birds could too; flamingos, for example. His mind busied itself with conscious thought, hoping to distract his senses and central nervous system from acting automatically, causing him to vomit.

My God, how does she live with herself? It was perhaps a rather uncharitable, even ungallant thought, but he was a man terrified for his life.

A low grunt came from deep within the animal's stomach and chest as she began to sniff the air. Her jaws parted once more with a crackling growl.

It's over, thought Miller. Visions of his wife and daughter shot through his mind, followed by the entire sixteen years of Rose's life on fast-wind, when suddenly he sniffed too. He was not given time to process the full ramifications of what he sensed before his thoughts were scattered by an enormous roar from the head of the Tyrannotitan, just a few metres away from his face.

Miller would have fallen out of the tree had Prentice not reacted with a soldier's reflexes and reached out to grab him.

At last, Miller's thoughts caught up with something the dinosaur had worked out several seconds ago – carried on the air were the unmistakable traces of an ancient enemy who, by luck or destiny, just happened to be man's best and most dangerous friend: fire.

Another roar caused them all to cover their ears and then she was off.

Running west along the trail, the Tyrannotitan known as Matilda left them behind.

The immediate forest, so subdued with silent terror in the presence of Matilda, suddenly exploded to life all around them. Screeches and calls assailed them from every direction, both on the ground and among the branches as a second migration began.

Amid the cacophony was one sound Miller had longed to hear. "Are you guys alright over there?" shouted O'Brien.

"I'm n-not sure! How are y-you?" he replied through teeth suddenly chattering as shock caught up with him.

"About the same," Henry called back. "That thing was running from the explosions, I think. And then it just stopped, right on top of us – can you believe it! What was it doing?"

"I think she simply stopped and went back to sleep," replied Miller. "Maybe she was asleep before all hell broke loose to the east?"

"She?" queried Henry.

"We've met before – please don't ask."

"Well, *I've* got a question to ask," stated O'Brien, a nervous edge to her voice. "Did anyone think to pack any beer?"

"We have teams out on the hull installing fixing points for the new lenses, gentlemen... and ladies," reported Singh.

The entire complement of the *New World*, barring Heinrich Schultz, Erika Schmidt and a couple of guards, currently occupied the officers' mess, drinking tea and coffee. The only females present were Kelly Marston and Dagmar Fischer.

Singh continued, "As the lenses are made from a polymer base, they're not overly heavy, so we're using a non-destructive adhesive to place the units. Mechanical fixings would be more likely to damage the hull. Jim Miller's team, currently led by Dr Patel, is already turning out a sample pair for us to trial. One will be fixed to the hull, the other aboard one of our remotely operated vehicles.

"We will fly the small ROV above the ship and align it with the lens on the hull. A second ROV will fly higher still, pointing its camera down at the *New World*. If part of the hull vanishes, as expected, we'll build the rest."

"Will we really have time to build enough of these things to cover the pointy end of this vast ship?" asked Marston.

Singh winced. "The *New World*'s proud and magnificent *prow* is indeed very large, but it's simply a matter of location and focal length. In other words, the further the lens is from the ship, the larger the area of deflection. Some of the lenses may even be fixed to the cliff face above us.

"We are also within the cauldron of a large volcano, so the angles from which any spycams may spot us are limited, too. This will reduce the required number of lenses dramatically. We calculate that, working together, our fixed and ROV-mounted lenses will cover a field of vision equating to a ninety-degree cone, and this should be adequate."

"Excuse me, I am not a physicist," interrupted Dr Klaus Fischer, "but are we relying on the lenses' *alignment* to complete the false image by remaining in sync with the spycam's field of view?"

"That's correct, Doctor," agreed Singh.

"In that case," continued Fischer, "how will we know where the enemy's cameras are going to be?"

"That's a good question," Singh accepted. "It's the problem which will surely present us with the most difficulty. To detect any ground based or low-level surveillance, we intend to set up a sensor array at the top of one of the mountains nearby. This system will only give forewarning and telemetry for vessels approaching at subsonic speeds, but if we are being hunted from the air, we assume they'll be searching carefully and so..."

"They will approach fairly slowly," Fischer completed. "What about weather conditions?"

"We are using sonics, rather than optics, Doctor, so freezing shouldn't be a serious impediment. However, we do have a little trick up our sleeve in that regard – the microphones' casings are already fitted with tiny vibrating panels which act like speakers.

"Although formerly designed with seismic geological surveys on Mars in mind, with a little tweaking, they will generate a pulse calibrated low enough to excite water molecules. Hopefully, this frequency will minimise icing but lack the modular strength to give us away – low frequencies create long wave patterns which degrade quickly. By way of analogy, *shortwave* radio was successfully used to send *long range* communications, even into the digital age, for exactly the opposite reason.

"The microphones themselves will be attuned to pick up on the ultra-high frequency which seems to bleed through the enemy's stealth technology from their engines.

"Despite all this, if the weather is bad enough to confuse our microphones, it will likely be too poor to see much on the ground either – perhaps even too poor to fly through."

Fischer nodded and looked around the group. "This is a very clever plan, Lieutenant Singh, but I have to ask the *other* question."

Singh chewed his lip. "You mean how do we position our lenses to block the view from ships we can't sense? Ships or cameras in orbit, perhaps?"

Fischer nodded again.

"The short answer, Doctor, is that we can't – at least, not entirely. What we *can* do is run the ROVs on an automated rota, allowing for charge and repairs downtime, so we always have *some* coverage. Of course, running the blind twenty-four seven *is* the downside with this plan.

"If we get an atmospheric flyover, our early warning system should give us the time to mobilise every unit we have, to cover all the angles. Fortunately, the view from space is pretty much straight down, so I believe we can protect ourselves against unfriendly eyes in orbit with fairly minimal coverage.

"Our other defence is the sheer size of the planet and the comparative smallness of our revealed prow. We're practically on the other side of the world from where we started out, just a few short hours ago, and the enemy have only a small number of craft with limited fuel and resources." He smiled. "It's also worth remembering that in the mid-Cretaceous there's no satellite network, so we'll be very unlucky if they come across us."

Captain Emilia Franke gazed dispassionately down from orbit at the virgin world beneath them. "Launch the satellites," she ordered.

Her ship was wounded, but it would be repaired. The topmost of the four main engines had been heavily damaged by flying debris from the *Eisernes Kreuz* during their escape. Configured in a diamond formation, like those of the *New World*, *Heydrich*'s engines not only controlled thrust but also orientation and attitude. Although these functions were augmented with flaps and air brakes during atmospheric flight, in space the ship needed all four engines to control pitch and yaw while under main power.

The damaged engine may have cost them a quarter of their overall propulsion, but the loss of controlled downward thrust provided good incentive for going into orbit.

Franke was more concerned about the damage sustained to their wormhole drive. This meant that, for now, they were trapped here.

The drive was essentially useless without engines to push the ship *into* the generated wormhole. Without forward thrust, any wormhole was just a light show. Subsequently, the drive, by its very nature, was linked to the main engines. The massive feedback loop from the explosion had damaged the main control interface. They had spare parts, of course, but the replacement processor seemed to be defective.

Franke found this suspicious. Theirs was a meticulously planned operation. It was hard to believe that any spare parts were not rigorously tested before loading aboard. It was possible they had a saboteur among them, but she doubted it. This had the feel of a 'built-in' problem and she suspected that the answer lay with Schultz himself. He clearly had at least one method of disabling his ships, perhaps he had others too.

Upon discovering the defective processor, she had immediately instructed her engineers to run every possible check on the original, searching for any form of self-destruct. Unfortunately, if there had been any such device, the evidence was well covered by the explosion damage.

It would make sense, at least to a mind like Schultz's, to be able to trap his people here with him, should any dissent arise. If he stopped them jumping back to the 22nd century, he could not have them simply fix the problem and leave anyway, could he?

Franke could not prove this, of course, but she knew how the man thought.

On the other hand, Heinrich Schultz had shown the foresight to include everything they might need to find their quarry. Especially a quarry as sneaky as Douglas had proven himself to be.

In a perverse and introspective moment, Franke could not help wishing they had him on their side, but she knew that would never happen. Douglas may not necessarily be a bleeding heart himself, but she knew he would always defend their right to exist.

"A waste," she said with a sigh.

"Captain?" asked her helmsman.

She held up a hand, shaking her head. The man returned to his sensors, tracking the tiny satellites as they shot from two small ports, one on either side of the *Heydrich*.

Franke could see some of them with the naked eye, briefly, before they powered up and shot off at immense velocity – each programmed to secure a specific orbit that, when combined, would drape a net over this ancient world.

"Have we heard anything about the hostage situation?" asked Meritus. He had borne a subdued air ever since Weber's betrayal came to light.

"This isnae your fault, Tobias," replied Douglas kindly. "Ah know what it's like to no' see something like this coming. There's been no answer yet, but dinnae worry, we've got one of our best men on point down there."

"Does he have much experience with hostage negotiations?" asked Meritus, lifting slightly.

Douglas smiled blandly.

"Alright or wha'?" Corporal Dewi Jones greeted Lieutenant Weber via the small video camera set within the hatch between them.

Weber, standing within the new medical isolation unit, offered no response, so Jones continued, "Well, it's like this, boy. The old man doesn't want to go, isn'it?" As an afterthought he added, "Sorry."

Weber's normally intense stare turned murderous. "You're lying!"

Jones scratched his ear. "There's no need to be like that, now. I don't know what else to tell you. He said no."

Weber opened his mouth to retort, but froze when he heard chuckling behind him. He turned to find Baines grinning from ear to ear. "It's coming unravelled, bucko! Didn't think this through, did you?"

"Shut your mouth," he shouted back at her.

White rolled his eyes.

Matron tutted.

Weber turned back to Jones. "Do I have to start shooting people to get your attention?" he snarled.

Jones brightened as an idea struck him. "Look, I'll tell you what, I'll see if Captain Douglas can pipe through a video call from the prisoner's cell. That way he can tell you himself, how's that?"

Weber squinted into the camera. "And how will I know if he's free to talk or whether you have a gun to his back?"

"I'm not being funny, like, but that'll be hellish tricky to prove, it will. I suppose you'll just have to trust us. After all, it's you who's waving the gun around, eh?"

"*Trust* you," mocked Weber. "Alright, I'll speak with him. Set up your call, but I warn you this will change nothing and if you've mistreated him, believe me, these hostages will be begging for death after I get through with them. When it comes to inflicting pain, I was trained by the best. I can keep them in torment for days, if necessary."

"No need for threats, boy. I'll call him now in a minute, see? I know what it's like to live in torment for days, so don't do anything rash."

Jones turned away, but Weber called him back. "What could *you* possibly know about anything like that?"

"Me mam forced me to stay in a caravan in Pontdolgoch for a week. Belonged to this fella she knew – total tosser! After a few days I was tamping!"

Weber's expression curdled further. "Do you really think I care about *your* petty enmities?" he asked, incredulous.

"No, no, he was a mate, like, you know?"

Weber opened his mouth to ask a question but gave up. "Make the call!" he bawled instead.

"Tidy," replied Jones, signing off.

White's shoulders were rocking as he tried to constrain his laughter. Baines did not bother. Matron tutted.

The smoke was acrid and choking. Electrical fires bloomed and wilted, fighting with automated suppression systems in a combustive symphony. Diminuendo followed crescendo as sparks flew everywhere carrying the stench of burnt metal and melted polymers.

Tim lifted his head painfully. There were almost fifty people aboard the *Eisernes Kreuz*. Enemies or no, he could not help wondering how many of them still lived.

Groaning, he pushed himself up. Rose lay motionless at his feet, hair draped across her face. His heart jumped.

Please no... he prayed.

Stiffly, he knelt and brushed her blonde locks aside. "Rose?" His voice sounded like it came from the bottom of a fish tank. He shook his head to clear it; something trickled down the side of his nose and into his mouth. He could taste iron. Pain followed hard on its heels and when he put a hand to his scalp, it came away bloody. Clearly, he had struck his head, but had no idea where or how.

"Rose?" he tried again, feeling for a pulse, but his hands shook so badly he could not discern her condition. *What should I do?* His mind would not focus, so he blearily turned her over. Fortunately, she began to cough and turned back on her own.

Unable to do anything more practical or useful, Tim held her to him.

Rose gestured for him to help her up and together they struggled to their feet. Heidi was also beginning to move and Tim knelt to help her. "Are you OK, cousin?"

She looked at him in confusion. Gradually, her intelligence seemed to reassert and she accepted his assistance.

They turned to find Rose kneeling over Del Bond. "He's not breathing," she cried out.

"Give him CP... er... CP..." Tim floundered, his thoughts wrapped in cotton wool.

"CPR," Heidi supplied brusquely. "Get out of the way, girl." She tugged Rose away from Bond and began working on him. Within a few seconds, he too coughed back to life.

Some of the bridge crew were also coming round. Others were less fortunate.

"*Kapitän* Muller?" asked Heidi. "*Kapitän* Muller?"

Rose saw him first and approached the man, bent backwards over a console. "Are you OK, Captain?" she asked. "Captain?"

Schultz walked unsteadily towards them. She could tell immediately that Muller was dead.

"Can you help him?" asked Rose.

"Don't be silly, girl. His back's broken. Come, we must go, before the whole ship goes up. Move!"

"I don't think sleep is on the cards for anyone tonight," O'Brien observed, drily. "What do you want to do, Jim? This is your party."

Miller appeared somewhat haggard, but did his best to think. "Obviously, I want to go after my daughter, but..."

"But?" asked Henry.

Miller shrugged. "We really need to know what's happened behind us. Rose might even be aboard one of those ships. If she was part of whatever happened back there…" he tailed off, his expression fearful.

"For what it's worth, Jim, I agree with you," said Prentice. "There's also the matter of that monster we just barely escaped. Taking the opposite direction to him is alright by me, if we're taking a vote?"

"Actually, it's a *she*," Jim corrected, distractedly – for good measure adding, "Matilda."

"That's nice," O'Brien commented caustically. "OK, kids, let's get packed up and hit the road! I'll take point. Adam, you've got our six. Jim and Henry, stay in the middle." She clapped her hands. "Come on people, let's go before *Matilda* realises she left without her lunch pail!"

Heinrich Schultz's demeanour remained cool, belying his fury underneath. The young fool could have been a serious asset aboard this ship. An asset he could have spent not only to secure his freedom, but more importantly, to assert his control. Now all he had was a wasted opportunity, and soon, a young idiot for a neighbour.

"Will you speak with him?" asked Douglas.

"I see Meritus is keeping a discreet distance from this," the old man replied.

"Do you blame him?"

Schultz shrugged. "And what do you wish me to tell young Mr Weber?"

"Something along the lines of 'stand down', perhaps? You must know that whatever he threatens, whatever happens, Ah cannae let you leave here with our coordinates, Schultz."

"Even if the boy makes good on his threat to kill people in order to secure my freedom, Captain?"

"Even then. What good will it do to save a couple of hostages if it gets everyone else killed?"

"Captain, you still refuse to see sense on that point. I have never threatened to kill all of your people."

Douglas glared back at him. "No. Just the ones you don't like the look of."

Schultz smiled serenely, making a palms-up gesture.

"Will you speak to Weber or will ye no'?"

Schultz nodded consent.

"Lieutenant Weber?" Jones enquired.

"Well?" Weber replied curtly.

"Your boss would like a word. It's being patched through to the doctor's office."

"Very well," said Weber. "Major White, remain where you are. Matron, let me know if he moves."

Matron Runde nodded.

Weber pointed at Baines. "You! With me."

"I'll need my crutches," she replied. "I still have a broken leg, you know."

"Get them and move." He turned back to White. "Any trouble from you and the one-legged woman gets it!"

"The name's Baines," she retorted. "*Captain* Baines, as it happens, *Lieutenant*."

"Everyone who was aboard the *Last Word* knows who *you* are. Now, move or die!"

With that he ushered her roughly towards Flannigan's office, as one of the unconscious patients began making sounds of distress.

Baines stopped.

Weber shoved her. "I said move!"

Recovering her balance, Baines turned. "She needs help." Seeing none in the young man's eyes, she tried again, "She's one of your own people!"

He glanced at the woman and replied coolly, "Then she will understand."

Baines glared at him with disgust, all traces of earlier humour gone. "This is the world you're trying to usher in? It'll be even more screwed up than the one we left behind. And with these levels of cooperation, I wouldn't give it a month before you're all *extinct!*"

"Matron Runde, keep the patient quiet," was Weber's only response before he pushed Baines, hard. "Sit there!"

She fell sprawling into the office. Clutching her fractured shin in silent concentration, she willed the agony to subside as she hauled herself into a seat.

A screen popped up from the desk's surface. Self-activating, it displayed an icon that flashed to denote a call waiting.

Weber accepted it and the face of Heinrich Schultz immediately filled the small monitor. Baines craned forward curiously, to see what he looked like.

"Sir!" Weber snapped a smart salute. "They told me that you—"

"*Listen to me, Weber*," Schultz interrupted curtly. "*You have bungled this opportunity. There is no way Douglas will allow either you or me to leave here now, not with knowledge of their location. You've made a shocking mess of things.*"

"But, sir, I have hostages—"

"*Imbecile! Douglas will not risk the lives of almost two hundred people in trade for two officers.*"

"But, sir," Weber tried again, plaintively, "one of them is Captain Baines, sir..."

"*Who is a serving officer. Serving officers die all the time, boy. It's par for the course!*"

"No, sir. I've been told that Baines is much more to Douglas than merely one of his officers." He grinned lasciviously. "Their relationship is more *inappropriate*, sir."

"*You've 'been told',*" Schultz mocked. "*Douglas is a by-the-book officer. Even if there were any truth in what you've heard, he would sacrifice his own well-being for the people under his command – that is their principal weakness, the reason they never do what is necessary! Do you understand nothing?*

"*Now listen very carefully, Weber. I am ordering you to stand down—*"

Weber's comm rang noisily in his pocket, interrupting them. He took it out to check the message.

Schultz's face reddened in fury while his voice calmed to a seethe. "*I am speaking, Lieutenant!*"

Weber looked up, wearing a stupid grin of disbelief. "Sir! They've found us, sir. A partial satellite net has been established and they've found us! All I have to do is hit respond—"

The eggshell clack as Baines' crutch connected with the back of Weber's head was nauseating. The comm flew from his hand back out onto the ward.

"That's what you get for messing around on your comm when you should be paying attention to the world around you!" Baines quipped, savagely.

Matron Runde picked up the comm before Baines could reach it. There followed a tense, uncertain moment as Baines *and* Schultz waited to see what the woman would do.

Eventually, she stated, "He was not able to send a response," and handed the device to Baines.

"*Traitors! Idiots!*" Schultz hissed furiously, slamming his fist down onto what Baines assumed was his thigh.

"Bad luck, Grandad!" Baines taunted. "You should have trained your boys not to mess with a girl on crutches!" She accepted the comm. "Thank you, Gloria."

"It's *Matron!*"

O'Brien slowed her bike and hopped off, pushing it into the brush cover, left of the trail. The others in their small party followed suit, walking the last few metres through the thinning foliage to the treeline.

Dawn was well on the way to full daylight. O'Brien knelt, pulling a pair of field glasses from a jacket pocket. The others came to kneel beside her.

The plain before them seemed strange without the immense bulk of the *New World* and Pod at its centre, completing the D-shaped enclosure. The huge earthwork and palisade remained, but open-ended, and without the ship herself, it was now useless as a defensive structure.

However, the real news was all taking place on the far bank of the river. It was hard for Miller's team to work out exactly what had happened. When they left the previous evening, there had been two vessels, lying parallel to one another. There remained two, although they could not tell if they were the *same* two; all that was clear was that they had moved.

The first seemed intact but was many hundreds of metres from its original location, while the second lay in a very peculiar position. Despite this, what really caught their attention was the fact that it was also on fire.

"There are people climbing amongst the wreckage," said O'Brien. "Many people."

Prentice pointed towards the intact ship. "Look, people coming and going from the other vessel, too – must be a rescue operation."

"Or the taking of prisoners?" suggested Miller.

"Maybe it's both," added Henry, darkly.

"May I see, Jen?" asked Miller.

"Sure," replied O'Brien, handing him the glasses.

The operation was well underway and must have been going on for some time. Miller adjusted the focal length and studied the people, the stragglers he supposed, running or staggering from the burning ship; some were alone, some escaped in small groups or with the help of others. It was a spectacle of tragedy, but there was courage at work here, also.

Suddenly, his eye alighted on one of the escaping survivors in particular. "Thanks," he muttered, passing the binoculars back to O'Brien.

"What should we do, Corp?" asked Prentice.

O'Brien shook her head, making a sucking sound while she pondered.

"I don't see what we *can* do," Henry added his two penn'orth. "What do you think, Jim? *Jim...?*"

Prentice looked around sharply. "Where's he gone?"

Hearing a rustle through the foliage, O'Brien followed the sound through the trees and out onto the plain. Once again raising her field glasses she noted, "Ah, hell – *it's in the sewer!*"

Captain Emilia Franke was alone in her stateroom. She reached for a towel, after splashing a little refreshing water onto her face. What a day it had been – a costly one.

Damn that girl! she thought, balling her fists. Heidi Schultz had always been a figure of respect, not merely family to the old man, but his chief disciple and strong right hand. How could she have betrayed him the way she had? Now things were bad. The *Dawn Fleet* originally consisted of the *Last Word* and the three smaller vessels, the *Heydrich* being Franke's command.

Now the *Last Word* and the *Eisernes Kreuz* were destroyed and the *Heydrich* would take days, perhaps even weeks to repair. Even the *Sabre*, though intact, had lost its captain. "Damn you too, Hartmann!" she cursed. "If you hadn't forced my hand with your talk of collaborating with that wretched traitor, Meritus – cowards all!"

At least she still had her operative aboard the *New World*. With the satellite net online, it should only be a matter of hours before she had the enemy's new location. With that information, the time for half measures would be over. As soon as her ship was battle ready once more, she would begin her assault and do what should have been done from the start.

She smiled at her reflection in the viewport. "I'll be with you shortly, Heinrich. *I* will take the Pod from that band of scum and miscreants to reinstate you – and *you* will owe me."

Jim Miller crossed the plain towards the river alone and at speed.

"What the hell is he playing at?" asked Prentice angrily.

"He's spotted his daughter," supplied O'Brien, shaking her head disapprovingly.

"Rose!" cried Henry, turning to retrieve his own bike.

"Adam, stop him!" barked O'Brien, getting back to her feet. "We can't just run after him, Henry."

"The hell we can't! You wanna let him go alone?" he cried.

He suddenly appeared very young to O'Brien. "No," she explained gently, "but he's revealed himself now. They still don't know we're here and I intend to keep it that way for as long as possible. Besides, I don't know how the hell he plans on crossing that river."

"Do we have any inflatable boats?" asked Henry, calming slightly as he tried to think.

"Not much call for those on Mars, lad," replied Prentice. "Maybe Captain Meritus' people came with some, but it's not the lack of a boat that's our problem."

"Indeed," agreed O'Brien. "The problem is those crocs on steroids. I suspect those people will need time to lick their wounds after this – quite possibly time to salvage anything useful from that wreck, too. Now, if it were me, I'd get everyone inside the working ship and bring it across the river to make use of *our* abandoned compound."

Prentice nodded his agreement. "Aye, it would only take a couple of days and a few strong backs to alter the walls – close part of them in to the new ship."

"But that ship's tiny," said Henry. "I mean compared to the Pod and the *New World*."

"Just a matter of shovels and graft, lad. Like I said, they would only need a section of it to make it viable."

"Adam's right," agreed O'Brien. "I was gonna suggest that we wait and watch, but now…"

"Sarchosuchus," muttered Henry.

"Eh?"

"Huh?"

"It's what Tim said those crocs were called," Henry informed them sadly. "Also, we should be careful about doing anything near the river that might attract the other critters. Particularly the—"

"Oh, don't tell me, let me guess!" interrupted O'Brien, once more looking through the binoculars. "Real ugly muthas, yeah? Long snouts? Heads like crocodiles, but run about, carrying most of their weight on their hind legs?"

"Lemme see," asked Henry.

She passed him the glasses and sure enough, emerging from the river further downstream were another group of predators that were not above scavenging a free meal; especially when smothered fires were replaced by the scent of death and distress on the wind.

"Irritators," Henry breathed the name like a curse. "We need to call Jim back."

"If we break radio silence we won't be able to help him, or any of the others we've come for, later," said Prentice.

Henry tried O'Brien. "But Jim's riding into an ambush," he pointed out, desperately.

They all turned to watch Miller move across the terrain at a speed that, while impressive, was unwise.

Now less than a hundred metres from the river, he closed quickly. Handlebars held in a death grip, eyes wide with terror, he noticed movement farther down the bank to his right, to the east. He *also* knew the river was full of crocodiles, some growing to twelve or even fifteen metres in length and weighing many tons.

They seemed to be keeping to the water for now, perhaps cowed by the fire and noise of the last few hours. As Miller approached the bank, he began to see them, moving just under the water, like vast tree trunks with nostrils. Occasionally one rolled. There were dozens of them.

Across the river, he could see several people milling about – many were female, most were blonde. He sought just one of them, and that was when the light of insanity supplanted the fear in his eyes.

Back in the forest, O'Brien almost dropped her binoculars as she called out, "What the *hell* is he doing?"

"No, no, no," muttered Prentice, shaking his head in horror and disbelief.

"Whoa! Back the truck up!" Henry cried. "Don't do it! Don't do it!"

Miller reached the riverbank, still travelling at close to fifty miles an hour. There was simply no way he would be able to stop on the sandy margin – he did not even try. Instead, he continued *on*to the river. The crocodiles were so tightly bunched that he rode over them, followed by an angry riposte of thrashing snaps as frustrated jaws closed on nothing but air, often mere inches behind *his* behind.

Almost at the other side, Jim's finale to this brand-new *Motocroc* sport[8] was a fifteen-metre dash along the back of the biggest of them all. The monstrous creature was barely aware of Miller's meagre weight until he passed the halfway point. Then its powerfully sensitive olfactory suite suddenly sniffed out that something was perhaps awry.

Miller was still a good ten or twelve metres from the far bank, when this mother of all Sarchosuchi began to rear. The rise gave the *lunicyclist* the exact trajectory he needed to attempt a suicidal leap from the enormous head.

Miller gunned the accelerator.

The powerful electric motor gave up all its torque in one massive surge to the rear wheel, sending the wildly fishtailing chemist skittering across the furious creature's incredibly sensitive nose.

Miller leapt for life.

Once airborne, he seemed unassailable, defying both gravity and art with a no-nonsense jump across predator-infested waters from the nose of a giant crocodile.

A hail of mud and destitute metaphors fell from the sky behind him, all snapped up instantly by the lightning lunge of a furious Sarchosuchus. Aiming for the rear of this most discourteous titbit, it caught Miller's back wheel, stopping the bike dead and snatching it from the air. The rider, perhaps fortuitously, continued his trajectory, reaching his zenith as water became sand again. Another five metres and he landed among the ferns to roll and roll and roll.

---

[8]   Later described by Henry as *Crocotrialing.*

Watching from the forest – now on the opposite side of the river – his compatriots were left wide-eyed, holding their hands over their mouths like three speak-no-evil monkeys.

In fact, the whole world seemed to take a breath after Miller's high octane leap.

A few accelerated heartbeats later, a man clambered unsteadily to his feet among the brush, staggering drunkenly. "That happened," he muttered blearily before continuing on foot towards the ruined ship and the daughter he loved.

"YEEEESSSS!" shouted O'Brien, Prentice and Henry, completely forgetting themselves until O'Brien came to her senses and pulled them back into the trees.

White awoke with a start. Remembering where he was, he hung his legs over the side of the hospital bed and rubbed his eyes.

"Bad dreams?" asked Baines.

He treated her to his lopsided smile. "Haven't been getting much rest recently," he admitted.

"Hmm, sadly, you'll have all the time in the world to catch up for a while, now you're locked up in isolation with us."

White looked nonplussed. "All I needed! Now we've arrived there'll be so much to do and to organise. And if that's not enough, I've lost another two security personnel taking Weber to the *New World*'s brig, too. Once they touched that young fool, they were cursed to stay aboard the infected ship!"

"You can give your orders from here, Ford. At least you haven't been signed off by your doctor!"

He snorted, despite his annoyance. "Becoming a little antsy about getting outta here, Jill?"

"Last night's action was the first thing to happen to me in days. I almost didn't want it to end!"

White laughed. "How are the other patients, Matron?"

"Settled and sleeping now," she replied. "A restful sleep. I think that they are coming through."

"And how are *you* doing?" White asked her, seriously.

She stared down at him for a moment, wondering if he was genuine. "I am fine, also. I do my job, Major."

"You did more than that," added Baines. "If you'd hit respond on that comm, it would've been a game finisher for us. Why didn't you?"

Again Matron took a moment before answering. "I have told you. I do my job. I obey my Captain. He says work with you, I work with you. There *was* no decision – you make too much of this."

"No, we don't," White chipped in. "It was a fine thing that you did and I for one am grateful to you."

"Me too," seconded Baines. "You hold Captain Meritus in great esteem, don't you?"

"Whatever you may think of me, I am a healer," replied Matron, slowly. "When you people destroyed our ship, sending us over into that steep ravine, you could have killed us all."

Baines looked slightly abashed, but answered, "I had to protect my people from a Nazi warlord. I didn't want to do it, but I make no apology."

Matron nodded. "Quite so. However, many more of my people would have died had it not been for the captain. He refused to leave until every injured man and woman had been retrieved from the wreckage and carried to the relative safety of our camp. Furthermore, despite heading into a hostile situation, he left a reasonable and well-equipped contingent behind to protect the wounded. Some among our leaders would have abandoned them to their fates and taken everything they needed with them into battle."

White nodded his understanding. "So I made the right call with Meritus, then."

"I have known Captain Meritus only for a short time," continued Matron, "but if we are to survive in this world, we have more chance with a man like him leading us."

"I'm inclined to agree," said Baines. "Pity he's locked down aboard the *New World* as much as we are here."

White sighed with frustration. "Never mind. We should use the time to plan what comes next. Jill, I have a few ideas."

Taking her crutches, Baines hobbled across the ward to take a seat beside White's bed. "Go on."

"I'm thinking about planting. We're already leaving it late and our rations deplete by the day, especially since we took Meritus' people aboard – no offence, Matron."

"I only had chance for the briefest look outside from a porthole, before Weber put a kink in my day. Best I could see, we're inside a huge crater partially filled with a lake. Around the edges there appeared to be some low-lying land inside the rim of the mountains.

"Now, I can't say whether these lands were floodplain or not, but they certainly appeared verdant and that gives me hopes for our crop."

Baines held her hand up as if in class. "Landing near fertile land is great news, but if we start cultivating fields, it might give away our position to any unfriendly eyes in the skies."

"True," White acceded. "So I suggest we cut down an area where the trees are youngest or undersized, leaving small copses every five or six metres apart. If we cut them at random intervals and vary the size of each, we'll still be able to machine plough between them. However, from above, the landscape will have a largely, no pun intended, organic look about it."

"What about protecting our people out there?" asked Baines, devil's advocate. "We've no idea how wild the wildlife gets in these parts. This isn't the Blighty we left behind, after all. Foxes and badgers never tended to swallow men whole. Even the occasional adder in the grass would seem a friendly face compared with what's likely to be waiting for us out there." She sighed, maudlin. "In fact, even a bit of grass wouldn't go amiss."

They both pondered a safer, softer world. "Come on," said White. "Let's not lower our spirits."

"You're right," Baines smiled, sadly. "I think I've just been staring at this ceiling for too long."

"I understand, Jill, and you do have a point about the land outside. It *is* full of unknowns. However, Sandy seems to have done real well in finding us a place closed off from the rest of the world. The mountains around us are high and look difficult to pass. However, there may be one or two rivers in and out of the lake. If there are any dangerous animals here, that'll be how they get around."

Baines raised an eyebrow. "That's not overly comforting, Ford."

He shrugged, palms up. "It is what it is."

Heidi, Tim, Bond and Rose watched the insane river crossing agog. Fellow survivors and rescuers alike, all stood frozen to the spot.

As the man fell among the ferns, so did a silence. When he eventually regained his feet, some little distance closer to them than where he had disappeared, a ragged clap began, followed by a blast of applause, calls and whistles.

Closing on their position, the dirt-smeared face soon became clear to Rose's young eyes and she screamed in joyful surprise. Pulling away from Tim's grip, she ran towards the heroic maniac.

Heidi reached forward to stop her, but Bond placed a gently restraining hand to her elbow. "Where's she going to go?" he asked, sensibly.

Rose ran as fast as she could into her father's arms. Miller, still a little disoriented from his ordeal, almost went down again, but held on to her, eyes tight shut.

When he opened them, tears obscured his vision. Nevertheless, he could not fail to note the approach of enemy personnel, and in good numbers.

They surrounded the pair and after the delight of finding his daughter, alive and whole, ice suddenly gripped at his heart. It was with great surprise that he noted the many smiles and heads shaken in disbelief, possibly even admiration.

Heidi forced her way through the ring of onlookers. "Are you alone?" she demanded harshly.

Miller swallowed and merely nodded.

"How came you to be here?" she asked.

"I stayed behind."

"Why?"

Miller's eyebrows rose in surprise. "You really need to ask? You have my daughter."

"And now I have you. I will be fascinated to hear what you think you have achieved? Apart from almost getting yourself killed, quite spectacularly, I might add."

Tim tugged lightly at her sleeve. "*This* is family, cousin."

She looked at him with genuine puzzlement. "*This*," she replied, "is stupid. A mistake. I had a young girl, of little worth – other than as potential breeding stock – now I have a world-renowned chemist. Moreover, I also have all the leverage I need to bend him to my will."

Tim put his head in his hands.

"I won't help you, Schultz," spat Miller, defiantly.

"Of course you will, you silly man," Heidi answered lightly, snatching Rose from his arms. "As you say, I have your daughter."

Weber awoke to pain. Groaning, he put a hand to his head and felt it wrapped in bandages. Opening his eyes made things even worse. The windows to his soul felt like someone had lobbed half a house brick through them.

While he wished for a way to lower the gain on his vision, the bright lights of the brig seemed to operate at a frequency not unlike the repetitive rhythm of sewing machine needles, stitching his retinas directly to their optic nerves.

It was excruciating enough, without dwelling upon the situation in which he now found himself. This really was all too much, but then things got worse.

"Imbecile!" hissed Schultz from the adjacent cell. "I had you where I wanted you and now look at us!"

Weber winced. The ferocity of Schultz's stare was almost worse than the lights.

"But I had a plan, sir—"

"Idiot!" the old man shouted, getting to his feet.

Weber cringed from the volume.

"You should have waited for my orders and now matters are worse. How could you not realise that Douglas was *unable* to let us leave? It would have cost them everything. If that were not enough, you had the chance to contact our ships in orbit and while you were busy telling me about it that *woman* took the opportunity away from you!"

"I'm sorry, sir. I thought—"

"You *thought*," interrupted Schultz derisively. "You have further thinned our list of assets. Note also that everything we do and say in here is monitored by the enemy, so think on that and keep your mouth shut!"

Schultz turned his back on the young officer. *There must be other loyal officers aboard this vessel*, he mused. *All I need is a distraction.* He smiled coldly. *Fortunately, I still know something my enemy does not.*

Beck was feeling much better. Although Dr Flannigan had been unable to find the physical cause of her recent collapse, she knew well that it had been a psychic attack; one that struck with a magnitude she had never before experienced.

Fortunately, her friends, both living and passed, had helped her through it.

She could feel Mario near, just checking in on her. *Bless him*, she thought. *I don't know what I would have done in this world without him, and the others.*

She lay back, focusing on her breathing. For days she had been afraid to open herself fully, but now she smiled serenely and relaxed. That was when she felt him.

The *New World* may have left her earthbound enemies behind, but this creature could not be shaken so easily. Beck knew that if the sub-creature found a way to affect more than her own psychic well-being, it could spell disaster for their people. She had to fight, but it was so *strong* – stronger even than before, she could feel it. A sense of malevolence, hatred, darkness, and it was growing, learning. Eyes wide, she cried out.

Flannigan was instantly at her side. "What is it, Beck?"

"Dave, you must listen to me," she cried out, breathless and in pain.

Her doctor, at a loss to find a single thing wrong with her, squeezed her hand. "Beck, stay with me. Come on, now. Let me help you sit up."

With a gargantuan effort, Beck sent out a psychic blast, backing the demon off – for now.

She sat up, grateful for Flannigan's help. "Dave, I know you don't believe in all my 'hocus-pocus' as you call it." She spoke painfully. "But I need to tell you something. I don't know what happened with Schultz, but that prompt Mario gave us panned out, didn't it?"

Flannigan looked uncomfortable.

"It's OK, Dave. I don't expect you to reveal the details of a security situation to a civilian, but I *know* Mario's advice was good."

"I don't pretend to understand what you've got going here," admitted Flannigan as kindly as he could, "but I will say that *your* insight led us to an idea which brought a solution. I'll say no more than that."

She smiled. The pain receded a little, leaving the light of mischief in her eyes. "Mario says he's sorry, by the way."

"*Does* he?" replied Flannigan, not believing a word. "For what, may I ask?"

"For tipping hot coffee into your lap, of course." She chuckled. "He just asked me to tell you that he hopes it didn't ruin your pants!"

Flannigan's jaw dropped. "How did you...?"

Beck smiled sweetly.

He threw his hands in the air. "OK, I'll bite. What do you wanna tell me?"

"Listen carefully. There are several spirits among us – people we've lost, mostly, but one of them is malignant. I believe that Captain Baines ordered someone's death, just before our attack on the enemy battleship. I don't know the details, only what I felt.

"Whoever that was, did not pass over well, Dave. They were probably as evil in life as they are now in death, but what I'm most concerned about is the fact that this entity is growing stronger."

Despite himself, Flannigan felt the hairs on his neck rise. *I'm not buying this... am I?* he asked himself.

Beck took his hand. "I know you have doubts. How could you not? But please believe me when I tell you, HE'S BACK!"

She jumped out of the bed, almost collapsing before Flannigan could grab her. "OK, Beck. It's OK, I got you."

"No! I mean he's back! He's here!"

Flannigan had a serious case of the chills now. What the hell was going on? "Nurse!" he called. "A little help here!"

"It's OK, Beck. We're just gonna give you something to help you rest—"

"NO!" screamed the medium. "You'll weaken me! I won't be able to fight! Dave, please. I beg you!"

Flannigan was at a loss. How could he believe any of this garbage? And yet...

"Beck, you have to calm yourself. We've got some real sick folks in here and they need rest."

She was no longer hearing the doctor and nurse as she crawled backwards up the bedstead. Before her, there stood a tall young man with a distinctive scar diagonally across his brow and down over his right eye. As he grinned at her, the scar turned white, standing out still further.

"Get him away from me!" Beck cried out.

Flannigan grabbed her wrists. "Nurse," he ordered with a nod.

The nurse filled the hypodermic needle with a clear liquid, squirting off the excess.

"NO!" Beck screamed once more.

The nurse walked *through* the young man with the scar, to approach Beck from the opposite side of the bed. He laughed, enjoying her fear and the chaos it was creating.

With every ounce of willpower she could muster, Beck attempted to calm herself, looking Flannigan in the eye. "If you put me out, Dave, I won't wake up – *please.*"

Seeing clarity reasserting itself in her eyes, he held up a hand for the nurse to stop.

Others circled her bed now, friends – some of them military and ready to fight for her.

The demon vanished.

"He's gone," she whispered quietly.

"Who?" asked Flannigan, completely at sea.

"Dave, that creature will bring us down if he can," she managed. "You must ask Captain Douglas to keep a round-the-clock guard on Schultz and no one should be left alone with him."

"What? He's well locked up. What do you think's gonna happen?"

"That *thing* may have been an enemy soldier once, but now all he cares about is bringing chaos to us all. He will use Schultz, Dave. I can feel it. He will speak to him, help him. The old man probably won't even know it."

Flannigan swallowed. "Look, I just don't know what to—"

"Dave!" she fired up again.

"Alright, alright," he said gently. "Doubling the guard will certainly cause no harm."

"Promise me!"

Flannigan helped Beck lie down once more. "I promise. Hey, it's gonna be OK. I'll get on to James as soon as I get you settled, huh?"

"You believe me then?" she asked hopefully.

He sighed deeply. "I don't know what the hell to think, but that coffee did trash my pants. Tell Mario, he owes me for the laundry bill, next time around."

Beck looked disconcertingly over Flannigan's shoulder and gave a brittle smile. "He says, there are two pairs in his locker. If they fit, they're all yours. He won't need them."

Flannigan snorted. "When I get outta here I might just do that."

Beck was suddenly serious. "Thank you, Doctor, for not putting me out."

"You bet," said Flannigan.

For most of the USS *New World*'s crew, the last several weeks of their lives added up to a string of dilemmas, dramas and crises – with intermittent explosions and running. Woodsey, however, was bored.

With most of his mates off doing who knew what, who knew where, he had taken to splitting his time between reruns of his favourite shows and exercising Natalie Pearson's faithful hound, Reiver.

He suddenly remembered his last conversation with Henry, just before the young American left to undertake a seriously dangerous mission. He looked down at the dog and grinned.

Reiver seemed to grin back. Indeed, though Natalie appreciated Woodsey's care of Reiver, especially during her often long shifts, she was less sure about the effects of this association upon her dog's behaviour.

"Come on, boy, let's go and keep a promise," said the New Zealander.

Presently they arrived at the Burnstein apartments. As the tallest of the pair, Woodsey pressed the bell.

The doors slid apart to reveal Henry's mum. "Hey, Mrs B," greeted Woodsey, familiarly. "I promised Henry I'd drop by now and then to check on Clarrie. Is she around?"

Chelsea Burnstein brightened. "Yes, she'll be glad to see a friend." Chelsea leaned in close to whisper conspiratorially, "She hasn't been right since young Tim disappeared. Then Rose was kidnapped and Henry went to follow her and…" She sighed.

"Chin up, Mrs B, I'll soon have her grinning again—" Before Woodsey could finish, Reiver began to growl, his hackles rising.

Sure enough, a large man entered from another room. "Who was it, honey— You!" Hank Burnstein snapped suddenly, pointing at Reiver, who responded by revealing some impressive canines.

"Get that *goddamned* critter outta here!" Burnstein bellowed. "You're lucky they wouldn't let me bring my shotgun cabinet aboard, you mangy S.O.B! Get the hell out!"

"Hank," Chelsea interceded. "They're friends of Clarrie's, come to see how she's doin'. That's OK, isn't it?"

Burnstein refused to take his eyes from Reiver's, which of course was exactly the wrong thing to do with an angry dog.

Woodsey's face split ear to ear into a grin. "Sorry, Mr B, I had *no idea* you were afraid of dogs – honest."

"I ain't afraid o' nothing! That monster's got it in for me, is all! Look at his face! That thing's a killer!"

Woodsey covered his mouth with his hand as he tried to stop himself from laughing. "He speaks highly of you, mate," he managed.

Burnstein snatched a large cushion from the sofa, ready to defend himself from any attack. The growling escalated and was now interspersed with barking as both males prepared for combat.

"He'll be OK in Clarrie's room, Hank," said Chelsea placatingly. She slapped her thigh a couple of times with her palm. "You won't hurt us, will you, boy?" she asked the dog in a high, friendly voice.

Reiver looked at her, his hackles dropping immediately. Lips covering teeth once more, his tongue lolled from the corner of his mouth as stupidly as his tail began to wag vigorously. Almost propelled across the room by it, he landed at Chelsea's feet.

Sitting proudly straight-backed, head held high, he was now ready to accept her praise and adoration... which was duly given.

"Oh, what a good boy," she gushed, stroking his head and tickling his ears. "My gosh, isn't he *gorgeous?* Don't you think, Hank?"

Burnstein pulled the cushion up close to his chin, as if readying himself to hide behind the sofa from a horror movie.

Woodsey followed Chelsea and Reiver down the hallway to Clarrie's room. "Nice talking with you, Mr B," he grinned.

Chelsea knocked on her daughter's door. "Clarrie, honey? There's someone here to see you."

They heard the hasty rustle of female panic, followed a few moments later by a nonchalant, "Come in."

As the door opened Reiver burst into the room and ran over to the bed, waiting to be invited up.

"*Hey*, boy," Clarrie greeted him, enthusiastically. "Hup, hup you come."

"Now, hang on. I've been told not to let him— Ah well, whatever." Woodsey gave up. With all the women's attention bestowed upon Reiver, he reasoned that no one was listening to him anyway.

"I'll leave you kids to talk," said Chelsea at last. She moved to the door, closing it behind her.

"You're lucky Dad wasn't here," said Clarrie. "He's got a bit of a phobia about Reiver. Apparently, he's still got a scar on his butt, too," she sniggered.

Woodsey grinned broadly again. *"Really?* I never knew. Look, kiddo, now there's just the two of us left here at the moment, I promised Henry I'd keep an eye on you. You know, just until he or the skinny Pom gets back?"

Clarrie continued to stroke Reiver, but her expression darkened slightly. "I'm so worried about them, Woodsey. Do you think they're OK?"

"Yeah, mate," he replied easily. "Look, I've brought you something. Dad has access to some of the recorded camera feeds during our flight over here. They're all busy, building something or other at the moment, so I felt sure he wouldn't mind if we log in and take a look. What do you say?"

"Yeah," replied Clarrie, excitedly.

"Hey and guess what, there's something I spotted which I think you'll find interesting…"

Henry watched Schultz's people lead Jim and Rose away. Through the binoculars, it appeared that Tim went with them willingly. He wondered at that, but shrugged it away, thinking, *I suppose he has no choice.* "Is there *nothing* we can do?" he asked O'Brien.

She shook her head, also frustrated by their lack of options. "I still think they'll bring the ship over to our compound, once they've scavenged the wreck. All we can do for now is stay out of sight, stay alert and most importantly, stay alive. Sorry, kid."

Prentice clapped Henry on the shoulder, reassuringly. "So, we settle in, lad. Why don't you break out a few breakfast rations from our packs while we keep watch, eh?"

Henry nodded and walked a few metres to where their bikes and packs were stowed.

Prentice turned to O'Brien, speaking quietly so as not to alarm the teenager, "How long *can* we wait around, Corp? Our resources are limited. Even the power in the bikes won't last forever and I don't fancy fighting those crocodiles for Jim's rations and equipment, do you?"

"I know," agreed O'Brien. "If we can't find or manufacture some kind of advantage, there may only be one option left to us."

"Surrender?" asked Prentice, stoically.

O'Brien gritted her teeth, unwilling to admit it to him or herself. All she could say was, "We're not there yet."

Ships, like many vehicles, take on a life which is tangible and real to the people who care for them. Dr Heidi Schultz was not such a person, but as she watched the last of the fires die within the *Eisernes Kreuz*, she could not help seeing a burnt-out ghost where there once had been power and vigour.

It was a sad sight, for anyone, but Heidi was not just anyone. She was what she had been made. To her, the destruction was expensive – her go-to reaction, anger.

She smouldered like the ashes of trillions of dollars outside her window. Feeling a presence behind her, she turned.

"You wished to speak with me, ma'am?" asked a young man.

She nodded briefly. "You are the lieutenant who reported *Kapitän* Hartmann's suspicious death?"

"*Hai*," he admitted gravely.

"You believe he was murdered by *Kapitän* Franke?"

"Yes, ma'am. She accused Captain Meritus of shooting him, but I know that Captains Hartmann and Franke were at odds about our mission before his murder.

"Also, Captains Hartmann and Meritus always enjoyed friendly relations – until Meritus' defection, of course. They would have gone into battle against one another, I don't doubt, but murder?"

"Indeed," she agreed sternly. "They both displayed a lamentable predilection for weakness."

"Yes, ma'am."

Heidi smiled coolly. "It seems that *Kapitän* Franke has now proven her guilt quite spectacularly and in no uncertain terms. However, your instincts were correct, Lieutenant. Therefore, I am promoting you. Congratulations, *Kapitän* Aito Nassaki."

The young officer smiled craftily while bowing courteously. *"Arigatou gozaimasu*. Thank you, Dr Schultz."

Heidi stopped a passing crewman. "Carefully pack away *Kapitän* Hartmann's belongings and prepare the vacant quarters for *Kapitän* Nassaki. Make sure Hartmann's rank insignia are saved and fixed to *Kapitän* Nassaki's uniforms."

The crewman looked surprised, but saluted them both before carrying out his orders.

"It seems that once again we must rise from the ashes, *Kapitän*." Heidi looked her new second in the eye – like Hiro and yet unlike. "Do not fail me," she added ominously.

Captain Aito Nassaki gave a smart salute and left her to her thoughts.

She had no sooner turned back to the smoking ruin out on the plain, than Tim appeared at her side.

"Where have *you* been?" she asked, tersely.

"Toilet," he admitted. "Thinking."

"About what?"

He wondered for a moment, how best to lead her. "I've been pondering how I can make you understand what family is meant to be."

"You naturally refer to the empty gesture of that fool Miller," she replied.

"That was no empty gesture, cousin. He went through extraordinary danger to be with his child."

She turned to look at him closely. "So you think that 'family' is doing stupid things for one another to prove that you care? For Miller, how did it help?"

"Rose is no longer alone on a ship of enemies – she has her father with her."

"Not if I split them up," she pointed out.

"Regardless, she will still know he's here and more importantly, that he *came* for her. Has anyone ever done anything like that for you? I'm guessing not."

She could not argue the point so she ignored it.

"What would it take, Heidi, for you to make a deal with the people of the *New World*, instead of trying to destroy them and take what we could all share? It seems so costly and ultimately, pointless. We're just making one bad decision after another and whittling away at what little resources we have left."

"And this is what you have spent an hour on the toilet deliberating?" she asked, wryly.

"What can I say?" he answered with chagrin. "It was quite a 'three-poop-problem'."

She snorted derisively. "Weakness and division must be stamped out. There is only one way to do this – eliminate all who oppose us. If we birth our new civilisation on the weaknesses of the old, we will simply make all the same mistakes again."

Tim stepped in front of the viewport, blocking her view to gain her undivided attention. "You already are."

Heinrich Schultz awoke a little disoriented. He never usually slept during the day, but incarceration was, at the heart of it, punishment through boredom. Even for a mind as powerful as his, there was only so much cerebral planning he could undertake before distraction gnawed. For the prisoner, any kind of self-determined routine was purposefully rendered impossible. It was an intolerable situation for such a busy man – it was meant to be.

Schultz never dreamed. Untroubled by conscience or concern for any living thing but himself, he slept remarkably soundly. Or at least he had, until now.

His last two sleep cycles had been troubled by horrible visions. With everything from the torment of repetitive non-events to the destruction of all life around him as he melted, undying, in a volcano's crucible; waking up came as a relief.

The young man in the next cell also seemed to have fallen asleep.

Schultz removed his shoes, a pretence of making himself more comfortable, which allowed him to note a scuff on the toe of his right. Buffing it with a sleeve gave him the opportunity to remove a tiny device hidden beneath the insole.

Any electronic devices would have been immediately picked up by the scans he underwent, both after his capture and again before his confinement. For that reason, the device was completely dormant, carrying no battery or power source of any kind, but when clicked into the back of a small button, which closed the inside pocket of his exquisitely tailored jacket, it became a very simple communicator. The metal content of the device was so small that it was easily missed amongst the everyday metallic apparel fixings upon his person.

The boy's pathetic attempt at rescue had served one purpose, at least – Schultz now knew that his people had managed to activate a partial satellite net. He also knew that any outgoing comm link would likely be noticed straight away by the *New World*'s staff, so he would get but one chance.

Ever since the boy's comm received a signal from one of his ships, he had been composing a simple message. His main problem was that he did not know for sure who would receive it.

Pathologically paranoid, Schultz had devised four unique communication codes; one for each of his captains. He could communicate privately with each of them, without anyone, even the *other* captains, being able to decipher any message's content.

It made sense to suppose that his granddaughter, believing herself betrayed, would have assumed control of the mission. If so, she would doubtless have taken the *Eisernes Kreuz* for herself. Knowing his granddaughter as he did, that would mean Captain Wolf Muller was now either compromised or dead.

Captain Aurick Hartmann was a good soldier, but less loyal to the cause than Schultz would have liked. Whereas Captain Tobias Meritus had proved the very embodiment of just how badly wrong a sense of duty and honour could go, when unrestrained by zeal.

If he was lucky, the listener in the sky would be Captain Emilia Franke. Franke was a true fanatic who enforced his every whim like her very essence depended upon it.

It was a gamble. Yet, if anyone was to rebel against his granddaughter's usurpation, it would certainly be Franke. So, it was a two-horse race. The recipient would be Franke or one of Heidi's people – and the odds, as far as he knew at that stage, were two to one against him.

The other problem he faced was twofold. Firstly, once sent, his enemies would jam any further transmission immediately, so he would never receive a response. Secondly, his order, which would be both sensible and wise to Franke, would be nonsensical gibberish to his granddaughter. However, it would eloquently pinpoint the *New World*'s position and he was unsure how drastic a response Heidi might mount. He needed this Pod, and preferably the *New World* herself, intact.

He drummed his fingers silently on the mattress of his bunk. Reaching a decision, he shook the device.

The act of clicking the unit into the button freed a tiny magnet from a secure dock, allowing it to oscillate through a coil of wire no thicker than a human hair. The magnet was made from neodymium. In an exotic state, the atoms within the element whirled like a helix, all weirdly spinning at different rates to create a colossally powerful magnet for its size – powerful enough to send a signal into orbit. Schultz's minimal shake of the wrist was all it took to build a charge inside a minute capacitor. Within moments the device was ready for action.

He sent the message, coded for Franke. To anyone intercepting it, it would be a burst of Morse code, but the packets and syntax would be meaningless.

If it reached the desired recipient, he would have a few months to kill, while eating someone else's food and all would be well.

If it did not... well, he would know soon enough.

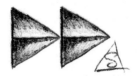

Chapter 12 | Montage

"Jen, how long can we live in this cave?" asked Henry, seriously. "We've been watching the enemy ship for... actually, I don't know. How long *has* it been?"

"Almost two weeks," supplied Prentice, sitting cross-legged across from Henry, around their small campfire.

"Right," Henry acknowledged. "Maybe I should carve a tally on the rocks!"

O'Brien did not answer at once. She understood the young man's impatience; he had risked all to find his girl and so far had only lost her father. They had seen neither hide nor hair of either since that day. She finished chewing a mouthful from a drumstick that tasted, perhaps unsurprisingly, like chicken.

"Thing is, Henry," she began, "nothin's changed. We still need to watch them and gather as much intel as possible, in case we find a chance to report back to the *New World*. Our only other alternative is to give ourselves up, yeah? And I for one am *not* ready to trust our lives into the hands of that psycho, Schultz. She was freaky enough when we thought she was on *our* side, but when she showed her true colours..."

Henry visibly deflated. "I thought we were gonna go in and try and get 'em out," he argued plaintively.

"I understand, lad," Prentice soothed. "But *you* need to understand that ninety-nine percent of soldiery is about waiting."

"And the one percent?" asked Henry.

"Sheer panic!" chuckled the private. "But even by waiting we *are* doing something."

Henry frowned. "And what's that?"

"Waiting and watching for the right moment to act. You're lucky, son."

"How so?" asked Henry, looking at the soldier askance.

"If we had a sergeant with us, you'd have spent the last two weeks with a shovel in your hands, digging up South America."

"What for?"

"Pretty much just to stop you complaining about being bored, I think. Maybe I'll understand the reasoning, if I ever get some stripes on my arm," he chuckled again. "That knowledge is still above my pay grade at the moment. What do you say, Corp?"

O'Brien grinned and opened her mouth to answer when a succession of beeps sounded from her comm, startling them. For a moment, they simply looked at one another before she reached for the comm. "We've got a message," she stated enthusiastically. "It says, 0845 hours. Burger. Bad Luck. Moon."

"Is that a message or answers for the pub quiz?" asked Prentice.

"Gimme a minute," replied O'Brien. Her forehead furrowed in concentration. "0845, 0845…"

"But it's already way past eleven, fellas," Henry could not help noting.

"No. When I made corporal, Major White forced me to memorise some code words – you know, in case we were ever lost in enemy territory, 12,000 klicks from our unit, that kinda thing."

"Awesome," Henry added fatuously. "And all this time I thought we might be in trouble."

"Tryin' to think here!" snapped O'Brien. "Don't make me unpack the folding shovels for you two! Right, now '0845' means west, that one's simple – you know, quarter to nine on your watch face? It's nothin' to do with the time, OK? Now, if I remember correctly, 'burger' means supplies or delivery or drop – somethin' like that."

"And 'bad luck'?" asked Henry. "What's that mean? Your delivery ain't comin'?"

"That's a shame. I was right looking forward to pizza, an' all," chipped in Prentice.

"Will you two save it!" O'Brien retorted crossly. "I'm tryin' to remember. Now, I'm pretty sure 'bad luck' means crashed or crash site."

"Ominous," said Henry quietly, afraid of getting his head bitten off again.

"So what's 'moon' mean?" asked Prentice. "Show us your ar—"

"Arrive at night!" O'Brien cut across the Yorkshireman, glaring at him. "Better keep those shovels on standby, Private! So, to recap – west, delivery or drop, crashed or crash site and come under cover of darkness."

They sat in silence for a moment.

"The *Last Word!*" They all spoke at once.

"Has to be," O'Brien elaborated. "They're making some kind of drop for us at the enemy's old crash site and, I assume, as we only just got this message, they're setting this up for tomorrow night." She clapped her hands enthusiastically. "Yeah! *Now* we're talkin'!"

0600 hours, one day earlier – The tropical island chain of Great Britain, 12,000 kilometres north-north-east of Patagonia

Douglas leaned against the wall outside Patricia Norris' convalescent room. He waited as patiently as he could for the British microbiologist to wake from her medically induced coma.

Primed for any complications, Dr Dave Flannigan was attended by a full emergency team as he began to bring her round.

Although the reptilian virus, inadvertently contracted from a snake bite, seemed to have run its course, Douglas still wore a mask; so fragile was Norris' condition. He was not usually an impatient man, but he could feel his nerves fraying on this occasion. Naturally, he was deeply concerned about Patricia's well-being, but additionally, he had to find a way to explain about her son, too.

Were it not bad enough that Tim was in enemy hands, Douglas' decision to leave him behind on another continent compounded matters, and if that were not enough, there was also the *other* problem.

How the hell am Ah going to explain to Patricia that her son is Schultz's grandson and Heidi's cousin? he thought wretchedly. *Let alone that some aboard this crew actually think he's collaborating with the Nazis for a piece of the pie if they win!*

Douglas did not subscribe to this theory. In fact he spoke out against and actively discouraged any talk of it.

He brooded, so deeply lost within these dark thoughts that the tap on the shoulder made him jump.

Flannigan smiled. "Sorry, James. Just thought you'd like to know she's awake."

Douglas visibly relaxed and breathed deeply, only now realising how tense he had been. "That's great, Davey," he replied, returning the smile.

Flannigan took him to one side. "Keep it light, James, please. I expect you will be wondering how to explain about Tim?"

"Aye," Douglas agreed.

"The first thing she said was 'Tim'. She has a memory of Heidi taking him so maybe you can work on that? Maybe even spin it – the boy's alive and healthy after all, isn't he? I would ask you not to tell her about Tim's possible associations."

Douglas shook his head. "No. That will have to wait for another day. Ah do have news that may provide some hope, however. The planting for the harvest seems to be going well. We've fully secured Schultz and made sure he doesnae have any more little toys on his person and Ah'm now free to think about a mission."

"A mission?"

"Aye. Ah assume you want to be in there with me to make sure Patricia's alright?"

"Yes, James. I hope that's OK with you?"

"Indeed. It'll kill two birds with one stone. Shall we?"

Douglas followed Flannigan into the private room. He was horrified by Norris' appearance.

She seemed near death, yet she recognised him and croaked, "Hello, James."

Douglas took the chair to her left, Flannigan drawing up a seat opposite. "You gave us all quite a scare there for a while, Patricia." He spoke kindly, trying to keep the concern from his voice.

"Tell me about my son," she said. Clearly, she was finding it difficult to speak.

Douglas understood and cut straight to the point. "Ah spoke to Tim a little after his capture. He's in good health and he doesnae seem to be in any danger. Ah suspect that, as the man who knows more about this time and world than anyone currently living, Heidi will be keeping him in luxury. So try not to concern yourself unduly. Ah willnae say dinnae worry, you're his mum, but he really is OK. OK?"

She nodded weakly.

"A lot has happened since you came in here," Douglas continued, nodding to their surroundings. "You'll be keen to be brought up to date in due course, but for now, everything seems to be quiet and surprisingly positive.

"We've begun planting for the harvest. In fact, Ah've an amusing little story about that. You remember Thomas Beckett, the armchair historian? He complained like hell when we told him he had to take a turn on the shovel. Practically screamed the place down!

"Well, it turns out that after a couple of days planting, he's a born gardener – loves it! We cannae keep the man in!"

Patricia smiled.

"There's lots more good news, but all in good time. You'll want to know just what Ah'm planning to do to get Tim back. So Ah'll tell you. Ah'm going after him, Patricia. We leave tomorrow."

Flannigan nearly dropped his clipboard, but Douglas shook his head for him to remain quiet.

"Ah'm not allowed to hold your hand, Patricia," said Douglas, kindly, "but Ah swear Ah'll get him back somehow. Ah willnae give up until he's here with us again, whatever the risks, Ah promise ye."

A single tear ran down Norris' cheek and she smiled bravely at him before her eyes closed and she lapsed back into the darkness.

Flannigan moved immediately to take her pulse. "She's asleep. She'll be fadin' in and out for a while," he whispered, gesturing towards the door. "I think that'll have to be enough for this sitting, James."

Douglas nodded and followed him out.

Once the door was closed firmly behind them Flannigan asked, "You're doing *what?*"

Douglas held up his hands in a calming gesture, ushering Flannigan towards the privacy of the ward office. He closed the door and began, "There's more to this than Ah could go into in there. Don't worry. Ah willnae be going alone."

"That's great, Captain. For a moment there, I thought you might be considering something reckless!"

Douglas snorted. "OK, Ah admit, this willnae be easy, but we have a problem.

"Satnam Patel has hit a snag with the development of our new wormhole drive. It's barely off the drawing board yet, but he can already see that manufacture of some of the parts is going to be difficult. He was banding around phrases like 'this will take about three years to develop'. Obviously, this is out of the question. With all the forces ranged against us we need to get from here way sooner than that, somehow. And this would seem the best way."

Flannigan listened attentively, but frowned in puzzlement. "What does this have to do with the search for Tim?"

"Our young Mr Norris and some of the parts we need are very close to one another. It'll mean getting back aboard that damned black monstrosity, where Schultz held me captive, but Ah think we can do it."

"James, stop, please," said Flannigan with finality. "They still have three warships in the vicinity – OK, if Old Man Schultz was attempting contact with someone in orbit, perhaps only two on the ground – but that's a huge amount of firepower and they'll see our shuttle coming by the time you're halfway around the planet!"

Douglas grinned. "Ah didnae know ye cared."

Flannigan breathed out something halfway between a sigh and a chuckle.

"Ah have a plan for that, Davey. We believe we can get in, get the parts we need, spring our people and get out. Besides, we may think we stopped Schultz's signal before it was received by anyone, but we've no way of being certain. We must act *now*."

Flannigan nodded, resigned. "Just make sure you bring all the pieces back."

"Pieces?"

"Yeah. So I can stick you guys back together again!"

"Sam! Satnam! How the devil are ye?" Douglas asked chirpily as he strode into Pod operations, bearing a tray of mugs.

Burton and Patel looked at one another and then back at the captain. "*What do you want?*" they asked in unison.

Douglas laughed. "Paint, gentlemen. Ah need some paint mixing, please."

Burton looked at him as if he were mad.

Patel said, "We're developing farming equipment at the moment. We've quite a large operation underway to sow seeds across many acres and organise stores until the crops are ready, Captain. Oh, yes, I almost forgot. We're also trying to build a completely new kind of wormhole drive, that none of our engineers have ever seen before, so that we can jump half a kilometre of ship a hundred million years into the future, to take us home." He turned to Burton. "Did I miss anything?"

"Only one small thing – hardly like to mention it really – we're trying to do all this in absolute secrecy whilst hiding under the noses of spy satellites and immensely powerful space-faring warships."

"Of course," agreed Patel. "You can see how a small matter like that may have slipped my mind. Perhaps you wouldn't mind 'redecorating' once we have these little chores out of the way, Captain?"

Douglas laughed again. "OK, OK, you two. Ah get it. No, Ah'm only asking for a small favour and in fairness, Ah think it'll be critical for getting the parts you need for the new drive."

Burton threw his pencil down on the papers strewn all across his desk. "Well, bladdy 'ell, when you put it like that, you should have just said."

"Have you boys managed to get any rest recently?" asked Douglas, not offended by their irascibility, merely concerned.

"I've had loadsa sleep, mate," replied Burton. "Musta wasted about three hours on it, not two days ago. What about you, Satnam?"

"My doctor told me that sleep can lead to 'unhappy captain syndrome' and that I should avoid it at all costs."

"Et tu, Satnam," replied Douglas. He set the tray down on Burton's desk to affect a dagger in his chest. "Ah thought that would be your reaction, so Ah brought hard currency."

He leaned across the desk to place a mug of steaming coffee before each man. "Now, gentlemen, about my paint – we need to camouflage some of our ships and vehicles. Ah know you already made some, for the truck we're using as a tractor – we simply need more, but with a few extra features. Ah have a plan!"

"Extra features like what?" asked Burton. "And I don't take milk, by the way."

Douglas chuckled. "Sorry, Sam. Mary was too busy to help me. And, as we cannae set off on our mission without the things Ah need from you, turns out Ah was the only one with nothing to do!

"Now, with regards to my paint, radiation absorbance would be good, for a start – of the non-ionising sort, naturally."

"Naturally," Burton noted, deadpan.

"Of course," seconded Patel.

"Gentlemen, Ah want the ships to be hard to see. Ah thought you could augment the camo paint you've already provided, turning it into a rubber solution and introducing iron and carbon fragments to make it repel radar. What do you say?"

Silence…

"Was that a tumbleweed Ah just saw roll by?"

0200 hours

The middle of the night, vehicles hastily covered with camouflage paint, every flight-capable lens-carrying ROV available in the air – it was time to go.

Captain Jill Baines sat once more in the command seat of the *New World* with her leg in plaster and her nose in a sling. She had impressed everyone by not wavering in her foul temper from the moment Douglas revealed his plan right into the small hours. Eventually, she had realised she could not change his mind, but acceptance dragged its heels.

She opened an internal comm link to the shuttle, for the moment, still within its berth aboard ship. "This is Baines to Douglas. You are cleared for launch, Captain. Can I try and persuade you out of this madness one last time?"

"Aye, course you can, Jill," he replied, the smile evident in his voice. *"Let me know how it goes. Ah'll see you when Ah get back."*

Baines' expression soured further. "For the love of God, take care, James. We need you here, all of you, and will continue to do so long after this action is over."

"This is only a wee camping trip. We're no' leaving home, Mum." After a short pause, he added, *"Thanks, Jill. We'll be careful, Ah promise. Take care of business for me."*

"I will. Good luck, James. Come back safely – *please.*"

The shuttle bay doors opened within the bow section of the *New World*, revealing a night sky so beautiful that it took Douglas' breath away. The twinkling of starlight on the still waters of Crater Lake, as they had named it, was almost too perfect to be real. He whistled softly.

"Looks like computer generated holography," said Hiro. This analogy was passion indeed from the chief engineer.

Douglas carefully manoeuvred the shuttle out of the bay, hovering above the beach at the lake's edge. A small team on the ground waited for the shuttle's winch to lower from her belly and connected it to the cradle, which held a three-ton mini digger.

While they carried out the procedure, three of the *New World*'s escape pods joined them, all carrying armed men and equipment.

Captain Meritus flew one of them. He had offered to bring his orbital attack fighter. With its stealth capability, he could have flown them to the *Last Word* much more quickly and attracting a lot less attention. Douglas had refused, stating that their only serious fighter craft should remain at the disposal of Lieutenant Singh, in case the *New World* was attacked.

Fully loaded, the tiny fleet set off south-south-west.

The officer monitoring sensors from the *Heydrich*'s bridge turned in her seat. "Captain."

Captain Emilia Franke left her command chair to see what was happening. "What do you have?"

With a hand wave above her console, the young woman flicked the information to a heads-up display for Franke to see for herself.

She watched with interest as the four tiny ships left their hiding place beside the lake to set off south. The picture was very sketchy, with vessels disappearing from the screen and reappearing elsewhere, sometimes only in part. "What is wrong with these scans?" she asked tersely.

"Nothing, Captain," replied the sensor officer. "They seem to have developed some kind of basic cloaking technology to confuse our cameras."

Franke's eyebrows rose. She may have loathed everything the enemy stood for, but their ingenuity impressed her nonetheless.

"In fact," continued the young officer, "had we not received that coded message from the surface, it may have taken us months, maybe even years, to find them."

Franke nodded dumbly. *We must not underestimate Douglas' people,* she reminded herself.

"Tag those ships and follow them wherever they are going. If you have to reposition our satellites, then do so – even if it causes black spots. We must know what they're up to. This ship will be factory fresh and ready for action again within the next ten days and I want to know where *every* piece is on the board before we act."

The young woman turned to face her. "But, ma'am, I thought we had orders to stand down until the enemy bring in their harvest, later in the year?"

Franke's eyes narrowed. "*Your* orders are to follow every move our enemies make. I also expect you to keep a close vigil on the *Sabre*. Have they answered any of our hails?"

"Negative, Captain."

"Very well. If the traitor, Dr Schultz, survived the destruction of the *Eisernes Kreuz*, it must follow that reconciliation with the *Sabre*'s crew may be impossible. Watch them carefully. Carry on."

0400 hours

Three lifeboats landed on the beach above the high-tide line. Douglas had chosen to set down upon the largest of a small chain of islands, out in the North Atlantic. They were perhaps a hundred miles west of what would one day be the coasts of Mauritania and Western Sahara.

Teams scrambled out from their ships to unhook the mini-digger, allowing him to land the shuttle too.

Over millions of years, tectonic movement had pushed the islands up out of the sea, tilting their rugged geology so that they sloped fairly steeply downwards from north to south. Wedge shaped and surrounded by ocean, they resembled iconic cheeses laid out upon a blue tablecloth; a description only enhanced by the buff colouring and pitted nature of the rock itself. The islands were a landscape of fissures and caves, all heavily forested on their southern slopes.

To the north, each sheared off severely; cliff faces fashioned by erosion to drop straight down to the sea. The *New World*'s topographical scans had shown some of these to be almost 800 metres high. However, after their low-level night flight and infrared scans, the shuttle and lifeboat crews learned that the razor sharp cliffs were also home to a veritable citadel of pterosaur and bird life; some vast beyond imagining.

Not for the first time had Douglas felt the lack of Tim's sage advice regarding the creatures of this world and their nature. Setting aside any obvious demonic references, he had only been able to discern that some of them appeared savage and possibly lethal.

He had naturally chosen to land on the gently sloping southern side of the island; a decision based in logistics, but reinforced by a desire to avoid any entanglement with the avian menace.

Although the *New World*'s sensors had noted the islands on her journey north, they had only become of specific interest to Douglas after Lieutenant Weber's comm had been fully downloaded. Rick Drummond, Major White's NASASEC consultant, had cracked the device to learn all of its secrets. He believed that Weber had harboured some hare-brained scheme to escape with Schultz; probably culminating in a meeting at these coordinates with his superiors, and this had given Douglas an idea.

There was a distinct likelihood that whoever controlled Weber was already aware of these islands, making them an ideal place to draw the enemy out.

The plan had several points in favour. Firstly, they were thousands of miles away from the *New World* and most of the people Douglas wished to protect. Secondly, it was an ideal place to drop a communications relay, being practically halfway between Britain and Patagonia. Should any signals be detected, they would not draw attention towards the *New World*. Lastly, this tiny and inoffensive group of islands was completely on its own in the ocean and really hard to miss, and this suited his purposes too – especially if his assumption regarding Weber's masters' knowledge of the place proved incorrect. After all, there was no point in creating a lure if the enemy could not find it.

Their lifeboats were equipped with the large-scale stunners developed by Jim Miller's people, making them more than capable of dealing with any threats from the natural world. They had no weaponry with which to take on the Schultz war fleet, but that was not their mission. Douglas' plan relied on cunning, not strength, to divide his enemies. It was, of course, a sad irony that he was as yet completely unaware that his enemies had already divided themselves.

He strode across the white sand, sparkling in the last of the bright moonlight, as he sought out Jones.

The corporal was spraying lines across the beach at the edge of the forest, setting out for their planned dummy dugouts and defensive structures. Meanwhile Bluey, the Australian construction worker, organised a team to set up the communications relay.

His brother, Red, fired up the digger and began a trench. Red had disgraced himself some weeks ago in Douglas' eyes. By refusing to bring his excavator back to the Pod when ordered, he and his team had cost a brave man his life. Despite acting with extraordinary courage after the fact, to save many more, Douglas still felt reticent to trust him.

His brother had proved stalwart from the start, arguing for his inclusion on this mission and Red certainly had the skills they required; Douglas just hoped he could be trusted to stick with the programme and obey orders, especially where they were going next.

Everyone busied themselves, hoping to get the better part of a shift in before the day's heat made the work unbearable.

The sky was already brightening in the east; a cool, deep blue, belying the furnace to follow.

"Good work, Jones," said Douglas, catching him up. "Ah've decided to take The Sarge with me, so Ah'll be leaving you in charge. You OK with that?"

"Yes, sir," replied Jones, unfazed.

Douglas clapped him on a meaty shoulder and marched off to find Bluey.

The Australian was shouting at a man who had dropped one of their power tools on the beach, filling the casing with sand.

"Everything in order, supervisor?" asked Douglas, grinning.

Bluey gave Douglas a sour look. "Talk about the great British skills shortage. These bladdy Poms you've given me don't know one end of a drill from the other! And they've *no* idea how hot it's going to get out here in an hour or two. Look at that stupid bagger standing there like a galah! *Oi!* Get it moving!" The Australian shook his head in dismay. "Sorry, Captain. What can I do for you?"

Douglas chuckled softly. "They'll no' let us down when the time comes," he assured. "Ah need to send a message to Jim Miller's team in Patagonia, Bluey. It's vital we send it soon, to give them a time frame. How long will you need to set up the array?"

"I spotted a cleft between the rocks as we flew over, Captain. I reckon this island is the biggest because it used to be a pair. The deep valley splitting the two land masses looks like a crumple zone to me. Anyway, that aside, it lies almost north-south. It's beaut', couldn't be any better for our purposes. If we set up the array within that valley, it'll send signals between the *New World* and South America, almost along a line of sight. The cliffs will force them into a narrow beam."

"So it'll be difficult to spot or intercept if you're off alignment?" asked Douglas.

Bluey nodded. "Like I said, beaut'."

Douglas pulled a scrap of paper from his pocket. "OK. Here's the message. I need it sent within the hour. Then get as much rest as you can throughout the day. We leave at sundown this evening."

Now

"OK, it's nearly midnight," said O'Brien. "We'd better get some zees. I wanna be outta here before sunup."

They rustled themselves into their sleeping bags. It took a moment for them to realise that, despite their having stopped rustling, the rustling had not stopped.

Lifting their heads warily, they exchanged a glance that was not exactly concern, but left room for development. At least the noise was outside the cave, which put it on the right side of their small fire.

Of greater concern was the fact that the rustling now clearly came from more than one source and seemed to have branched out into snuffling.

O'Brien slowly pulled her rifle from her sleeping bag and sat up in one fluid and near silent movement.

"You sleep with that thing?" Henry mouthed silently.

Prentice attempted to unzip his sleeping bag without making a sound, but this proved agonisingly slow. He had just freed one arm when a high-pitched, angry growl entered their cave.

This time they looked at one another with confusion. Did the Cretaceous have Jack Russells? It really did sound for all the world as if a small pack of terriers had congregated outside their hiding place.

Slipping from their sleeping bags, they moved forward irresistibly, squinting to see past the blinding firelight. O'Brien and Prentice stepped left and right to the narrow cave mouth, while Henry trod awkwardly around the fire to stand in the centre.

As their eyes adjusted to the night, Henry suddenly cried out in alarm. Military training on full automatic, the soldiers snapped towards the new threat, weapons up.

Henry seemed to be involved in some kind of one-legged dance around the cave's entrance as a small, badger-like creature tore at his trouser leg. Two more of the little furry quadrupeds joined in; one assailing the young man's other trouser, the second snapping for its packmates' swishing tails.

Henry went down in a fur ball as another six, of various sizes and ages, joined in the mêlée. Once on the ground, Henry felt the natural urge to protect his face, but the animals only seemed to be interested in his jacket. After a scramble, one tiny set of jaws clamped around the half-eaten chocolatey fruit bar in his breast pocket, tearing open both pocket and package to spray crumbs and raisins all over the floor.

The tiny pack fell upon this sudden bounty in a frenzy – all but one. The first intruder still hung on to Henry's trouser leg determinedly as it tried to drag him around the cave floor, yowling and barking its frustration past a mouthful of canvas.

Prentice would have helped, but he was struggling to see clearly through tears of laughter. O'Brien covered her mouth with a hand as she tried not to compound Henry's suffering with further ridicule.

She clapped her hands sharply and called, "Out! All of you, out!" Grabbing two of the little creatures as gently as possible by their scruffs, she manhandled them outside.

Henry attempted to eject his antagonists more forcefully, but they were so quick and dexterous that he simply ended up scrabbling around the floor getting more and more filthy.

The pack of nine regrouped at the cave mouth, yipping and whining as they looked for a further opening to explore the interesting smells the weird looking two-legs had about them.

They stayed well away from the fire, so O'Brien knelt to their small, circular stone hearth, retrieving what was left of their 'chicken dinner'. She broke up the still-warm pieces, handing one to the nearest, and apparently bravest, member of the pack as he approached cautiously. Sniffing at the proffered morsel, he suddenly snapped and took it away to devour in a corner, before the others could react and steal it from him.

"There's some for everyone," said O'Brien, now smiling and showing a kindly side to her nature the others had hitherto never suspected.

Divvying out the remains, making sure that even the pups and the old, retired matriarch got a fair share, she stepped back. Having eaten, fairly well for such small creatures, the pack turned to other matters and began to give themselves a bath.

The three humans retreated slightly, to once again take up sitting positions around the fire. "If that's a mouth wash, I don't think Listerine has much to worry about," Henry chuntered, still grumpy.

O'Brien wrinkled her nose. "Gross!"

Remarkably, the pack had now settled in the corner of the cave, climbing over one another to huddle for warmth. They were asleep in no time at all, but interestingly, and without any obvious organisation, two of them always remained alert. O'Brien noticed two pairs of beady little eyes, twinkling in the firelight. After a little while, the eyes would close, but two other sentinels would take their place.

"Maybe we should take a leaf out of their book," Prentice commented.

"Right," agreed O'Brien. "I can't believe how cute they are, though – now they're asleep."

"It's weird how they've decided to stay with us," noted Prentice.

"Actually," said Henry, "I'm pretty sure they *are* us. They're mammals, just like you and me."

"Speak for yourself, pretty boy," O'Brien acknowledged with a grin.

Henry smiled. "They're probably some long lost ancestor of the wolf." He sobered slightly. "Rose would have loved this. Tim would have been fascinated. Woodsey..." he paused, frowning, "would have probably tried to get them drunk to see what happened."

"Well, at least we seem to have made our first friends here," said O'Brien. "Let's take the win."

Pretty soon, they were all asleep.

Less than a mile away, Jim Miller felt as if sleep would never come again. Dr Schultz had forbidden him any contact with his daughter until he agreed to work for her. That was bad enough, but he also knew she was being forced to share accommodation with Del Bond. He did not trust that man as far as he could throw him, but the situation was further complicated by the fact that they seemed to have developed some kind of strange friendship.

Miller knew they had been through a lot together, during their gruelling and deadly walk through the forests to the enemy camp. He understood that a shared experience like that could bring even enemies together – he was simply worried about how *close* it would bring them together. Bond looked a good decade older than Miller himself.

He brooded. It was a father's worst nightmare.

Give me tattooed bikers or pierced punks, give me flighty literary types... give me anything but this.

In the next solitary cell, Tim also lay awake. He had refused one of the small suites aboard the *Sabre*, preferring the austerity of his prison. Heidi had thought this strange but made a concession in that his door was now unlocked, from the outside, at least.

In truth, Tim was concerned about how far he was slipping into his role of Nazi collaborator and hoped his prison would remind him of who he really was. He could feel Heidi beginning to trust him a little more each day – as much as she ever trusted anyone – and it was like the gradual, inexorable tightening of a snake around his soul.

He was helping the enemy. There was no other way of describing it. He had his reasons, good ones, he hoped, but every day he educated Heidi's soldiers a little more about the world around them. Giving them the edge deprived to his own people, now that he was here.

His own people... The phrase went round and around in his head. Who were *they?*

The only good thing about Jim Miller's capture, aside from providing comfort for Rose and reaffirming just how loved she was, was that he now knew his mum still lived.

When Miller left the *New World*, Patricia was desperately ill and in a medically induced coma, but she was *alive*.

The constrictor around his soul seemed to relax as thoughts of her flooded his mind. Even memories of her being furious with him, about some high-spirited misdemeanour in which Woodsey had involved him, allowed a little hope back into his world.

Chains seemed to break, and he began to see clearly for the first time in weeks. His mum was alive, some of his friends were actually with him and he had a job to do.

Henry, O'Brien and Prentice woke up simultaneously with a jolt. It sounded like all hell was breaking loose at the entrance to their hiding place.

Despite their best intentions, tiredness had overpowered them, but their nine furry friends had remained resolutely on duty.

As O'Brien ran to the entrance, rifle in hand, she saw the flick of a long tail vanish back into the trees. The deep blue tones of a fast approaching dawn offered just enough light to make out the disappearing rear of a man-sized theropod dinosaur.

The small mammals continued making an awful racket, taking no chances until they were sure the predator was gone. Their noise caused several smaller rustles in the undergrowth as other animals were startled awake to scurry away too.

O'Brien fired off two stun bolts into the bushes. Her sentinels stopped barking at once, cowering away from the sudden flashes of light. The corporal parted the bushes and grinned. "We have breakfast," she called back. "Henry, bring the fire back to life."

She strode back into the cave bearing two small dinosaurs with crooked necks. They looked like turkeys and were about the same size. O'Brien wasted no time in laying them out on a rock they had used to prepare previous meals, before she carved them up with a bowie knife.

Passing the choicest pieces to Prentice for cooking, she at last turned to her small band of spectators. All of them sat patiently in a line, drooling, as they studied her with huge, sad eyes.

O'Brien chuckled. The little critters' acting may have left much to be desired, but their behaviour was so recognisable, so *normal*, that it instantly transported the corporal. Her family home had always been filled with the antics of pets. She sighed, such bittersweet feelings.

"Now, who's gonna take a piece nicely?" she asked the little monsters dressed as teddy bears. One at a time she gave them a generous piece of meat, surprised at how they waited patiently for her to feed them. They pushed and shoved each other mercilessly for position, but they waited with manners for the woman to dispense their reward.

"If you ever wondered how dogs and man became so joined, then here it is," she said, smiling ruefully. "It really wasn't that hard, was it?"

"What did you expect?" replied Henry, cynically. "We think the same. If you want to understand humans, follow the money – if you want to understand dogs, follow the food!"

Prentice's cooking was already beginning to smell good and O'Brien's tummy growled.

"Once we've eaten breakfast, we'll get outta here. The road in front of us is long and rough."

"Once we've had our evening meal, we'll get ready to leave," said Douglas. "Ah want to hit Patagonia around 2100 hours – local time. Hopefully, that will have given Miller's people long enough to get into position – assuming they got our message. Are our preparations in place?"

"Almost, Captain," replied Hiro. "They should be easily finished by the time we get back with the rest of what we need. May I remind you, Captain, that we'll cross another time zone as we head south? If we leave too early, we'll catch the sun up."

"Aye, you're right. Ah havenae run the numbers yet, but Ah'm sure there'll be time for a wee nap after dinner. Ah want us as rested as we can be before we hit our targets.

"Now, gather round, everyone. It's time for the second half of the plan."

Meritus, Hiro, Gleeson, The Sarge, Bluey and Red all dutifully sat in a circle on the sand in the shade of a huge cycad.

"Did anyone bring a wee guitar?" Douglas quipped, causing a small round of chuckles.

Oblivious, Hiro asked, "I never knew you played guitar, Captain?"

Douglas gave a bland smile, scratching his head. "Right… Ah'll begin then, shall Ah?"

"Please do," said Gleeson. "We've still got Hiro's health and safety talk to look forward to, yet – and I intend to be asleep by then."

"When we start taking apart extremely high energy equipment that may still be holding a charge—" Hiro rounded, hotly.

"Alright, alright, gentlemen, please!" Douglas interceded. "Ah know it's hot, but let's try and stay calm, eh? Now, as you already know, we're going to attempt a salvage mission aboard the wreck of the *Last Word*. Captain Meritus will take us in and help us find what we need."

A shadow passed over Douglas' face. "Unfortunately, a lot of people died that night, some of them good people. To one of them, Elizabeth Hemmings, Ah owe ma very life. Unfortunately, the initial explosions – before Captain Baines dragged the ship over the edge of that ravine – apparently killed all of the *Last Word*'s engineering staff."

A silence followed Douglas' words. No one was sure how to break it.

Gleeson suddenly felt wretched. It was bad enough that he had set the bomb that killed them, without having to sit opposite their commander, who was well on his way to becoming a friend.

Eventually, Meritus swallowed. "Some of them were indeed good people," he acknowledged quietly. Looking Gleeson in the eye and seemingly reading his mind, he added, "Some, *not* so good. I would that the whole situation could have been avoided, but here we are. And let's not forget who the true architect of all of this mayhem is. He's the one who should carry the guilt, not people forced to make impossible choices to save their people."

"Well said, Tobias," agreed Douglas. "And to that end, Ah want to try one last time to bring all of this to a peaceful conclusion."

"What are you saying, Captain?" asked The Sarge, speaking for the first time.

"While you boys go shopping, Ah'll be taking one of the lifeboats, alone. Ah'm hoping Captain Meritus will give me a suitable enemy ident code, so that ma ship will read as one of their own. Ah don't expect them to be fooled by this, Ah simply hope that it will provide a symbol of my peaceful intentions."

Bluey leaned forward to speak. "I'm sorry, Captain, but it's more likely that it'll pop a symbol on their tactical board, painting you as a target, so they can launch a missile from halfway around the world to blow you outta the sky!"

"Aye it's a possibility, Ah'll no' deny it."

"A possibility?" asked Hiro, askance. "This is Heidi we're talking about, Captain. Heidi, who practically fed me to that Mapusaurus after forcing me to get her off the ship that first time. She *hates* us!"

"The Health and Safety Executive's right, Captain," added Gleeson.

"Will you stop calling me Health and Safety?" snapped Hiro.

"Sorry, mate. Do you prefer safety officer?"

Douglas sighed. "*Gentlemen.*"

Gleeson looked at him directly. "You shouldn't do this, Captain."

"Crocodile Elvis is right, sir," agreed Hiro.

Gleeson gave him a scathing look, but before he could respond, The Sarge said, "Let me come with you, Captain."

"No, Sarge, Ah think you'll be needed at the *Last Word*."

"Me and my brother are strong, Captain," said Red, earnestly. "We can carry the stuff outta there. You shouldn't go alone, sir."

Douglas nodded his gratitude for the young man's sentiment. "It's not as simple as that, Red. You see, to bring back the equipment we need, you're going to have to go in as light as you possibly can. That means a skeleton crew, and very few of you are trained soldiers.

"The thing is, no matter what Ah do to distract Heidi, she's going to know you're there and she's bound to send some people of her own – probably *all* soldiers.

"Hopefully, Jim Miller's people will make it there and be able to provide support, but there's no guarantee they even got the message."

He looked around them seriously. "Ah've made my decision, gentlemen. Bring back what we need and save our people. Ah'll do what Ah can to make things a little easier for ye from within the enemy camp."

Henry laughed genuinely for the first time in what seemed to him like forever. "I can't believe they stayed with us all this way!"

"Well, you keep feeding them," said Prentice. "Contrary to popular belief, animals aren't stupid."

"Perhaps not," allowed O'Brien, "but we're gonna have to shake 'em. We're headed into a dangerous situation and we're supposed to be *sneaking* under cover of darkness. Those guys haven't stopped yipping for the last fifteen klicks!

"OK, it's cute, but we can't go in like that. We don't know what's waiting for us."

Henry fed a morsel, dotingly, into a little mouth; they were taking food readily from his hand now.

"No, you can't keep him!" said O'Brien, reading his mind. "Come on, we still have about thirty klicks to cover."

Thomas Beckett removed his hat and wiped his brow, gazing up into the clear blue sky. He too was falling in love. His previous life had given him no inkling that nature could have such a powerful draw. The very idea of returning to the concrete sprawl of England was abhorrent to him now. He knew Dr Patel's team still worked diligently on the new wormhole drive project, in the hope of taking them home, but in his heart, he wanted them to fail.

Replacing his hat, he looked out over Crater Lake and breathed deeply of air that was so fresh he could almost drink it. Returning his attention to the soil, he smiled as he placed seeds within the furrows fashioned by machine for him and his fellow workers.

Eventually, they would build machines to handle the whole process and yes, they would be far more efficient, use less seed and produce more crops, but they would not *feel* their surroundings, as he did now. *I'm working the soil in an ancient, beautiful, completely unspoilt land,* he thought, happily. *I really am!*

As if the moment were not perfect enough, several small and vibrantly pretty birds fluttered around him. Beckett was a city dweller, as was almost everyone else in the 22nd century, so he had little experience or knowledge of birds. However, to his untrained eye, they would not have looked amiss hopping across any metropolitan park bench in Europe. They had beaks, rather than teeth and were so colourful that the historian stood mesmerised – even when the tiny creatures began to steal the seeds from the furrows he had so recently sown. Eventually, he found the will to shoo them away, gently. Naturally, they did not go far and although contra to his efforts, he was glad of this. Their melodious song may have been a frank and deliberate death threat to any other species of bird in the area, but it lifted Beckett's heart more than he would ever have thought possible.

He really could not wipe the grin from his face. It had to be wiped for him.

A sudden sound from behind made all the hairs stand up on his neck and head. Turning slowly, he heard the sliding of a large body across the ground.

He grimaced. *Not again?*

The creature making its way towards him stopped as he turned. "*Sneaky*," said Beckett. "Watch out everyone, we have a visitor!"

As far as Beckett was concerned the animal was simply a crocodile – a crocodile with darned big flippers. However, Natalie Pearson, his friend and doctor of zoology, had insisted they were part of a subgroup of freshwater Mosasaurs.

She approached Beckett cautiously. "They like *you*, don't they?" she teased.

"Hmm. Have you managed to find a name for them yet?"

Natalie shook her head. "Nah. Don't know if we ever will find out the exact species – an ancestor of the slightly later Pannoniasaurus, perhaps? They may even represent a species formerly unknown to science. Tim might have known, but there are many creatures here we've never found any record of.

"I *can* tell you they're potentially deadly – especially in or near the water."

"You don't say," Beckett replied drily.

"Apparently, freshwater Mosasaurs are really rare – at least they were, in the fossil record, I mean."

"And yet, I seem to encounter them daily – lucky me."

Natalie laughed. "Oh, Thomas, don't be such a misery – he didn't get you, did he?"

"Didn't stop him damned well trying, did it?" he snapped, giving her one of his cross looks, which only made her laugh again.

The adult specimens grew large. Farmers from the *New World* had spotted them at up to eight metres in length. Fortunately for Beckett, and everyone else, they never left the lake; their immense weight and lack of dexterity out of water made it all too easy for them to become beached and fall prey themselves to other killers more suited to life on land.

However, the younger animals seemed a little more adventurous. Quite often they would attempt to sneak up on the people working their new fields. They were not fast on land, but at up to three metres in length, they would be more than capable of causing serious injury to anyone caught unawares.

"OK, everyone – cover your ears!" Beckett took one of Gleeson's now famous dingo wingers from a pocket, activated the small cigar-shaped device and threw it to land between himself and the Mosasaur.

The bang echoed all around the mountains encompassing their little world. The effect on the animal was immediate; initially curious about what had been thrown its way, it suddenly turned in panic, slithering back to the water as quickly as it could. Once buoyed by the lake, it shot off at great speed, away from the shore.

Beckett watched with satisfaction. "Not today, my lad!"

Natalie clutched urgently at his sleeve. "We need to get to the safe house. Look!"

Approaching them along the lakeshore came another creature, not completely dissimilar to the Mosasaur, but clearly far more capable on land.

"That one I can name," hissed Natalie. "*Sigilmassasaurus!*" she bellowed, and everyone ran for their emergency bunker.

Disguised by undergrowth, it looked like no more than a group of bushes from the air, but its construction of concrete and steel had saved the workers several times already.

Once sure everyone was in, Natalie closed the door and opened the small shutter set within it. "Damn it! Those Sigilmassasaurs keep finding their way in here from the rivers," she cursed.

"Catchy handle," Beckett commented sourly.

"Sigilmassasaurus brevicollis was the closest match I could find within Tim's files. In fairness, the fossils found in the 1990s were far south of where we are. There are enough large landmasses and island chains to link our locations, though. And as you see, they swim really well!" she added, pointedly.

"So, what now?" asked Beckett.

She shrugged. "Wait for a rescue?"

A scream came from farther back in the bunker, followed by the metallic twang of someone wielding a shovel with prejudice.

"Open the door, open the door," someone called. The Sigilmassasaurus was close but not yet upon them, so Natalie obliged, allowing the man to throw the remains of a huge scorpion outside. "Everyone, look around," he shouted. "There may be more of them."

"Ooohhh," Beckett pined, "and I was having such a lovely day."

Chapter 13 | Rough Wooing

Douglas crossed the Southern Atlantic alone. The rest of his insurgency team were aboard the shuttle, 500 metres off his starboard wing. Crossing the sea was not their most direct route, but was by far the easiest way to fly low.

In its hastily applied camouflage paint, the shuttle had lost much of its slick, white spaceship-of-the-future appeal. The rough work served to break its lines and disguise its shape, but in the process made it look more like something left on the back lot of a film studio; the remnant of a broken down set from a military science fiction movie.

Douglas sighed deeply, his heart heavy. They were less than a thousand miles from their old enclosure in Patagonia and so, with grave misgivings, he activated the beacon announcing his arrival to Heidi's people.

Opening a tight-band comm link to the shuttle, he said, "Douglas to Meritus – head west and approach your destination from the North. Ah'll try and draw their full attention."

"*Understood, Captain. And James – good luck.*"

"Thanks, Tobias. You too. All of you, Godspeed. Douglas out."

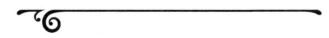

Franke studied the two little ships on her main viewscreen. They appeared to be heading back to their original encampment; straight towards Heidi Schultz. "What are they playing at?" she muttered to herself. Turning to her comms officer, she began, "If there is any comm traff—"

"We have a signal, Captain," the officer interrupted.

"What is it?"

"A beacon, ma'am. The smaller of the two craft is broadcasting, and they're using one of our codes."

Franke's eyes narrowed and her mouth puckered as she scowled. "*Meritus*," she hissed.

"That's most likely, Captain," the young officer agreed. "The larger of the two vessels, the *New World*'s shuttle, has veered off west, taking a separate course."

Damn these orders, thought Franke, clenching her fists. *We should be taking them down, one at a time. I hope all this waiting turns out to be* worth *the wait!*

"Captain Nassaki, we have a vessel inbound, broadcasting on one of our frequencies."

Aito Nassaki stepped across his bridge to lean in close. "Do we have identification?"

"Negative, sir. They're simply broadcasting a beacon."

Aito called across to his sensors officer, "Are there any other vessels in our vicinity?"

"Scanning, sir."

Aito turned back to comms. "Call Dr Schultz to the bridge."

"Yes, sir."

With that he moved to stand behind the sensors station. He could clearly see the flashing marker which represented the small vessel heading straight for them; tagged in green, it was denoted 'friendly'.

Moments later, Heidi strode onto the bridge. "What have you, *Kapitän*?"

Aito gestured towards the screen. "Are we expecting anyone, ma'am?"

Heidi shook her head distractedly. "Are they alone?"

"Running scans now."

"Send your orbital fighter to intercept the vessel, just in case," she ordered.

Aito coughed awkwardly. "We no longer have one, Doctor. It was destroyed, during the *incident* that led to the capture of your grandfather," he stated, diplomatically.

Realising that he meant the ship *she* had destroyed, she frowned in frustration. "So Franke has the only fighter still in our possession and Meritus has the other?"

"*Hai*," he answered with a brief bow.

She cursed inwardly. Her own attack ship had been destroyed with the *Eisernes Kreuz*. The icon representing the incoming vessel was approaching quickly when the sensors officer spoke again, "Captain, I have a second vessel."

"I knew it," said Heidi. "This is an attack."

"I can't speak to that, ma'am. All I can say for sure is that the second vessel is not heading for us at this time. The first will be here in three minutes."

Heidi turned to Aito. "*Kapitän*, assemble a commando team."

"Certainly, ma'am. What are their orders?"

Before she could answer, the sensors officer reported, "The second ship seems to be headed for the crash site of the *Last Word*, Captain."

"Do you still have your armoured personnel carrier?" asked Heidi.

"We do," Aito replied with a nod.

"I urged *mein Großvater* to strip the *Last Word* of anything useful, but he would not listen! He just locked me away." Heidi smiled unpleasantly. "See how that worked out for him. *Kapitän*, assemble your team and get to the *Last Word* with all haste. Save anything you can, destroy everything you must. We cannot afford them any advantage."

"Yes, ma'am. You wish me to lead the team personally?"

"I do, *Kapitän*. I will take care of things here. It seems we are about to receive a guest. Go quickly."

Aito saluted and made for the exit. Anxiety, fear, even excitement were all natural emotions for a man about to go into what could easily turn out to be a combat situation. However, the thoughts foremost in his mind were of Heidi being left to 'take care of things'. Wherever Dr Heidi Schultz led, it seemed death and destruction followed.

Worries and suspicions niggled at him, and as he was about to leave, he turned to take one last look around what had briefly been *his* bridge.

O'Brien waited just inside the treeline as she kept vigil over the enemy's original compound. Over the edge of the ravine, lay the ruins of possibly the most horribly beweaponed vessel mankind had ever conceived, saving nuclear ordnance. She could not help but wonder at how lucky they had been. The fact that Captain Meritus was an honourable soldier and not a mad butcher had certainly helped, but more than that, the real reason they were all alive was the fact that the enemy needed *Factory Pod 4.* Unfortunately, so did they.

Heinrich Schultz had clearly believed the mere threat of his terrible machines would overwhelm the crew of the *New World*, quelling any resistance before it began. He had been wrong – a mistake doubly compounded by the defection of Captain Meritus and most of his surviving crew. All of whom preferred their chances with an unknown enemy, over an unforgiving master.

I wonder what he would have done if he'd found them here? Reckon the loss of that battleship would have taken some explaining.

Prentice cut into O'Brien's thoughts, "I can hear a ship, Corp."

Tilting her head, she could hear *something* – just on the edge of hearing. Listening hard, it became clear that it was indeed an approaching ship.

The weather had taken a turn for the worse during late afternoon, with even some distant thunder. Heavy cloud blocked any moon or star light, so that when the sun finally set, it became almost completely dark.

Seconds ticked by and it began to spot with rain again.

"There!" Henry suddenly pointed due north.

Between two peaks, just about discernible as black ridges against a very nearly black sky, they saw the flare of rocket engines. Within moments it was upon them, hovering overhead. The pilot switched on the craft's flood lights, clearly looking for a place to land.

Prentice waited for the noise of the landing thrusters to abate before he whispered, "What is it?"

O'Brien shook her head and then realised the private would not have seen the gesture. "I'm not sure," she said instead. "Doesn't look like *New World* fleet. Even in this light we would have seen something of it. That thing's practically invisible now it's on the ground."

"Maybe they painted it," suggested Henry, helpfully.

"Perhaps," O'Brien allowed, "but I can't say I'm comfortable with the idea of stepping out to introduce ourselves. What are they doin'?"

A hatch opened in the side of the craft, barely discernible as a dim, squarish glow. Six vague silhouettes jumped out carrying an assortment of boxes or possibly cases. The faint light vanished as the ship sealed itself again.

Glad of their heat-deflecting ponchos, which hid them from infrared scans, O'Brien donned a pair of night-vision glasses.

"Can you make out who they are?" asked Prentice.

"Not really. They're dressed in heavy raincoats with their hoods up."

"Sensible," said Henry as a trickle of cold water ran down his neck. "Think I'll do the same."

"What do you want to do, Corp?" asked Prentice.

"Well, I think the kid's right. That looks like the *New World*'s shuttle with some kind of camo paintjob. That should be good news for us, but we're so far outta the loop we can't be sure who's driving. Whoever they are, they seem to be heading down into the ravine."

"Some kind of salvage mission from the *New World*?" asked Henry.

"That would be my guess," agreed O'Brien. "We'll hold position here and see what happens when they return. Maybe we'll glimpse a few faces before we commit, yeah?"

"Sounds good to me, Corp," replied Prentice as they settled in to wait.

Douglas landed within a hundred metres of the still-functional enemy warship, orienting his lifeboat's stun cannon towards anyone who might approach from that direction.

Completely staggered by the destruction of the other ship, hope rose in his chest – could Heidi finally be a distant memory?

Before leaving the relative safety of his tiny craft, he opened a comm channel. "Remaining warship," he began, with some relish, "this is Captain James Douglas. May Ah come aboard?"

His message was answered directly. "*What do you want, Douglas?*"

He went through an entire gamut of swear words in his head before he could trust himself to answer calmly. "Flight Officer Schultz, is that you? Ah'm so relieved to find you alive."

"Indeed, and it's Doctor *Schultz,"* she answered coolly, across the channel.

Douglas noted that, like so many who inspire fear in others, she had no grasp of sarcasm at all. *Understandable, Ah suppose,* he mused. *Anyone who knew Heidi would doubtless feel it unwise to demonstrate the concept.*

"At the risk of repeating myself, may Ah come aboard?"

"At the risk of repeating myself, *what do you want?"*

Ha, perhaps she's learning, he thought. "To talk, Heidi, that's all. Isn't it time we tried to end this conflict? Ah see something has happened to your wee ship over there..."

"These ships may not be as large as the New World, *Douglas, but they are far more formidable, I assure you!"*

Douglas smiled. Even digitised, the bridling was evident in her voice. Heidi was the very epitome of unbalanced, but if he could just keep her *off* balance, their plan might have a chance. "So what happened, pilot error? Or do they just not make them like they used to?" he needled further.

After a brief pause, where Douglas could almost hear the grinding of teeth, Heidi replied, *"Give me one good reason why I should not blast you into many pieces, right now?"*

He had expected this. "Because Ah may have something you need," he stated simply.

"You are willing to render Factory Pod 4 *to me?"* she asked, disbelieving.

"Yes and no. Do we talk?"

"Very well, Kapitän. *You may come aboard,"* she agreed reluctantly.

"Gladly," agreed Douglas. "Ah just have one small favour to ask. My sensors are showing a pack of small predators heading this way. Ah believe Tim would call them Buitreraptors. We met previously and Ah've no wish to reacquaint. Could ye no' fire off a couple of shots into the air, to clear the area?"

"Very well. Someone will meet you at the portside airlock. And, Kapitän, *do not try to conceal any weapons."*

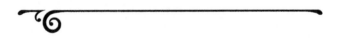

Hiro stared balefully at the wreckage within the *Last Word*'s engine room. Everything appeared the worse for being at a thirty degree angle. The intrepid scavengers had to climb for everything, even for things mounted to the floor.

Gleeson clapped him on the shoulder. "It could have been worse, Nasso. At least the place isn't full of dead bodies."

"I made sure of that before we moved out," said Meritus.

Gleeson winced. He had not realised the Captain was behind them. "Sorry, mate," he said with feeling.

"All of the people we lost were given a decent military burial." Meritus spoke lifelessly, quietly adding, "It was the least I could do, having failed them so badly."

"You didn't fail them," said Gleeson. "Schultz did that, when he sent them off to kill our people instead of joining them. You saved everyone you could."

"You saved *me* too," said Hiro, "from Godzilla's god-daughter, back at the *Newfoundland*, remember?"

Meritus raised an incredulous eyebrow. "*Do I?* I've dreamt about little else since."

Gleeson chuckled. "Now that's something I understand," he replied knowingly.

"Where did you bury your fallen?" asked Hiro.

"Aaaarrrgghh!" screamed Henry. "Oh my God! Oh my God! *Oh my God!*"

"Where's he gone?" asked Prentice.

"He's disappeared," replied O'Brien. "Kid? Where are you?"

"Oh my God! Oh my God! *Oh my Gaaarrghd!*"

"Henry?" added Prentice.

"*Down here!*" the young man bellowed.

"Alright, lad, stay calm."

"Stay *calm?* I'M IN A GRAVE!"

"Just up on the plateau – south side," answered Meritus. "I'm glad to say that, thanks to a few miraculous recoveries, some of them were never filled."

"At least some were fortunate, then," agreed Hiro.

"Lucky? I'm in a grave *goddamnit!*" Henry screamed. Realising he sounded like his father, he took some deep breaths to calm himself.

"I just meant that you're unharmed. You *are* unharmed, aren't you?" asked Prentice with irritating calmness as he reached down to pull the young man out.

"Thank you!" said Henry, stiffly. He shivered massively. "As I don't have night-vision goggles can we *please* use a torch?"

"We may as well, now," O'Brien acquiesced. "Your hollering was loud enough to wake the—"

"Don't say it!" snapped Henry.

Douglas was route marched through the *Sabre*, with little courtesy, to a state room he assumed was the captain's quarters. Heidi was already seated at a table under a large starboard viewport.

"Very nice," he remarked drolly. "Was this the old man's suite?"

"*Mein Großvater* had his flag aboard the *Eisernes Kreuz*." She nodded out of the window into the darkness where the ruined ship lay. "He would never have travelled in accommodation as spartan as this."

Douglas' eyebrows rose as he took in the opulence of his surroundings once more. "Maybe Ah *did* sign up to the wrong team."

"Indubitably. Now tell me how you propose to hand me the Pod," she answered, peremptory as ever.

"Not *the* Pod. *A* Pod," replied Douglas, obliquely.

"Explain."

"Very well. We've taken many scans all over the planet in recent weeks," he embellished. "Ah've had people pawing over them, but believe it or not, it was actually a couple of kids who spotted the location of greatest interest.

"Tim's young friends found an active volcano, perhaps not so surprising, but all our scans lead us to believe that it is fairly stable. More than that, it's likely to remain so for hundreds of thousands of years, maybe longer."

"You are suggesting a geothermal vent as a power source?" asked Heidi.

"That's part of it."

"And the rest? I could find one of these for myself, once I have the Pod," she stated belligerently.

"The rest is that Ah'm authorised to offer you a Pod of your own – almost identical to ours."

Heidi leaned forward, interested despite herself. "Go on."

"You will already be aware of the *Newfoundland*, not far from here."

"Of course."

"Well," continued Douglas, "she's no' in great shape, but she's fixable over time and with appropriate resources. She also carries a rescue Pod."

"I am aware of all this, *Kapitän*. The rescue Pod only has three decks and nowhere near the resources or capacity of *Factory Pod 4*. Tell me something of interest."

"Ah will, if you'll let me finish, lassie!" snapped Douglas, feigning agitation to give her the impression that he was rattled and therefore likely to make mistakes.

"Now, where was Ah? Oh, yes. We're suggesting that we move the *Newfoundland* to the location of the geothermal vent. With a treaty in place between our two peoples, we would then bring the *New World* to join her.

"This next bit may be something ye didnae know. The rescue Pod utilises the same hanging chassis as *Factory Pod 4*. So, in plan, they're the same size. With the almost infinite power of the vent, we could begin to manufacture a new factory Pod onto the chassis of the rescue Pod, you see? A vastly easier task than starting from scratch."

Heidi remained impassive, but was secretly intrigued by this offer. "Very well, *Kapitän*. I now understand that. What is to stop me from taking *Factory Pod 4* by force and simply undertaking the project myself?"

Douglas had expected this too. "Two things. Firstly, Ah have some of the finest minds from our time, willing to work for *me*, to give *you* what you want. You only want to kill them or make them homeless – which will pretty much add up to the same thing – and could even make the whole endeavour impossible for you. Ah couldnae help noticing you've lost quite a few of your Nazis since beginning this little excursion of yours. Maybe some of *your* best minds have already had their last ideas?"

Heidi coloured. Douglas noted it, but continued before she had chance to interrupt, "Secondly, if you try and take the Pod by force, you will lose even more people and possibly destroy the thing you are trying to steal."

He spread his hands wide upon the table as he leaned forward. "For God's sake, see sense, lassie! Before there are nae enough of us left to survive."

Heidi leaned forward too. "As always, Douglas, you fail to grasp the full complexity of the situation."

He leaned even further forward and, almost in a whisper, added sweetly, "Then why don't ye enlighten me?"

"I can hear another vehicle," said Henry.

O'Brien and Prentice stood still, listening hard. After a few moments, they began to perceive what Henry's younger senses had already picked out – the moan of a diesel engine.

"I wonder what this could mean," O'Brien thought aloud.

"Nothing good," said Prentice. "It can only be one of theirs, surely."

"OK, take cover," snapped O'Brien, warming to her element. "They're bound to come sniffing around the shuttle, so we'll hide behind the attack ship, over there."

The wrecked fighter was an artefact of the stampede, in which O'Brien had played a part. A huge, male spinosaurid dinosaur – Oxalaia – had rushed from the bank to step, and partially fall, upon the machine, causing structural failure to the starboard wing as it capsized.

It now lay roughly twenty metres from the shuttle. They sprinted the distance and dove under its portside wing.

The ruined husk had obviously been cannibalised, probably during the enemy's second habitation of the plateau. By happy chance, they had also left it open.

O'Brien pulled the hatch a little farther open and stepped inside cautiously, weapon raised. Not seriously expecting to find enemies inside, she was nevertheless alert, just in case other things had set up house within the cosy, abandoned shell.

"They're close now, Corp," Prentice hissed through the hatch.

"The rear compartment is clear, Adam. I'm gonna check the cockpit."

"Go on in, lad." Prentice ushered Henry inside, just as a piercing shriek came from the front of the little ship. Prentice barged past Henry, shoving him aside to get to the threat. "What the hell's happening?"

In answer to his question, a dozen or more tiny feathered dinosaurs ran squawking and flapping past them.

"What the—?" Prentice cried out in surprise.

"Whoa!" exclaimed Henry.

They pressed themselves against the bulkhead, scrambling out of the way as the furious little creatures ran and flapped for the exit.

O'Brien stepped back into the aft compartment, nudging the last of them out with her foot nonchalantly. "They're only little ones."

The men looked at one another and blew out their cheeks, crisis passed.

They could hear the rumble of a powerful diesel motor through the hull now. Clearly, whoever it was had arrived.

O'Brien ducked back into the cockpit. "Keep your faces covered," she whispered. "They're bound to be scanning for everything. I would."

Squinting through the darkness, they could just about make out a tracked people carrier as it left the forest. Descending the low bank, it growled to a halt on the plateau. O'Brien tucked her night-vision goggles away, in case the vehicle's sensors picked up their signature.

The rain grew heavier, battering the shell of their hideout.

"I'm glad we found this thing," Henry muttered. "It's raining whatever passes for cats and dogs around here."

O'Brien held a finger to her lips.

"Sorry," Henry mouthed.

The armoured vehicle had stopped roughly halfway between them and the shuttle. A sudden light showed as the rear hatch opened. Troops spilled out quickly, taking up positions around the vehicle.

"Stoopid," whispered O'Brien.

Prentice nodded, also counting their forces. "I make it fifteen, Corp," he murmured.

"Agreed," O'Brien replied softly. "That little guy at the back seems to be giving the orders." She turned to the others and sat back down. "Now, if that were me, I'd have left a couple of guards in the APC, too."

Prentice nodded again, a grin forming. "Doubt there'll be any more than that."

O'Brien grinned back. "We'll give them time to disperse – they're bound to head down for the *Last Word* – then we go."

"We go where?" asked Henry, in a nervous whisper.

"The last time I was here, I bagged a new set o' wheels," replied O'Brien.

As she spoke in hushed tones, her words were almost obliterated by a crack of thunder. She looked up at the sky. "And if I'm not mistaken, that's the sound of lightning striking twice!"

"*Quiet!*" hissed The Sarge, waving a hand towards the trio behind him. They stopped disassembling the *Last Word*'s wormhole drive and listened.

"What is it?" asked Hiro.

"*Sshhh!*"

The Sarge checked his rifle's charge and pulled a small periscope from his pocket. The cylinder itself was telescopic; he extended it to see around the corner and up the corridor.

Hiro stepped silently over to where The Sarge stood guard, collecting his own rifle on the way. The Sarge nodded, holding up a count of five, before reaching for his comm to give the pre-agreed double-click sign for trouble. Gleeson and Meritus would now be on their guard – he could do no more for them.

Bluey and Red carefully placed the parts they had scavenged into flight cases. Nervously, they pulled stun pistols from their holsters and braced themselves.

Bluey took his brother's hand and Red nodded – if they were going down, they were going down together.

"Let me tell you what *I* think, *Kapitän*," said Heidi. "*I* think you are here, hoping to distract me while your companions do whatever they need to do aboard the *Last Word*. Brave but stupid – that seems to be the way you people operate."

Douglas had never really believed his team would make it to the wreck site without being spotted, but something in her manner made him feel like a rock had just settled in his gut.

"Of course," she continued, "you will have assumed that your people were bound to be spotted, sooner or later, and planned for this, too. So why don't you tell me what your real plan is here, *Kapitän?* Then, if you're a good boy, I might tell you what I am about to do to your people over there."

For such a beautiful young woman, she had a smile that made Douglas' flesh crawl. It was as if something else was just beneath her skin, synthesising human behaviour.

He stretched the muscles in his neck and shoulders to stop himself from shuddering. "What are you planning?" he asked quietly.

"No, *please*," she replied, feigning courtesy, "you first. It might keep your people alive a little while longer."

The muscles in Douglas' jaw bunched as he literally chewed over how to answer. "They're after some parts for ma ship," he admitted at last.

"Now, I ask myself, what could your crew possibly want with parts from our battleship and I find I can only come up with two options – parts for the wormhole drive and weapons. How am I doing so far, *Kapitän?*"

Seething, he replied, "We dinnae have a wormhole drive, thanks to you!"

"I think you mean thanks to Geoff Lloyd, another of your *loyal* crew, don't you, *Kapitän?*"

Her constant needling had Douglas bridling like a shire horse in a wedding dress. Mindful of this, he decided to use it to help his friends. After all, the longer she was enjoying herself, the longer his people had to acquire what they needed and get the hell out of there. He sat back and folded his arms, testy yet anxious.

Heidi seemed on a roll, determined to get a rise out of him. "You really expect me to believe that your mealy-mouthed band of do-gooders are not working towards building a new drive? Especially that clever Indian – when he's not moonlighting as a politician. No, I think you are after parts *and* weapons." She smiled again.

Douglas' fists clenched, his right eye twitching slightly at her contempt for his companions. Most of his crew were good people and he was not a man given to hating. However, he made an exception where the Schultzes were concerned.

"What you don't know," she continued smoothly, "is that I have the *Last Word* – now, what is the correct phrase – *rigged to blow?* Yes, I think that adequately describes the situation."

She grinned, dropping a remote detonator on the table, daring him to make a move.

Anxiously, he thought, *Come on, Meritus – get my people out of there! Och, damn her and damn my pride, too – lives are at stake.* "Heidi, *please*," he begged. "Don't do this. We can make this work. We *have* to make this work."

"You did not really expect me to believe that you would be willing to build me a new Pod, did you? And that story about volcanic vents? Please, *Kapitän*, we both know you would never give me the means to build a civilisation based on my beliefs – as I will not allow you to build one based on yours—"

"But there must be *some* common ground, surely? We're all human beings and we're so *few*," Douglas tried, playing for as much time as possible. "Surely, you must know that if your explosion detonates that ship's power-core, you'll flood half the continent with radiation, rendering it uninhabitable for centuries! That's not even taking into account what effect that might have on the wildlife – most of them are halfway to being Godzilla already!"

"No. *Our* ships were designed to be far tougher than NASA's *cargo* ships," she placed a very deliberate sneer on the word. "The core is protected and will survive – may even be salvageable after the fact."

Despite his desperation, Douglas was both surprised and impressed by this. However, he needed to buy more time. Grappling for inspiration, he asked, "What happened to your third ship, over the way there?"

Heidi drew the detonator closer, then put it aside. Drumming her fingers on the table, she gave him a sideways look.

The Sarge fired, dropping the first man instantly with a heavy stun blast. He was not killed, but the jolt was powerful enough to make sure he stayed down.

Return fire was immediate and rather unsportingly consisted entirely of traditional ordnance. Bullets rang and ricocheted off the walls and bulkheads all around the hatch where The Sarge hid. He naturally ducked backed into wormhole drive control.

"This is it, lads. Fall back and find cover. Make sure it's not cover that explodes if its hit! I want this doorway in a crossfire. We'll bottleneck 'em!"

Bullets continued to rain down the hall for a few seconds, but withered to a halt when no return fire came.

The enemy advanced cautiously. One man jumped across the open hatch to take up a position on the opposite side of the doorway. Unfortunately for him, The Sarge expected this tactic and was ready for it. He fired with exquisite timing and took the man out of the air, sending him sprawling across the corridor floor.

No one else tried to cross the hatch.

"We have you penned in," a man shouted, "and we have more troops on the way. Why don't you throw down your weapons and come quietly? There's no way out of this."

"You want our weapons, come and take 'em!" The Sarge shouted back. "I haven't killed any of your people yet, so why don't you leave now, in case I change my mind!"

The enemy officer's sardonic smile was evident in his voice. "Or why don't I send a gas grenade in there, wait a few minutes, and drag you all out? I was considering non-lethal gas, so why don't you comply before I change *my* mind?"

The Sarge gritted his teeth. This had been their problem from the beginning. They were just not kitted out for any kind of serious military engagement. The enemy, on the other hand, had popped back in time with all the tools they needed to prosecute a war.

While he frantically mulled over his limited options, Hiro called out, "Aito? Is that you?"

The Sarge was angered at first; now the enemy would certainly know who they had. However, by the time his second thoughts caught up, he had to admit that, just maybe, this would save their lives. *Here's hoping brother dearest still believes in family,* he thought. "Give us a minute to think this through," he called back.

"No," replied Aito. "You will drop your weapons and come out now. And Hiro, don't try any fancy engineering tricks. I really don't want to shoot you – but don't force the issue.

273

"And if you think your other team members are going to take us from the rear and save you, you should know they're being detained as we speak. *They* were wise enough not to try and make a fight of it. I suggest you follow their wisdom."

The Sarge quirked a half smile. *No matter how clever they think they are, the smarmy gits always make a mistake*, he reflected. Quite simply, he could not imagine a world in which Commander Gleeson would ever come quietly. His musings were borne out almost immediately by an explosion. The already unstable hulk rocked.

Another of Aito's men fell across the doorway as the ship lurched. The Sarge fired from his stable, crouched position, bringing the enemy numbers down to two.

However, it appeared that Hiro's brother was a man of his word if nothing else, and they soon heard the booted, running feet of reinforcements.

The Sarge gritted his teeth. *Oh, Turkish delight!*

Heidi seemed suddenly pensive. She remained unmoving for some time after Douglas' question; every fibre of her being telling her to quash the enemy sitting across her table and all of his followers – to remove all resistance to her plans.

However, the traditional Schultz approach had proven itself flawed recently. Her cousin had his ridiculous philosophy on family. Douglas had his weak, committee-based style of leadership, and yet they kept surviving against all odds.

She had considered making Tim a part of this meeting to see how he would react, but something within her, some small part to which she would never admit, was afraid to do so. If he saw Douglas, she may lose the boy, if indeed she ever had him. This bothered her, no matter how she trounced her... *feelings?*

Added to this, there was the uncomfortable truth that, in terms of resources and position, Franke had the upper hand. Worse, Heidi knew she had not the strength to fight a war on two fronts. If the *Sabre* and the *Heydrich* faced off, there was every chance that the last man standing would actually be the *New World* – their entire mission, their dreams for the future, all lost forever.

For himself, Douglas was happy to sit there in silence all day while she deliberated, if it gave his team more time to effect their escape.

"Very well," said Heidi, reaching a decision. "*Kapitän* Franke has turned traitor. She is now a rogue element, and in case you were forming any ideas along the lines of 'my enemy's enemy', let me be clear – Franke is neither on my side nor *yours*," she stated adamantly.

Douglas shrugged. It was a fair cop.

"What did you do to send her rogue?" he asked.

Heidi narrowed her eyes angrily. "Why do you suggest that this was my doing?" she asked, with her characteristically Germanic syntax.

"Just a hunch," he replied nonchalantly. "So, what did you do?"

Her eyes narrowed further. "*Mein Großvater* betrayed me, supplanting me in favour of my cousin. Franke refused to accept the new chain of command."

Douglas felt a stab to his heart as she referred to Tim Norris as 'my cousin'. He tried not to show his distaste.

"Ah thought the old man might have booted you out because you lost his near-priceless battleship," he stated innocently.

Her expression soured further, causing Douglas to smile on the inside while outwardly wearing his 'I only wish to help' face.

Deciding it would be best to move her along before she lost her temper altogether and pressed the button, he asked, "You really *don't* want your grandfather back, then?"

"No," she answered coldly.

"Do Ah presume that Captain Franke does?"

"Yes."

Douglas sat back, mulling over the potential ramifications for his crew after such a revelation.

"She is a fanatic," Heidi embellished disdainfully.

This statement took Douglas by surprise and it must have shown on his face because she quickly followed by asking, "You think that *I* too am a fanatic?"

"Erm…" he answered weakly.

"Franke follows *mein Großvater* slavishly. Many of us did – perhaps some still do. It was not until we…" She broke off, changing tack. "Let us just say that I no longer feel that way."

"You mean he turned on ye?"

"If you like," she admitted, tetchily.

"Will ye no' see?" Douglas argued plaintively. "Evil cannae thrive here. There are just no' enough of us. If we don't find a way to work together, we willnae make it. Surely, this is proof – even for you.

"Ah hate to sound dramatic, but come over to the light, Heidi, before it's too late – not only for us, but for you too."

"And we arrive at the same impasse," she replied.

"Aye," Douglas admitted. "Ah hold the key to the future of humankind, or at least the tools they'll need, and you're holding a detonator."

"And if our roles were reversed, what would you do, *Kapitän*?"

"Ah'd make a deal. My offer for a second Pod was genuine. We can even feed your people while it's being built, then we can go our separate ways – or not. Ah hope we can all learn to live together. This world is vast, far bigger than the one we left behind. There are no people in it! What are we? Three hundred souls?"

"And the timeline?" she asked.

"Ah didnae think you cared about that," he replied cautiously.

"*I* don't, but I know that you do. Am I to believe that you have turned your back on our set-piece future?"

Douglas whished. "Heidi, what's it going to take?"

"A lot more than that!" snapped Gleeson. "Give it here." He snatched the small package from Meritus' grasp and slapped an extra pack of plastic explosive to the detonator taken from one of his dingo wingers. Complete, he threw the whole device down the corridor.

Covered from both ends, at least six enemy soldiers had them pinned down in one of the *Last Word*'s large-ordnance storage bays. Gleeson's explosive fell at the forward end of the connecting corridor, against an external bulkhead. "Fire in the hole!" he screamed, covering his ears.

The explosion was catastrophic. A large part of the outer hull vanished, along with the enemy soldiers unlucky enough to be at that end.

The fireball and shrapnel cloud traversed the whole corridor, tearing past Gleeson and Meritus' weapons locker. With power down across much of the ship, closing the hatch was impossible. They could only leap away from the doors, diving beneath the under-stuffed mattress of hope.

Judging by the terrible screams from out in the corridor, hope had temporarily abandoned their enemy.

"This is our chance, mate!" Gleeson shouted excitedly, past the ringing in their ears. He grabbed Meritus by the lapels to bring him to his feet.

Captain Tobias Meritus swayed slightly, both stunned by the proximity of the explosion and his companion. "You're a raving bloody lunatic!" he exclaimed at last.

Gleeson grinned. "You're starting to sound like me, Tobo. Quick, grab the other end of these flight cases."

Still a little wobbly on his feet, Meritus complied. Between them, they carried two cases, each about a metre and a half in length. Gleeson took the handles at the front of the boxes and Meritus followed, bringing up the rear.

They were soldiers, but as they made their way down the corridor the cries of the injured still gnawed at their souls. With no choice but to ignore them, they made their way to the brand new hole in the side of the ship.

"Sorry about the paintwork," Gleeson quipped, trying to cheer his teammate.

Meritus took a deep, shuddering breath. "I don't like leaving those injured men down there."

A shot pinged off the ceiling above their heads. Gleeson ducked. "Perhaps I can change your mind?"

"Right!" agreed Meritus.

They jumped.

The Sarge, Hiro, Bluey and Red came out with their hands up. Once reinforcements arrived, Jackson knew that any continuance would only get his men killed. Although Lieutenant Nassaki was technically in charge, he was no combat soldier and bowed to The Sarge's judgement with frustration, but no argument.

"Brother," greeted Aito, cheerfully. "Please, gentlemen, lower your hands – you will need them to carry away my plunder. I see you've disassembled much of the wormhole drive, Hiro. Speaking as an engineer myself, it would be churlish to leave all your hard work just lying around here, wouldn't it?"

"You're no engineer! You ditched our honourable profession to go into politics!" Hiro spat accusingly.

Aito shrugged. "Just because I can carry two careers, there's really no need for sour grapes, brother."

"So, does that make you a jackass of all trades, then?" Bluey piped up, finding his courage once more.

Hiro muttered in Japanese, just loud enough for Aito to hear.

"OK. Perhaps I'm not the engineer you are," Aito agreed resentfully, speaking over a few disrespectful sniggers from both sides, "but surely *no* engineer would leave such valuable equipment lying around, would they? Now, you and your men will carry the items you've salvaged up to the plateau and then we'll come back down here, to see what else we can find." He grinned, suddenly. "Guess what? I found a nice little ship up there to carry all my goodies away in."

Hiro glared at him. "How could you do this?"

"Enough!" barked Aito. "Sergeant, collect their weapons and get them carrying – let's go!" He clapped his hands together and strode from the room, pulling out his comm. That was when a second explosion shook the ship.

Much larger than the first, the entire vessel groaned as the aft end slid a little farther down the embankment. The *Last Word*'s back, already broken, distorted still further as the superstructure parted with a rending squeal of tortured metal.

For a fleeting moment, The Sarge hoped he might use the opportunity to turn the tables, but there was real fear in his people now. Added to this, the enemy were more on their guard than ever as everyone attempted to keep their footing.

"Get this equipment out of here," shouted Aito, angrily.

The ascent was gruelling. Hauling two heavy flight cases up such a steep embankment was backbreaking in itself, but the torrential rain really heightened it to a Sisyphean task.

Each box weighed close to fifty kilograms. Even between them this was a lot to carry, but the slope, so recently turned over by the *Last Word*'s downhill slide, was now almost entirely made up of slippery, loose material turned to sludge.

By the time Gleeson scrambled over the brow, he was covered head to foot in mud and thoroughly done in.

Meritus slipped, right at the top, causing them both to slide back before they could catch themselves.

"Bladdy 'ell, Tobo," Gleeson called out above the roaring wind. "If you drop these babies back down there, you can bladdy well bring 'em back up on your own!"

"Sorry," Meritus replied with the last of his breath. The two men collapsed in the muck, but they had made it.

After a minute's respite, they decided it was time to head for shelter. "Do you think they've left a guard by the vehicles?" asked Gleeson.

"I would have," Meritus replied, squinting through the darkness and the rain. "I can just about make out our shuttle, to the north. What's that next to it?"

Gleeson peered. "I reckon it's probably one of those tracked personnel transports your side uses."

"*My* side?"

"Sorry, mate."

"You say that a lot."

"I usually need to."

They lapsed into silence.

Gleeson stood. "OK, let's get these boxes a little closer. Then we'll see what's to be done."

"Fair enough," agreed Meritus. "By the way, be careful on this part of the plateau. There may be an open grave—"

"Aaarrgh!" *Splash.* "Bladdy 'ell!"

"He found it," Meritus muttered to himself as he leaned over a hole of 'manly' proportions. "You OK down there?"

"You could have told me!"

"I was just— Look, never mind, I'm sorry. Here, take my hand."

Gleeson had fortunately fallen on his feet. However, his full weight on two relatively small surface areas had forced those feet well down into the muck at the bottom of the pit. This left him sunk to *plum depth* in a very small and variously unpleasant pool.

Their first attempt to raise HMS Gleeson almost ended with them *both* in the hole. The Australian was once again forced to express his dismay. "Bladdy 'ell!"

Using his arms, he tried pulling one leg at a time – stuck. "Damnit! I need help. If I pull my leg out I'll lose my boot."

"What can I do?"

Gleeson had an idea. "Hang on – I've got some straps in me pack. Brought 'em in case we had to hold the cases closed. Here…"

A wet nylon strap lashed out of the dark hole to strike Meritus in the face. "Thanks!"

"Welcome," replied Gleeson, oblivious below. "I've tied it round my leg. We need to work together, so when I tell you to tug, don't go mad! I don't wanna end up doing the splits with my head down in that sh—"

"Should I pull now?"

"*No!*" Gleeson panicked for a moment, but by grappling for a handhold in the slimy walls managed to regain his balance. "Are you trying to wind me up, mate?"

"Well, I'm pulling your leg," Meritus called back down. "Does that count?"

Gleeson developed the giggles, which cost him more than half his strength. "Now you've gone and done it," he wheezed.

After a few moments of useless effort, they regained their composure.

"Right. *Pull!*" said Gleeson. With a horrible sucking sound his foot came free, and to prove that luck had not deserted them entirely, it retained its boot. They repeated the exercise with his other leg, managing to upgrade his situation to semi stuck. "OK, Tobo. Now, let's go for it!"

Meritus leaned down to pull one last time. With much grunting and effort, a thoroughly wretched Gleeson eventually slid over the edge on a ripple of foul-smelling sludge and even fouler language.

"Bladdy 'ell, mate! I bet you were one of those kids who loved to dig holes all over the beach. Leaving 'em open for some poor devil, on a pleasant evening stroll with his dog, to break his neck in!"

Meritus fell back, laughing.

"I'm glad you think it's funny!" Gleeson snapped, testily.

"We're a couple of mud-men," began Meritus, "carrying four deadly missiles, out in the dark, battered by the weather, with enemy forces everywhere, and we're arguing about whose fault it was that one of us fell into a hole?"

Gleeson tried to hold on to his temper, but eventually roared with laughter – a sound lost to the howl of the wind. "For the record it was *your* fault! But I suppose that, after the last hour of our lives, we should be a bit more grateful, eh?"

Meritus nodded. Still laughing, he got to his feet and held out a hand to help his companion.

Their laughter lifted them, but ended abruptly as the heavy, concussive thud of fifty-calibre machine guns sent them diving for the mud once more.

"What if Ah could take care of Franke and your grandfather both, in one fell swoop?" asked Douglas.

Heidi raised a delicate eyebrow. "Go on."

Douglas placed his hands on the table. "Look, what Ah'm about to tell you, is so abhorrent to me, that Ah hope you'll see the truth in it."

Her eyes narrowed. "Are you going to ask me to *believe* you again, *Kapitän?*"

"Aye," admitted Douglas sadly. "Ah suppose Ah am. But if you'll hear me out, Ah'm sure you'll see that a scheme like this would ne'er have come from me."

Heidi leaned forward with interest, linking her fingers. "You intrigue me – for the first time."

Disapproval flashed across Douglas' face, but he let it pass. "Ah'll need some guarantees from ye, before we go any further."

"Ha."

"That's your last word?" Douglas pressed.

"My *Last Word* is in the bottom of a ravine fifty klicks west," she answered, threateningly. "But I will guarantee you this – show me your last hand or I will destroy that ship while your people are inside it."

Douglas was outraged. "Your people are inside it, too!"

She picked up the detonator. "Do, or *someone* dies, *Kapitän.*"

"OK, OK," he replied quickly. "This whole situation is very different from what Ah expected – Ah'll no' deny it. The situation with Franke changes everything, but Ah really do have a way to deal with your enemies. Ah'll give ye my terms and then lay out my proposal. No tricks,

Ah promise." He leaned forward again. "This is a good deal for you, Heidi. Now, get Del Bond in here."

Captain Aito Nassaki fell to the floor. His men and their prisoners followed him down immediately. The thump of the heavy machine gun fire, just above their heads, was so loud it made the muddy ground throb. Everyone covered their ears.

The short burst ended abruptly and was followed by a voice. A female American was shouting above the roar of the wind, "Drop your weapons or I'll turn you into red mist!"

Aito leapt backwards over the edge of the steep bank. "Return fire!" he shouted on the way down.

The Sarge, Hiro and the Australian brothers dropped the cases they were carrying and dove to the side. They crawled around to the south of the tracked APC in the confusion, hoping for the best and keeping their heads down.

"I did *not* see that one coming," muttered Gleeson.

Meritus pulled at the Australian's sleeve, grinning wolfishly. "They don't know we're here."

"Which means they won't see *us* coming, either," replied Gleeson, catching on.

Leaving the heavy cases behind, they pulled their stun rifles from around their shoulders and crawled across the plateau, heading for the action. Once within thirty metres, they could just about pinpoint the enemy from the minuscule light thrown by the *New Worlders'* stun blasts and from occasional muzzle flare from other weapons.

Seeking cover, they scrambled towards a large boulder at the edge of the promontory. With rifles set to heavy stun, they poured fire into the completely unsuspecting enemy flank with impunity.

It seemed like an age for all concerned, but after what was actually less than a minute, Gleeson hollered, "Have you baggers had enough yet?"

The front of the armoured carrier lit up with immensely powerful spotlights. Blinking, Aito, and the remainder of his troops who were still conscious, threw their weapons over the top and climbed up with their hands in the air.

Despite the lashing rain, Henry, Prentice and O'Brien met The Sarge and his team with a round of back slapping and cheers.

Henry's whoop of joy at seeing friendly faces was answered from the forest. Turning towards the trees, everyone could hear the distinct howling of several creatures.

As the sound came closer, Gleeson and Meritus snapped to, rifles up.

Henry waved them down. "It's OK, it's OK. They're friends."

"*How's* that again?" asked Gleeson.

Scanning the eastern edge of the plateau with torches, they soon made out a small pack of furry bodies, skittering across the puddles and mud of the old enemy camp.

The shuttle crew greeted these new arrivals with some alarm, but less so than the recently disarmed and suddenly defenceless prisoners.

Henry knelt down and was instantly mobbed.

"What the hell is this?" Gleeson tried again.

"They're coming back with me," giggled the teenager. "I can't leave them here."

"You wanna bet?"

Henry stood. Squaring up to the Australian, he stuck his jaw out belligerently. "Look, I've been out here for two weeks and I've never asked for nothin' – now I'm askin'!"

Once it was obvious that the threat had passed, Hiro moved forward to stand in front of his brother. "*Captain* Nassaki, eh?"

Aito grinned ruefully. "*Hai.*"

"I'm not sure father would have approved," continued Hiro. "All I know for sure is that I'm so glad you're alive." The driving rain hid his tears. "It will be alright now, little brother. I'm taking you home."

Chapter 14 | Wheelbarrows

Thomas Beckett was often an irascible man, but today he really felt he had cause.

"What's wrong?" asked Baines.

"What's wrong, my dear captain, is that you left us in that damned bunker for close on sixteen hours!"

"We explained that, Mr Beckett," she replied patiently. "We had three satellites practically parked over us! If we'd done anything, even so much as sent you a message, we'd have been detected."

"Well, it's some good sending Corporal Thomas out there to protect us if he won't fire on anything!" Beckett challenged.

"He has strict standing orders to only fire if lives are at stake. *Yours* weren't. He also knows that *if* we're forced to leave you alone out there in the bunker, it's only because we're under close surveillance and have to proceed under blackout protocols. Corporal Thomas assures me that he explained this to you, quite clearly."

Beckett looked away, aloof. "He may have mentioned it," he acceded, then fired up again. "If you'd spent sixteen hours in that concrete sweat box, you'd really understand the full horror of what blackout means, Captain."

Baines gave him her schoolmistress' glare. "Corporal Thomas explained the gravity of the situation to you – more than *a dozen* times. After that, he stopped counting!"

Beckett threw his hands up in the air. "Fine! *Fine.* But I'll have you know that, by the time we bring in the harvest, I'll have spent more time entombed than Howard *chuffing* Carter!"

The reference was lost on Baines so she offered no response, allowing Beckett to continue with his grievances, "And furthermore, Captain, I've lost my wheelbarrow!"

"Oh, *no,*" she offered, "not your wheelbarrow?"

"Indeed. That wretched leviathan stepped on it whilst rooting around outside our hiding place – saw it with my own eyes! Flattened! That was *my* wheelbarrow, Captain. I specifically painted my name on the side because other planters kept *borrowing* it, with absolutely no respect for property!"

Baines tried hard not to smirk. "Were they *wheelborrowing?*"

"You may laugh, Captain, but when it comes time to bring in the harvest—"

"I'm sure we can find you another one, Thomas," Baines placated. Struggling to keep a straight face, she added, "You can paint your name on that one, if it will make you feel better."

"There are only four spare barrows left, Captain, and when they're gone, they're gone," he pontificated, throwing his hands up in the air. With that, he strode away.

Baines called after him. "*Oi,* Beckett! Was that a flounce?"

The overloaded shuttle came in to land upon the south-facing beach of a small island, roughly a hundred miles off the West African coast.

Cramped, uncomfortable and wet, the miserable crew stepped out onto cool sands to stretch and were instantly bathed in bronze.

A stunning red-sky dawn set the eastern emptiness aflame, while the gentle lapping of black waters soothed their weary souls. Each ripple twinkled gold as troughs and peaks played upon the sand, sharing their early bounty from the sun.

The survivors took deep draughts of purest sea air, sweetened by the scent of primeval forest fruits.

The elements combined for a perfect moment, lifting tired minds and aching bodies from somnolence and fear.

For some, it was hard to believe that the storm, the cloying muck and the fighting had ever happened. For others, the headaches and nausea were stark reminders that they had been stunned. Aito's troops bore the grogginess without complaint, acutely aware that for six of their number, there would be no dawn.

For everyone, nature's spectacle drew them in, poignant, beautiful, fleeting. Even for such hard men and women, a tear was not too high a price to pay for acquaintances that could never be renewed.

Meritus allowed the prisoners to sit and reflect, leaving them under guard while he slipped away to arrange a hearty meal for them all.

Slowly, he made his way up the sloping beach, losing one step in two as his feet slid. His muscles complained in reminiscence of their scramble up the muddy slope just a few short hours before. He was exhausted.

Corporal Jones met him halfway. Meritus returned the young Welshman's salute awkwardly, shuffling upright on the shifting sand.

"How'd it go, sir?"

"Wasn't pleasant, but it could have been worse. We got what we needed and all of *our* people made it out – thank God – all except Captain Douglas, of course." Meritus turned once more to face the radiant glow of the rapidly approaching day. Shaking his head sadly, he added, "He's a brave man. I hope he's alright."

"Actually, sir, we had a message from him about an hour ago," replied Jones, brightly.

Meritus snapped alert immediately. "What did he say?"

"It seems there have been a few surprises, sir. Not at all what the Captain expected."

Meritus frowned. "Better or worse?"

Jones appeared at a loss for a moment. "Not sure I can answer that, sir. Captain Douglas plans to lead Dr Schultz's ship here, eventually, but we're no longer to blow it out of the sky."

"Run that by me again?" Meritus replied. "Does he have any idea what we went through to get those missiles?"

Jones shrugged his massive shoulders. "He still wants them, just not here. Perhaps I'd better play you the message, sir."

"Captain, the enemy's shuttle has left the island off the African coast again and is leading a small fleet of shuttlecraft on a heading for the *New World*."

Franke placed her elbow on the arm of her chair and held her chin with thumb and forefinger, a habit subconsciously borrowed from Schultz himself. "Are there any people remaining on the island?"

"Many life signs, ma'am, but I'm fairly sure none are human – mostly avian. It seems their camp has been abandoned."

Franke's brow furrowed. "How singular. Comms – have you monitored any communications between the *New World* and the *Sabre*?"

"None we've been able to detect, Captain."

"Do we allow them to continue, Captain?" asked her weapons officer, barely disguised excitement in his voice.

Franke encouraged a certain zeal in her bridge officers, particularly at tactical. Her lip curled slightly. She understood his eagerness to dispatch their enemies, but would have to rein him in on this occasion.

"OK, everyone," she announced. "Until we know more about the situation down there, we follow our orders and wait."

Reading disappointment in the young man's face, she added, "Do not worry, Lieutenant Devon, we shall deal with the pestilence aboard our *Factory Pod 4* soon enough. In the meantime, you may paint the shuttle and small fleet as targets, in case the situation should change."

Tactical officer Devon smiled cruelly, eyes alight with temptation. The draw of the 'big red button' was clearly consuming him, but Franke was unconcerned. Her hounds may drool and whine, but they tasted blood only when *she* commanded it. It was the only way to run a ship. Heinrich Schultz had made a mistake with Hartmann and Meritus. They were too soft.

Repairs to her ship's wormhole drive may have run into problems, but otherwise the *Heydrich* would be ready for battle again soon. The delay tallied with her orders, so she would wait – for now.

Meritus stood aside as teams of people unloaded the prisoners and equipment from the shuttle and lifeboats in the Pod's main hangar.

They had left the islands near Africa almost at once, in line with Douglas' orders. Wearier than he could ever remember, Meritus could barely stand. To take any more caffeine or stimulants would probably be to risk a coronary, so he leaned quietly against a wall out of the way, instead.

The scientists and engineers were very excited about the wormhole drive parts and paraphernalia; the military were equally happy with the missiles stripped from the dead husk of his ship.

He had known going back there would be bad. If anything, the calamities they had faced once aboard her probably made things simpler for him, emotionally. They certainly made it easier to ignore the ghosts around every corner.

All that anguish, all those deaths, he thought. *And now look at me, alive at their expense and working with the very people who killed them.* He knew things were not that simple, but the guilt gnawed at him nonetheless. He had never felt so lost.

Having accepted the human world was coming to an end, he had signed up to a plan that he did not really believe would work, but the only other choice was to go down with the ship and save no one. So he had turned his back on his old life and come here – hoping to at least save a few. He had never expected to *belong* within the Schultz regime, but the few days spent with Heidi Schultz aboard the *Last Word* had proved even more intolerable than expected.

By going against them, and his orders, he had perhaps turned a small and very localised genocide into a full-blown war. Unable to go along with such evil against unarmed civilians, he was now unsure if *any* of them would survive this insanity. Had he made things even worse?

"You did well, Tobias," said Major White, gently.

Meritus jumped.

"Sorry, I didn't mean to sneak up on you."

"It's OK, Ford. I was a little lost there for a while."

White nodded understandingly. "It must have been tough – going back there, I mean."

Meritus sighed, rubbing his stubble. He seemed unable to answer, pale with exhaustion.

White placed a hand on the other man's shoulder. "It's bad to lose people, I know, but you didn't start all this—"

"Didn't I?" Meritus bit out harshly. "I see people walking around here, people Schultz would have thrown out and abandoned to the monsters outside, or simply shot. I'm glad that didn't happen, but I can't shake the feeling that my actions may have led to even more lives being lost by the time this crazy business is through."

White thought for a moment before answering. "Sometimes the right decision is painful – painful and costly. I believe that all these people would choose to go down fighting for what's right, rather than live at someone else's expense, Tobias. Whatever the final score, you've acted with honour – no one can ask any more."

Meritus closed his eyes and was instantly assaulted by a parade of faces – all gone. He dropped his head into his hands to hide his tears.

White moved, blocking him from view to provide some measure of privacy. "You need to rest, my friend, because we need you. We *all* need you." With that, he led Meritus away, unresisting, to a private billet.

The Sarge strode into the brig aboard the *New World* at the head of a three-man security detail, with all the confidence of his rank. Twenty-four hours had passed since their return; he was rested, clean and wearing a fresh uniform. His arm was now almost completely recovered from his fall from the lorry, when he had leapt to escape a Tyrannotitan – now known affectionately by some, less so by others, as Matilda – and he felt *great*.

"Mr Schultz!" he barked. "It's your lucky day – you're going for a ride!"

The old man eyed him suspiciously. "Going where exactly?"

The Sarge pulled his stun pistol from its holster. "Now if I told you that, I'd have to shoot you." He fired.

"Hey!" shouted Weber from the next cell, jumping to his feet. "You shot him but never told him!"

"Really?" replied The Sarge. "Oh, maybe you're right. Never was much good at threats, me – always more of a 'man of action'.

"So here's some advice – keep your mind on your own problems, boy. Now take that stupid look off your boat race and sit down, savvy?"

Weber swallowed and sat while his master was dragged unconscious from his cell. "He's quite old, you know," he pointed out plaintively. "I mean, to stun him like that…"

The cockney sergeant took a step back towards him. "And I wonder how many folks never got the chance to get 'quite old', because of 'im."

Weber looked away and The Sarge turned on his heel, following the guards from the brig.

As the door was closing, Weber ran to the bars of his cell. "What's a *boat race?*"

The door to Franke's private quarters chimed. "Come."

It slid open to reveal Lieutenant Devon. "Ma'am," he greeted courteously. "The *Sabre* has lifted off from Patagonia and is heading north-north-east."

"Is she now," Franke replied. "We'd better get to the bridge then."

Within moments she was in her command chair demanding reports from her officers.

"They appear to be making a straight line for the— stand by, Captain." The young woman operating the scanners suddenly bent to her screen. "Sorry, Captain. They're heading for the island off the coast of Africa – where the people from the *New World* set up a temporary base a few days ago. Also, we have a contact leaving the *New World* in the north."

Franke leaned forward in her seat, intrigued. "Heading?"

"Computing, ma'am. Yes, it seems they too are headed for the island."

"Captain…" The comms officer looked around in surprise. "We're being hailed, ma'am."

"Who is it?" snapped Franke.

A shadow crossed the officer's face. "It's Dr Schultz, ma'am."

Franke quickly ran through possibilities in her mind. "Very well – on screen. Dr Schultz, to what do I owe this pleasure?"

Heidi sneered at her greeting. "*I am offering a truce,* Kapitän. *We have an opportunity to reclaim* mein Großvater *from Douglas' people and refocus our efforts towards the real enemy.*"

"Really," replied Franke, not believing a word of it.

"*Indeed, Kap*— Emilia."

"Well, as we're on first name terms, *Heidi,* would it surprise you if I asked for a little more information?"

Franke enjoyed the flash of anger that crossed the younger woman's face. Keeping her own expression neutral, she thought, *Heidi really is a hopeless politician. Perhaps there* is *an opportunity here.*

"I have Douglas and some of his people captive aboard my ship," Heidi continued. *"He came to me requesting a summit. A contingent from the* New World *is already en route and we are also on our way to attend – as I am sure you are already aware."*

"I know this," agreed Franke, feigning boredom.

"Well here is something you may not know – mein Großvater *is with the* New World *contingent."*

Franke was indeed taken aback.

"The summit is to be a meeting of all parties," said Heidi, taking pleasure in Franke's obvious surprise. *"Douglas' fools think they can broker a peace agreement with us, so that we will leave their mongrel society alone. They wish to offer us,"* she paused to smile nastily, *"a 'fair share' so that we can all live happily ever after. Surely, I do not need to spell out what an opportunity this could be for our cause, Emilia?"*

"One big enough for us to forget any…"

"Misunderstandings?" supplied Heidi. *"Yes, indeed I believe so. Will you attend?"*

After a moment's deliberation, Franke nodded once.

"Good. I will send you the details and look forward to seeing you shortly."

The Sarge had pushed the engines of *Lifeboat 3* to the limits in order to arrive before Heidi's *Sabre*. The old man, still zip-tied in one of the rear seats, had regained consciousness about an hour ago and was furious about the indignities he had endured.

The Sarge grinned. He had others yet to bestow.

Leaving Schultz with a guard, he and Corporal Jones stepped outside. Their small ship was almost hidden under the shadow of a vast cycad at the top of the sloping beach.

Every time a vessel roared across the islands, there was an alarming display of flapping aggression from the indigenous inhabitants. Historically, angry colours and the beating of giant wings had always scared intruders away – but this was before the arrival of man.

Among the several groups to call the northern cliffs home, the two largest and most visible were quite similar in appearance; they were also similarly huge. Yet despite a few death-defying feints, they did not directly attack the little ship. Indeed, once it had landed on the opposite side of the island, they seemed to forget about it.

Perhaps it doesn't register with them because it doesn't smell alive, thought The Sarge. *Bird brains – you've gotta love 'em!*

Despite this withering appraisal, the pterosaurs were still roused. Now displaying at altitude, they circled the entire island, defending their wider territory. The screeching cacophony put The Sarge's teeth on edge.

Some were perhaps twelve or thirteen metres across the wing with the merest nub of a tail between their short legs. Many had rounded, bulbous crests to their upper and lower jaws which formed an upright ridge, rather than the flat spoon-like bill of a pelican.

"What *are* those ugly sods?" he asked Jones, not really expecting an answer.

Jones surprised him. "I looked them up on one of the lifeboats' computers, Sarge – while you were raiding the *Last Word* in Patagonia, a couple of days ago.

"The closest pictures I found for those massive ones were... erm, hang on..." He frowned, trying to remember the names. "The smaller one, if I got it right, is called Anhanguera – that's Portuguese apparently. Don't ask me how the hell you're meant to pronounce it."

The Sarge gave his Welsh-speaking friend a mildly ironic look, but did not interrupt Dewi Attenborough-Jones' crash course in Cretaceous pterodactyloid pterosaur spotting. He had not the heart; this was one of the longest speeches he could ever remember the corporal making.

"The name means something like, spirit protector of the animals from a bygone age..." He wore a look of Celtic mysticism, utterly ruined when he added, "...isn'it?"

Jones beckoned for The Sarge to follow; he had spotted something. "Look at that," he gestured.

"What is it?" asked The Sarge, looking at a huge pizza of white sludge on the beach.

"Let's just say, you shouldn't wander around here without a hat!" replied Jones, knowingly. "The really big sods might be Ornithocheirus. I'm not a hundred percent sure about the dating, but they looked like them from the pictures Mr Norris uploaded to the main library. There seemed to be some disagreement among the experts about how big they grew – just goes to show how strange life can be, eh, Sarge? *These* are certainly damned big ones. Maybe they're relatives – the geography seems pretty close."

The Sarge gave him his 'impressed' face. The huge Welshman smiled back proudly.

"You're full of surprises, Jones. A man of many talents, it seems. Next time you volunteer for a suicide mission, I might have to ask you to step back!" He slapped him companionably on the shoulder.

As with irony, flattery also bounced off Jones with all the effectiveness of ordnance fired from a pop gun, and he replied simply, "Them giant birds buzzed around us non-stop, after you left with the shuttle party, Sarge. They were tamping about something. So I thought it might worth knowing a bit about what might be trying to eat us – before we got et, like?"

This was of course quite sensible, but before The Sarge could say as much, their attention was drawn to the far-off roar of powerful rocket engines. Shielding their eyes from the noonday sun, they could just make out a black speck flying low, approaching rapidly from the south.

"Devon, you have the bridge," said Franke.

"Yes, ma'am."

"However, I'm taking your usual bridge crew with me. You may call on elements from duty shifts two and three, at your discretion. I've received a secret communiqué and have expectations. It's just possible that we may not leave this so-called summit empty-handed."

"Captain?" asked Devon.

"I can't say any more at the moment. You have our landing coordinates and you have my special instructions. I rely upon your judgement, Lieutenant."

"I won't let you down, Captain."

"You have never done so, which is why I leave you in command. Good luck, Mr Devon."

"Good luck, Captain."

He held his salute until Franke returned it.

She turned on her heel and left for the *Heydrich*'s small hangar, where her orbital attack ship was berthed. Soon joined by five chosen men and women, she led them aboard the deadly little craft and waited for the hangar to go through its depressurisation cycle. The bay doors opened after a short interval, and within moments they were free-flying in space, heading away from their ship and temporary home, towards the Earth.

The *Sabre*'s landing thrusters twisted the white sands into a maelstrom. The Sarge and Jones shielded their eyes as best they could, but found it difficult to turn away from such an impressive spectacle.

The Sarge had to admit that, although most of the Schultz line was technically several generations South American, his ships had a sleekness and obvious build quality which could *only* be German. As far as he knew, Heidi was the only Schultz to have actually spent her early childhood in Germany. He could only guess that her grandfather had turned her into what she had become, later.

"That's a good-looking ship," he called to Jones over the rocket noise.

"A good-looking woman in command, too," replied Jones. "Pity they were both made to kill us, isn'it?"

The Sarge gave him a nod and a wry smile. From time to time Jones' perceptiveness surprised him – he was certainly 'on it' today.

As the *Sabre* lowered to within ten metres of the ground, she generated a sandstorm obscuring her lower half completely as it beat the gently lapping waves into a spray.

She eventually came to rest with three stanchions on the sand, the aft starboard just into the shallows. The self-levelling hydraulics kicked into action as soon as they sensed the ship's full weight upon them, compensating for the slope of the beach.

After the shocking noise, the silence seemed even more so, at first. Despite their vast size and prowess, the avians had not dared query *this* visitor, opting instead to stay on the north side of their island and make themselves small.

No sooner had the waiting soldiers' ears begun adjusting to the gently lapping waves and rustle of breeze through the forest, than another roar came from the east.

The newcomer was smaller and already on top of them before the wash of its engines caught up.

"There's nothing subtle about these guys, is there?" The Sarge cried into Jones' ear above the din.

With much less ado than the *Sabre*, the comparatively small vessel practically *plonked* itself down, landing more like a Harrier Jump Jet.

A boarding ramp lowered from the *Sabre* while the port access hatch opened on the smaller craft, facing the sea.

The Sarge was unaware of this until a group of officers began to appear from around their ship. Looking back towards the larger vessel, he sighed. Heidi's blonde hair shone in the noonday sun as she disembarked. She too seemed to be surrounded by at least half a dozen guards. The only comfort for The Sarge and Jones was their first glimpse of Douglas, following the Nazis down the ramp.

The three groups convened about twenty metres down the beach from the *New World*'s lifeboat. The Sarge quickly tallied the forces ranged against them and wondered how the hell he had allowed himself to be talked into this. All they had going for them was their faith in James Douglas – he hoped it would be enough.

"Captain," he greeted.

"Good to see you, Sarge, Jones," he replied with a nod to each.

"Yes, sir," The Sarge grunted with what he hoped was more enthusiasm than he felt.

Douglas' mouth twitched slightly; he could fully understand how they felt.

"Emilia," Heidi greeted.

"Heidi," Franke returned. "Captain Douglas," she added with a nod. "We meet in person at last. You looked younger on the viewscreen."

Douglas grinned. Not willing to get into petty insult trading, he simply said, "Aye, Ah've gotten pretty good at staying alive over the years."

The Sarge chuckled and Franke gave him a scathing look. "Where is Heinrich Schultz, *Sergeant?*" she demanded, imperiously.

The Sarge straightened smartly, only his smirk betraying contempt. "He'll be along soon, Captain. It is OK if I call you Captain?"

"Of course," replied Franke, curtly.

The Sarge nodded. "Good, only I didn't want to offer a faux pas – you know, in case you'd promoted yourself to Admiral or Empress, perhaps?"

Heidi chuckled.

Franke had clearly never been gifted with a sense of humour. "Watch your mouth, Sergeant. Your people organised this little *soirée*, Douglas. Are we to sit upon the sand?"

Douglas was at a loss for a moment, but Sergeant Jackson stepped forward and saluted. "No, ma'am," he barked. "Corporal Jones! Break out the beach seats! And tell Corporal Thomas to bring the old man over 'ere."

"Sarge," rumbled the giant Welshman and set off back to *Lifeboat 3*.

"Now, ladies and gentlemen," The Sarge stated loudly, "you must understand that our expedition to Mars was a little light on beach furniture, so we had to use our initiative." He winked at Franke, ingratiatingly. "We hope it will serve, ma'am."

Corporal Thomas joined them quickly with Heinrich Schultz, still in wrist restraints.

"Captain Douglas," Heinrich spat without preamble. "The indignities I have endured at the hands of your people do you no credit. I will remember each and every one of them, and who caused them. *And* hold *you* responsible!"

"Just one moment, sir." The Sarge held up his hand, forestalling his prisoner. "Sorry to interrupt your list of indignities, but we haven't finished yet."

From behind them, Jones brought four, rather ungainly stacked, substitute beach chairs. Having picked up a little trick from Bluey, he had managed to slide the front rim of a wheelbarrow over the handles and under the rear rim of a second barrow, lifting the second completely off the ground. This technique allowed him to link all four barrows, balancing them precariously on a single wheel.[9]

Douglas' eyebrows rose even further when he read the name 'Thomas Beckett' painted very neatly on the side of one of them. He scratched his head in bafflement. "Sarge?"

The Sarge helped Jones unlink the barrows and set them upon the beach, one at each point of the compass, with their handles down into the sand.

"Alright, *mein Führer*, sit!" he commanded the old man, pushing him down.

---

[9]   According to Bluey, the linking together of as many wheelbarrows as possible in this way and then pushing them around, was often considered a sport on building sites, reaching back as far as the early 21st century.

"*What!*" bellowed Heinrich Schultz as he was forced into the wheelbarrow.

Douglas felt his face twitch, then his shoulders began to rock and before he knew it, he was in full blown hysterics.

More shocking still was Heidi's Bavarian belly laugh. Douglas had not imagined such a thing possible. For the last month of his life, every day really had been a new world.

Franke flared incandescent. "How *dare* you?"

To offset any further outbursts, Douglas dropped into one of the impromptu bucket seats himself, finding it surprisingly comfortable.

His was clearly new and still had a label inside. He read, "Fully galvanized tub, non-puncturing tyre, lifetime warranty. Well, as ye can see, we've spared no expense. Will ye no' sit, Captain Franke?"

Heidi surprised Douglas again by lightly settling into the next barrow along.

"Captain?" Douglas tried again.

"I will stand," replied Franke. Rigid with anger, she kicked her proffered seat aside.

"As you wish," Douglas answered, easily. "Ah'll begin with our offer." He explained about the stable volcanic vent and its possibilities for almost unlimited power generation. He further illustrated the opportunities offered by the NASA Rescue Pod.

Franke listened intently, her eyes boring into Douglas'. When he had finished, she asked, "Is that it?" Turning to Heidi she added, "You brought me here for this? They offer nothing we cannot simply take!"

"I agree," affirmed Heidi, clicking her comm once.

Franke looked around to see a large detail of armed troops descending from the *Sabre*. "*Treachery!*" she spat.

Heidi stood easily, lithe as a dancer. "You didn't really think I would allow you to get away with destroying the *Eisernes Kreuz* with me aboard her, did you?"

"What's this?" asked Heinrich, outraged.

"She had given you up to the enemy, Heinrich," explained Franke, a pleading edge in her voice. "Usurped your power. I couldn't let her get away with it!"

"You destroyed my *flagship?*" the old man bellowed. He jumped to his feet, showing virility belying his years.

"She would have left you to rot with Douglas' mongrels, Heinrich. I—"

"Did it not occur to you that I might be exactly where I wanted to be? Am I completely surrounded by fools?"

This statement sent a shiver down Douglas' spine. He too regained his feet. "What do you mean?" he asked.

"Be silent!" snapped Heinrich.

Heidi's troops had now surrounded the small party. "How did you know I wouldn't just kill you for betraying me, *Großvater?*" she asked.

"Because I trained you better than that, foolish girl!" he bit back. "If you had killed me you may have faced a full revolt when you tried to take control. With me alive, but safely out of the way, you could always take a backward step if necessary. I knew *exactly* how you would figure your options and what course you would take. Just as I knew Douglas' weaklings, instead of executing me, would treat me with sickening softness.

"Sometimes the king must involve himself to bring about the final checkmate. And by allowing myself to be captured, I intended a lull in hostilities – a false and temporary stalemate, allowing the crew of *Factory Pod 4* to gather in a good harvest. Then I would have instigated a takeover, bringing to bear both internal and external resources.

"All that has now been ruined by the infantile machinations of you idiots!" he raved. "Now I must risk destroying the very thing I need most and take *Factory Pod 4* by force! *Imbeciles!*"

Heidi waited for him to finish. "*Mein Großvater,*" she began quietly, "you seem to be labouring under the misconception that I will forgive your betrayal, allow you to replace me with the Norris boy and relinquish power back to you."

"What you wish is not important, girl. Only our work matters – the project to which we all gave our oaths."

"Plans change, old man," she answered coolly. Turning to her sergeant, she ordered, "Disarm Franke's people."

Franke's officers were relieved of their sidearms and forced to kneel. For the first time, Douglas saw Del Bond among Heidi's newcomers.

Franke stared balefully at the young German woman. "You take me for a fool, Heidi?" she asked calmly.

Heidi merely raised an eyebrow.

"If I do not contact my ship in," she checked her wristwatch, "three and a half minutes time, my gunners will carry out their standing orders and turn this beach into glass."

"Are any of you people capable of straight dealing?" exploded Douglas. "What the hell is wrong with ye?"

Franke did not break eye contact with Heidi. "You may think this is an opportunity to take the remaining pieces off the board, my girl, but you will not survive such an act, should you do so."

"What do you suggest?" asked Heidi.

"That you allow us to leave, with your grandfather. If you are lucky, we may allow you the time to come to your senses. However, if your ship moves a millimetre we will, regretfully, reduce it to slag."

"Hmm," Heidi pondered. "Or I could just have you killed right here, right now, and take control of the whole fleet as is my birthright."

"*I* command this fleet, *Enkelin*. Never forget that," said Heinrich menacingly.

"*Nein, Großvater*, what I *forgot* was to mention that I will end you too, this time. I can neither trust you, nor do I have need of you any longer."

"And you seriously think my crew would follow you after my murder?" asked Franke.

"They might, Emilia. After all, who else will they have? Besides, it is you who murders our captains, I believe. You shot Captain Hartmann for your own ends. I will *execute* you, for treachery – see the difference? I would then control the only credible military force on this world."

"Ahem," Del Bond broke into the moment's silence that followed. "Firstly, I'm afraid I can't allow that, Heidi. Secondly, I rather think Captain Franke should contact her ship before we all end up as reconstituted beer bottles, don't you agree?"

"What have you to say on the matter?" Heidi sneered.

Bond drew a rather nice ballpoint pen from his jacket and clicked the pocket clip back, aiming it at Heidi.

"If this is jest about the pen being mightier than the sword, your timing is lousy, *Derek!*"

As ever, the use of his name made him flinch slightly. He quickly aimed at the ground near Heidi's feet and fired a small round into the beach, causing a plume of sand to rise from the impact.

"It's a simple three-shot repeater," he stated airily. "I constructed it from, oh, this and that – just bits and pieces I found lying around on your shiny new ship, over there."

Heidi's eyes narrowed. "Rubbish! How did you really get the equipment to manufacture that?"

"Well, I suspected that you may not be one hundred percent reliable, when the chips were down – I'm sorry, my dear – so I developed my own little side-scheme. All it took was a little bribery and, well, here we are."

Douglas began to laugh at their situation with a mixture of disgust and despair.

Heidi ignored him. "Bribery?" she asked, dangerously.

Bond nodded, sagely. "You wish me to tell you which of your people were responsible, so that you may exact some frightful revenge, I expect? I'm afraid I cannot help you."

"What could you *possibly* have had to bribe my crew?" she asked, incredulous. "When I saved you from the dinosaurs you did not even have a change of clothes!"

He had the decency to look a little ashamed. "Well, I had no power or currency to trade, so I had to sink to base appetites, I'm afraid."

He stared meaningfully at Douglas for a moment. "I'm rather ashamed to say that I was placed in a position of trust, sharing a room with a very beautiful and rather innocent young woman. Knowing the sort of people your grandfather tended to favour, I suspected – correctly, I might add – that a few *discreet* photographs of the young woman disrobing might get me the things I needed to construct a weapon. I mean, the man in question was hardly likely to turn me in, was he?"

He turned to Douglas again. "I hope that one day she will realise it was all for the greater good."

Douglas could only stare, guarding his emotions carefully. Although he could not approve, he could certainly understand that Bond's mission was so important he simply had to use whatever resources were available to him. Under normal circumstances he would have been tempted to say 'Ah'm sure she'll live' but that remained to be seen.

Bond continued, "I'm afraid, Heidi, that I will have to ask you to stand your men down. Now, please release Captain Franke and her people, and your grandfather, of course."

"Traitor!" Heidi spat.

Now it was Franke's turn to laugh; the grating sound of a hinge not oiled in many a year.

"I'm afraid I'm going to have to press you," urged Bond, almost apologetically pointing his weapon at Heidi's head.

She nodded for her sergeant to give the order to disarm and release their prisoners.

"Unfortunately, that is not all, Heidi," continued Bond. "I also require you to order your entire crew off the ship."

"*What?* What the hell are you doing, Bond?" she hissed.

He replied calmly. "I cannot let you have all the toys, Heidi. You are the most dangerous loose cannon I have ever met. Regrettably, I must leave you your life to retain my leverage, but do not push me, *girl*." The last was delivered with a savagery belying his preferred urbanity.

Franke continued to laugh unpleasantly as she ordered a couple of her officers to collect their former captors' weapons. "Why don't we use a couple of Captain Douglas' lovely new wheelbarrows to get them aboard *my* new ship?"

"Franke!" snapped Heidi, furiously.

Franke made a point of looking sidelong at the *Sabre*, before she turned and smiled nastily. "I think you had better make that *Commodore* Franke, young lady, don't you?"

As Heinrich passed her, he said, "Do not think you will escape punishment for this, *Enkelin*." With that he turned his back on her, perhaps forever, and boarded with the others while Heidi's crew were abandoned on the sands.

Franke ordered one of her lieutenants to fly their attack ship back to the *Heydrich* before following him.

"Heidi, I must ask you to accompany me," said Bond, courteous and cultured once more. He gave Douglas a nod of farewell, ushering her away at gunpoint.

On the way back to the *Sabre* they passed, among others, Rose Miller and her father.

"Del?" asked Rose, looking afraid. "What's happening?"

"Don't worry, my dear. I'm going to have to leave you here, unfortunately, but there we are – Captain Douglas will explain, I'm sure. Please understand that I am very sorry you had to be involved in all of this." He gave her a sad smile and Jim Miller a brief nod before leaving them behind.

Upon reaching the boarding ramp, Heidi turned to him. "This was not the agreement we made, *Derek!*"

"No, my dear, you already broke that agreement, remember? But still, you have your life and..." he glanced at the lost-looking group further down the beach, "the dubious loyalty and support of your Nazi followers down there. And I... I have my duty."

"Who *are* you, Bond?"

He smiled enigmatically. "Goodbye, Heidi. I urge you, look after young Mr Norris. He may just save you – in the end."

He backed away up the boarding ramp, keeping her covered. Pausing at the top for a last look around, he breathed deeply of the sweet, unsullied air of the natural world. "This is a beautiful place, isn't it? Farewell."

He disappeared inside the ship as the boarding ramp rose behind him.

Chapter 15 | Paladins and Demons

The *Sabre* lifted from the beach. As she gained altitude, her abandoned crew were lost from sight in the sandstorm driven by her engines.

Left almost defenceless on a small island populated by pterosaurs, all Heidi and her people could do was watch as their ship left them behind, taking hope with it.

No. Not all hope, Heidi reflected. Bond may have disrupted the first phase of her takeover bid, but as long as he kept to the rest of their bargain she would have options again soon enough.

The small clique from the *New World* banded together without even meaning to. They were suddenly alone among well over seventy strangers, most of whom were enemy soldiers.

The Sarge caught Douglas' eye and they began moving slowly back towards *Lifeboat 3*. The partial cover offered by the billowing sand was abating quickly. Soon their stranded enemy would get past their shock and realise that *they* had the only ship within several thousand miles. Fortunately, Bond had never requested, and Franke's people had never insisted, that they drop their sidearms. They were only stunners, but they could fell a man temporarily and were a lot better than nothing.

The *Sabre* was a mere dot in the sky once more.

"You did well, Bond," Schultz remarked with unusual courtesy. "Very well."

"Indeed," Franke added her appraisal.

"*Herr* Schultz, Captain Franke," Bond nodded, accepting their commendations. "Would it be possible to have a private word in Captain Nassaki's quarters, please?"

"Of course," replied Schultz. "Captain *Nassaki*, really? There appear to have been some changes since I stopped minding the shop."

Before leaving the bridge, Franke barked orders to her skeleton crew, "Pilot, set course to rendezvous with the *Heydrich* – I want us parked in a parallel orbit within the next few minutes. Comms, inform *Heydrich* of our status and ETA. I don't want Devon taking pot-shots at us!"

"Aye, Captain."

Within the quarters recently vacated by Captain Aito Nassaki and before that, rather more permanently, by Captain Aurick Hartmann, Schultz and Franke took seats at the table while Bond remained standing.

"Thank you for seeing me," he began. "There is something that I..." he smiled secretly, "that I need to get off my *chest*."

"Very well, what is it, Derek?" asked Schultz, peremptorily – goodwill already forgotten.

Bond smiled again. He did not wince at the use of his name. He was on the home run now. "Of course, sir. I'll come straight to the point. You will, I'm sure, have heard of the Order of the Silver Cross."

Schultz leaned forward slightly. "I have," he confirmed.

"I have not," admitted Franke.

"They're a bunch of traitors and zealots," supplied Schultz. "They began their sordid pact at the end of the Second World War – enemies of our great work."

"Indeed," agreed Bond. He turned to Franke and continued, "But in fact the movement goes back to 1940, just after the Nazi invasion of the Netherlands – despite the Netherlands being neutral at the time. They're mostly Dutch nationals, or of Dutch descent, and have spent the last century and a half hunting down Nazi war criminals. Once the war criminals had all expired, or were executed, they continued their work to track down anyone propagating or disseminating Nazi sentiments or ideals, and those directly supporting the movement itself, of course."

"*Our* ideals," interrupted Schultz, forcefully. "*Our* movement."

"Of course," Bond acquiesced. "Our ideals."

Schultz relaxed a little. "You're saying that we have a Silver Cross operative amongst us? Here?"

"I do very much fear it, *Herr* Schultz."

"Impossible! I would have known about it. I know *everything* about my people and more about the *New World*'s crew than NASA themselves. That's how I was able to place you, Mr Bond."

"Quite right, sir, and I'm very grateful to meet you in person at last, so that I may thank you for the opportunity you have so kindly given me. However, the Silver Cross should not be dismissed lightly. They have more than a hundred and fifty years' experience of spying and infiltration into some of the most dangerous organisations in the world – our world, that is— was. Actually, perhaps I should have said, will be?"

"Move on! Who is it, *Derek?*" asked Franke. She knew he hated being called by his full name.

Once again, he only smiled.

"Forgive me," Franke added insincerely. "I had forgotten that you prefer 'Del'. Why *is* that, by the way?"

"Well, that's a funny story, Emilia. You see, I always hated it when people called me Derek in case my real name ever occurred to them. We need nerves of steel in our business, do we not, but no one's perfect, as they say. Accents can slip, names can become known."

Schultz's eyes narrowed. "What do you mean, *real name?*"

"Forgive me, sir. I mean, of course, my real *codename.*"

Schultz rose steadily to his feet. "You had better explain yourself immediately, Bond."

Bond retrieved his pen from a pocket. They were all aware that it still had two shots left, so he did not reiterate. "Perhaps this thing really is mightier than the sword," he mused, still smiling. "But not mightier than the *Cross*, I think."

Franke knocked her chair over as she jumped to her feet.

"You will both remain quite still, please," said Bond, calmly. "I will tell you my real name first, Heinrich. I was born Lucas Jansen in the old municipality of Amstelveen, Greater Amsterdam, in 2057. But by all means, continue to call me Derek Bond. Not a name I would have chosen for myself, perhaps – as you will soon understand – nevertheless, I've grown rather fond of him over the last month or so.

"You will also remember my niece, I think. Lieutenant Audrey Jansen? Pilot of the USS *Newfoundland?* Of course you will. You had *her* murdered too, didn't you?"

Schultz raised his hands, but his options were limited. Franke stepped around the table to stand in front of her master, shielding him.

"Well, isn't that nice," Bond remarked with genuine surprise. "Here at the very end you have one doggy who still loves you. It warms the heart, Schultz. Not that you would understand anything about that type of thing."

"What do you want, Derek?" asked Franke.

"I can give you anything," added Schultz.

"But you've already given me everything I want, Heinrich. I have *you*. Don't you want to know my codename?"

Schultz could not have cared less, but was willing to do anything at that point to stave off death for a few more moments. Once they made orbit, someone would surely check on them for further orders.

"Very well, Derek. Please, tell me," he answered slowly.

"Of course I will, Heinrich," replied Bond, pleasantly. "I've waited what seems like an age to tell you what I've been waving in front of your superior Aryan face the whole time! Interestingly, my codename means almost exactly the same thing in both German and Dutch. It's wonderful how things come together sometimes, isn't it?"

Schultz was happy to let Bond witter on; someone simply *must* check on them soon.

"In Dutch, my name is De Wreker – in German, I'm known as Der Rächer, quite a similar pronunciation, you will agree?

"So now you know my name. I would like you to speak it, just once and in English, please."

Schultz swallowed. "The Avenger," he spat the name like a curse.

Bond's smile was beatific. He took a moment before announcing, "The *Avenger!* That felt good! You see, my niece, Audrey Jansen, was also a member of the Silver Cross, *mein Herr*. It is in her name that I will now take your life and end your disgusting organisation.

"It's a shame I couldn't also destroy the creature you constructed from your own granddaughter – I will just have to leave that task to others now, but at least I removed the monster's teeth, when I helped you take this ship from her."

Schultz, seeing his very last chance, launched Franke bodily at Bond, while he made for the door. Bond fired, twice, expending his weapon.

Franke gazed up at Schultz in full horror of his final betrayal.

Bond knelt down next to the woman. "So sorry you won't be in at the end, Emilia, my dear. Do you see, now it's all over, that you were on the wrong side all along?"

He sighed sadly, but she was no longer listening to him and he closed her eyes with gentleness. Standing once more, he turned to face the running footsteps suddenly converging on the captain's quarters.

Three armed officers appeared at the door.

Bond smiled broadly. "You know what, ladies and gentlemen, when I recall all of the terrible atrocities you and your kind have ordered, or at least orchestrated across the world, it amazes me that none of you ever even considered the possibility that... Ah, never mind. You'll find out."

"Considered the possibility of what?" the senior lieutenant demanded. "Tell me, now!"

"Or you'll kill me?" Bond began to laugh.

The officers eyed him warily. The man was behaving as though he had won; it made no sense.

"What have we not considered?" the lieutenant asked again.

"Oh, alright, if it puts you out of your *agony*." Bond's laughter reduced to fits and starts, but still had a maniacal edge. "You never once considered that 'the good guys' would send someone like me, did you?"

The lieutenant's expression suddenly cleared. "Search him!" he snapped, urgently.

"Oh, I'm not carrying anything. Maybe I'm not that much of a good guy, either, come to think of it. Not sure.

"If you're hiding round the corner, Heinrich – much good may it do you! All that remains is for me to say..." Bond took a long, deep, calming breath.

"What? *Well?*" shouted the exasperated lieutenant.

Again, the beatific smile. "Goodbye," said Bond, softly.

He relaxed his neck and shoulders. Reaching up, he grabbed his chin and the back of his own head, and twisted. The snapping of his spinal cord severed all electrical impulses from his brain to the myriad devices embedded deep within the bone marrow of his ribcage and sternum, creating an open circuit.

The entire forty-five metre length and many thousands of metric tons of material that were the *Sabre*, vanished in a flash of white light.

The last thing the officers heard before their existence winked out forever, was laughter –Bond's voice chorused with another, raised in rapture to chaos.

Chapter 16 | Home

"Where do you think you're going?" asked Heidi, haughtily. "You seriously think I will let you take our only ship?"

Douglas sagged. They were close, but he had not really expected to get away with it. He turned to face her. "So, what do you suggest?"

When she did not answer at once, Douglas began to suspect that she was unsure what to do next, herself. With a disparity of more or less seventy to seven, this hardly gave him the upper hand, but he would snatch at *any* advantage right now, however small.

He spoke loudly enough for all to hear, "We're all stuck here, people. We've virtually no food, water or resources. What Ah propose is this: We contact the *New World* and get them to send enough ships to take us all from here and to a place of safety. What do you say?"

"Place of *safety*," mocked Heidi. "You mean back to *your* ship, where *we* will be prisoners."

Douglas shook his head sadly. "Heidi, can ye no' see it's over? Our only chance is to work together, now – it's what we should've done in the first place!"

Anger crossed Douglas' face, anger at the loss and waste they had all suffered and for nothing. "Ah suggest we take a vote!" he called out loudly – once more, for the benefit of the whole group.

"A vote!" screamed Heidi, suddenly furious. She rounded on her people to say more, but stalled when she realised they were all transfixed.

Following their gaze upwards, she shielded her eyes from what appeared to be a second sun in the sky. It was done, then.

The explosion must have taken place very high in the atmosphere because the boom, when it came a few minutes later, was surprisingly faint for such an apocalyptic event. The *Sabre* must have been so high when she blew that the extremely thin air transmitted the sound poorly.

Douglas bowed his head for a moment, in reverence for Bond.

Heidi felt no such compunction. "Now for my idea, Douglas."

He looked up. "That's it? Your grandfather is gone and that's it?"

"I am what *he* made me, *Kapitän*. I would not shed any tears for him if I were you."

"What about the other people aboard? Maybe they could have been saved. What about Bond?"

"You agreed with Bond's intent!"

"No!" Douglas roared, adamantly. "Ah deplore what he came here to do, but he was a ticking time bomb – there was no way out for him, you know that, and he knew it. Realising he was trapped, he disclosed his situation to a senior officer aboard the Pod to avoid hurting any of the innocent people back there.

"He knew his time was running out. His mission failed early – ironically because so many of *your* people joined the opposition, once they realised there was another way to live!

"Ah would have done anything to remove the curse he carried around with him, but tinkering with the nanotech devices in his chest would have killed us all and probably destroyed everything within several miles of the blast.

"Can we no' put an end to this destruction now? Please, Heidi – think!"

"Are you finished?" she asked. "I wish to use your ship's communications array. Now, it has not escaped my attention that three of your men are still armed. I assume they have your usual *toothless* stun weapons?

"So I will make this simple. We can overpower you with our numbers – which will be very unpleasant all round, especially for you – or you can just allow me to make the call." She tilted her head to the side and raised an eyebrow, waiting for his response.

Douglas seethed, but he nodded stiffly.

"Good," she said lightly.

"But Ah'll be coming with you!" he snapped. "Don't want you getting any ideas about abandoning us all here, do we?"

Once again, Douglas made sure everyone heard the exchange.

Heidi strode towards the ship but Tim intercepted her. "What are you planning?" he asked quietly.

She smiled, patting him lightly on the shoulder. "Timothy, we are alone now, the last – or the first – of the Schultz line. Stay close to me and you will see what we are going to do next."

Tim gave Douglas a look of concern, but followed Heidi inside.

Douglas took a weapon from The Sarge, keeping it trained on her from a safe distance at all times. It did not pay to get anywhere near the reach of a killer like Heidi Schultz.

It took some time before any communication was possible. The ionisation in the atmosphere from the blast had essentially produced a complete blackout over the entire hemisphere.

Eventually, a weak signal was received via an analogue band, allowing Heidi to contact the *Heydrich*.

"Lieutenant Devon here – who am I speaking with? We thought everyone had bought it."

"Dr Heidi Schultz, Lieutenant. As you will have no doubt observed, the *Sabre* has been destroyed. *Kapitän* Franke and *mein Großvater* were both aboard at the time. You now serve *me*, Lieutenant."

Douglas and Tim sat in stony silence as the tension built. Only the sound of white noise filled the lifeboat's cockpit.

"Stand by..."

After a painful two-minute delay, the comm came briefly back to life. *"Acknowledged."*

Douglas' heart sank still further. Would this never be over?

"Dave, please stop giving me the runaround," said Patricia Norris, wearily. "You're supposed to be keeping my stress levels down, remember?"

Dr Flannigan gave an exasperated sigh. "That's what I'm trying to do, Patricia."

"So you're keeping the efforts to retrieve my son a secret – good job!"

Flannigan frowned. "Alright, alright." He sat on the side of her bed and checked her pulse, more as a delaying tactic than because it was necessary.

"All I know is that James is in talks with Heidi Schultz and that she has Tim, but he's safe. Really, Patricia, I can't tell you much more than that. When the other guys came back from the *Last Word*'s crash site, they hadn't seen Tim *or* James. There's no more news."

She gave him a sideways look, clearly trying to decide if he was giving her the whole truth.

Flannigan took her hand. "Hey, I promise, that's all I know – all any of us knows. I get it, you're about as low as you can be right now, but *I'm* gonna take *no* news as *good* news, OK?"

"I need him back, Dave. He's all I have."

"I know, honey," he consoled, "but if anyone can find a way to bring him back, it's James Douglas.

"Heidi, your transport is en route. Will ye no' let us go now?" asked Douglas. "You've got everything you wanted, it seems."

"Why on earth would I do that, *Kapitän?*" she replied, looking genuinely puzzled. "Your ship may be small, but it is still a valuable asset – as are all of you, as prisoners."

"Ye really are a piece of work, aren't ye?" he snapped viciously.

"You may have your stunning weapons, *Kapitän*, but if you try and take off, I will have no choice but to order the *Heydrich* to destroy you."

Douglas muttered angrily.

"I'm sorry, I did not catch that, *Kapitän* – your accent…"

"Aah, awa' n' bile yer heed, damn ye!"

"Let them go, Heidi," said Tim, quietly. "What difference will it make?"

She gave him a hard stare. Eventually, she asked, "Let *them* go?"

He nodded. "I'll stay with you, cousin."

"Not a chance, laddie!" Douglas cut across them. "Ah swore to take you back to Patricia. Ah'll no' leave without you."

Tim ignored him, focusing on Heidi. "Cousin?"

"So you expect me to believe, truly believe that you want to stay here, with me?" she asked.

"*No!*" snapped Douglas again, but Tim held his hand up to forestall further comment.

"This is *my* choice," he said quietly. "That *is* my choice," he reiterated more forcefully.

Their conversation was ended by the approach of a large vessel. A few minutes later the *Heydrich* landed and, with spooky *déjà vu*, almost precisely where the *Sabre* had been less than an hour ago.

A detachment of troops descended the boarding ramp and the *New World* soldiers were disarmed.

Douglas turned to see Rose, tugging gently at his sleeve. "What is it, lassie?"

"Is Del really dead?" she asked.

Douglas was surprised to see tears welling in her eyes. "You cared for him?"

She nodded. "He saved my life, when we were on the run through the forest. He was on my side, when that monster Lemelisk tried to..."

Douglas checked that Jim Miller was out of earshot before asking, "What happened to you?"

"Nothing," she said quickly, then shuddered, "but if Del hadn't been there..."

Douglas put a fatherly arm about her shoulder. "He was a brave man and, if Ah get ma way, he'll be remembered by our people as a hero – along with Elizabeth Hemmings."

Rose frowned. "Who was she?"

"While the Nazis were seeding our crew with their people, it turns out we had a few very brave people in *their* camp, too. Elizabeth Hemmings saved my life when the *Last Word* was destroyed and it cost her..." He choked, swallowing. "She lost her life. Remember her name, and Del Bond's. When we get back Ah'll tell you what little Ah know of them."

He had absolutely no intention of telling her about the photographs Bond had taken during the course of his operation to save them all. The man had obviously been ashamed of the fact and she had no need to know. Furthermore, he would make sure that The Sarge, Jones and Thomas never breathed a word about it back on the ship – if they ever got back to the ship.

"Ah'd better tell Geoff Lloyd, too," he said instead. Smiling sadly, he added, "He'll probably freak out."

"Why?" asked Rose.

315

"You've heard the name Audrey Jansen? One of my friends our archaeological dig uncovered? Del Bond was her uncle."

Rose's blue eyes opened wide.

"Very few of us knew, and even then only very recently," he continued. "If we ever get back to the future, at least we may be able to contact his family or friends – try and make sure they know…" He trailed off as Rose began to cry.

"He showed me a side of himself that no one else saw. He could be funny and he was my friend," she said.

Heidi walked back down the *Heydrich*'s boarding ramp. She strode across the beach purposefully to where Douglas and the small group from the *New World* waited.

Tim greeted her. "What have you learned?"

She smiled, but her eyes always hid something dark. "It's all good news, Timothy. In fact, I *have* decided to let your friends go."

Tim's eyes widened. "Really?"

"Indeed. Why don't we go and tell them together?"

He looked at her askance for a moment, but fell in behind.

"*Kapitän*," she called brightly. "I have decided to let you go."

Douglas was clearly also taken by surprise. "Ye have?" he asked, dumbly.

"Yes, you may go and take your people, and your little ship, your *escape* pod, and leave!" She was obviously in a very good mood, but with Heidi, this merely made her seem even more unstable. "Go now!"

Douglas was very concerned by this change in their circumstances. Nevertheless, he had no choice but to act. "Sarge! Get everyone aboard the lifeboat." He turned back to Heidi. "Ah want Tim to come with us. His mother is seriously ill – she needs him."

"I know how ill she is, *Kapitän*. *I* shot her, remember?"

Douglas' blood boiled but he fought to keep his voice even. "So will ye let the laddie go?"

"No. And if you do not go now, I will not let any of you leave."

"Captain," said Tim. "Tell her I love her, please. Also tell Clarrie… Well, I hope someone can make her understand, I *have* to stay here."

Rose leapt into his arms. "Oh, Tim," she sobbed.

"It's OK. You've been the best friends I've ever had. You, Henry, Clarrie, Woodsey." He tried to laugh bravely but choked. "Yes, even Woodsey." He held her for one last moment and whispered in her ear.

Rose leaned back slightly, to look him in the face, but Tim gave the slightest of headshakes. She kissed him on the cheek. "We all love you," she said and boarded with her father, who gave Tim a nod of respect.

"Take care of them, Captain," said Tim, offering his hand.

Douglas took it and pulled him into an embrace. "Ah'm staying with ye."

Tim broke the embrace. "No, Captain! You *must* go. I have to do this... *alone.*"

Douglas gave him a long, measuring look before taking a step back.

"It's OK, Captain," Tim added quietly. "Trust me."

Douglas' eyes shone with pride as he smiled at the young man. Standing to attention, he gave Tim a salute. "Take care o' yeself, son. Ah'll see you soon. Ah promise." Turning on his heel, he boarded *Lifeboat 3*.

Tim watched them lift and set off in a northerly direction. Within moments they were gone and he was alone again – alone in a crowd, like always, and very unsure of his welcome.

"You said you'd give that to me!" Clarrie complained. "Henry, tell him!"

"Come on, Woodsey. You did say that."

"I never!"

Picking up on their heightened emotions, Henry's small pack of new pets began to yip and jump up excitedly. Reiver, lying quietly at Woodsey's feet, scrambled from under the table and began to bark loudly.

Clarrie was not to be dissuaded by the chaos. "You did, Woodsey! Henry, tell him!"

"Give me chance, Clarrie. I'm telling him, I'm telling him! I heard you, dude. I was there too, remember— Will you guys be *quiet!*"

The yapping and barking continued.

"Nepotism, that's all this is, mate. Ganging up on poor old Woodsey."

"Haha, right! Poor you."

"You told me I could have it!" Clarrie repeated. "Henry, tell him, he did!"

"I just told him!"

One of Henry's new friends leapt up onto the table and began to spin around yipping, forcing the three teenagers to hold the drinks they had brought with them up out of the way.

"Look, the truth is, I don't actually have it... Well, not any more, OK?"

"*What?*"

Henry shook his head. "Oh, *man.* You never had it, *did you?*"

The New Zealander looked shifty. "Er... a bit."

"*Woodsey!*"

Rose watched her friends from the entrance to the Mud Hole. She had no idea what they were squabbling about and it really did not matter, she was just so glad to see them all again. Moreover, seeing them acting like kids *again.* She had heard all about Henry's heroic fortnight in the Patagonian forests, dodging dinosaurs, and worse. She could hardly believe he would do that for her. At least he seemed undamaged by his trials, even seemed to have picked up some new pals, and the others were the same as ever.

A smile tugged at her lips as Clarrie began to slap Woodsey, completely ineffectually, with a beer mat – but of course, there was an empty seat.

Without meaning to, she began to cry and for the first time, they noticed her.

"*Rose!*" they shouted together.

Henry jumped over the seats, knocking them down in his haste to embrace her and she fell into his arms without a moment's hesitation.

Clarrie literally jumped at them next, joining in the hug. Woodsey joined a little later, rubbing his shin where Henry's fallen chairs had tripped him, sending him sprawling across the Mud Hole's carpet.

Eventually, they were reunited and then came the inevitable, "Where's Tim...?"

"He stayed behind, of his own volition." Douglas sagged, putting his head in his hands. "Ah failed."

Mother Sarah took his right hand. "That's nonsense, James. You achieved an incredible amount over there."

Baines took his left. "It's nothing short of a miracle you made it back at all, Captain. I can't believe you managed to rescue Jim and Rose too. Not to mention you gave Del Bond his chance…"

Douglas looked up at her with bloodshot eyes and she realised she had said too much.

"What happened to Bond was nothing short of an abomination!" he stated angrily. "If there had been any way to stop it Ah would never have gone along with it. As it is, Ah'll never forgive myself for my part in his death."

"James," Sarah interrupted, "you cannot and must not take responsibility for his actions. He made his choice. None of us here could ever condone it, but by confessing the way he did, he saved all of us here. God forgive me, I could never excuse killing, but Bond had little time left and he used it well. If he had not acted the way he did, Schultz would have murdered many of our closest friends – maybe all of us."

Douglas sighed heavily. "Can you imagine what Bond went through? He had to be reviled by us, to make his cover stick with the enemy. He had to be just about competent enough to be included in their schemes while superficially weak enough for them to ignore any threat he might represent.

"Hated by us, denigrated by them, oh, and of course, he also carried a ticking time bomb in his chest!

"Wouldn't you give almost anything to go back and send him on his way with just a kind word – just one kind word!"

"Del Bond knew how it had to be and accepted it, James," Sarah replied, kindly. "As we must, now, it seems. We should honour him. And we should honour you, too. You showed extraordinary courage going there. And let's not forget Tim Norris' sacrifice."

"He's no' dead!"

"I know," Sarah answered calmly. "And if there is any way at all we can get him back, we should try it. We owe him that – and poor Patricia."

"Has anyone told her yet?" asked Baines.

Douglas shook his head. "That job has to be mine, but Ah don't know what the hell Ah'm going to say."

"That you saved everyone you could and Tim's choice to stay behind is what gave you that chance. He's a hero, *and*… it's not like we're leaving him there, right?"

Douglas gave her an intense look. Gradually a smile began to form on his lips, stripping him of ten years' load in a single instant. "Aye, you're right. That Ah will never do!"

Dr Sam Burton, *Factory Pod 4*'s head of operations, slammed his fist on the machine's drive housing in a fit of exasperation. "I've been working forty hours straight on this damned thing and I still can't get it to—"

"It's working!" shouted Patel incredulously.

"Eh?"

Patel grabbed his dumbstruck colleague and proceeded to dance him around the manufacturing bay in a manner most unseemly.

Burton whooped in delight. "Two years! We've caught up two years' development in two days!"

"I know," laughed Patel. "It's amazing how much time you can save by stealing someone else's work!"

"And by giving it a thump!" shouted Burton joining in the exuberance.

Hiro sat at a desk checking over a few equations. He had glanced over them several times already, but they were not sinking in. When Burton and Patel attempted to share their euphoria, he smiled and shook their hands, it was a remarkable achievement, but his mind was tied up with a darker matter – one involving his brother.

Aito was now in an overcrowded holding cell, with no hope of parole or indeed any clear future at all. Everyone expected to be under attack again soon and there was no time to consider captured enemy soldiers – they were simply to be housed, to be fed and to be content.

Hiro did not know what to do, had not visited Aito since their return, and the longer he left it the harder it became to do so.

"Wassup, Hiro?" asked Burton, jovially.

The chief shrugged. "Just wondering about my brother."

A shadow crossed Burton's face. "It's a hard one, mate. Maybe, if you're wondering about him, you should go and see him."

Hiro nodded, noncommittal. "I know he's OK. I was just wondering whether he would help us or try and sabotage our efforts. He's the only one here who's actually worked on the enemy's wormhole drives. He's not *that* bad an engineer – not really." He tailed off.

"Do you think he could help us?" asked Patel, soberly.

"I'm pretty sure he *could*..."

"You're just not sure whether he would," Burton completed.

"Why don't you find out?" suggested Patel.

The chief scratched his head and sighed. "Firstly, if I introduced him to what we're doing, he might ruin everything we have. Secondly, if I brought him down here, the captain would probably skip my court martial and go straight for the firing squad!"

"Douglas doesn't trust him?" queried Burton.

Hiro gave him a sour look, not even dignifying the question with an answer.

"Fair enough," Burton accepted.

"You could appeal to Captain Baines," tried Patel.

Hiro shook his head. "No. She would go straight to shooting Aito. I don't know what to do. All the years I thought he was dead, I wanted him back more than I can say, but now... what? I just watch him rot in prison?"

Burton and Patel shared a look. "You could try throwing yourself into your work," the New Zealander attempted. "We've missed you."

Hiro sighed, with a grudging smile. "I'm sorry. I know I haven't been pulling my weight since we got back."

"Quite understandable, my friend," reassured Patel. "The way I see it is like this: there are too many uncertainties right now to take any further risks, but when this current crisis passes... Well, I know both Captains Douglas and Baines to be the most honourable of people. If we survive this trial, there will be a lot of us requiring forgiveness, and if the regret is genuine, most will receive it. That is what I believe."

Burton placed a hand on Hiro's shoulder but spoke to Patel, "You know what, we've had a hell of a success here at last. It's late and about time we all got some rest." He winked. "We've got Chief Hiro Nassaki starting back tomorrow, that'll get things moving!"

Hiro smiled at the compliment and stood to be away for his bed. He did not need telling twice.

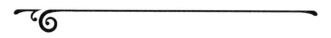

Tim had slept very little. With the first rays of dawn, he had taken himself down to the beach. Removing his boots and socks, he walked a few hundred metres from the *Heydrich* to sit upon the sands and ponder.

It was so beautiful and so peaceful here, it was a pleasure just to *be*, but the pondering was getting him nowhere.

Every thought started out as a plan to change his circumstances, but inevitably derailed each time a memory surfaced. Spiralling depression sought him out and he was tired of fighting.

A screech from above made him look up sharply to see a large pterosaur, also greeting the dawn. It glided across the rusty sky in silhouette, unmissable, yet unbelievable, the undeniable master of wind and wave.

Despite his sadness, Tim's mouth turned up into a smile. "Catch those early fish, boy."

"Who are you talking to?"

He jumped, turning round to see his *cousin*. "You startled me," he responded redundantly.

"Who were you talking to?" she asked again.

"Ornithocheirus," he breathed the name with a dreamy sigh. "Or one of his relatives." Then he noted something different about Heidi. "You've taken your boots off?" he asked incredulously.

"There is no threat here," she stated simply, compounding his surprise by sitting next to him and taking in the view.

Tim could not help recoiling slightly. "Are you alright?"

"Of course, why shouldn't I be?"

"It's just that I've never seen you, erm... *relax* before."

She tilted her head back and gave a lilting, almost girlish little laugh.

Where's the monster gone and who the hell are you? he thought, suddenly on edge.

"We have time," she answered obliquely. "*Mein Großvater's* plan was to wait for the *New World's* crew to gather in the harvest before making our move. Time *is* running out for food production after all. We will lose the season, if we are not careful."

"Well, he was right – about that, at least," Tim agreed. "They would share it with us, you know." Wondering at this *other* new side to her, he threw that nugget out, just in case.

"I know," she replied simply.

He tried again, "I mean, we don't need to attack them or hurt anyone."

She smiled secretively, playing sand through the fingers of her right hand. "I like this place," she said at last. "Maybe we will build an island retreat here, yes?"

Tim nodded, not knowing what else to do.

"Timothy, it is time you began your training."

"Training?"

"Yes, cousin. You are soft. We need to toughen you up, teach you how to survive. You have a fine mind – and that is important – but it is not enough in a world like this. You must learn how to fight."

"*Fight?*"

"Indeed. Do not worry, young one. I will teach you. And what better place or time can there be than here and now, yes?"

"Erm..."

Three weeks later

"I hate this," Thomas Beckett admitted sadly. He had been leaning on his shovel, taking a breather, when Natalie Pearson and Reiver happened by.

"*Why*, Thomas?" she asked. "You've done a beautiful job here. When Captain Baines told me you were building a rockery, I thought she was winding me up! You know what she's like."

Beckett soured even further. "Indeed. She was here yesterday, *exercising* her mended leg!"

Natalie tried to keep a straight face. "Why do you let her get under your skin? You know she only teases you because you fall for it every time."

"Never mind that," he replied, irascible as ever. "I didn't mean I hated my rockery, or this place. I mean I hate the idea of leaving it!"

Natalie's first reaction was surprise, but taking in their *almost* perfect little world of Crater Lake, she had to agree. "You know, Thomas, I can hardly believe those words came out of your mouth, but looking around... I think you'd have to be crazy to think otherwise."

She bent to pick up a stick and threw it towards the water's edge. Reiver naturally brought it straight back. "No, boy, we don't play with sticks – they splinter." She stroked his ears lovingly. "My fault," she admitted.

"Imagine if that stick got buried under the fluvial silts hereabouts," said Beckett. "Try explaining border collie teeth marks in hundred-million-year-old fossilised driftwood to your students, Miss Zoologist."

"*Thomas*, are you teasing me?"

"I never tease, Dr Pearson."

"Of course you don't." Natalie looped her arm through his as they stood together, admiring the view. "Besides, I'd just pass the headache on to the boys in palaeontology – they love that stuff!" Sobering slightly, she asked, "Do you think they'll be able to do it? Get us out of here and back to our own time, I mean?"

"Well, I didn't think you were referring to explaining away your dog's fossilised chew-stick." He winked.

Leaning more heavily upon his shovel he sighed. "I rather fear that they will, my dear."

As they looked out over the lake, it felt like a fantasy coming to an end. Pretty soon the cinema would close and then it would be off home to bed and up for work the following morning.

"I hate this," said Natalie.

Douglas and Baines made their way to the bridge. Singh was on duty, running a series of habitual passive scans. His call had been unexpected and sounded urgent.

Baines arrived first. "What is it, Sandy? You sounded worried."

Douglas burst onto the bridge just behind her. "What's happening?"

"Sirs, erm, sir, ma'am, er... Captains! We're being hailed, sir-ma'am."

"*What?*" they exclaimed together.

"Who is it?" asked Baines.

"Bet Ah can guess!"

"They've found us," replied Singh. "There's an enemy attack vessel hovering above the lake. One of the small ones."

"Get Meritus on the line and tell him to be ready to scramble!" snapped Douglas.

Baines sat in her old commander's chair. "Well, I suppose we'd better acknowledge, Sandy. Is it AV?"

"Just audio, Captain," replied Singh. "Responding now. This is Lieutenant Sin—"

"*Put me through to Douglas,*" a haughty and all too familiar voice cut across him.

Singh turned to face the captains, wearing an expression of annoyance. "I hadn't finished."

Douglas' mouth twitched a half smile. "Douglas here. What do you want, Heidi?"

"*Really,* Kapitän, *where are your manners?*"

"Save it, Schultz, get to the point."

"*Don't you wish to know how we found you?*"

"Ah cannae see how it makes the damnedest bit of difference. What do you want?"

"*I want the Pod,* Kapitän – Factory Pod 4. *That has never changed. The only question remaining is how reasonable you are going to be about surrendering it to me.*"

"Ah didnae expect to be having this conversation until we brought in the harvest. It seemed obvious that was what ye were waiting for. Ah knew ye'd find us in the end."

"*How omniscient of you,* Kapitän. *However, you seem to have accelerated our plans for us, wouldn't you agree?*"

"Explain."

"*Come now, Douglas, don't be coy. Did you really think we would fail to notice the wormhole tests you've been running? Within atmosphere, too. Very naughty,*" she tutted.

"We're getting an invitation for a video link, Captain," muttered Singh. Douglas nodded unhappily.

The main viewscreen lit up to reveal a beautiful face marred by an ugly sneer. "Kapitän," she nodded. "*I just could not deny myself the pleasure of watching you squirm and then bluster. See how well I know you?*

"*Is that Commander Baines there, too? How nice to see you again. Last time we met, you were crippled by a broken leg, I believe. I trust that you are back to full strength now, and are crippled only by your ongoing incompetence?*"

"That's *Captain* Baines," growled Douglas.

"*Oh, please do forgive me – I'll inform the dinosaurs at once!*"

"Do you have a point, Schultz?" prompted Baines.

"You are probably wondering how your rather ingenious cloaking technology failed, allowing us to spot the wormhole, Kapitän?"

Douglas said nothing.

"Of course you are. The truth is we have known your exact location almost since the moment you landed. Naturally, we have kept abreast of your developments ever since."

"Why are ye telling us this?" asked Douglas.

"Just to make it clear that you cannot fool us. You are outclassed at every turn. It would go better for your people if you simply surrendered, now!"

"So it was the seismic tremors that gave us away," said Singh. "They would have been unremarkable, wouldn't they? Had you not known exactly where to look."

"Very good, Lieutenant. You always were a bright boy. It's a shame that your services will not be required in the future."

Singh swallowed, nervously. "Your outlook really does belong here with the dinosaurs!"

Heidi sneered. *"I have someone here who wishes to say hello, Kapitän."* She widened the field of view to show Tim in the co-pilot's seat, and they could clearly see other uniformed bodies in the background.

The young man looked different. For one thing, his face was a mess of half-healed cuts and bruises.

Douglas jumped to his feet. "What the hell have ye done to him?"

"I'm OK, Captain," said Tim, quietly. *"My cousin has been* training *me."*

"Damn you, Schultz," hissed Baines.

"For teaching the boy to survive? What else could I do? He is family, after all." Once again she smiled that smile that Baines wanted to reverse a car over, several times, just to be sure.

"I've been thinking about your offer, Douglas, regarding the Newfoundland *and the Rescue Pod."*

"Ye have?" asked Douglas, unable to hide his surprise.

"Indeed." She nodded. *"No one wants a war, Kapitän."*

"Is that a fact?" Baines commented drily.

Heidi ignored her. *"With a few minor changes, I think your plan might actually work, Kapitän."*

"What changes?" Douglas asked, suspiciously.

"It seems to me that the main bugbear – for you – is that I will not share with your other *people."* She placed a deliberate contempt on the word 'other', enjoying the rise this provoked in Douglas.

"Get to the point!" he barked.

"The 'point' is that we are willing to offer you *the Rescue Pod, and what is left of the* Newfoundland. *She may not be flightworthy but she is big enough to provide a home for your menagerie – as long as you enforce strict* breeding *controls.*

"Meanwhile, my people will take control of the New World *and* Factory Pod 4. *We would even be willing to provide you with some basic necessities and enough food to get you through the winter. In essence, we get what we want, you save the lives of your people."*

Douglas straightened, his hands linked behind his back. "And you would leave us alone otherwise – allow us to live in peace?"

"James!" Baines cut in, outraged.

He raised his hand to silence any further outburst. "Well?" he prompted Schultz.

"Of course, Kapitän. *It is the Pod and ship I want. That is all I have ever wanted."*

"Ah have three conditions."

Heidi raised an eyebrow. *"Name them."*

"Firstly, Ah will need twenty-four hours to gain the complete agreement of our people before Ah can officially make a bargain of this magnitude. Secondly, should our people agree to your terms we will need at least three days to put everything in order and collect our belongings – that's three days without bullying or interference!"

Heidi wore a bored expression. *"Very well, and your third condition?"*

"Tim Norris should be allowed to visit his mother. She's critically ill, but when she does come round, she's desperate to see him. Ah fear that her survival may even be contingent upon his presence. Well?"

"I will consider *it,"* she answered coolly.

"Do we have a deal or no'?"

"I suspect a trick, Kapitän. *This would be unwise."*

"You came to *me* with the deal, damnit! What's it to be?"

"I will have your answer in twenty-four hours, Douglas. You will have mine then, also."

The viewscreen went blank and then settled on standby.

"James, we can't make a deal like that," said Baines, calmly this time.

Douglas shrugged. "Probably not."

Baines' eyes narrowed. *"You've* got a plan."

He smiled. "It's been known to happen."

"You may be wondering why Ah've called this emergency meeting," said Douglas, as he paced the small stage at the front of the cavernous embarkation lounge.

Everyone with any connection to engineering or manufacturing had been summoned and Douglas could feel their tension. His very demeanour made it obvious to all that his address was going to include bad news.

Realising, he stopped pacing and forced himself to stand still in the centre of the dais. He used the plinth housing the stage's audio-visual electronics as an anchor, and leaned heavily upon it.

"Ah'll come straight to it. Our enemy has found us."

As expected, a collective moan and rumble gusted through the assembly. He gave them a moment to collect themselves before raising his hands for calm.

"Apparently, they have *always* known our location – which leads me to surmise that the only reason they stayed their hand was because they were waiting for us to gather in the harvest. However, our experimentation with wormhole technology has accelerated their plans, it seems."

He explained the enemy's offer of relocation to the *Newfoundland*, with the further offer of limited resources to get them through the winter.

Fairly soon, the gathered men and women were in uproar.

Douglas raised his hands again for calm, but it made no difference. Having little choice, he gave the nod.

"SHAT IT!" bellowed The Sarge.

"Thank you, everyone," continued Douglas into the relative calm. "Ah know this is shocking news, but it was always to be expected.

"Now, Ah don't need to tell you that we cannae altogether trust our enemy to even keep these ridiculously one-sided terms. However, they are now offering life as opposed to... Well, at least it would be a continuation of sorts."

"What's brought about this sudden *humanitarianism* within the Schultz camp, then?" Sam Burton called out.

"You want the truth?" replied Douglas. "Ah think it's the effects of Tim Norris on Heidi Schultz. For whatever reason, she has accepted him and seems to want to keep him – by that, Ah mean keep him on side.

"Whatever the cause, Ah think agreeing to this is a mistake, and so do the leading council.

"So, ladies and gentlemen, Ah want *you* to tell *us* what you think we can do about it."

"Well, what do you suggest?" asked Burton again.

Douglas' response was blunt. "That we use the wormhole drive and take our chances."

Again, uproar.

This time, Douglas beckoned Dr Satnam Patel to join him up on the dais. Patel had been so busy working on the wormhole drive that Douglas had barely seen him in weeks. He could not help noting that his fellow councillor was thinner and his skin, always so dark from the hot Indian sun, now had a greyish pallor to it. Eventually, the hubbub quieted out of respect for their most senior scientist.

"My friends," he began, "Captain Douglas has bought us three, maybe four days' grace. We have that much time to complete our work and leave."

"It can't be done!" someone shouted.

"We've barely even tested it!" cried another.

"How will we even get into space with their guns on us?" asked a third.

Patel raised a placating hand. "All reasonable questions, but this is the situation we are in. We will not only have to expand the power output to create a wormhole large enough to encompass the vast bulk of the *New World*, but we will have to do it all in secrecy with no possibility of a physical test."

"This is crazy," a female voice stated flatly.

"No, my friends," continued Patel, as calmly as he was able. "This is *desperate*."

Three days later

Heidi lunged. Tim blocked. She launched a roundhouse kick to his face, redirecting at the last instant to strike low at his knee. He saw it in her eyes and blocked low with his left forearm, stopping the kick. Heidi placed her weight on her forward leg, launching a lightning back-fist across his face to his right temple. His right forearm twisted upwards ninety degrees to form a rigid block.

Tim smiled. This earned him a vicious slap across the face.

"Fool! Do not waste time smirking, like a monkey brandishing a stolen windscreen wiper! If you get into trouble on this safari there will be no one to tow you to a safe zone! Pay attention!"

She sighed angrily. "Right. Assume defence position one. We shall try again."

"Wait, Heidi, wait. Please." Tim waved her away for a moment and sat heavily upon the sand, looking out to sea.

Heidi was about to strike him again for turning his back but, noting the boy was sucking blood from a broken lip, she softened. Realising *that*, she immediately stiffened. This boy was clearly having a deleterious effect on her state of mind.

With another sigh, she sat beside him. "What is wrong with you now, Timothy?"

He turned towards her. "We travel back to the *New World* today."

"I am aware."

"When they agreed to your terms, two days ago, you said I could see my mum within two days."

"As long as they hand back my team, captured during their salvage mission to the *Last Word*, at the same time, yes, it's today, I know. I was there when I made the deal."

He gave her a long, searching look. Despite herself, she began to feel a little disconcerted by it.

Maybe he has somehow inherited the Schultz stare too? she mused.

"Will you keep your word?" he asked, finally.

She returned his stare, but Tim did not look away. "And what will you do, Timothy, if I allow you to visit their ship and see Dr Norris?"

Heidi found that she was holding her breath. She was afraid to admit the truth to herself, but she really did not want to lose him. He was, after all, the only family she had left, but it was more than that. To Heidi, 'family' was little more than a description. Spending time with her cousin seemed to be filling in many holes within the whole. She both enjoyed and despised those feelings. It was very disconcerting.

Tim broke into her musings. "You don't believe I'll come back to you?"

"Will you?" she asked, just a little too quickly.

"If you promise to let them live and help them to stay alive, I will never leave you, cousin."

She felt a thrill at his words, even while her conscious mind attempted to divine the truth in them. "*Why?*" she asked at last.

"Because you need me," he replied simply.

Her eyebrows shot up in surprise. "*I* need *you?*"

"Yes."

"How and why?"

"Because you've had such a horrible life, Heidi."

"I was heiress to a global organisation and destined to become one of the richest women in the world – you grew up in a ghetto with your single-parent family and you feel sorry for *me?*"

It was impossible to keep the disbelief from her voice, but Tim was undeterred.

"That's right. My mum loved me – my dad too, when he was alive. Before your creatures had him murdered," he added bitterly.

"That was not my doing," she murmured, feeling the need to explain.

"That is the only reason I can forgive you. That and because the terrible, evil thing you did to my mum may also have failed. No one has ever cared for you, have they?"

"Nonsense!"

"Is it? Your grandfather made you into a weapon and discarded you as soon as a male heir resurfaced. Who else have you ever had to turn to?"

She had no answer to that, so she asked another question, "And what can you possibly offer me that is so much better?"

"A home?" he postulated. "For the first time, someone you can trust?"

They fell into a moody silence. Eventually, Heidi stood. "Come, we must get you cleaned up before you meet with your mother."

Hiro faced his brother as they stood next to the pedestrian airlock in the Pod's main hangar. "I don't want us to be separated again, Aito."

Aito swallowed. "Nor I, brother. But at least this way, we'll both be free. To stay here would mean a cage for me, maybe for life."

Hiro shook his head. "Why did you always have to make such poor, no, such *stupid* choices, Aito?"

Aito grinned. "We never agreed on anything, did we?"

Hiro snorted, wiping away a tear.

"This isn't goodbye, Hiro."

"So why does it feel like it? You can't possibly trust that monster, Schultz."

"Actually, my life has been quite comfortable within their organisation," Aito rebutted.

"Maybe, but I suspect the reasons for this are not good ones." Hiro took a step closer. "Please reconsider, brother."

The voice of Lieutenant Singh boomed from the tannoy, breaking up their conversation, *"Yellow alert. The enemy vessel* 'Heydrich' *has set down approximately five hundred metres along the beach, before our crop plantations. An armed contingent is making their way towards us. All security personnel should assume their posts immediately – repeat – all security personnel to your posts. Yellow alert. Message ends."*

Douglas placed a gentle hand on the chief's shoulder. "It's time, Hiro, Ah'm sorry."

Hiro turned. "Can't we refuse to release him, Captain."

Douglas hesitated. "We *could...* trouble is, that might blow the whole deal."

"But, Captain—"

Douglas cut him off. "Ah know, son. Ah know what this means. But there are two factors we must consider. Firstly, it would risk the lives of the almost two hundred souls aboard this ship, and secondly, he *wants* to go."

Hiro slumped.

"Ah'm sorry laddie, but at least you know he's alive. Isn't that something at least?"

"Something," Hiro muttered.

"They're approaching on foot – that was the deal. So we have a few minutes. Ah'll leave you to talk, but be careful what ye say. You can come with us for the handover if you wish."

Hiro nodded and returned to Aito.

Heidi waited impatiently within the vast cave as the *New World* contingent approached.

As they neared, Douglas greeted them. "Only two guards, Heidi? How trusting of you."

Heidi yawned disdainfully. "My ship has heavy weapons trained on the *New World*, Douglas. At the first sign of any failure to comply with our terms, you will be destroyed."

"Ah thought you needed ma ship."

"I do, but if people refuse to listen, then what is a girl to do? My patience is not infinite. After all, if things don't work out here, *I* can simply go home, should I choose."

Her guards looked uncomfortably at one another. Heidi had her back to them, but Douglas saw it. He would have to ponder the meaning of that little wordless exchange later.

To divert attention away from what he had just seen, he greeted Tim. "How are ye, laddie?" He glared at Heidi. "Still covered in bruises, Ah see."

"I'm OK, Captain. Is mum alright? I only have today and then I must return to Heidi. That's the deal."

A look of sadness crossed Douglas' face. "Aye, Ah know, son. Patricia's stable, for now. She'll be right glad to see you. That'll help more than Dr Flannigan's medicines, Ah'm sure."

"Dr Schultz," Heidi's comm crackled.

"Go ahead," she snapped, suspecting a trap.

"There's a large animal heading into the cave, ma'am. We think it may have picked up your scent. It looks dangerous."

"Acknowledged."

"We'd better speed this up," said Douglas.

Heidi nodded.

"Release the prisoners, Sarge."

"Can you at least untie our hands?" asked Aito. "We've given you no trouble."

Douglas was about to refuse, but Hiro stepped forward and cut the zip-tie restraining his brother with a folding pocket knife. They exchanged a hug.

"Welcome home, Captain Nassaki," Heidi remarked drily.

Aito treated his sibling to a boyish smile. "Take care, Hiro."

"Goodbye, brother," replied Hiro, quietly.

"Yes, this is very touching but we need to move!" snapped Heidi.

"Too late!" someone cried as a roar echoed around the vastness of the cave.

The small group from the *New World* knew, or suspected, that the creature striding towards them was their old friend, Sigilmassasaurus brevicollis – a spinosaurid that, at a glance, bore a certain resemblance to the crocodilians, also indigenous to the area. However, the upright hip arrangement of the theropod dinosaurs made it stand much taller, and if anything, gave an aspect even more frightening and otherworldly.

The stun pistols carried by The Sarge and his security detail may have been adequate for their intended duty, but they barely tickled the giant bearing down on them. It did not run, but at over ten metres in length, its long strides ate up the distance easily as it crossed the sandy cave floor towards them.

Schultz's men fired. The small, rapid-fire rounds from their assault rifles *did* have an effect. They made it *really* angry.

They were still firing when the creature ran them down. Had the situation not been so horrific, the dinosaur's confusion at the sudden disappearance of its quarry would not have been out of place in a cartoon.

The recently released men and women ran terrified, in all directions. Most of them still had their hands bound.

Hiro shouted, "Aito! Come back! Come back to the ship!" He could not tell if Aito had heard him among all the screaming. Perhaps he was simply too panicked by events to understand, but either way, he made a mistake.

Running around to the right of the dinosaur, he attempted to dive under its tail as it swept around in an arc. His dive was successful, and when he regained his feet, Hiro dared hope, but the creature had seen him. It spun around quickly.

Aito waved his hands in the air in a hopeless attempt to protect his head and the huge jaws closed around his left arm, lifting him bodily from the ground. Hiro opened his mouth in silent scream as his brother was tossed in a ten-metre bloody arc to slap dully against the cave wall.

The creature swallowed Captain Nassaki's left hand, hardly noticing the morsel. With people running all over the place, it was spoilt for targets.

Heidi drew her trusted nine-millimetre and began pumping rounds into the dinosaur's head.

Unable to protect itself from the deadly hot needles pricking its flesh, its small intelligence was faced with a decision: run from the cause of the bangs and the pain, or kill it. Its antagonist was within the distance of its own length, so it charged.

Heidi stood her ground; dropping an empty clip to the sand, she slapped another in its place.

Douglas began to manhandle Tim away from the altercation, bellowing for The Sarge and his people to retreat – there was nothing they could do.

Heidi stood, implacable as a goddess, before the giant carnivore, pouring lead into its face.

It lunged and the spell was immediately broken. A mere mortal once more, she was flung through the air like a ragdoll in one direction while her gun went in another. She rolled and came back up into a crouch.

Tim saw where the gun landed. He pulled away from Douglas' grip and ran for the pistol. Seizing it, he pointed the muzzle at the Sigilmassasaurus and froze.

The dinosaur was still fixated on Heidi. "Fire!" she screamed. "Fire!"

Tim looked at it dumbly. "It's just an animal," he called, at last.

She ducked and rolled, coming back to her feet a little closer to him. She looked furious. "You had no problem shooting me!" she thundered.

Instantly, she regretted the outburst. Yes, Tim had shot her, but only because she had shot his mother. *Damn!* her inner thoughts railed at her stupidity.

Sigilmassasaurus lunged again, clipping a leg as she dove, sending her spinning across the sand. Standing unsteadily this time, she tried another tack. "Tim, you swore you would not leave me! Please, help me!" Terror thrust all further translation from her mind. "Tim! *Hilf mir, bitte! Hilf mir!*"

The young man's face crumpled, a damburst of emotion arriving so quickly it overwhelmed him. He fired the gun into the air, which attracted the predator. "That's all I can do, I'm sorry." With that, he threw the gun to the sand and ran for the Pod's airlock.

Granted a temporary reprieve, Heidi watched in shock as he ran from her. "You promised," she mouthed.

The moment her cousin disappeared inside the ship, the unmistakable sound of thrusters firing forced Heidi to cover her ears.

For the dinosaur this was simply too much. Shaking its head in distress at the noise, it stooped to pick up a dead body for its troubles and made all haste towards the mouth of the cave and the cool fastness of the lake.

Heidi came to her senses, realising that she would be in a lot of trouble if they burned the main engines. Looking around, she spotted a deep nook within the cave wall – it would have to do. She sprinted.

Drawing her comm from a pocket, she yelled above the din of the engines, "Lieutenant Devon. Take off immediately and destroy the *New World!* Repeat, *destroy* the *New World!*"

She dropped the comm to the cave floor as she flung herself into the comparative safety of her crease in the rocks.

The *New World*'s main engines fired. It was so loud, Heidi's senses closed down and she could hardly breathe.

Slowly the leviathan began to lift and move. Terrible scraping sounds came from the hull where she caught the roof of the cave, bringing down tons of stone in her wake.

Half a klick away, the *Heydrich* also began to lift. Lieutenant Devon glared at his instruments with demonic intensity. He began to laugh, causing some of his crewmates to glance at one another with concern.

"Helm, bring us around," he barked. "I want a clean shot!"

The *Heydrich* crept out over the lake as the vast bulk of the USS *New World* left her safe berth.

"The fools!" cried Devon. "Where do they think they can hide on this worl—"

His crowing ended abruptly as the unthinkable happened – the *New World* opened a vast wormhole in the middle of the lake.

"FIRE!" screamed Devon, despite being at the tactical controls himself.

Two missiles launched from the *Heydrich*'s forward batteries, instantly connecting with their targets. The first missile hit the rear of *Factory Pod 4*, throwing a vast cloud of metals and ceramics in all directions, but the second struck the *New World* herself, near the topmost of her diamond shaped bank of engines. The explosion, in conjunction with the firing of the engine itself, was enormous. The ship leapt forward with astonishing speed and a boom that shook the earth for miles around.

Devon suspected he had done enough, but the bloodlust was on him and he fired again anyway.

Before the second volley could connect, the USS *New World*, the debris cloud, the explosion and the wormhole, all winked out of existence. Only falling shrapnel, thrown high into the air, remained as proof that they were ever there.

Epilogue

The escape pod barely stayed ahead of the destructive wave on its tail. Entire-vehicle-shudder numbed the man at the helm. The atmosphere around him thickened, increasing friction in line with acceleration, but to slow down would be to die.

He could state the toughness and combined durability of the tiny craft to ten decimal places, but this was a most earnest trial. Fire suppression systems coughed to life all around him as he fought the controls.

The Earth below him spun. The continents, already well outside the lines of any standard geography map, were just shapes without meaning to a man struggling to remain conscious.

He sought a name, *North Africa?* That would do. The little craft, sensing possible incapacity from its pilot, automatically opened air flaps to reduce speed. The sudden forward g-forces *made sure* the man blacked out for a few moments.

Screaming in from the lower atmosphere, the lifeboat trailed fire in its wake. The pilot regained consciousness to see land-sky, land-sky from the main viewport. Regaining command over pitch and yaw, he stopped the spin and brought his dive mostly under control at last.

Far below was a crisscross of rivers and rocky islands, cutting through a carpet of thick jungle, opening to a vast delta in the north.

"*One thousand metres,*" a digitised voice pointed out, unemotionally. He was falling fast. The controls seemed to have been damaged and despite shedding much of his speed, this would be a hard landing.

"*Five hundred metres.*"

He scanned ahead, desperately looking for anything that might be considered *soft.*

The rivers were mostly heavy sludge haulers, conveying silt to build new lands and that gave him hope. *Clean* rivers tended to be *rocky* rivers. He lined up to use one of the delta's large tributaries as a landing strip.

"*One hundred metres.*"

Despite a lifetime of discipline, the man screamed, bracing for the shock of impact as the river rushed towards him...

He shook awake, bathed in sweat. *Damn that nightmare again!* Stretching, he wiped his face and checked the lifeboat's scanners for wildlife. Satisfied, he opened the hatch to let the hot, fetid humidity in – though hardly invigorating, it was preferable to his dreams. He stepped out.

Behind the escape pod, he could still see the path his crash had smashed through the brush.

After skipping the water's surface like a skimmed stone, a bend in the river had forced him, slewing and sliding, up a shallow rise. Although the jungle foliage thinned as the bank rose, a cluster of dead trunks remained near the top. That was where he had come to a fortuitous and very final stop – just a few metres from the edge of a small promontory.

That was almost a month ago, but even in his dejected state, he had to admit that the view from his solitary crash site was tremendous.

He soaked it up a moment longer before deciding to fully banish the bad dream with a nip of fifty-year-old single malt. One of the finest he had ever tasted. It had been prescient of him to include such things within all of his escape pods – one never knew, after all – and Heinrich Schultz had always appreciated the finer things in life.

Author's note:

To everyone working in the field of natural history and dinosaur research, I once again send a massive thank you for your constant inspiration. As always, a few liberties have been taken...

Ornithocheirus and *Anhanguera* were vast flying reptiles (pterosaurs), and related. Size estimates for *Ornithocheirus* are still disputed, but range anything up to 12m across the wing – although other researchers believe they may have been little more than half that size and very comparable to *Anhanguera* in that respect also. Both animals probably lived a little earlier than the setting for 'Allegiance' – perhaps as much as 10 million years further back, hence Tim's comment, "Ornithocheirus, or one of his relatives." *Ornithocheirus* remains have been found in Britain and *Anhanguera* in north-eastern Brazil (either side of the fictional island where our heroes discover them off the west coast of Africa). For animals that fly and eat fish, it must be a palaeontologist's nightmare to guess where they were actually from! I chose to feature *Ornithocheirus* because it is so well known from the BBC's *Walking With Dinosaurs* series. Sometimes it's nice to be able to provide an actual face to a name! Although a flying pair do feature on the cover of the next novel in the New World Series, 'Reroute' (Oops! Spoiler alert!).

Cronopio (the little critters that savaged Henry's trousers) were small mammals. Probably no larger than terriers, one of the palaeontologists who discovered them described *Cronopio* as bearing a marked resemblance to 'Scrat' – the cute and immensely industrious little chap that chased the ever-elusive acorn in the film *Ice Age*. The idea that they behaved in a very dog-like manner was a complete liberty on my part, for the sake of the story – but then, if those ancient mammals had come across a pack of wild humans, maybe they would have developed a symbiotic relationship and, dare I say it, become friends in an age of deadly reptiles?

I try and stay away from gladiatorial contests among the dinosaurs. As stated on previous occasions, large predators, then as now, may have made a lot of noise when defending their territories, but would most likely have avoided direct conflict with one another. Injury could so easily mean death. However, a few scraps must have happened down the years – what a tremendous piece of good fortune that one such occurred while a couple of our heroes just happened to be crossing the river, so we got to see it!

Ekrixinatosaurus was a relative of the much more widely known *Carnotaurus sastrei*. As depicted in my amateurish sketch at the head of chapter 8, its arms were almost completely vestigial and probably useless. Subsequently, not being able to reach to cover his ears was a really cheap gag, but sometimes you just have to go with the classics. However, what I really like about this animal is its size. Unlike the behemothic *Mapusaurus* or *Oxalaia*, *Ekrixinatosaurus* was small enough to easily follow you through a forest and would likely have had the stamina to go all day – nowhere to hide – *shudder.*

Talking of shudders, the fanatical Emilia Franke's ship, the *Heydrich*, was named after Reinhard Heydrich, one of the main architects of the Holocaust. Considered one of the worst of a very rotten bunch within the Nazi leadership, it is fair to say that few have left such a trail of murder and chaos in their wake – millions dead. Even Hitler took this man very seriously, describing him as "the man with the iron heart". Fortunately, in 1942 he got what he deserved. History crucially remembers these monsters in order to give future generations a chance at stopping the next one. In the past they have tended to rise from a world where the vast majority of people are afraid, or simply consider it wise or easier, to hide their real thoughts from view. Within his Cicero Trilogy, Robert Harris wrote a lovely little piece where Cicero says something to the effect of 'we only have the knowledge of our own lives, but if we read history, we can call on the wisdom and knowledge of generations'.

The '*Schutzstaffel*' was more commonly known as the infamous 'SS', a major paramilitary organisation under Adolf Hitler and the Nazi Party.

The *Eisernes Kreuz* (Iron Cross) was a medal for valour and service to one's country (in Germany). Unfortunately, it is commonly tainted with association to the Nazi movement (the Nazi iron cross can be differentiated by the *swastika* emblem at its centre), but the honour goes back much further; in fact all the way to the Napoleonic era, and was awarded to some very courageous men and women who were most certainly *not* Nazis. The idea of Heinrich Schultz identifying himself with such an icon seemed entirely in keeping with the deluded self-importance of his character – the man was not even German!

The German people are, and have always been, clever and industrious. The Nazis are in no way synonymous with them. However, when it comes to writing 'bad guys' for the purpose of fiction, they don't come much 'badder' than the Nazis, do they? After all, where would our much beloved Indiana Jones have been without them?

Once again, thank you so very much for reading,

Stephen.

Coming soon:

REROUTE

THE NEW WORLD SERIES | BOOK FOUR

Stephen Llewelyn

Other titles in the New World Series

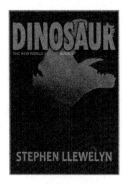

...

BOOK 1
DINOSAUR

BOOK 2
REVENGE

BOOK 4
REROUTE

DINOSAUR audio - performed by

CHRIS BARRIE

(Red Dwarf, Tomb Raider)

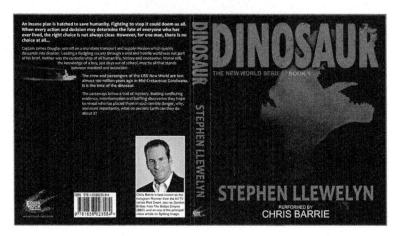

Printed in Great Britain
by Amazon

57184596R00200